Also by Kimberly K. Fox

A Distant Star, Volume One
A Distant Star, Volume Two

To Be a
STAR

KIMBERLY K. FOX

iUniverse, Inc.
New York   Bloomington

To Be a Star

This is a work of fiction. All of the characters, names, incidents, organizations, and dialogue in this novel are either the products of the author's imagination or are used fictitiously.

iUniverse books may be ordered through booksellers or by contacting:

iUniverse
1663 Liberty Drive
Bloomington, IN 47403
www.iuniverse.com
1-800-Authors (1-800-288-4677)

Because of the dynamic nature of the Internet, any Web addresses or links contained in this book may have changed since publication and may no longer be valid. The views expressed in this work are solely those of the author and do not necessarily reflect the views of the publisher, and the publisher hereby disclaims any responsibility for them.

ISBN: 978-1-4502-6466-2 (pbk)
ISBN: 978-1-4502-6469-3 (cloth)
ISBN: 978-1-4502-6470-9 (ebk)

Library of Congress Control Number: 2010915442

Printed in the United States of America

iUniverse rev. date: 11/9/2010

For: Andrew

With all of my love,
Mom

CHAPTER
ONE

TAYLOR BOUDRAIN GLANCED AROUND the crowded ballroom, champagne glass in hand and the latest bimbo of the month on his arm. Disdainfully he noticed all the big movers and shakers in the movie industry schmoozing each other. The bleached blonde giggled on his arm as he listened with half an ear to his agent berate him.

"Taylor, I don't think you really get it! People in this town don't like you. Now I know to you that might not be a big deal, but when casting directors don't call you anymore..."

"Ah, come on, Frank," Taylor interrupted. "You know as well as I do that ain't gonna happen. Not for a long time." Taylor wondered briefly how many glasses of champagne he had had. At last count, he thought it was three.

Frank Zimmerman sighed in frustration. "Yeah, I know you got it all, Taylor. Looks." His gaze traveled up and down the man in front of him. Taylor was tall, lean and muscled. He had a beautiful head of golden blond hair and deep teal eyes. He had been compared in the press to a Greek God on more than one occasion because of his fantastic looks. "Money. Lord knows you make enough of that. But your ego is getting in the way here. If you make enemies in this town, you make them for life and they have a way of getting back at you, buddy."

"Frank, you worry too much. You really do." Taylor lightly pinched the arm of the blonde and she squealed in reply, batting her fake lashes at him. She wasn't drop dead gorgeous, but she had one helluva body and that was all he was interested in anyway. To get away from this boring party and screw her brains out. But first there was Frank to deal with. He tuned back into his conversation.

"Why won't you let me release the information that you donated five

1

million dollars to the new children's cancer hospital? It would go a long way to soothe some ruffled feathers and paint you in a more benevolent light. I could have the publicist release a statement—"

"Nah, you know I don't want to do that. Listen, I ain't worried about egos in this town. I'm not in this business to win a fucking popularity contest. I'm in it to make money. And I've made a helluva lot and as a result, so have you, Frankie my friend." Taylor sipped at his champagne, teal eyes sardonically studying his agent.

"Taylor everyone knows you're king in this town. Your movies consistently are box office smashes. Hell, you've even won an Academy Award. You're gold in this town, but barracudas abound in Hollywood and I'm telling you to watch your back. As your friend and as your agent." Frank's dark eyes studied Taylor carefully, hoping he was getting through to his biggest asset, Taylor Boudrain, the Texan that blasted Hollywood away six years ago and still ruled.

Taylor sighed. "Frank, they're all jealous. Jealousy also abounds in this town. Fuck 'em. If they can do better, let them try. I ain't holdin' anyone back. I'm just doing my thing."

"Taylor, your publicity is bad right now. Hell, last week some rag caught you having an orgy in your hot tub, right out in the open where they could splash pictures all over the place! How do you think that looks to your fans? And—"

"Frank, there ya go. Exaggerating again. I had three women in there, it was hardly an orgy. And the pictures they managed to snap hardly showed anything but four people's heads. So don't lecture me about the damn press. They are, as you say, barracudas."

People waved and smiled and tried to gain Taylor's attention. He waved back perfunctorily, flashing his dazzling smile. Everyone in the room was trying to get his attention, which belied his agent's words.

"And then there was the affair with a married actress. Really Taylor, none of this looks good..." Frank continued.

"She wasn't married at the time. She was separated."

"Says who? Certainly not her husband."

"Yeah, she neglected to tell me that little detail until after I ended the affair. Who knew?" Taylor snorted, but Frank was not amused.

"Am I getting through here, Taylor? Are you even listening to me? That's what you pay me for, to give you my advice."

"I'm listening, Frank. Ya know, I'm thinking of taking a little sabbatical anyway. I've been working six years non-stop and I'm thinking of taking a vacation. Go off on my own for a bit. Blow this town and travel around. Get a different perspective on things."

"Oh honey, no!" the blonde protested.

Frank's silver brows rose. "Oh, really? How long are you thinking of being away?" This news greatly surprised him. Taylor lived to act and he was damn good at it.

"Six months. Just hop on my bike and ride around, see the great U.S. of A. up close and personal."

"Six months! That's way too long to be away from this town, kid. They forget about you in weeks if you don't have a movie out. I can understand wanting a break. Maybe two, possibly three months, but six is *way* too long."

Taylor flashed his famous grin. "Don't worry, Frank. I'll keep in touch. In the meantime, you can live off of the commission royalty fees. You'll hardly go broke," Taylor joked.

Frank sighed again. Taylor was one of his most difficult and hard to predict clients, but he also made him the most money. For now. "Taylor, reconsider. Please. That's way too long to be away—"

"My mind's made up, Frank," Taylor said adamantly. "Been thinkin' about this for awhile and I need to do it. Ya know, fresh air, nothing but me and the bike and the endless highway. Should be heaven."

"What about me, Taylor? Are you gonna take me?" The blonde looked up hopefully, squeezing Taylor's bicep.

"Sorry, darlin'. It's just gonna be me and my mean machine." He squinted and pointed off into the distance. "Heading east and keep on going until I see the other shoreline."

The blonde pouted as Frank scowled. "Taylor, this is a hare brained scheme. Think about this some more."

"Sorry, hoss. Ain't gonna happen. Made up my mind."

The blonde sighed. "Oh, Taylor. I just love that southern drawl."

"You're about to love something else a whole lot more," he leaned down to whisper in her ear.

"I'll leave you two alone," Frank interjected sarcastically. "Keep in touch, Taylor."

"Will do, Frank."

Taylor took the blonde outside. The glitzy ballroom of the hotel glittered with lights behind them. The valet drove Taylor's black sleek sports car up, but Taylor waved him off, flipping him a one hundred dollar bill.

"Not yet, buddy. We're gonna take a little stroll."

The young guy grinned as he caught the bill adeptly. "Yes, sir."

Taylor pulled the blonde around the corner of the building, down a pathway leading to pretty tended shrubs and a gazebo off to the side. Walking casually down the path, he pulled the blonde along. She was wearing a sequined skimpy black evening gown which should come off very easily. Taylor silently thanked the fashion gods for little favors. Taylor was wearing a collarless black tux but that wouldn't present any problems either.

"Taylor, where are we going?" the blonde huffed, trying to keep up with his loose limbed walk, tottering along in spike heels.

"Oh, just for a little stroll. Yeah, this looks about right." Taylor surveyed the long granite wall of the hotel only partially concealed by shrubs.

The blonde tried to tuck her hair behind her ear, it was coming loose from her carefully upswept style. "Right for what? Taylor, let's go back inside. They rented the penthouse suite for you. That would be SO romantic!"

"I ain't into romance at the moment, darlin'. I want something and I want it *now*."

"What?" she asked innocuously.

"Why, to fuck. What else?" His teal eyes grinned down at her.

"Here?" she squeaked.

"Yeah, right here." He picked her up bodily and gently placed her back against the building. Quickly he put on a condom, tossed up her dress and nailed her against the building.

Taylor had his customized Harley up to 100mph, the wind shearing around him as the endless highway ribboned in front of him. He decided to be smart and wear his helmet, the patriotic one with the flag and stars emblazoned on it. He figured it would impress any local yokels and he wouldn't get into too many bar fights. Being tall and strong Taylor usually never lost any bar fights because he could be a nasty son of a bitch. Men read that in his eyes and left him alone. But Taylor tried to avoid fights if he could. Messing up his pretty face wouldn't help his career, although he did bear a slight scar on his right cheek below his eye. It was small and crescent shaped but visible. Women said it only made him look sexier.

As he rode along he recalled how he received that scar and other nasty beatings from his dear old dad. Taylor grew up in bumfuck Texas, Beaumont to be exact. Oil refineries employed most of the town and his father worked there until his dying day. The prick used to beat all his siblings and mom too. Taylor had three older sisters and a younger brother. He was smack dab in the middle of the passel. One day Taylor got big enough and smacked his dad down hard when he was beating on his mom. The old man never touched her again but he did everyone a favor and died of cirrhosis of the liver a few years back. Taylor was the only one in the family born with the looks of an angel. The rest of the brood were pretty plain. He also inherited all of the height in the family, which his mom claimed came from her side. Taylor sent her money every few months (heck, he was worth 3.3 billion, he could afford it) but he dusted his boots of that Texan town long ago. He lit out at sixteen and never looked back. He went to Holleeywood to become a star and damned if it didn't happen.

He was waiting tables one day and a producer came in for lunch, told him to go audition for his studio. He showed up for his screen test and wowed 'em. Who knew he could act? He certainly didn't. But he wasn't an uneducated hillbilly. Taylor was a voracious reader. He read everything he could get his hands on. Thus, though he barely had a high school education, Taylor's native smarts and book learnin' made him smarter than some people with several degrees.

Taylor shook off thoughts of his past. He never thought of his family much. The only one he had any use for was his mother. His siblings came with their hands held out long ago and he told them all to get jobs. Hadn't heard from them since, which was just fine by Taylor. He was free, he had a great job and he answered to no one. He had women in his life when he wanted one, and didn't when— well, when he didn't want one. Like now. Just him, the open road and his awesome bike.

It took Taylor about five days to cross the country and that was with stops along the way. He camped out briefly with his gear here and there, but if there was a town with a decent hotel, he stayed. People recognized him and he dutifully signed autographs. Taylor was smart enough to show appreciation for his fans. They got him where he was and he wanted them to keep him there. But it was secretly tedious to him. Even though he came across as a guy with an ego the size of Antarctica, Taylor was basically a humble guy who just wanted to act. The whole Hollywood ego thing was to keep people at a distance and it worked. He didn't want anyone getting too close, not even Frank. Taylor was the original Solitary Man. Thank you Neil Diamond for giving me a moniker. Taylor grinned under his helmet.

He was wearing jeans and a white tee shirt and black cycle boots. He didn't need his shades right now, the sun was setting on good 'ol Western New York. Taylor had decided to drive up to Niagara Falls to check it out and it was an awesome sight for this Texas boy, even from the American side. He could see the Canadian side was more magnificent and bigger, but he didn't want the hassle of crossing the bridges into Canada. Right now he was on a highway taking him by the large cement hydro electricity power grids on the New York side. He recalled seeing a sign a little ways back saying he was in Lewiston,

New York— wherever the hell that was. He was thinking about stopping for the evening and finding a place to stay and eat. Head out tomorrow for New York City, then his coast to coast journey would be complete.

As Taylor was ruminating on these thoughts, his attention shifted to the huge cement barriers down below through the gated barricades. He only shifted his attention for seconds but it was long enough for Taylor not to see the huge semi that swerved into his lane.

Taylor acted instinctively to save his life as his Harley was shaved alongside the huge metal behemoth.

Everything went dark and black and the last thing Taylor recalled was flying through the air and terrible pain. Then it was lights out.

CHAPTER
TWO

EVERYTHING WAS WHITE. EVERYWHERE he looked, white. White, white and more white. Where was he? Was this heaven? Couldn't be. He would be going in the opposite direction, he was sure of that. Hell. Was hell white? Taylor tried to think, but his head hurt. If his head hurt, he couldn't be dead, could he?

Taylor became aware of a slight beeping noise. Slowly he opened his eyes and saw more white, this time a white ceiling. Okay, for some reason he wasn't dead.

Then the face of an angel came into view. A woman. Her hair was an abundant mane of brown with gold and red glints, her eyes were a whiskey brown color and she was the most beautiful woman Taylor had ever seen. Surely he was dead and this WAS heaven! Then the apparition spoke.

"Mr. Boudrain? How are you feeling? Do you have pain?"

Taylor tried to wrap his brain around the moment. Gingerly he turned his head to take in his surroundings. He was in a hospital bed, and looking further, he could see he was alone in a room with glass walls at the far end where he could see nurses and doctors and NA's busily scurrying around. The beeping he had heard was an IV hooked up to his arm which was feeding him fluids. So, a hospital. He focused his attention back on the woman. He could see she was dressed in white (white again, when he died he probably would see only white. The thought scared the beejeebers out of him). He read her I.D. tag: T. Patterson. He tried to speak but only managed a weak croak.

"Here, this should help," the soft voice said. A hand held out a small paper cup. She helped support his shoulders a bit as he took a sip of the water. It hurt like hell to move. She eased him back and he looked up into that beautiful face again. What lush lips. Kissable lips.

"Where am I?" he finally managed to say.

"You're at Lewiston Memorial Hospital, Mr. Boudrain. You were in a very bad motorcycle accident. Do you remember?"

Taylor frowned and just that movement had him wincing in pain. "Yeah. I was driving along…a semi. I think a semi hit me." He closed his eyes, sighing heavily. "Oh, God. How bad am I?"

He opened his eyes to see her golden eyes smile down at him softly. "You were very lucky. Wearing your helmet saved your life. You have a slight head concussion and your ribs are very badly bruised. Nothing is broken, but you are in ICU to monitor you for the next several days. A cat scan has been administered and the doctor can tell you more about that. But your biggest injury was to your ribs. They will hurt badly for a while, but they will heal up."

As she spoke, Taylor looked down at his ribcage and could see it was heavily bound and restricted his breathing. And breathing in and out hurt like a bitch. He looked back up at Nurse Patterson.

"Fortunately for you also, there was a doctor who witnessed the whole scene and called 911 promptly and the quick response probably also saved you."

"And my bike?" he asked.

Tessa looked down at the gorgeous man in the bed. Even as banged up as he was, she had never seen a finer specimen. But his question seemed strange to her. He was worried about a motorcycle when he was in the ICU?

"Your bike was pretty mangled. It ended up under the semi. You were thrown clear. Another event that probably saved your life." She continued to study him as he took stock of his injuries. She knew he was that famous movie star. His gear and effects had survived the crash too, landing nearby him. He was just as terrific looking in person as on the big screen. What kind of person was he? Would he be a difficult patient, or was he a good man? Tessa had no clue from their conversation so far.

"So, again Mr. Boudrain. Are you in pain?"

"Yeah. My head hurts pretty bad and my ribs, when I breathe—"

"Okay. I'll be right back. The doctor has prescribed some pain medication for you." She turned to go.

"Wait." His word stopped her and she turned to him with brows raised in question. "What is your name?" he managed to say.

"Tessa. My name is Tessa." She turned and left him.

After Tessa gave him his medication, no matter how hard he tried to stay awake to speak to her, he couldn't do it. He nodded right out and when he woke, he could see it was now evening. He looked around for Tessa and what he saw hovering over his bed actually startled him.

"Yikes!" It came out before he could bite back the words.

Battleaxe Nurse leaned over him. She had to be seventy if she was a day. Her face was deeply lined and she had scraggly grey hair, but she did have kind brown eyes. Groaning, he closed his eyes again. Maybe it was a nightmare and she would go away.

No such luck. "Mr. Boudrain? I know you're awake. I need to take your blood pressure and administer your pain medication. Mr. Boudrain?" she repeated.

Slowly Taylor opened his eyes. Yep, she was still here. Where was the other one, Tessa? Must be off shift.

"Yeah. Okay, fine," he answered Nurse Battleaxe.

"Ya know, you're lucky to be alive, sweet thing," she informed him as she put the cuff on his arm.

He winced. Christ, even his arm hurt.

"Got some bad bruises and such, but you should mend. Big strong guy like you."

Taylor grunted in answer. "Just give me the meds. I want to go back to dreamland. Where is the other one? Tess—"

Battleaxe smiled. "Ah ha! Got the hots for our Tessa? Forget it! She ain't available."

"Oh, isn't that nice?" Taylor dropped back into unconsciousness.

The morning sun pouring through the far window woke Taylor. He looked around the room and could see a very curvaceous female with her back to him. When he saw the luxuriant mane of brown hair, he knew immediately it was Tessa. She was fussing with some tray across from him or something.

"Hey," he said weakly.

Tessa turned to him, turning up the wattage on her smile. Be still my heart, he warned himself. He made a half hearted attempt to return her smile. Christ, his ribs were killing him again.

"I have some breakfast for you, Mr. Boudrain. The doctor has ordered only light broths and juice for now, but you should get some hardier fare tomorrow if everything seems okay." She placed the tray on the swing arm table and elevated his bed enough that he could easily reach the tray. It contained soup broth, green jello (yuck) and what looked like apple juice.

He groaned. He'd rather go back to sleep than eat this slop.

"Are you in pain again, Mr. Boudrain?"

Taylor grimaced and looked up at her. "Yeah. And it's gonna be a whole lot worse if I gotta eat this stuff. No thanks."

She smiled sweetly. "Sorry, but it's this or nothing. And nothing isn't a choice. Eat." She pointed to the food. She shook a paper cup invitingly. "And if you do, you'll get some of these. Pills to make you feel better." She smiled saucily.

"Do you treat all your patients like this, Tessa? Like they are little kids begging for a treat?"

She smiled again. "Only the stubborn ones."

"Okay, okay. I'll give it a shot. If I barf, it's on you."

"I am a nurse, Mr. Boudrain. I've cleaned up a lot of what you call barf."

Surreptitiously Taylor studied her hands for signs of a ring. What did the old Battleaxe say last night? Tessa was unavailable? He looked hard. Nope, no rings on any of her fingers. No flashy diamond, no gold wedding band, no nothing. Hmmmmm…

Hurriedly Taylor finished up the breakfast. When he ate his last spoonful of soup, Tessa smiled and gave him his pills with water.

After that, it was back to dreamland for Taylor.

When he woke up, he was alone. The clock on the wall told him it was mid afternoon. He pressed the nurses' button, summoning Tessa. Hopefully she hadn't gone home yet.

Within five minutes she appeared in his door, approaching the bed with yet another tray in her hands. She smiled at him.

"I'm glad you're awake. It's time for your sponge bath."

"Wha— a sponge what?" Taylor eyed the tray warily. It contained a sponge, what looked like antibacterial soap, wash cloths and towels.

"Yep. Time to clean up a bit."

Taylor reconsidered. It might not be so bad having her touching him, giving him a 'sponge bath'. He flashed his famous grin. "Okay, darlin. Whatever you say."

At this comment, Tessa glanced over at him, wringing out the sponge. "I can see you're feeling better."

"A bit. Never had a sponge bath. Is it fun?" he grinned wickedly.

"Don't get any prurient ideas, Mr. Boudrain. A bath is a bath." She got to work, scrubbing at his arms and chest, being very careful around the bandaged ribs. She was gentle and had slim, beautiful hands. As she continued to bathe him, he addressed her.

"Why don't you call me Taylor, okay? Everyone else does. Mr. Boudrain is so formal."

Tessa looked up from her chore. "Very well. Taylor."

He liked the way his name rolled off of her tongue in the upstate New Yawk accent. "And I'll call you Tessa, darlin."

She rose to her full height, throwing the sponge down and picking up towels. "You may call me Tessa. But drop the darlin. I'm not your darling." She dried him off as Taylor attempted to get more information.

"If you're not my darlin, are you anyone else's?" Teal eyes studied her closely.

Tessa finished with the sponge bath and gathered up her tray and supplies. "That, my dear Mr. Boudrain, is none of your business." With that comment, she left the room.

Taylor sighed. Eventually he slept again.

When he woke, Battleaxe was back. She was putting something into his IV. He hoped it was something that would send him back to sleep, because he felt wide awake now. And only had Battleaxe for company. Maybe he could worm some information about Tessa out of her.

"Hey," he said by way of greeting.

"So, you're awake. How are you feeling?"

"The pain's not as bad, still there, but bearable. Pretty awake, though."

"That's a good sign." She went back to whatever she was doing with his tubes.

He strained to see her I.D. tag. After all, he couldn't call her Battleaxe if he wanted to get on her good side. He caught a K. S. something or other. He cleared his throat. "So, Nurse— ah, what do I call you?"

She turned to him. "You call me nurse."

Now he could read her I.D. tag. It said C. Wilson. Okay, his vision was seriously messed up. "Well, I guess it must be Nurse Wilson. What does the C stand for?" He smiled at her.

As usual, his smile worked. The old Battleaxe actually grinned back at him. She wasn't too bad actually when she smiled. "It's Cathy. Cathy Wilson. And you're Taylor Boudrain, that hot shot movie star."

Taylor did the humble act. After all, he *was* an actor and could pull it off. "Yeah, that's me. Don't let on to anybody, though. Wouldn't want your hospital to become a riot zone from the stampeding of fans."

She threw her head back and laughed at that one. "You're something, you are." She put her hands on her prominent hips. "Say, I know you must get asked this all the time, but my daughter and granddaughter are crazy about you. Could I get your autograph for them?"

"Sure. Got paper and pen," he offered generously.

She produced a notepad and pen, handing them to him.

"What are their names?" he asked.

"My daughter is Kaitlin with a K, and my granddaughter is Emily."

She waited patiently as he wrote a little note to both mother and daughter. Nurse Wilson took the notepad back and noticed he had written a little note to both women and signed it with his sweeping autograph. "Well, that was very kind of you." Her brown eyes rose to his.

"Well, if you're going to give an autograph, give an AUTEEGRAPH!" Again the grin flashed. As she turned to go, he stopped her. "Hey, about Tessa—"

Nurse Wilson turned back to him, smiling. "That's right. You got a thing for our Tessa."

"Well, I don't know if it's a thing. But I was just curious about her. You said something about she is unavailable. What did you mean? I didn't notice any rings on her fingers." He waited expectantly for her reply.

Nurse Wilson was silent for a moment, holding her notepad and eyeing him. Finally she relented. "What I meant is; Tessa's got a lot on her plate. She doesn't have time for men. Even famous ones."

Taylor frowned and immediately got a headache. "I don't get it."

"Sorry, Taylor, my boy. That's all you're going to get from me. If you want to know more about Tessa, you'll have to ask her yourself. I'm sure a handsome stud like you usually has no problems with women. But Tessa's different. I don't think she'll be as easily impressed with you as some others." She smiled at him. "Now you get some rest. I did put something in your I.V. that will help with that."

As she left, Taylor didn't have time to speculate on her words. He conked out.

The next morning a different nurse was in attendance, some little blonde. Tessa must have the day off. Just great.

"Hi there, blondie!" When she turned to smile at him, he continued. "When do I blow this pop joint?"

"Well, doctor says it will be at least a couple more days. We are going to take a walk down the hall today. Get you out of that bed." She smiled perkily.

Oh Christ. Where was Tessa when he needed her?

CHAPTER
THREE

TESSA STUDIED THE MAN sleeping in the hospital bed. His glorious blond hair was spread across the pillow and his face was turned away from her so that she could not see his perfect features. He had one arm flung wide and slept deeply, his chest rising and falling gently. She noticed his fair eye lashes were long and brushed his cheeks as he slept. He looked like a fallen angel, too beautiful to be earthly. Tessa silently snorted. The man was well aware of how gorgeous he was and made no bones about it, flashing that dazzling grin and spreading it around like diamonds to charm the female species. Tessa didn't need the complication of a man in her life and she had no plans to get involved with this one, but even she could not ignore the sheer brilliance of his looks. Steve had been good looking too, and look how that had turned out...

He turned and groaned slightly in his sleep and she moved to him to check his pulse. As soon as she touched him she saw his eyes flutter open. The laser beam teal eyes speared her and she smiled tentatively.

"Hi," she said.

"Hey," he mumbled, clearly still half asleep.

"How do you feel? Any pain? Did you sleep okay?"

He sighed, running his fingers through his glorious hair. She noticed the darker honey strands threaded throughout the lighter gold. She knew it was his natural color, there was no way you could fake those shades. She shook off her thoughts.

"I slept okay. I am tired of just sleeping. Would it be possible for you to bring me some books today?"

Tessa's brown eyes widened. "Books?" She said the word as though she had never heard of the item.

"Yeah, you know, books to read? Any kind, I'm not fussy. There must be

13

some down in the gift store. Could you get a bunch sent up? At least I can read if I gotta lay here. Can't stand watching TV." He gestured to the overhead television high on the wall.

Tessa was just so startled he was a reader, he didn't seem like the type. She also loved to read and was amazed that she had *anything* in common with him.

He waited for her answer as she rose, looking down at him. "Certainly. I'll have a PA go down and pick some up. How many would you like?"

"At least ten or so. How long am I going to be in this joint? Doc didn't say."

"The doctor will be in to speak to you shortly. There was something found on one of your X-rays that he would like to speak to you about."

Taylor arched a golden brow. "Oh really?"

"I can't elaborate. You need to speak to the doctor about it. Can I get you anything else? Are you hungry?"

"Can I get some pancakes and orange juice? You know— real food?" he asked with a slight smirk.

Tessa smiled as she prepared to leave. "I think that can be arranged."

The doctor arrived soon after Tessa left him. She was true to her word. He received several books from an aide and he was perusing them when the doctor entered.

He was an older man, probably mid sixties, with gray hair and eyeglasses. Looked like your typical efficient doctor. He knew since he had been in an accident he was assigned to the doc on duty. He seemed to recall his name was Dr. Franklin. What a hoot! If Frank could see him now...

"Good morning, Mr. Boudrain. How are you feeling this morning?"

Taylor shrugged a bit. "Better than two days ago. Still have a lot of pain in my ribs. My head is much better, no pain there."

"We were worried about a slight concussion. You can remember all of the events leading up to your accident?" The doctor studied him as he laid a notepad on his lap.

"Yeah. Everything. I was on my Harley just cruisin' along and then BAM! Some dummy in a semi hits my bike and I go sailing. That's all I remember until I woke up here."

"Okay. How about past memories? Do you remember everything about yourself?"

Taylor snorted. "Yeah. Too well."

"Fine. Now let's talk about your physical injuries. As you know, your ribs were badly bruised. I've taken another look at the X-rays we ran the night you arrived and a tiny hairline fracture was missed by the tech that night. On your left ribcage, about here," he indicated the area on his own body, "you have a tiny fracture in your third rib. What this means is your recovery will take a bit longer than we originally thought. Bruised ribs can heal fairly quickly. A fractured rib takes longer, meaning your ribs will need to stay wrapped and you will need someone who can help you do that once you are discharged. Do you have anyone who can help in this area?" The doctor's dark eyes studied him closely.

"Hell no, doc. When I'm discharged, the only place I have to go that is actually home is all the way in California. And no, I don't have anyone to help out." Taylor didn't want to get into the reasons why he didn't employ help at his mansion back there. Hell, he was never there.

"Hmmm…that's going to be a bit of a problem. We can't discharge you yet, not for several days. But soon and you will need this medical care. Perhaps hire a visiting nurse?"

"Wait a minute, doc." If they were thinking of discharging him, how the hell would he get to see Tessa? Bottom line, he wouldn't. "If my rib is fractured as you say, shouldn't I be staying in here for a while?"

"For a while, yes. I would say several more days, just to keep an eye on that rib. In fact, we're moving you out of ICU today to a regular room. It will be private, of course." He was well aware Taylor was a VIP patient.

Taylor didn't like this idea at all. Not only would he not get to see Tessa after discharge, he would not get to see her *at all*. "Listen, doc." The teal eyes swung to the doctor's, a bit of entreaty in them. "I really like being up here in ICU. They are taking such good care of me. Do I really have to move? If you need the bed, I understand, but unless it is absolutely necessary, I prefer to stay here."

Dr. Franklin studied Taylor. They didn't have an immediate need for the bed and he could accommodate Taylor's request. He suspected this had something to do with the pretty nurse, Tessa.

Dr. Franklin smiled. "Okay. We don't need the bed right at the moment. So if you want to spend your remaining time here, I can speak to the head of ICU. I'm pretty sure she will okay it. She has a crush on you, as do all of the nurses on this floor." The doctor chuckled.

"Maybe not all," Taylor mumbled.

"I'm going to examine you now and then I'll speak to the ICU head." He leaned over and inspected Taylor's bandaged head, gently tapping. "Hurt?"

"No." Taylor was surprised by that.

The doctor moved his hands down to the ribs, compressing slightly, especially on the left side. "Again, hurt?"

Taylor's breath whooshed in. Yes, it hurt like a bitch! "Yes!" he gasped.

The doctor's brows knit. "Okay. I'm going to authorize you stay on the pain meds. And something to help you sleep too." He glanced at the pile of books on Taylor's night table. "Good thing you have those, you may be here for a little while."

This news cheered Taylor a bit. Good, Tessa hadn't escaped him yet.

She was back shortly with his breakfast, steaming pancakes, o.j. toast and black coffee. Hot damn! Taylor grinned. "Yeah, this is more like it."

Tessa looked down at him coolly. "The doctor has informed me you won't be moved to a regular room." This went against all protocol for the hospital when a patient was well enough to be moved.

Taylor flashed his grin. "Yep. I talked him into letting me stay in the ICU. Aren't you happy, darlin'?"

Tessa remained silent making sure his bed was elevated so he could reach his food. Straightening, she looked down at her patient. "It's not my decision to make."

"That's not what I asked you, darlin'."

"Taylor, we've been over this. Please don't call me darlin'. It's condescending." She moved his pillow up a bit for his back so he could sit straighter.

Taylor was a bit taken aback. This thought had never occurred to him and the women he had so addressed had never had a problem with it. Obviously Tessa did.

At his silence, Tessa rose to meet his eyes. He had a serious and contemplative expression. "Sorry. I never thought of it that way. I won't say it again."

He dug into his food, chewing and not meeting her eyes. Tessa suddenly felt very down, she had no idea why. Like she had kicked a puppy or something. For him, it was probably just a friendly expression. After all, he was southern. Frowning, she left the room as Taylor continued to eat his breakfast.

When Tessa returned to remove his breakfast tray and give him medication, she found Taylor reading a book. A Dean Koontz novel, *Watchers*. She recalled reading it a long time ago. It was scary but a very good read.

As she swept up the tray, Taylor's eyes rose. "Can I ask you a question?"

Tessa's eyes turned to him. "Yes. What is it?"

"Don't you like me for some reason?"

Tessa was startled. "Whatever gave you that impression?"

Taylor shrugged. "I don't know. You just don't respond to my usual female magnet personality." He laughed slightly, the grin curling around his full sculpted lips.

Tessa put one hand on her hip, holding the tray in the other. "Well, let's put it this way, Taylor. You do have quite the ego. But that is probably a movie star thing, huh?"

Taylor contemplated her words. "Yeah. I guess you're right. An ego as big as Texas. Thanks for answering my question." His eyes went back to his book.

Tessa left more bewildered with her patient than ever.

Tessa stopped into Taylor's room before the end of her shift. She really didn't need to, he was taken care of for now, but she felt a need to speak to him. Their earlier exchanges left her feeling a bit uneasy, as if she had somehow been unkind to him and she didn't like the feeling.

She entered his door and could see he must have been tired of reading. His book lay on his lap and his eyes were slightly droopy.

"Hey," she said softly. "You asleep?"

Taylor turned his head at the sound of her voice. He was amazed to see her, he knew her shift ended fifteen minutes ago (he had checked) and even more amazing, she was in street clothes. She wore faded snug jeans that clung to a very slender, curvaceous figure and a light blue vee neck tee, sneakers on her feet. Her beautiful brown hair was pulled back in a ponytail, emphasizing the whiskey colored eyes and her high cheekbones. She looked marvelous.

"Hey," he responded. "No, I'm not asleep."

She tucked her hands in the back pockets of her jeans. "I just wanted to stop by and see you before I left. I just felt—" she hesitated and he watched her keenly. Those teal eyes shot through her like laser beams. "I just wanted to say I didn't mean to hurt your feelings or anything earlier. I didn't mean to sound so— so abrupt," she ended awkwardly.

Taylor flashed a grin. It lit up his whole face. "I forgive you, sweetheart. See ya tomorrow, same time, same place?"

Tessa smiled slowly. "Yeah. Uh, huh."

"It's a date!"

Tessa smiled, turned and left.

Taylor laid his head back on the pillow, his own smile soft and wistful.

Nurse Battleaxe was back. 'Scuse me. Nurse Wilson.

She leaned over his bed, placing a blood pressure wrap on his arm and pumping the balloon end for all she was worth. Taylor decided Battleaxe owed him more answers for those generous autographs.

"Hi, Nurse Wilson. How are ya?"

"Just fine, Taylor, my lad. Just fine. And how is our most famous patient feeling?" She looked down at him as she slowly released pressure on the cuff.

"I've had better days."

The nurse looked down at him. "What do you mean? Something wrong here?"

"No, no. Not with the hospital or your wonderful care. I just have some questions and I'm hoping you can answer them."

"This is about Tessa, isn't it?" Nurse Wilson rose to full height, removing the blood pressure cuff, making notations on her chart.

"Yeah, it is. I want to know more about her. Does she date? Have a guy in her life? C'mon, Cathy," he cajoled. "Those autographs have to be worth *some* information."

Nurse Wilson did the silent bit again. Then she relented like before. Damn, he was good. "It is common knowledge, but it's not really my place to be telling you this. Tessa will tell you herself, if she wants you to know. But I can answer your basic question. No, she doesn't date and doesn't have a man in her life."

Taylor squeezed his eyes shut. "Oh God. She isn't gay, is she?" That would be a nightmare come true in his case. He had the hots for her, big time.

"No, Taylor. That's not why. She has a son, a little son. And he has autism."

Nurse Wilson turned and marched out of the room as Taylor digested this information.

Autism? What was that? All he could recall was that movie *Rain Man* and it didn't inspire great feelings. Tessa had a son with a disability!

CHAPTER
FOUR

"So, you finally decided to call me. You've only been gone two weeks and do I hear a word from you. No!" Frank's voice berated Taylor through his cell phone. It had miraculously survived the crash with his effects and Nurse Battleaxe had returned it two days ago, but Taylor hadn't felt up to dealing with Frank until now.

"So, where are you?" Frank's voice demanded.

Taylor was starting to get a bit of a headache. His agent could do that sometimes even when his head wasn't batted around in a cycle accident. He sighed, answering his agent. "I've been around. Actually, you won't believe where I am." He looked around the hospital room as he spoke.

"With you Taylor, I can believe anything. Are you in Alaska, for Christ's sake? St. Thomas? Where?"

"No Frank. Nothing as exotic as all of that. I happen to be in a hospital. In upstate New York," he calmly replied.

Frank went ballistic. "Are you shitting me?! What the fuck, Taylor—"

Before he could go off on his expected rant, Taylor interrupted him. "Look, Frank. Obviously I'm okay or you wouldn't be speaking to me. I crashed my cycle and I've got some ribs that are hurtin' big time, a slight concussion, but they tell me I'll live. So I'll live to make another movie for you, pal."

Frank felt a bit of chagrin. "Taylor, I'm worried about *you*, not my money making star."

"Well, that's mighty nice of you, hoss."

"Where exactly are you at? I can have the private jet out to you in moments and we can get you back here and properly cared for. Just—"

"No, no. I'm getting fine care. Remember, I'm taking a sabbatical. I plan to stay around this town for a little while. And Frank," he continued, "I don't want the media knowing about this accident. I really don't. I don't want the locusts descending on these fine people. I mean it, Frank."

Frank knew when Taylor used his given name he was dead serious. Frank sighed. "Okay. Where are you exactly anyway?"

"A little town above Niagara Falls, called Lewiston. They got me here right away and probably saved my life."

"What the hell happened?" Frank demanded.

"A semi decided to collide with my bike. I went sailing but was wearing my helmet, so I'm here to talk about it. It's a cute little town, especially now with the leaves changin' and such. Beautiful scenery around here."

"Taylor, cut the crap. When are you coming back?"

"Not for a while, hoss. Told you. Gonna hang out here for a little while. Six months, remember?"

"Why there of all places?" Then it dawned on Frank. "It's a woman. There's a woman there you're interested in."

"Got it in one, Frankie."

Frank sighed. "All right, Taylor. Keep in touch. I'll send flowers." Click.

Frank hung up before Taylor could assure him he didn't want any freakin' flowers.

Sighing, Taylor tossed the phone aside.

The morning got brighter when Tessa appeared at his door, carrying in his breakfast tray. She was silent as she placed his food in front of him, adjusting the table. Taylor was content just to watch her. She had her glorious hair pulled back into what looked like a tight French twist (Taylor knew these little details from all of the women he dated). The style showed off her incredible features and eyes. She straightened and looked down at him.

"Do you need any pain medication, Taylor? It's been several hours. How are you feeling?"

She was all business, business, as though their conversation yesterday afternoon had never occurred. Taylor remembered what the Battleaxe had told him about her son and wondered about that. Had she been married? Was she divorced? It was none of his business, but of course he wanted to know all about her and he knew he only had a few days to accomplish that task.

"Are you busy right now, Tessa? Got a moment to talk? And no, I can hold off on the pain meds just for now." He flashed his winning smile at her, hoping she would be chatty.

She placed her hands on her hips, studying him warily. "Talk? What do you want to talk about? And yes, I *am* busy. I have other patients."

"Okay. I'll cut to the chase. I know about your son and I know he has autism. I'm just curious about you, Tessa."

Tessa's brows arched. "I see the resident gossips have been in here."

"Nope. I wormed it out of someone and I'm not saying who." If he needed more info, he didn't want to blow his spy's identity.

"Yes, Taylor, I have a son. And yes, he has autism. Any other questions?" Tessa crossed her arms over her breasts.

"Tell me about him. And what exactly is autism?" Taylor's teal eyes studied her carefully.

Tessa was thoughtful for a moment, looking down at her patient. Most people had no interest in finding out what autism was or caring about those who suffered from it. Of the men she had dated, as soon as they found out she had a son with a disability, they were shortly gone. And who could really blame them? Taking care of Andrew was a full time job, but totally worth it. She loved him with her whole heart and soul and was fiercely protective of him. But she could see that Taylor seemed to be genuinely interested in her answer. Of course, she had already figured out he had the hots for her, as he probably did for any attractive woman. Tessa was aware she was a beauty; she had dealt with too many jealous women in the past not to be aware of that fact. These thoughts flew through her head as she decided how to answer him. Her private life was very personal and Taylor was a total stranger. Or was he? Something in his eyes made her feel she knew him quite well already, which was totally absurd.

She finally answered him. "Autism is a developmental disability. A child can be quite normal until maybe the age of eighteen months. Then suddenly he changes. He doesn't speak, he has an abnormal attraction to objects or things and will line them up, instead of playing as a normal child will. He may not even interact with those around him. Those are the stereotypical aspects of autism. As with any group of people, autism varies greatly from person to person. My son is verbal and is in a very good school that is helping him to learn social skills and academics. He is my life. Does that answer your question?"

Taylor frowned slightly, taking in all of this information.

"And his father?" he asked tentatively.

"Was killed in a motorcycle accident. See how lucky you are to be here, Taylor? I'll have a PA pick up your tray when you're through with your breakfast." She turned and left the room.

Taylor just looked at his food. He wasn't hungry at all and needed some time to ruminate on all Tessa had just told him.

He didn't see her for the rest of the day. A nurse's aide brought him his meds and his lunch. Taylor spent the time reading, wondering what he would say to Tessa when he finally did see her. I'm sorry that your son is autistic? No, she didn't want pity and obviously loved her son exactly as he was. He wondered if she was married to the father. Yeah, most likely. He couldn't see Tessa being in a relationship with a child without being married. So, Tessa was a widow and according to Battleaxe, didn't date. Where did that leave him? And how could he convince her she was a guy he could trust, especially with his awful reputation? Yep, he certainly had his work cut out for him.

His ribs still hurt when he moved around, but not as badly. He made sure he took several walks a day around the floor, trying to get his strength back. In his perambulations, he never saw Tessa. He was aware she had other patients, but he also knew she was avoiding him. And what if she had another day off? Oh hell, then what?

Taylor decided to take each day as it came. If he rushed her, he would just scare her off. At least now, with her job, she *had* to interact with him. He would have to use those moments wisely.

An elaborate flower arrangement came for Taylor that afternoon from Frank. The thing was freaking HUGE. It had every flower imaginable tastefully arranged in a large white wicker basket all tied up with a festive bow. In the center, he saw one perfect pink rose just starting to bloom. He immediately pulled it from the arrangement, inhaling the delicious aroma. Maybe flowers weren't such a bad thing after all. He read the card Frank sent briefly. "Get well soon. And get your ass back here soon, too. Frank." Taylor chuckled.

One of the other nurses came in to rewrap his bandage, not Tessa. He smiled at her as she did her job and when she was through, he pointed at the gorgeous floral arrangement. "Hey darlin'. Why don't you take that arrangement out to the nurses' desk? Y'all can enjoy them."

The nurse gasped. "Oh sir! You don't want those lovely flowers?"

"Yeah, they're pretty and everything, but it's my way of saying thanks to everyone here. Could you do that for me?" He smiled up at her.

"Of course. Thank you! Thank you very much!" She was all smiles as she lifted the large basket of flowers and carried it proudly out to the main desk, which he could just glimpse through the glass walls. He saw all the nurses exclaiming as the arrangement was placed on the desk. Shortly every single nurse and aide was in to thank him, with the exception of Tessa.

The sun was waning and he could see another day was ending. He only had maybe two more days here and had to figure out where he would stay after leaving. It was a dilemma.

A slight noise at his door drew his attention. Tessa stood there with her purse slung over her shoulder and a sweater on her arm. She still wore her uniform but it was apparent she was leaving for the day.

"Hi. I just wanted to stop by before leaving to say thanks for the flowers. That was a wonderful gesture." Her dark eyes were solemn.

"Yeah, I wanted to thank everyone here. They've been great. But—" he paused, pulling the perfect pink rose from the table, "I saved the best for you." He handed her the perfect bloom and she accepted it hesitantly. He smiled softly as she inspected the perfect flower.

"Well, thank you, Taylor. I don't know what to say—" she seemed at a loss.

"'Well, thank you, Taylor' will do just fine."

Tessa's golden eyes lifted to his. "I have to go. Andrew will be home soon." She hesitated. "I'll see you tomorrow."

Taylor crossed his arms. "I hope so. Hope you don't avoid me like you did today."

Tessa's cheeks pinkened. "Goodbye, Taylor."

Taylor spent the remainder of his day and evening in his usual fashion. Reading and bantering with the Battleaxe.

CHAPTER

FIVE

TESSA DROVE UP THE driveway to her home and parked her mid sized SUV in front of the garage. There was a three car garage that Steve had wanted to work on his motorcycles and it had a very cute and spacious carriage house above. She had been trying to rent it out for ages, but most single people preferred apartments or condos. The extra money the rent would bring in would definitely help pay for the home tutor she wanted to hire for Andrew. She didn't want to touch the trust fund money she had set aside. That was for Andrew's future so they lived strictly on her salary.

As she emerged from the vehicle, she thought about Andrew's caretaker, Rose Hamilton. Rose rented the bottom flat of the Victorian duplex Tessa owned. She and Andrew lived in the top portion of the house. It was a lovely old home that was on a slightly wooded lot and even possessed a beautiful front porch, which seemed to be a dying breed on homes built these days. Tessa had an old fashioned swing suspended on it and she and Andrew spent many summer days talking and playing there. Mrs. Hamilton was an elderly widow who was responsible for Andrew's care until Tessa returned home from work. She was wonderful with Andrew and Tessa thanked her lucky stars she had a support system for her son. She knew many families were not that lucky. Since Steve's family had disowned her, and Tessa didn't have any living family, Rose was all she and Andrew had.

Tessa slung her purse over her shoulder, heading toward the back door which would lead into the large old fashioned kitchen. She looked around at the blazing autumn colors of the trees. It was mid September and soon winter would be coming. Unfortunately Lewiston was located smack dab in the middle of two of the Great Lakes, Lake Erie and Lake Ontario, and always received the brunt of storms from both lakes. There were times Tessa sorely missed having a man around, mostly when things like winter storms hit and she had to try to shove the snow blower around herself. Although Tessa was tall at five eight, she was slender and sometimes she had to throw her whole slight weight against the thing and with the inclined hill it could be a real pain. But there was no one else to handle the chore. Rose was too old, and Andrew was too young. Her whole face lit up as she thought of her little son.

She unlocked the back door and stepped into the roomy kitchen. "Hello! It's me! Anyone home?"

She heard the pitter patter of running footsteps as Andrew ran into the kitchen from the front living room. Rose was a few steps behind, smiling.

"Mommeee! Mommee! Look! Look!" He held up a drawing proudly and bending down, Tessa took him into her arms, hugging him tightly. She took the proffered drawing, inspecting it. She could see it was a drawing Andrew had made in crayon of herself and her son. Andrew drew the human figures as huge blobs, with blob hands and feet and circles for eyes and noses, but she could clearly see herself with all the brown hair he had added and he had drawn them holding hands. Tears pricked her eyes as she looked down at her perfect looking son.

"I drew! I drew!" he exclaimed.

"It's beautiful, Andrew." She set him down and pointed to the paper. "Who is this?" She pointed to the larger figure with brown hair.

"Mommmeee," he answered.

"And who is this?" she pointed to the smaller figure.

Andrew frowned for a moment, his big brown eyes looking up at Tessa. He was a miniature replica of Tessa. He had her long lashed brown eyes, although his were a shade darker and perfect features. He was six years old and Tessa had cut his brown hair into the wedge cut that looked so cute on little boys— long length all around with long bangs, shaved up the neck and sides. Tessa had to cut his hair herself with scissors because he could not tolerate buzz clippers and she had to do the style on her own, which was a real challenge. But Tessa considered it one of the smaller challenges they faced. Andrew was a beautiful child with a pleasant demeanor and as a result he was very popular at school with the teachers and students.

Finally he answered her question hesitantly. "Me." He pointed to his chest.

"That's right!" Tessa exclaimed, hugging him tightly. Smiling, she rose to look over at Mrs. Hamilton. "How are you, Rose? How are things going?" Tessa smoothed Andrew's hair as she spoke.

"We're doing just fine. No problems getting off of the bus today. It was a beautiful day, so we collected some leaves. Want to go get the leaves to show your mommy, Andrew?"

"Yes, yes!" he exclaimed, running back into the house toward the front room.

Tessa set her purse down on Rose's kitchen table, her eyes rising to meet Rose's. Rose was average height, about sixty six and a real sweetheart. She had kind brown eyes which shined behind the eyeglasses she habitually wore, her grey hair pulled back from her face which she usually wore in a bun or upswept style. In Tessa's opinion, she was an angel from heaven.

"How have things been today?" she asked Rose. Andrew had good days and "off" days. On off days, he could be quite a handful.

"He's been in a very good mood today. Here is the communication book from school and his backpack." Tessa accepted the items as Rose studied her. "Would you like to stay for dinner tonight? I made spaghetti and there's more than enough."

That sounded heavenly to Tessa. She wouldn't have to cook and she loved Rose's special sauce. She would have to make Andrew his usual peanut butter and jelly sandwich. He ate a very limited diet and Tessa was working with the school trying to get him to expand it.

Tessa took a seat at the table. It was wonderful to finally get off of her feet. "Oh Rose, that sounds great. Thanks. I'll make Andrew his sandwich in just a bit." Sighing, she ran her hands through her hair.

Rose moved toward the cupboards. "No, no. You sit. I know you've been on your feet all day. I'll take care of everything."

She went to get china to set the table as Tessa looked up at her.

"Well, you can at least let me set the table," she remarked.

"I've got it under control, Tessa. You really do look tired."

It had been a long day all right, and dealing with Taylor added to that. She hadn't mentioned Taylor to Rose Hamilton yet. She was a big Boudrain fan (imagine that) and Tessa just didn't want to get into that yet.

Andrew came skipping in with a bunch of leaves, red, bronze, copper and orange. As Tessa oohed and ahhed over them, Rose smiled and went about preparing dinner for mother and son.

In a few hours, after visiting with Rose and helping to clean up after dinner, Tessa and Andrew went upstairs to their own home.

Tessa had been fortunate (if you could call it that) when Steve died. He had believed in making sure his family was well insured. Tessa and Andrew would never be in need. Tessa took the bulk of the money and put it away in a trust for Andrew. She bought the old Victorian house with the remainder. It was lovely and spacious with cherry wood accents throughout. Tessa had bought cozy and comfortable furniture. Since she had the upper flat, she had lovely wooden French doors that opened out onto an upper level porch. She had lace swaged drapes gathered at the center of the doors but when the doors were open, the scenery and view were perfect. It was possible to just make out the Niagara river over the abundant trees. When the leaves started falling in a month, you would be able to see the river and part of the lake. It was a barren view in the winter but right now with the trees changing into beautiful hues it was spectacular.

Tessa opened the French doors to let the gentle evening breeze blow through the front living room. The doors were screened in the summer to prevent her house being full of insects. She stood with Andrew looking out at the view, her hands resting lightly on his shoulders.

She looked down at her son. "Would you like to watch Barney for an hour before bed time and bath?"

This was his evening ritual. It was very important for Andrew to have a routine.

Andrew turned and flopped on the pale, puffy cushions of the sofa. The entertainment unit was directly across the room on the far wall. "Yes, mommee. Barney, please."

Tessa smiled as she slotted in a Barney DVD. Things couldn't be more perfect at the Patterson household.

As usual, Tessa was up bright and early to see Andrew off on his school bus if her schedule allowed it. It was her opportunity to get a final hug and kiss and they had to last her all day. She was working a longer shift today and would not be home until well after dinner.

She hugged her son tightly, leaning down to kiss his cheek.

Andrew laughed, hugged her back and scurried up the steps into the bus. The aide came over and seated him, clicking his belt securely after placing his backpack beside him. The driver greeted her and she chatted with him a few moments before waving goodbye.

Tessa watched as the yellow bus moved down the road, praying for her son's safety as she did every morning.

Sighing, she turned to walk up the driveway to her SUV.

Taylor woke when he heard someone bringing in his breakfast tray. He could see it was Tessa and his heart immediately grew lighter. What was it about her anyway that could make his heart go pitty pat? He hadn't quite figured it out yet. She was certainly beautiful, but Taylor had known many beautiful women. There was something— poignant about her. She had an aura of sadness and hope— a very disturbing combination. Of course, now he understood that a bit better knowing about her son. How had her evening gone?

"Good morning!" she said cheerily.

"Hey you. Missed ya last night," he responded, lifting a piece of toast.

Tessa straightened, arching a brow. "Oh?"

"Yeah. Bantering with the Battleaxe isn't half as fun as looking at you."

"The Battleaxe?" Tessa was baffled.

Taylor laughed, quickly bringing up his napkin. "Whoops! Shouldn't have said that. She really is great. I was referring to Nurse Wilson."

Tessa smiled. She could see where Cathy's first impression could be intimidating. As Taylor had learned, she was a big softie. And now Tessa finally knew who had spilled the beans about Andrew. It didn't matter. It wasn't a big secret and Tessa was very proud of her son. However, she was not in the habit of speaking about him to total strangers or her patients. That was her private life.

"Cathy is a very nice person, Taylor."

"I'm well aware of that. I don't know— it just kinda fits somehow and in my mind I still think of her that way sometimes. My bad." He flashed her his delicious grin.

Tessa tried to ignore how it made her insides flutter.

"Say, Tessa. The doc says I'm probably going to get sprung tomorrow and I was wondering about a place to stay around here. I don't suppose this rinky dink town has any hotels, does it?" Teal eyes studied her as he casually sipped coffee.

Tessa was a bit startled by this statement. She read his chart. Sure enough, he was due to be released the next day. "No, Taylor. We don't have any swanky hotels or such. The best we can do is probably a bed and breakfast."

"Yikes! Never stayed at one of those. Seems like the type of places a Norman Bates would frequent."

Tessa laughed as she caught his reference to the movie *Psycho*. Then she grew thoughtful. She did have the carriage apartment available at her place. Should she mention it? She wasn't quite sure how that would work out with Andrew and everything. Maybe it would be a good thing for her son. He didn't have any male influences in his life. His father had died when Andrew was only one and there were no male teachers or tutors at his school. However, she didn't know how well Taylor took to children. Perhaps she should feel him out a bit before making the offer.

She fluffed his pillows a bit and looked down at him. "Where are you from, Taylor?" she opened casually.

"Why, from Texas, darlin'." His eyes met hers as he scooped up corn flakes.

"Yes, I know. Where at in Texas? What was your family like?"

This was the first time Tessa had ever shown any interest in Taylor beyond her duties as a nurse and Taylor was intrigued. Hmmmmm... "Oh, I grew up in a dirt poor family in Beaumont, Texas. Not far from Houston. There's a bunch of us. I'm smack dab in the middle. Got some sisters and a younger brother."

Tessa took his blood pressure, frowning slightly, avoiding his eyes. "So, you've been around kids a bit?"

"Sure. Kids all over the place when I was growin' up." Again, he wondered where these questions were coming from.

"Do you like kids, Taylor? I mean, you know, like other people's kids?" Her brown eyes studied his as she finished her task.

"Wee-ll, never thought much on it. I haven't been around other people's kids too much. But I've always had a soft spot for kids. Want some of my own. Someday," he answered wistfully, stirring his corn flakes.

It was the right answer. She decided to go ahead, hoping she wasn't making a huge mistake.

"About having someplace to stay—" she tried tentatively.

Taylor's blonde head rose, his teal eyes piercing. "Yeah?"

Tessa tucked away the blood pressure cuff in a pocket, eyeing him warily. "I do know of a place if you're interested."

"Oh, yeah? Where would that be, darlin'?"

"I have a carriage house apartment in the back of my house that I've been trying to rent out. It isn't a huge place, but it's comfortable and has a bunch of windows. It's above a large three car garage that's back away from the house above a slight incline in the drive. If you're interested—"

"Say no more," he interrupted. "I'm interested."

"But Taylor, you don't even know how much I want for the place."

"How much do you want for the place?"

"Well, I was thinking maybe five hundred a month. You would have to pay your own utilities and heat, phone, etc—"

He interrupted again. "I'll pay you a thousand a month and the utilities myself, yadda yadda."

"Just like that." She snapped her fingers. "You're going to pay me double what I want."

"Yep. A problem?"

Tessa put her hands on her hips. "Well, Taylor— maybe. There is my son to consider. He hasn't been around men at all and I don't know how that will work out. I want you to know that if it becomes a problem, I'll have to need you to leave. So I guess we can't sign a formal lease or anything. We'll just have to sign something informally and have a good faith agreement. What do you think about all of this?"

"How old is your son, Tessa?" Taylor chewed his breakfast as he studied her.

Tessa was startled by the question. "He's six, Taylor."

"I'm not afraid of no six year old. And I can assure you, he doesn't have any reason to be afraid of me. Any other objections?"

"No, Taylor. None."

"So tomorrow, when they let me blow this joint, I'll go home with you?"

"You'll be coming with me, but to *your* new home, the carriage house. I have to warn you. There isn't any furniture."

"That's just fine, darlin'. I'll manage until I can purchase some."

Tessa was silent a moment, gazing down at the glorious-looking blonde man. He glanced up at her silence. "Any more concerns, Tessa?"

"No, Taylor. Not at the moment. We'll see." She turned and left.

Taylor contemplated this new chain of events. "Oh yes, Tessa. We will definitely see." He went back to his corn flakes.

CHAPTER
SIX

TAYLOR GLANCED IMPATIENTLY AT the clock on the wall. It was eleven a.m. and he was still in Lewiston Memorial. Tessa had not been in yet to see him this morning, a little blond nurse came instead. She had re-wrapped his ribcage securely, knowing he would be released soon.

Finally the doctor showed up and gave Taylor last minute instructions for the bandage and pain medications and muscle relaxers. Taylor's head bandage had come off days ago and he was able to shower and inspect his face. No lasting damage at all. His ribs still hurt a bit when he breathed but the doctor assured him that was normal and should lessen within weeks.

The doctor stood, clapping his thighs with the file. "You're a big strong guy, Taylor. You'll mend just fine." He smiled down at his famous patient. "One last request, though. An autograph for the wife. She'll kill me if I come home without one. She's been great about not giving away the secret that you're here, and *that* is killing her." He chuckled.

"Sure doc." Taylor took the paper the doctor handed him and wrote a personal note to the doctor's wife.

The doctor inspected it and smiled. "Thanks a lot, Taylor. She'll love that."

"No problem, doc. When will I get out of here?" Taylor arched a brow. He had already changed into his street clothes, the extra pair of jeans and tee shirt salvaged from the accident. He had added an open plaid red flannel shirt over the tee and was forced to wear his sneakers. He was told his boots did not survive the accident. Damn, they were fine boots too.

"I'll have all the discharge papers in shortly. You should be able to leave by noon."

Noon. Taylor checked the clock again. It was eleven fifteen. Where was Tessa?

She showed up at his door right at noon with a wheelchair. Taylor stood to his full height and Tessa's head rose. She didn't realize just how tall he was seeing him in bed every day. He must be at least six four, she thought. She maneuvered the chair so he could sit in it, but Taylor waved it away.

"I don't need that thing, Tessa." He picked up his bag with his personal effects. "I'm ready and can walk out just fine."

She was also in street clothes, wearing faded jeans and a pale pink sweater. She looked sweet with her brown hair tumbling over her shoulders, the lights picking out golden glints in it. "Taylor," she began firmly, "we have a strict rule that all patients—"

He waved it away again. "I don't care what the rules are, Tessa. Never followed 'em in my life. Why would I start now?" He gave her a sardonic smile, looking down at her.

She pushed it aside. "Fine. But if you fall flat on your face, don't blame me."

He grinned then swept his hand toward the door. "After you, Tessa."

She led the way down the halls and everyone came over to say goodbye to Taylor. He was quite popular in the hospital and it took a while for them to get disentangled from everyone before they were on their way to the garage.

"I was able to park in the underground garage. It is closer than employee parking, so you won't have to walk as far." She opened the main hospital door as they crossed over the street to the garage. She noticed Taylor grimace slightly. "You okay?" she asked.

"Yeah," he grunted. "It's just my ribs. They just hurt a bit here and there."

"Did you take your last prescribed pain med?" she asked as she guided him to the elevator which would take them to the floor she parked on.

"No. I didn't want to. Things make me woozy. I'm only gonna take them if I really need to."

"Taylor, you are given meds for a reason. Take them. You are just now being released. You will have pain for a while." She led the way toward her SUV as Taylor rolled his eyes.

"I'll live."

She popped the trunk on her vehicle. "Let's hope so."

Taylor glanced around at the scenery as Tessa drove to her place. He noticed the trees were really changing now. Bronzes and gold dominated instead of summery green. What was it, mid September? He couldn't remember.

He turned to Tessa. She had on sunglasses that he thought made her look very sexy. "What date is it?"

She turned to him briefly, then her eyes went back to the road. "Today is September 17th."

Taylor acknowledged that statement with a nod. "When does winter arrive? September 18th?" he smirked.

Tessa laughed a bit. "No. Not quite that early. But don't be surprised if you see snow swirling in October. It's been known to happen. Which brings up a question. How long are you planning on staying? Don't you have to get back to film some movie?"

Taylor sighed, laying his head back and closing his eyes. "No. I'm on hiatus. Told my agent I was taking six months off. That's why I was in your good little town on my bike. Just cruisin' around to see the country. I don't have to worry about being back for a while. Besides, I need to heal up. Can't do stunt work with a bad rib."

Tessa was greatly surprised by his last statement. "You do your own stunt work?"

"Sure do. If I can do it, I should. It's part of my job." He opened his teal eyes to study her. "Say, do you have an extra pair of sunglasses? This bright light is kinda giving me a headache."

"Sorry Taylor. No."

"I'm gonna need a bunch of basic things, like some food and stuff, some more clothes. Can we stop at a store along the way?"

"I guess so. There's a Target not far from here."

"Okay, great." Taylor laid his head back again and closed his eyes.

After collecting some bedding, towels, extra briefs, food and other essentials, Tessa swung her vehicle toward her home. She pulled up the drive and braked in front of the carriage house.

Taylor emerged from his side of the vehicle, looking up at the carriage house through his new mirrored sunglasses. They had helped to back his headache off. What he saw pleasantly surprised him. It wasn't what he was used to. He was used to large and elegant but the carriage house was quaint and picturesque. It was white and had the intricate Victorian carvings that he noticed on the main house as they passed it. There were four large windows across the front and he could see more on the sides of the structure. He would definitely have to invest in window shades soon. In fact, he needed to furnish the place from the ground up. He turned to Tessa, smiling. "Cute. Can I see the inside?"

Tessa had been holding her breath, wondering how the hot shot movie star would react to her carriage house. "Sure." She pulled keys from her purse, and handed him an extra one. "Here is your key." He accepted it silently and followed her up steep stairs.

The stairs ended and to the right of him there was a long ledge that separated the stairwell from the rest of the apartment. It was spacious and well lit with shiny hard wood floors.

Tessa gave him a tour, showing him the main bedroom. It was pretty spacious, again with more windows. She showed him the bathroom and he was pleasantly surprised to see it had recently been upgraded with new brass fixtures for the sink and shower. It was modern, clean and was tiled in dazzling white. Unlike the other rooms, there was not a window.

Taylor walked out into the main room and could see the ceiling was a slight cathedral height. The room had many possibilities but he wasn't much in the decorating department. He had always hired people for that.

He turned to Tessa, smiling. "I love it!" he grinned.

At his words, she smiled.

"But I'm gonna need help in getting it all furnished and decorated. Know how to do that, or anyone I can hire?"

Tessa had tons of ideas for the carriage house. She always had but her imagination took her in directions her budget did not. That should not be an issue with Taylor, however.

"Well, I've always imagined what I would do with the place. I'd get a big comfy sectional and put it in the center of the room. Then I'd place big wooden tables all around with pretty jewel colored lamps. Lots of big cushions. Maybe an antique rocker in the window over there. A big bookcase over there. And a huge sleigh bed for the master room. Then of course, personalize it with any artwork or favorite photographs. Flowers always add a pretty touch too. I have a lot of late blooming roses that would look great in some pretty vases." She blushed, turning to him. "But of course, it's your place. Do what you want."

"I like your ideas. When can we go shopping?"

"Really?" She looked at her watch. "Andrew won't be home for several hours. We have some time to go now, if you like."

"Let's go now." As they turned to go, he directed another question to her. "When do I get to meet your son?"

"Let's take one thing at a time, Taylor. We'll get your furniture, get you settled in and we'll see. There is plenty of time."

"Yep. That I got a lot of."

Taylor was able to convince the furniture store to deliver his sectional that evening, along with the rest of the furniture he chose. He and Tessa decided on a sage green velour type material that was huge and cushy for the sectional, with oversize evergreen throw pillows to place on it. For now, Taylor decided to go without a rug, preferring to leave the hardwood floors bare. If he was still around when winter came, he might re-think that. He wasn't sure exactly how long he would be around. They also chose mahogany tables, a huge square cocktail table, end tables and several sofa tables. He took her advice and bought a beautiful king size sleigh bed and they stopped at some linen place and picked up a navy satin duvet and tons of pillows for it, as well as white sateen sheets. The set came with a dresser, an armoire and night stands. Tessa helped him pick out lamps and accessories to make his home more comfortable.

After everything was delivered in the evening, Taylor spent his time getting his home organized and arranged as Tessa went back to her own home when her son returned.

They had gotten along well as they shopped, just like old friends or maybe even a married couple. Now, where had *that* thought come from? He had never considered marrying anyone in his life. And he admitted that all he really wanted from Tessa right now was sex, a roll in the sack. Was that fair to her? He didn't want to hurt her, she had a son she had to care for and she didn't need grief from him.

Well, there was time to see how this all played out.

Taylor flopped on his sofa and flicked the remote for the huge screen TV hung on the opposite wall.

Tomorrow— window shades.

CHAPTER
SEVEN

TESSA MET HER SON that afternoon at his bus, bringing him in to have his habitual snack after school. She had taken a rare week day off to help Taylor get established. Tessa had long ago made sure her schedule was flexible enough to be with Andrew as much as possible. She had enough seniority to work the days and hours she requested. Weekends she was always home and she didn't work any late shifts; always back in the afternoons by five. She rarely worked holidays although there were a few that she couldn't escape. Nurses were in high demand as there was a shortage of them and Tessa had a very friendly relationship with the head nurse, so her work hours did not interfere with her job as a mom. She thanked her lucky stars for that. Andrew needed her as much as possible. She was fortunate to have Rose, too.

Tessa and Andrew entered the big kitchen Tessa had decorated in a country style. Andrew flopped his back pack on the kitchen table and then ran into his bedroom off the main hall. The first thing he did was check on his Barney to make sure he was still situated in the middle of his bed. It was one of his many "rituals" that Tessa respected. Soon he was back to sit at the table and have the snack that Tessa had prepared.

He started on his snack as Tessa read the communication book from his teacher.

Andrew seemed a bit out of sorts today. I don't know what exactly was bothering him. Nothing unusual happened. He just seemed sad and more "zoned out", which is not like Andrew, as you know. We worked on his reading primer and he did very well, and he got 100 on his spelling test! I was so proud of him! His O/T said he needed extra sensory input today also. Otherwise, he had a pretty typical day.

Tessa frowned as she read these words. Her son had a pleasant disposition and was popular with both the other students and his teachers and therapists. She glanced up at Andrew who was eating his snack with apparent unconcern, occasionally glancing up at her.

She went to her son and kissed him on the top of his head. "Hey, buddy. How did school go today?"

Big long lashed brown eyes swung to Tessa's. Her heart ached. Her son was so physically beautiful. He didn't reply, so Tessa repeated her question.

Andrew frowned a bit, as though he didn't understand the question and Tessa knew he did. Receptively, Andrew understood almost everything one said to him. He had a difficult time expressively with language, which was quite common with children afflicted with autism.

"Ya know, school? Mrs. Carrel? Mrs. C.? How did it go?" Tessa persisted.

Andrew gave her his sunny smile. "Like Mrs. C."

"Yes, I know. But did you like school today? What did you do?"

After a moment, he answered. "Reading."

Tessa waited a few more moments, watching him expectantly. She was trying to cut back on prompts so Andrew would speak more spontaneously but it was so very difficult. Andrew only responded with prompts. "Okay. Reading. What else?"

After another pause, his smile turned into a frown. "Didn't like it, today. No." He turned back to his snack.

Tessa leaned forward, pulling Andrew around so that he faced her directly. Looking directly into his eyes, she asked him very clearly "What didn't you like, Andrew?"

"School."

Tessa frowned. "But Andrew, you love school. All of the other kids, Mrs. C. Did something happen at school you didn't like?"

Andrew frowned and Tessa knew he was having a hard time processing this. Sighing, she tried another tact.

"Mrs. C. said you got 100 on spelling. Hooray for you! High five!" She smacked his hand in the traditional manner.

He smiled, fiving her back.

"So you did great! What's not to like?"

Andrew's attention went back to his snack and Tessa knew she would not get anymore information out of him for now.

Andrew finished up his snack and put his dishes away, as he had been taught. "Watch TV?" he asked hopefully.

Tessa knew his favorite show Barney was on. "Sure, Andrew. You can watch Barney."

"Yeaaah!" he ran into the front living room to watch his show.

Tessa called Rose and asked her if she could come up for a cup of coffee. She needed to let Rose know about Taylor (who was already moved into the carriage house) and to get her advice on how to broach that news to Andrew. Since his school day had not gone the best, it would be even tougher.

Rose came up the back stairs that connected the two stories and sat down at the kitchen table as Tessa poured coffee for the two of them.

Rose accepted the delicate china cup, sipping the hot liquid slowly. Her warm brown eyes smiled at Tessa through her eyeglasses. "Thanks, dear. A nice hot cup of coffee on a chilly fall day is wonderful." She studied Tessa and noticed the younger woman was fidgeting with her own cup, barely drinking it. "What's wrong, dear?" she asked, sipping her coffee.

Tessa's lovely brown eyes moved to Rose and she sighed. "I guess you must have noticed all the moving vans and such today in the back."

Rose put her cup back in the saucer. "Yes. I did notice all of the activity. You finally have a tenant?"

Tessa sighed. "I guess you could say that."

"Well, that's a good thing dear. Who is it?" Rose watched Tessa with interest, sensing her disquiet. Was it Andrew? Or this tenant she was worried about?

Tessa's mind went into mental gymnastics. She knew Rose Hamilton was a huge Taylor Boudrain fan, declaring him one of the finest actors to come along in quite a while. Tessa had never really seen any of his many movies because her movie time was spent with Andrew who only watched Disney movies. She knew Rose could keep a secret. She didn't want Taylor's identity here known because it would disrupt their quiet life and that was the *last* thing Tessa wanted. She had bought the property for its privacy and Tessa fiercely wanted to protect that for Andrew's sake.

She finally answered Rose's question. "Our new tenant is none other than Taylor Boudrain." She waited for Rose's reaction, finally sipping at her coffee.

Rose's grey brows knit in confusion. "Taylor Boudrain? A man then? Young, old?"

Tessa could see that she had no idea she meant Taylor Boudrain, THE movie star. "No, Rose. You know that movie star you like so much? That Taylor."

Rose gasped, both hands going to her mouth as her eyes widened. "Oh, my!" she gasped. "Taylor Boudrain— here? Renting our carriage house? I don't understand—"

"Long story short: he had a motorcycle accident and ended up at our ICU. I was on shift for him most of the time and he told me he was looking for a place to stay. When I mentioned the carriage house to him, he wanted to stay here. I have my reservations, mostly because of Andrew. We'll see how it works out," she picked up her coffee cup, studying Rose.

"Oh, I would *love* to meet him!" Rose said with a huge smile.

"Well, since he lives right behind us, I'm sure you'll have an opportunity." Tessa's smile vanished and she became serious. "Rose, I don't want anyone to know he's here. I've already explained that to Taylor too. He's a big star and I don't want hordes of people around here for the obvious reasons."

"Of course, dear. My lips are sealed. You can count on me."

"I know I can, Rose. That is why I asked you up for coffee also. I need your advice. How should I broach this to Andrew? It will be a big change, having a man living in the back. Andrew hasn't been exposed to men, so I guess it could be a good thing. It all depends on how they interact. Taylor seems to like kids, but Andrew is not an ordinary kid. What do you think of all of this?" Tessa's brown eyes were worried and concerned.

Rose reached over and patted Tessa's hand. "Don't be concerned, dear. If Taylor likes kids, they'll find their own relationship and their own rhythm. It may take time, but it will happen. I think having a man around for a role model will be a very good thing for Andrew."

Tessa frowned a bit. "I was hoping so, too. But what if Andrew doesn't take to Taylor for some reason? I mean Taylor has a HUGE ego. I just don't know—"

"Tessa, my advice would be to just be open and honest to Andrew about Taylor living in the back. Andrew has no idea Taylor is a big star, so that's probably a good thing."

"Yes, I hadn't thought of that. I keep thinking about Taylor through my own eyes, not Andrew's."

Rose sipped her coffee. "What's he like? Taylor? Is he as glorious looking in person as he is in the movies?"

Tessa rolled her eyes. It seemed every woman in the world was infatuated with Taylor. "If by that do you mean is he good looking, yes, definitely. And he knows it too!"

Rose arched a brow. She detected a hint of animosity toward Taylor. "What about you, Tessa? Are you going to have a problem with Taylor living here?"

"That remains to be seen."

That evening, as Tessa prepared Andrew for bed, she tucked him in as was her habit and read him a story. Andrew sometimes listened and sometimes she could tell his attention was diverted, but she insisted on this little ritual. She wanted her son to become accustomed to words.

After reading the story, she leaned over to plump his pillows. Andrew smiled, knowing his goodnight kisses were coming next, but his mommy leaned back for a moment.

"Andrew, there is something mommy needs to tell you," she looked down at her son all tucked snug in his bed, Barney by his side. Andrew's brown eyes met hers, listening. Good, she had his attention.

"We have a new neighbor in our back house. He is a nice man and his name is Taylor Boudrain. Can you say his name?" Tessa watched her son for his reaction.

Andrew frowned a bit, then yawned. "Go sleep, mommy. Kisses," he said hopefully.

Tessa leaned down and gave her son several kisses all over his face, making him laugh and giggle. Then she leaned back up. "I hope you will welcome our new neighbor, Taylor. Say hi when you see him."

"Hi." Andrew responded automatically.

"No, honey. When you see the man in the back, Taylor. You can talk to him. I know I've told you not to talk to strangers, but Taylor will be our friend, so it is okay to talk to him or say hi." She paused. "Honey, do you understand me?"

"Say hi Taylor," he echoed again.

Tessa knew Andrew was responding in echolalia, a common problem with children when language was such a barrier for them. They would typically fall back on this tactic. Tessa's eyes welled with tears. She wished she knew what Andrew was thinking, *really* thinking. She knew he was bright and so much went on inside that head of his but that he just didn't have the means to communicate it to her or the world.

"Yes, say hi Taylor," she whispered. She leaned down again to kiss him once more. "Good night, Andrew."

Andrew smiled and snuggled into his pillows.

Tessa made sure the night light was on for her son and left for her own room, leaving Andrew's door open.

Taylor contacted his agent and gave him several instructions. He had Frank make sure a black Suburban SUV would be delivered the next day with all the bells and whistles. He needed to get out and shop for several different things, chief among them clothes. Then he arranged for the storage facility that had his mangled bike to return it to him. If there was enough of it left, he planned on spending his time restoring it. He had glimpsed through the garage windows downstairs a complete workroom set up with various tools and equipment and it would be a perfect spot to work on the bike after he got Tessa's permission. It would give him something to do with his time as he recuperated. He was lucky he had Tessa around to help him change his bandage as he could not do it on his own. One of the advantages of having his own personal nurse.

He had not seen her since they returned from shopping. He knew she had to get Andrew off of the bus and he had not seen hide nor hair of anybody. Evening was here and it was very quiet with few lights on in the big house across from him.

After Taylor finished up his business with Frank, he headed off to bed. Tomorrow he would settle further into life here in Lewiston and he absently wondered what Tessa's son was like.

Time would tell, he supposed. He drifted off to sleep in his brand new bed, dreaming of a very sexy brunette with lush, kissable lips.

CHAPTER
EIGHT

THE BRIGHT MORNING SUN blazed through the undraped windows of Taylor's bedroom. Groaning, he turned in the bed to cover his eyes with his arm. Raising his head up a bit, he checked his watch. Christ, it was six thirty in the morning. He hadn't been up this early since he shot his last movie several months ago. What the hell?

Looking around the room, memory came rushing back to him. The carriage house. Tessa's place. The accident. Oh yeah.

Grunting, he sat up. Man, his ribs hurt like a bitch. He looked down at his bandage. Tessa had told him she would change it later on today for him and he wondered when she returned home from work. If he wasn't mistaken, today was Friday. He looked at his watch again. Yep, Friday, which meant she wouldn't be around until later and her kid was in school until— well, who knew when kids got home from school. He certainly didn't.

Walking gingerly into his bathroom, Taylor inspected his face in the oval mirror hanging above the sink. Yep, he needed to shave and that long mane of blond hair needed to be washed. Taylor wore his hair unfashionably long when he wasn't filming, almost brushing his shoulders. He was blessed with thick hair that fell in waves around his neck and the only maintenance required was to run a comb or his fingers through it to get it back off of his face, which he quickly did. He brushed his teeth, shaved and hopped into the shower. The water pressure was good and he took a nice long hot shower, careful to keep his bandage from getting wet. It was a real pain in the ass, but he would do what Tessa said. For now.

Toweling off, he inspected his drawers in his armoire. Man, he needed clothes. Choosing a pair of battered Levis, a navy henley he had managed to pick up yesterday, he dressed, finally lacing up his sneakers.

Putting his hands on his hips, Taylor looked over at the bare windows. Time to do something about this non-privacy issue.

He picked up the phone book Tessa had left yesterday and flipped to the appropriate page. As he did so, he remembered that Mrs. Hamilton should be home. After he made arrangements for shades and accessories (hmph!) he would go introduce himself to the fine lady.

Taylor knocked at the back door of the big house in front of him, hands on his hips, leisurely glancing around. There were several large rose bushes nearby that had large pink blooms. He could see under the September sun they added a beautiful splash of color by the door. Looking further around the yard he could see large evergreens nearby and lining the driveway. Planted by the previous owners for privacy, no doubt. He could not see any evidence of a nearby home, the property seemed secluded. He could hear an occasional car pass by the road out front, but other than that, just birds twittering. Since Taylor was used to big city noises, this total quiet was a bit eerie. He shook off the thought as the door was opened by a woman in her sixties.

Rose Hamilton had been an attractive woman when she was younger, he decided. She possessed thick silver hair which she wore clipped back in one of those old fashioned combs and warm brown eyes sparkled behind her eyeglasses. She was wearing a pale pink printed summer dress and comfortable shoes. She smiled up at him with delight and Taylor grinned back at her, well aware of his appeal with women.

"Well, hello!" she said. She extended a hand to him while holding the door open. "I'm Rose Hamilton. You must be our new tenant."

Taylor shook the proffered hand. "Yes, m'am. I'm Taylor Boudrain. It's a pleasure to meet you. Mrs. Hamilton, right?"

Rose waved that away as she beckoned him inside the kitchen. "Oh please. Just call me Rose. Would you like to come in for a bit?"

Taylor grinned, putting his hands in his back jean pockets. "Thanks, Rose, but I was just on my way out to do a bit of shopping. I wanted to introduce myself so you know it's me coming and going. I'm having some things delivered today too. I hope all of the activity won't bother you." Taylor gave her his winning smile.

"Oh tush!" Rose dismissed this thought. "It will be nice to have some activity around this place. Usually I'm just here all by myself. It will be nice to know someone else is here. I'm alone all day until Andrew and Tessa return."

Taylor tipped a finger to his chin then looked down at Rose. "Speaking of Tessa, what time does she usually return from work?"

"Tessa is always home by five. I take care of Andrew and get him off of the bus until she returns." Rose studied the tall man in front of her. Oh my, she was talking to a *movie star* and such a handsome one at that. And she had to keep this secret to herself. How delicious!

"And what time does— Andrew?— get off of the bus, Rose?"

"Three thirty every day like clock work. We amuse ourselves until Tessa returns. I have the downstairs flat," she waved behind her. "If you need anything at all Taylor, please don't hesitate to ask me."

Taylor smiled again. "You've been very kind, Rose. It was a pleasure to meet you. I'll see ya around." He waved as he moved down the back steps.

Rose watched him as he walked over to that brand new fancy SUV she noticed was delivered last evening. Hmmmm…he might have possibilities for Tessa. Tessa was too young and beautiful to be on her own. Wouldn't that be something if they hooked up? Smiling, she closed the back door.

Taylor finished up his shopping by around two. He unloaded his purchases and moved up the steep stairs to his place quickly. The interior decorator he had called was coming at 2:15 to install blinds (Taylor had already given them all measurements) and add other things such as artwork, plants, yadda yadda. He hadn't paid attention to everything the man said.

He quickly dumped a bunch of stuff on his bed and proceeded to put away new clothes in his closet and new dressers. He purchased enough clothes for several months, including some warm clothes. He was assured by the saleswoman who helped him he would need them. He managed to get everything organized and put away by the time he heard the buzzer downstairs.

Quickly, he trotted down the stairs to open the door to a diminutive man standing in front of him. He was balding and looked to be fortyish and he grinned broadly up at Taylor. Taylor figured he probably came to his mid chest, if that.

"Ah, you must be Mr. Patterson!"

Taylor had already decided to use an alias so no one would know he was here and the only name that occurred to him to use was Tessa's. "Yep, that would be me. Ya got everything?" Taylor craned his neck to see around the little guy and could see a van parked behind his SUV.

"Yes, yes, Mr. Patterson. Everything is in the van. May I come in and take a look around and discuss where you would like everything?"

"You can come in Mr?—" Taylor arched a brow, waiting for a name.

"Oh you can just call me George!" the man gushed.

"Okay, George. C'mon in. But I hired you to place everything. That's your job." Taylor led the way upstairs as the little guy kept gushing.

"Oh yes, I know, I know, but I want you to be HAPPY! I want you to be— oh my!" he exclaimed as they reached the top of the stairs and he took in the spacious beautifully furnished room with the cathedral ceiling with intricate moldings. "Oh this is SUCH a beautiful room! What I could do with it—"

"Yeah, yeah," Taylor waved these remarks away. "I'd like all the shades put up first. Damn sun woke me up and I don't want to wake up at six again."

"I have *just* what you ordered in the van, Mr. Patterson. You chose wisely. The almond cream shades are the *perfect* color to offset the sectional—"

"George, I would kinda like the work to all be done soon. Like *as soon as possible*." Taylor emphasized.

"Of course, I will go get the shades and install them immediately." He paused, studying the handsome man. "Has anyone ever told you you look exactly like Taylor Bou—"

Taylor grinned. "Yeah, I get that a lot. The shades, please?" Taylor arched a brow.

"Of course, Mr. Patterson. Coming right up."

George was still puttering around at three thirty and Taylor was washing the new SUV. It didn't need it, but it gave him something to do and to keep out of George's way. Mostly he didn't want the little guy chattering at him. After inspecting the shades and finding them to his liking, he left George to do the rest of his thang.

Rinsing out his sponge, he looked up as Rose emerged from the back door. Smiling, she waved at him and he waved back. She walked down the slight incline to the end of the driveway where Taylor could see a small yellow school bus. It wasn't one of those normal big bus sizes, but smaller. Oh yeah, that stupid phrase 'riding the short bus' used to ridicule people. Taylor's back arched at the thought. He hated injustice or prejudice of any kind, mostly because his dad had been such a bigot and Taylor had spent most of his life trying to be as *unlike* his father as possible.

Taylor watched closely as he pretended to wash the roof of the SUV, standing on the foot bed. Taylor wore mirrored sunglasses out here in the sun and had tied his hair back a bit to keep it out of the way as he usually did when doing any physical work or riding his 'cycle.

A young boy came down the stairs of the bus to meet Rose, wearing blue jeans, a red jacket with a back pack on. As they moved up the driveway Taylor got a closer look. Andrew's brown hair was cut into one of those cute wedge cuts popular for little boys. It was shiny and thick and Taylor could see he was a miniature male Tessa. He had big beautiful brown eyes with long lashes and perfect features. He looked over Taylor's way and Taylor prepared to wave but he turned away and followed Rose into the house. Rose returned his wave as they disappeared into the bigger house.

Taylor put his hand down, feeling chagrin. The boy had not so much as acknowledged his presence. Frowning, Taylor went back to his chore.

An hour later, George came to fetch him, rhapsodizing about how great the place looked. Taylor followed him upstairs and was pleased as he looked around. George had placed a huge vase of real roses in a beautiful crystal vase in the middle of his huge cocktail table, placed what looked like a real tree in a large wicker basket in a far corner where it would get abundant sunlight from the many windows. He had framed some posters and artwork. Taylor recognized a Renoir print and a black framed Marilyn Monroe on the far wall. Taylor grinned at that. He had also added some Aubusson throw rugs here and there in the sage green and cream color scheme. It all meshed and blended and it was nicer than his barely furnished mansion in Beverly Hills.

"Well, what do you think?" George asked anxiously.

Taylor grinned down at the little man. "You did a heckuva job, Georgie. What did you say your fee was?"

"Well, I did need to charge a bit extra for some prints and art and—" he began nervously.

Taylor interrupted. "George? The fee? What is it?"

"Five thousand," George said tentatively.

Taylor arched a brow. "Accept a bank draft?"

George stumbled over words. "A bank draft? Of course, that would be fine. Make it out to me, please, George Manney, if you would, please."

"Fine." Taylor took out the book and scrawled out the information and his signature, making it illegible as he intended. "Here ya go." He handed the paper to George.

George inspected it and gasped. "Mr. Patterson! There must be some mistake! This says *ten* thousand dollars! Why—"

"Just think of it as a tip, George. Now it's getting along to dinner time. I need you to leave."

"Okay. I just have a few things to finish up—"

"*Now,* George. I have a dinner date and don't wanna be late!"

"Of course, of course, Mr. Patterson. I'll get right out of your way."

"That's a good fella. Thanks! Everything looks great!"

"Please recommend me to any friends, Mr. Patterson—"

"Yeah, yeah," Taylor led George down the stairs and out the door. Tessa would be home soon and Taylor admitted he couldn't wait to see her. He had missed her.

Evening came and Taylor prepared a small dinner. His kitchen was located in a far corner of the large room and Taylor had delineated the space by placing a bar with stools there. He would eat all meals at his bar. If he needed a bigger space, there was always the huge cocktail table. The kitchen was modern and small with white appliances. George had tried to dress up the area by putting some dried flower arrangements around. Taylor ditched them. His kitchen could be utilitarian; it didn't need to be fancied up.

Since Tessa still hadn't shown, Taylor flopped on his sectional and turned on the evening news. He loathed watching TV and vowed tomorrow to get some books to fill his bookcase. He would much rather read then watch the tube.

Finally around eight p.m. his buzzer rang downstairs. Taylor went down and opened the door to Tessa. She was wearing jeans and what looked like a teal vee neck sweater and boots. Her glorious brown waves fell around her shoulders. She was carrying a canvas bag. Oh yeah. The new bandage.

"Hey, Tessa! How are ya?" Taylor grinned, motioning her up the steps.

"I'm fine, Taylor. How are you? How are your ribs and the bandage holding up?" she questioned as she moved up the steps and then into his main room. She gasped as she looked around.

"Wow! You had more work done! It looks wonderful!" Her brown eyes moved to his, wide with surprise. She moved over to his sectional and Taylor followed her.

"Yeah, well, I can't take the credit. I hired some designer guy named George. Mostly I wanted shades." He motioned to the cream cellular shades George had installed. Taylor had them half down at the moment.

"Oh yes. Shades too. You did need those. Well, it looks wonderful. Back to you." She eyed his midsection. "It's been several days. I'm sure that needs changed."

"Yeah, I think so. Really hard trying to keep it dry in the shower too."

"Did you try the towel trick?"

"Yeah, I knotted it around as you suggested, but it keeps slipping."

Tessa blushed, thinking about a certain part of his anatomy.

Taylor noticed the blush and wondered what that was all about.

"Well, here, let me take a look," she said in her professional nurse's voice.

Taylor removed his henley, revealing his well toned torso and biceps. His washboard abs were hidden by the bandage that wound around his waist. Tessa carefully kept her eyes on the bandage as her gentle fingers unwound it. She was very careful to be gentle but Taylor still winced, his breath whooshing in a bit.

"Well, I guess that answers my earlier question about does it hurt. You know, you've only been out for two days. I think you're doing too much. Don't push yourself, Taylor. This needs time to heal up. You need to take it easy."

"Yeah, well I had things I needed to do," Taylor answered as he watched her wind a clean bandage around his ribs and secure it snugly. When she finished, he gingerly put his navy henley back on, breathing a bit easier. Tessa took the old bandages and put them in her bag. "Say, I saw your son get off of the bus today."

"Oh?" Tessa fussed with her bag, not meeting his eyes.

"Yeah, I waved to him but I guess he didn't see me. He didn't wave back."

Tessa's brown eyes met Taylor's deep teal eyes. "Are you surprised by that?"

Taylor arched a brow. "Yeah, actually I was a bit taken aback."

Tessa stood, preparing to leave. "You know Andrew has autism, Taylor. Perhaps you should educate yourself on it." She turned to go.

"Hey, wait a minute! I haven't had company all day except for George and he doesn't count since I avoided him. Care for a glass of wine or something?" Taylor followed her to the top of the stairs.

"No, Taylor. I'm not here to keep you company. You are my tenant and I come by to help out with your bandage. That's the extent of our relationship." She turned to go.

"Hey, wait a minute again, Tessa. Thought we were friends?" He smiled. "I don't expect you to babysit me, but I did think we would be seeing each other, ya know, here and there?" Taylor arched a brow.

"Yes. Here and there. When I change your bandage. If I see you outside. That kind of here and there." Again she turned to leave.

"Okay. Got it, Tessa. One question, though."

She tuned back to him, brows raised.

"I noticed the garage downstairs has a decent workshop. I'm having my motorcycle delivered here and I'd like to see if I can restore it. Would it be okay if I used the garage and equipment down there for that purpose?"

Tessa frowned a bit. She had set up the work shop for Steve to work on his motorcycles but he had died before he could use it. Thus it had sat empty for about five years. Tessa studied the handsome man before her and her heart fluttered. What was there about this man that affected her this way? No other man had been able to reach her since Steve. And that's the way she wanted it to stay. But his request was not unreasonable.

"Of course. I'll see you get a key for it tomorrow. But there may not be everything there you may need to restore your bike."

"Not a problem. I can purchase whatever I need."

"Yes. I can see that. Good night, Taylor." She moved down the stairs and out the door.

Taylor frowned. Tessa had always been friendly toward him in the hospital but now she seemed downright frigid.

He decided a trip to the library was in order tomorrow to stock up on books relating to autism. He needed to know what he was dealing with here, especially if he wanted to get closer to Tessa.

Chapter
NINE

Saturday morning arrived and this time the shades Taylor purchased prevented the sun from waking him. Groaning, he moved over in the bed and looked at his watch. Christ, it was nine o'clock! He was usually always up by at least eight. The new shades had sufficiently done their job and he had slept longer with the darker room. Well, time to get up and at it. He had some errands to run and his motorcycle was supposed to be delivered today, too.

He hopped into the shower, again being careful of his bandage. His ribs didn't hurt as much today as yesterday, but they were still sore. Tessa and the doctors had warned him it would be a good month before his ribs would be feeling back to normal. That would be October. Would he still be here in October or would he be moving on?

He ruminated about Tessa as he showered. She had not been particularly friendly last evening and Taylor wondered what it was about her that so intrigued him. Yes, she was beautiful but Taylor had been involved with many beautiful women, too many to count. There seemed to be a certain vulnerability about her, although she was so self sufficient. Her husband was gone but she had built a life for herself and her son and he found that— courageous, I guess is the word, he thought. He frowned. He had no idea what she dealt with as far as her son's disability; he needed to learn more about autism. One of his errands was to stop at the library and pick up some books.

After showering, he dressed quickly. It looked like it was a beautiful September morning. He chose a denim shirt to wear open over a white tee and jeans, donning his cowboy boots. He quickly threw the bed into some kind of order and grabbed his wallet and keys and headed downstairs.

As he proceeded to his SUV, he glanced over at the bigger house. He knew Tessa was home on the weekends and he saw no sign of activity, but it was a bit early yet.

Coffee. He needed coffee. Then he would run his errands. Hopefully his bike would be here when he returned. He needed tasks to keep him busy and his mind occupied.

He started up the SUV and backed down the driveway carefully, making sure no little boys were around. Taylor took the road into town.

Tessa saw the SUV leave as she was sipping her morning coffee and wondered where Taylor was off to. Shrugging, she figured it wasn't her business. Since she knew he was gone, now would be a good time to leave the keys to the garage for him. She could put them in his mailbox with a note. That way she would not have to speak to him directly. She tried to ignore the reasons for that, but she knew she found Taylor extremely attractive and knew that was a huge mistake on her part. Taylor would be moving on someday (possibly soon) and she didn't want to get too close to him.

She moved downstairs and over to the mailbox hung directly underneath the outdoor lamp. She had scrawled a hasty note that she left partway out of the box so he would notice it and inserted the keys into the mailbox. That done, she returned to the house. Since it was such a beautiful autumn day she was planning to take Rose and Andrew to a local orchard to pick apples. Rose made the most wonderful apple pies and cobbler.

Tessa moved her face up to the warmth of the sun's rays and tried to let it help dispel her troubles.

Taylor returned a few hours later and noticed Tessa's vehicle was gone. So, they were out somewhere for the day.

As he parked his SUV, he noticed his mangled bike placed in front of the garage doors. Groaning, he took in the completely mangled heap of metal.

Hopping out of the Suburban, he went over for a closer inspection. The entire front of the motorcycle was bashed in, like a giant fist had clobbered it. However the back of the bike was fairly intact although badly scraped. It would take a lot of work and money to get the Harley back into the fine looking machine it had been before the accident, but it was certainly possible. Taylor had learned how to work on cars and motorcycles as a teen at a local garage. He got a job as soon as he could to sock money away for his imminent departure to wherever he would eventually leave for. That had turned out to be Hollywood and damned if it hadn't been the right decision.

He carefully circled the bike, noting what parts he would need and thankful he had stopped to purchase a laptop today. He would need to get on the 'net to special order custom parts. The more mundane things he could pick up at the local hardware store.

Sighing, he turned toward his door and noticed a note sticking out of his mailbox. Curious, he plucked out the yellow sheet of paper and read the note quickly: *Taylor, I've left the keys to the garage in the mailbox for you. Feel free to use it whenever you like. Tessa.*

Taylor fished in the box and sure enough, there was a gold key on a ring chain in the bottom. Twirling the key, he moved up the stairs. He had everything he needed to get started on his bike. And tonight he could read some books on autism so that when he met Andrew, he would have some idea of what he was dealing with.

Tessa pulled her SUV into the driveway, into the park space behind the house. Over to the left was the carriage house and she could see Taylor was outside working on a mangled heap of metal. The garage doors were up and the lights were on and his big black SUV had been moved to the side, out of the way. He was dressed in denim and had his long glorious hair tied back as he used a tool to remove something from the motorcycle. As they emerged from her vehicle, he looked up and waved.

Tessa waved back and Rose and Andrew also emerged from the vehicle.

"It looks like he's getting right to work on that thing," Rose commented.

Tessa had informed Rose about Taylor using the garage to repair his bike.

Rose craned her neck to look further. "It's a wonder he wasn't killed on that thing." Rose immediately felt chagrined at her comment, remembering Tessa's husband was killed in exactly that manner. "Andrew, would you like to help carry a bag of apples in for me?" Rose turned to the little boy who stood beside her, staring at the tall man near the carriage house.

Andrew did not respond and Tessa took matters into hand. "Here ya go, Andrew. A bag of red apples for you to carry upstairs for mommy. You're such a big boy! Thank you for helping!"

Andrew smiled and took the small bag his mommy handed him and went into the house, forgetting about the man outside. Rose followed closely with some bags as Tessa moved over to Taylor.

"I see you have your bike back. What's left of it, that is."

She was wearing snug Levis and a soft ivory sweater that looked terrific on her.

Taylor smiled down at her. "Yep. Ordered some special parts for it from the Internet today. They should come in a few days but I have enough to get started on some basic stuff."

"You surprise me, Taylor. I didn't think movie stars were mechanics too." Tessa crossed her arms over her breasts, looking up at the handsome man in the bright sun. With his hair pulled back it really showed off his magnificent features. Mirrored sunglasses hid his beautiful teal eyes.

Taylor grinned down at her. "I'm a man of many talents, Tessa."

"I just bet you are." She turned to go but his words stopped her.

"I see you were out apple picking. It's a great day for it."

He wanted to prolong their conversation for a bit.

She turned back. "Yes. Rose makes great apple pies. They are out of this world." She smiled and Taylor's heart flopped. What *was* it about her?

Taylor was silent a moment, wiping his hands on a rag. He threw it down and put his hands on his hips. "So, when do I get to meet the little guy?"

She arched a brow. "I'm sure you'll meet him soon. He usually comes out to ride his bike around the yard if it's nice out." She paused. "I want to be sure you know he may not talk to you."

"Yeah. I know that. In fact, today I got some books from the library on autism. I took your advice."

This surprised Tessa. "Oh really?"

"Yep. So don't worry, Tessa." Taylor turned back to his work and Tessa moved over to the trunk of her SUV, carrying apples into the house and wondering about the man behind her.

Taylor went into his house briefly for lunch, then came back out to do some more work on the bike. He noticed immediately that Andrew was out riding a red small bicycle in the yard. This meeting had come sooner than Taylor expected and he hadn't had a chance to read any of his books yet. Oh well. He'd have to wing it. He was a kid, right? Treat him as a kid.

Taylor waved to the boy. "Hey, Andrew! How ya doin', buddy?"

At the sound of his name, Andrew turned toward the man. He came a bit closer on his bike, looking up at a tall man with very light colored hair. His eyes were a different color too. Andrew felt a bit uneasy because the man was so big. He turned to back up a bit.

"Whoa, wait a minute, buddy. I just wanted to introduce myself. I'm your new neighbor. I live there, in that house," he pointed to the carriage house.

Andrew stopped and looked at the carriage house and Taylor could see he had his attention. "Your mom let me move in for a little while. I got hurt." On inspiration Taylor lifted his white tee shirt so Andrew could see the bandage wound around his waist.

At this action, Andrew moved closer to inspect the bandage and then looked up at the man again. "Boo boo," he said to the man. "Hurt?"

Taylor believed this was definitely progress. The boy was talking to him and Tessa informed him Andrew rarely spoke to others.

"Yep. Does hurt bad sometimes. But your mommy. Tessa? She helped me feel better." Taylor studied the beautiful brown eyes to see what effect his words would have.

"My mommy?" Andrew seemed bewildered.

"Yes. Your mommy is a nurse. She helps people."

Andrew smiled and Taylor's heart melted. He had never seen a more beautiful smile, with the exception of Tessa's. "Yes. Mommy helps me."

Taylor was silent and smiled. "Yes. Your mommy is a good person. I like her."

Andrew cocked his head then his attention went to the motorcycle Taylor was working on. He moved closer on his bike to inspect it. He frowned down at it, then looked into the garage. He clearly didn't like the fact the doors were open. He frowned, pointing. "No garage. Close doors." He looked over at Taylor.

"Well, they are open because I am trying to fix my motorcycle. See, it is crunched up? I am going to fix it," Taylor tried to explain.

Andrew still continued to frown, pointing to the doors. "No doors! No doors!" he shouted.

At this, Taylor was at a loss but fortunately he could see Tessa moving toward them. "Hi, Andrew. Hi, Taylor. What's going on?"

Right away Tessa could see there was a problem. Andrew was scowling and pointing at the open garage doors and Taylor looked a bit confused.

"Tell him, no doors!" Andrew demanded.

Tessa sensed the problem immediately. Andrew was a creature of habit and the doors had never been open since they were living here. He was accustomed to them being closed.

"Okay, Andrew. I'll talk to Taylor about it. Why don't you go ride your bike?"

With a final scowl for Taylor, Andrew pedaled away, further into the yard and out of sight.

Taylor turned to Tessa. "I'm sorry. I don't know what the problem is.

We were just talking and all of a sudden he got upset about the doors." He gestured behind him.

"He isn't used to seeing them open, Taylor. Andrew is a creature of habit, it is part of his disability. Seeing them open throws him off, especially seeing a stranger standing in front of them. For now, can you just work with them closed? I'll try to get Andrew to accept that sometimes the doors will be open, but it is a process. He's not mad at you or anything, so don't take it personally." Tessa studied the tall man, wondering if he would understand.

"It's not a problem for me to bring out whatever I need and keep the doors closed. Had I known it would be a problem, I certainly would have done so. I didn't mean to upset your son."

"I know you didn't, Taylor. But that's just Andrew."

"Well, our first meeting certainly didn't go all that well." Taylor's full lips curled ruefully.

"And your second and your third and fourth might not either, Taylor," Tessa warned as she walked away.

Taylor turned back to his bike, thinking he better spend his Saturday night reading about autism.

Evening came and Andrew was safely tucked in his house and Taylor was reading library books. He sighed. He never in his life thought he would be reading books on autism. Think of it as research Taylor, he told himself. So you're not screwing some blonde on a Saturday night. Who cares?

His thoughts went to Tessa. He wouldn't mind screwing a brunette, though. Ha! In your dreams, Taylor!

CHAPTER

TEN

SUNDAY ARRIVED AND TAYLOR dressed quickly so he could go work on his motorcycle again. He dressed in beat up Levis and a white tee and his sneakers. It looked sunny and warm, a perfect day to be outside.

He had spent Saturday evening reading until he fell asleep on the sectional and he had learned quite a bit about autism, especially that it was vastly misunderstood in the general population. There were certain "do's" and "don'ts" and Taylor tried to commit these to memory. He understood a bit more what Tessa was dealing with and admired her even more. She was fortunate to have Rose to help out. What about family? Did she have family? He really didn't know too much about her other than her husband had been killed in a motorcycle accident. Taylor thought it very ironic that was how they had met, because of his accident. Fortunately, he had survived it. He was young and his entire life was ahead of him. Perhaps it was time not to be so reckless with his life...

Taylor was ruminating on these thoughts as he worked on the bike, careful to have the garage doors closed. All of the tools and equipment he needed had already been moved outside and placed close by. He was again wearing his mirrored sunglasses because it was so sunny out. He did still tend to get headaches on and off and the bright sunlight didn't help.

Suddenly the back door to the house opened and Andrew appeared. He was wearing jeans with a yellow and white striped shirt and sneakers. His brown eyes widened when he saw Taylor, clearly surprised. He took a step backward into the house, but Tessa appeared behind her son. She gently pushed him out the door and guided him down the few steps, also noticing Taylor's presence. She wore a white sundress that hugged her curves and her thick brown hair was pinned up, tendrils of hair escaping from the style at

56

the nape of her neck, which looked very kissable to Taylor. He shook off his thoughts as the two of them approached him.

"Hello, Taylor!" Tessa greeted.

Taylor grinned down at the two. "Hi, guys! Where you off to today?"

"Oh, Andrew will be playing outside today; it is such a nice day. We may swing on the front porch too. We have to enjoy these sunny days while we still can." She smiled up at him then looked down at the bike. To her it still looked like a tangled mass of metal, not much seemed to have changed despite his work.

"So, this certainly looks like a big project," she remarked, one hand on Andrew's shoulder as she spoke to Taylor.

Taylor smirked a bit. "Yep. It ain't gonna look like anything even remotely resembling my bike for a while. It'll give me something to do, though."

Taylor switched his attention to Andrew. "Hi, buddy. How are you today?" He made sure to make good eye contact with the boy, one of the hints he had read about.

Andrew avoided the eye contact, instead pointing down at the bike. "What?"

Taylor followed the pointing finger then looked back at the boy. "That is my motorcycle. I had an accident with it and crashed. I am trying to fix it." Taylor looked up at Tessa. "Will it be okay for me to work if he is out here? Some things I'll be doing will be making some noise and I know sensory wise that could bother him."

Tessa's brows arched. "Why, Taylor. You *have* been reading up on autism, haven't you?"

"Yep. Last night."

"What will you be doing, specifically?"

"I have to use a drill bit for a while and it does buzz a bit. Won't have to use it for long, but it can be noisy."

"Well, while you are doing that, Andrew and I will go to the front porch. When things quiet down a bit, I'll let him play in the yard. It shouldn't be a problem. He just needs to get used to seeing you around and that may take some time." Tessa was planning on bringing lemonade out to the porch and relaxing there with Rose and Andrew.

"Okay. I'll get that part over with first and let ya know when all is clear."

"Great. And thank you for understanding."

"You don't have to thank me, Tessa. This is your place and I don't want to intrude." With that, he went back to his work and Tessa and Andrew moved around the house to the front porch.

Tessa was very surprised at Taylor's manner with Andrew so far. He was being kind and careful, not at all the arrogant man she thought he would be. She had read all the usual magazines; you couldn't help it working in a hospital. *People, Us, Insider* those kinds of gossip mags and Taylor was always portrayed as a very talented actor but a playboy also, going through women like water. The two images of Taylor didn't quite mesh with Tessa's personal experience, but then Taylor was an actor too. This could all be an elaborate act to fool her. She chided herself. For what purpose?

As she poured lemonade, she tried to put Taylor from her mind.

Taylor finished up the drilling process and then moved around the house to the front porch. Rose, Tessa with Andrew in the middle were swinging on one of those big old fashioned swings. It was white with bright floral cushions and he could see a white wicker table nearby that held lemonade. He was sweaty from working out in the sun and the frosty drink sure looked good.

He moved up the stairs and smiled at the three. "All done with the noisy stuff for now." He wiped his brow off, removing the band that held his hair back and shook out his blond mane, running his fingers through it. He could see two wicker chairs placed on the opposite end of the porch with the same bright floral cushions. It was a cozy and inviting place to spend a late summer afternoon.

Tessa smiled and rose. "Can I get you a glass of lemonade?" she offered.

Taylor smiled. "That would be great. Sure is hot today for late September."

Tessa handed him a glass of lemonade with ice. "Yes, sometimes in late September we'll have a bit of Indian summer. It doesn't last too long. When October arrives, it can get cold very quickly." Taylor sipped the drink in appreciation, standing as he listened. "Sit, Taylor. Relax." Tessa waved to one of the wicker chairs.

Taylor grimaced. "My jeans are a bit dirty from working, ya know. Don't want to—"

"Nonsense," she interrupted. "It's not like those cushions haven't seen any dirt in their day." She chuckled and returned to the swing as Taylor gingerly sat in the wicker chair.

"Thanks. This is a nice break. Hi there, Rose."

Rose smiled at him. As usual, she was impeccably dressed, wearing a dark blue summer dress with a smattering of white flowers, cool white sandals on her feet, her hair up in a clip. Taylor really liked Rose; she was one friendly classy lady. "Hi, Taylor. So good to see you again. Tessa has been telling me about your adventures out there to try to fix your machine. I must say, it looks like quite the project."

Taylor finished his lemonade in one long gulp and Tessa rose to pour another. He accepted it gratefully as he answered Rose. "Yeah, it's in pretty sorry condition. I figure it will take at least a couple of months to get it back in mint condition. But I like tinkering. A bit of a hobby, I guess."

Rose couldn't believe she was talking to a real live movie star and was very curious about him. She wanted to ask him many questions but did not want to appear pushy. "Taylor, do you have family back in Texas?" She knew he was from Texas, the whole world did. Andrew was silent during these exchanges, looking at a book as Tessa moved the swing back and forth gently.

"Yep. I come from a big brood. Have three older sisters and a younger brother. Don't know what they're up to. We're not close." His lips twisted wryly.

"Oh, I see," Rose said in a subdued manner.

Taylor smiled. "My mom's the best, though. I try to get back and see her every once in a while. She's very proud of me and my success." He paused. "Her life wasn't always easy so I try to help out as much as I can." Taylor stopped speaking abruptly, looking down and swirling the ice in his glass.

Rose thought this was very admirable and smiled. "She sounds like a lovely person."

Taylor's teal eyes rose. "She is. My dad put her through hell, but he's gone. Died several years ago." Taylor's eyes moved away, out across the lawn to the street and both Tessa and Rose picked up on his reluctance to speak about this subject.

Tessa rose. "Who's hungry? It's time for lunch!" She turned to Taylor. "Taylor, would you like a sandwich?" she offered.

Taylor placed his empty glass on the wicker table, rising. "No thanks, Tessa. Gonna get back to work. Thanks for the offer, though."

Nodding to Rose and Andrew, Taylor moved down the stairs and around the house out of sight.

Tessa was very surprised he had turned down her offer of lunch. Shrugging, she went into the house carrying the lemonade and glasses on a tray.

Taylor worked straight through Sunday afternoon, not even breaking to eat. Andrew came out to ride his bike but he stayed far from Taylor and Taylor did not encourage him to come nearer as he had yesterday.

On the porch, drinking lemonade with such a nice family was a pleasure, but Rose's questions had started to hit too close to home and were too personal.

There were things about his life *he* didn't want to examine too closely and to talk to an almost complete stranger about it was— well terrifying to Taylor in a way. He didn't want to get close to people, especially these people. He knew he would be moving on eventually and he didn't want to hurt anyone or especially disrupt their lives. He snorted. He was already doing that by the very fact that he was living on their property. But Tessa had weaved a spell around him and he wasn't ready to leave until he managed to break it or she surrendered to him.

And fall and winter were coming. He decided to stick around at least until then. Take each day as it came.

CHAPTER
ELEVEN

THE WEEK WENT BY and Taylor continued to work outside. The weather continued to be on the mild side. Not as warm as Sunday, but crisp and clear, with a bright blue sky. October was only days away and Taylor could see some of the trees were starting to flaunt their autumn colors— bronze, gold and red. It was a beautiful area around here, very different from Texas where there were hardly any trees. During evenings when Taylor tired of reading he would hop into his Suburban and explore around the area. He had made sure the SUV came with a GPS unit so that he didn't get lost. He knew Toronto was close by and so was Buffalo, New York, neither of which he had had a chance to explore yet.

As he worked outside during the week, sometimes in the afternoon after school Andrew would ride his bike. He mainly stayed clear of Taylor, but Taylor caught him shooting curious looks his way once in a while. Taylor would smile and wave every time and eventually he coaxed a smile out of Andrew. Taylor thought this was progress. As the week went by, Andrew would inch closer and closer. Taylor kept his conversation brief and friendly, not wanting to frighten Andrew. He knew strangers were more bewildering to children with special needs and he was careful to speak slowly and enunciate properly. Sometimes his Texan accent interfered with that but for the most part the boy did not seem afraid of him and Taylor thought this was definitely progress.

Rose would come out occasionally and speak to him, but he did not see too much of Tessa. She seemed to be keeping her distance.

She had changed his bandage Monday for him. He went up to her place to make it easier for her, so she wouldn't have to haul bags over. She changed the dressing in the kitchen area and Taylor looked around curiously. Her kitchen was decorated in an old fashioned country style that Taylor found cozy and comfortable. He couldn't really see too much of the rest of the house from where he was sitting, but he was sure it was just as nice and inviting. She didn't let him stay long. Bandage changed and bye Taylor.

He sighed as he worked on his bike. Except for Rose, no one was really talking to him and Taylor was not used to this total silence and aloneness. In Hollywood, there were always people in his face. He even actually missed Frank. Imagine that! But, he told himself, this is why you wanted to get away. Get a different perspective, peace and relaxation. He was definitely getting an abundance of that.

Taylor turned his attention back to his work to try to dispel his unsettling thoughts.

Tessa watched Taylor through her back kitchen windows as he wrestled with that hunk of metal. As usual, he was wearing casual work clothes—jeans, a white tee, boots and a dark green flannel shirt he wore open over the tee. It was a bit chillier now, today was October first, a Friday. Taylor had been living in the carriage house for over a week now.

She had observed his interactions with her son when he was outside with their new tenant. Taylor was always friendly and smiled and waved to her son. He kept doing it even when Andrew didn't respond. Eventually her son let down his guard a bit and would approach closer and she could see Taylor smiling and talking patiently with Andrew. She frowned as she considered all of this. She was very grateful that Taylor was being kind to her son, but when he left, it could leave a hole in their lives and Andrew could get hurt if he got close to Taylor. She could too, that was why she was careful to keep her distance. She was very attracted to Taylor and she had not felt this way about a man since Steve. Oh sure, she had dated, but she had never met anyone besides her late husband that could make her heart race. Being around Taylor, it not only raced, it galloped! Danger, Tessa, danger! She did not need her heart broken. The famous movie star would be moving on soon.

She had changed his bandage on Monday and since it was Friday, she was due to change it again. She called him to let him know she didn't mind coming up to his place this time. She was a bit uncomfortable with Taylor in her home. She didn't know why. Maybe he was comparing it to his luxurious life style and found it lacking? She tried to imagine what sort of home he must have back in LA; probably something palatial and huge. Tessa was proud of the nice home she had made for her little family and did not want anyone looking down on her accomplishments. She frowned again. She could be doing Taylor an injustice; he certainly did not seem to be snooty in the least which also didn't jibe with what she had expected from him.

Sighing, she gathered up her bag with the new bandages and left for the carriage house. Andrew was downstairs playing a game with Rose and it was early evening, so now would be a good time to do it.

Taylor heard the door bell downstairs. He was reading the evening newspaper. He finally broke down and subscribed even though he now had a pretty good personal library. His bookcase was filling up quickly. Basically he spent his evenings reading and sleeping if he wasn't roaming around in his SUV. He threw the paper down on the big cocktail table, knowing it must be Tessa coming to change his bandage.

He ran his fingers through his blond mane, pushing it off of his face a bit. He had dressed casually as usual, but wore a teal sweater with his jeans tonight. It was starting to get chilly with October upon them.

He headed down the stairs to open the door for her and his spirits lifted immediately as he took in the lovely brunette holding a canvas tote. She had her hair back in one of those clips, which emphasized her high cheekbones. She was wearing jeans and a red sweater and the color looked terrific on her.

"Hi!" He motioned her in and up the stairs.

"Hi, Taylor," she said in a subdued voice. She proceeded to climb the stairs and Taylor tried to keep his eyes off of her terrific ass, but it was hard. Damn, but she had a fine body.

When they reached the upper level she moved to the sectional and he followed her. She sat, looking around. His gorgeous place was as neat as a pin, only a newspaper thrown casually on his table. In her experience most men were sloppy. Her eyes moved to Taylor, who took a seat next to her, smiling that famous grin. Reluctantly she smiled back.

"Well, let's get to work. Shirt off," she said.

"Yes, ma'm." Taylor drew his sweater over his head as Tessa carefully kept her eyes averted.

She rummaged in her tote, found bandages and started to unwind his old dressing. Although she was gentle, he hissed in a bit. His ribs still bothered him now and then. How long had he been out of the hospital? Ten days, two weeks? He couldn't remember.

At this reaction, Tessa looked up at him. "Still hurts, huh?"

"A bit, now and then." He watched as she carefully removed the old bandage and inspected his stomach and waist. He was still badly bruised, the purplish bruises not yet healing.

Tessa gently started to rewind the new bandage. "You know, Taylor. You need to take it easy. All of that physical work you are doing on your bike is probably not helping. And take your pain meds," she added as she worked, carefully trying to avoid looking at his magnificent body.

"Tessa, I gotta have somethin' to do. Otherwise, I'll go stir crazy. Can only read so many books." He watched intently as she worked.

She finished up with the bandage and looked back up at him as she packed away the old dressing. Taylor gingerly put his sweater back on, covering the bandage up once again.

Taylor looked up at her. "What do you do for entertainment around here? Are there any good night clubs, restaurants or shows? I know you're pretty rural here but surely there must be something *somewhere*." Teal eyes moved to Tessa's face.

She smiled. "We are not all that provincial, Taylor. Lewiston has several good restaurants, as does Niagara Falls. Then if you want to drive into Buffalo, there are tons of places to go. Buffalo is famous for its great food."

"Yeah. Buffalo wings, right?" Taylor arched a blond brow.

Tessa laughed and Taylor thought it sounded like bells chiming. "We don't call them Buffalo wings around here. Here they are just chicken wings or wings."

"What is your favorite restaurant?"

"Oh, I haven't been out in ages. But one I really like is right here in town. Shamuses. On clear days, you can see all the way to Toronto." She started to gather her things, but Taylor wanted her to stay longer. He hadn't seen her all week.

"Are you going to run away again, Tessa? Can't you stay for a bit, have a glass of wine? I am *dying* for some company."

Tessa realized that the only people he really saw besides herself were Rose and Andrew. She knew Rose and Taylor had become friends but Taylor was used to having people around. What could it hurt to have a glass of wine? "Okay, Taylor. A glass of wine sounds fine. Do you have any chardonnay?"

Taylor was surprised she had accepted his offer. He was prepared to come up with several reasons to convince her. Her capitulation was unexpected. "Chardonnay, white wine? Yeah, I stocked up." He moved over to his wine rack, located on the kitchen wall. "Kendall Jackson okay?"

"Yes. Perfect."

He chose a Merlot for himself, pouring the wine into balloon wine glasses he had purchased somewhere. He carried the glasses over to the sectional and settled in, handing Tessa her glass. He clinked his glass against hers. "To new friends."

Long lashed brown eyes studied him over the rim as Tessa sipped. Lowering the glass, she responded. "Are we friends, Taylor?"

"Of course! Did you doubt it?" He studied her as he sipped.

Tessa looked away a moment, then focused back on Taylor. "Yes, I guess for now we're friends. But you'll be moving on someday Taylor."

"Probably. But not for a while." He studied her intently, wondering why she had brought this up. She was still an enigma to him and usually Taylor had no problem figuring women out. This one was much tougher. Taylor was used to frivolous women such as actresses and models who were pretty transparent and let you know right up front what they wanted. This one— Tessa— had really lived through some tough times and probably would continue to considering she had a child with special needs. One of the reasons Taylor was so attracted to her was the vulnerability mixed with such courage that she displayed. He admired her and he had never met a woman he *admired*. He had met many he was sexually attracted to and with his looks and fame he could sleep with just about anyone he wanted to. He could jet back to Hollywood tonight and get laid but here he was in upstate New York trying to figure out what made a gorgeous nurse tick.

Tessa glanced over at Taylor. He had been silent for several minutes after his last comment. She sipped her wine, studying him as he in turn studied her. What was he thinking? She knew he was attracted to her, but he probably only wanted sex and Tessa did not do casual sex. She had not had sex since Steve died, what five years now? Yeah, she missed it but with Andrew her life was so full and she had learned to do without it. She did not need a man in her life to complicate things, but she realized things were already quite complicated by just having Taylor around. Should she ask him to leave? He and Andrew seemed to be developing a bond and that was good for her son's sake. But what about later in the future when he left?

"You're awful quiet," she finally remarked.

He decided to be blunt. "Just thinking about you, Tessa."

She arched a brow. "Oh?" She waited for him to elaborate.

Taylor placed his wineglass down on the table and ran his fingers through his glorious hair, disrupting the blond waves. Tessa unglued her eyes when he spoke. "Yeah. Just wondering about your life here and stuff. I know your husband is gone but didn't he have family? You seem to be alone with just Rose. What about— Steve I think you said— what about his family? Do you see them?"

Tessa glanced away, uncomfortable. This was a very touchy subject. Steve's family had wanted nothing to do with either her or Steve after they found out their grandson was autistic. Steve came from one of the old wealthy families in the area and they could not accept the fact their grandson was not perfect.

Steve was their only child too and now he was gone. Tessa thought they probably blamed her for that too. They had never approved of her, thinking a lowly nurse was not good enough for their son. She really didn't want to share any of this with Taylor. Not yet. It was too personal.

She turned her attention back to the man next to her. "Steve's family is not around. Let's just leave it at that."

Her tone and closed expression told him he had hit a sore spot. "Okay, Tessa." He picked up his wine, sipping again.

Tessa shook off her mood, turning up the wattage on her smile as she turned to him.

My heart be still, he warned himself.

"What about you, Taylor? Tell me about life in Hollywood. It must be quite fascinating. I'm sure you have a lot of stories to tell."

Taylor sighed. "Hollywood's Hollywood. Everyone climbing all over each other to get to the top. They all pretend to like each other, but it's a sham. They would all stab you in the back and walk over your corpse if it meant they could take your place. I make a ton of money, know a ton of people, but no one that is really my friend. Maybe my agent Frank. But that's about it."

Tessa considered his words. "That's sad, Taylor. It doesn't sound like the glamorous world it is painted to be."

"Oh, it's glamorous if you're into that sort of thing. Parties, people wearing jewelry they really can't afford, mansions galore and all the pretty people. It's all a façade. To get caught up in it is when you're gonna start heading down. Successful people in Hollywood know the business is what counts and concentrate on making good films. Some just glide by. Me, I just like to act." He shrugged broad shoulders. "The money doesn't mean squat to me anymore. It did at one time when I was dirt poor, but I have more money now then I can ever spend, even if I don't make another movie. Does that answer your questions?"

He sipped wine, teal eyes studying her lovely face.

Tessa felt a bit uncomfortable. "Yep." She finished her wine, setting the glass on the table and standing. "I have to get back to Rose and Andrew now, Taylor. Thanks for the wine." She started to collect her tote as Taylor stood too.

"Wait, Tessa. I want to ask you a question."

She paused, turning to him. "Oh? What would that be?"

"Can we have dinner tomorrow night at that place you like, Shamuses? I need to get out a bit and I want to treat you to a nice dinner. To thank you for everything you've done." He put his hands in his back jeans pockets, looking down at her, holding his breath, hoping she wouldn't refuse.

"Thank me? You don't need to thank me, Taylor. You pay me good money to live here. I was able to hire a tutor for Andrew with the extra income. You don't owe me a thing."

Taylor sighed. "Okay. I don't owe you a thing. But I'm getting a bit lonely, Tessa. Please say yes."

Tessa considered the drop dead gorgeous man in front of her. She had not been on a date in ages and when she did go, it was just a date. That's it; that was all. With Taylor, she suspected it would be so much more. But his imploring beautiful teal eyes were getting to her and it would be so nice to be wined and dined again. Treated like a woman again instead of just a mom and a nurse. She hesitated a bit further, then sighed.

"All right, Taylor. You'll have to make reservations. They are in the phone book. Around six p.m. should work. I'll have Rose watch Andrew."

Hot damn! She had agreed! Taylor grinned. "Okay. I'll do that. Tomorrow night at six. I'm looking forward to it."

As she turned to go down his flight of stairs, she glanced back over her shoulder. "I have to warn you. I haven't been on a date in a long time."

"That's okay, Tessa. I'm sure it will come back to you."

She snorted, descending the stairs as Taylor grinned hugely.

He went and poured himself another glass of wine to celebrate.

Chapter

TWELVE

Saturday was dreary and rainy. Taylor spent his time running errands, buying groceries, that kind of stuff. He usually wore his sunglasses and tied his hair back to hide his identity but with the rain it would just draw more attention to him, so he tied his hair back and clapped a ball cap on.

When he returned to his place, he called up the restaurant and told them he wanted reservations at their very best table, one with a good view. After being denied such accommodations Taylor had to use his considerable charm to get the table he wanted. Usually all he had to do was say his name and like magic he received whatever he requested. This being a regular Joe stuff was much harder than Taylor had been accustomed to in recent years and it was certainly interesting.

Taylor prepared for his date with Tessa, taking a nice long hot shower. He shaved and groomed his hair so that the long waves fell off of his face and brushed his shoulders. He found the dark blue suit he had purchased, adding a white shirt and pale blue tie. He was able to find Bruno Magli shoes at some men's store and he bought several pairs. He pulled out the black ones and put them on. Straightening his tie in the mirror, he inspected himself. Not bad. Conservative and not over the top. He felt Tessa would feel more comfortable with that style than some of his other wilder styles.

Sighing, he checked his watch. He had called her to tell her he would be by around five thirty. It was now five twenty. He would wait five minutes and then go over and knock on the back door. Fortunately the rain had let up and a warmer front had moved in. Thank God for little favors.

When Tessa informed Rose she would need her to come up and watch Andrew on Saturday evening because she had a date with Taylor, Rose screamed in delight. Tessa didn't think it was cause for *that* much celebration but she knew Rose wanted her to be paired up with a man. Why, Tessa did not know. She was doing just fine on her own. But Tessa was very nervous.

Trying to decide what to wear was nerve wracking. Tessa had not shopped in a while, but she had several very nice evening dresses and cocktail dresses from her days of socializing with her husband. She finally chose a dark navy satin sheath that had a matching bolero jacket to hide the strapless style and for warmth. The dress was very form fitting and showed off her curvy figure. Was it too much? She did her hair up in a curly French twist and added a single strand of pearls and black pumps. She inserted pearl studs into her ears and carefully applied her makeup. Adding lipstick, she closed the tube, turning to exit the bathroom and found Andrew standing in the entrance watching her. Rose had already arrived and was probably in the living room. Andrew's big brown eyes looked up at his mommy.

Andrew had never really seen her dressed up, with the hair, makeup, etc. She smiled at him and leaned down to kiss his cheek.

Andrew smiled, accepting the kiss and then tentatively touched her satin dress. He smiled, liking the texture, smoothing his hand over the material.

"Mommy prettee..."

"Thank you, honey. Mommy is going out tonight. Mrs. H will be here to stay with you and put you in bed while I'm gone. I will be home soon though and come in to give you good night kisses." Tessa wanted to assure him that this ritual would not be forgotten.

Andrew frowned. "You go out?"

"Yes, honey. I'm going to dinner with our new neighbor who lives in the back, Taylor. You know Taylor, right?" She watched his eyes and expression and could tell this news wasn't going over well.

"No, mommy. Stay with me," he insisted.

This reaction surprised Tessa. She had dated in the past and Andrew had never had a problem with it. "Andrew, I won't be gone long. And you know Taylor. He is a nice man."

The beautiful lips pouted and he turned to go down the hallway to the living room. Tessa followed him, grabbing her black evening clutch from a table, depositing her lipstick and keys in the clutch.

Andrew moved to sit next to Rose on the sofa who currently had a game show on that Andrew usually liked to watch. He continued to pout as he sat next to Rose.

When Tessa appeared, Rose gasped. "Oh, Tessa! You look beautiful!"

Tessa moved to stand in front of the two. "Thank you, Rose. But we have a bit of a dilemma. Andrew is not too happy I'm going out. Perhaps you could make a special treat?"

At these words, Andrew perked up. "Ice cream?" he asked hopefully.

Rose put her arms around Andrew and hugged him; leaning back she smiled at him. "We can make ice cream sundaes while mommy is out. How does that sound?"

"Yes!" Andrew was all smiles now.

Tessa sighed. Thank God that trick had worked. Sometimes Andrew could be difficult to handle if something upset him.

Tessa leaned down to kiss Andrew on the cheek, careful to wipe the lipstick off. "I'll see you soon, honey. I love you," she whispered.

Andrew kissed her back and then turned his attention to the television screen as the doorbell downstairs rang.

Taylor waited impatiently for Tessa to answer the summons of the doorbell. He debated about bringing roses or flowers or something but decided against it. He wanted her to feel as comfortable as possible and he usually never went the flower route anyway. He shoved his hands in his suit pocket, glancing around as the outside lamp lit up the back door area.

Soon he could hear heels clicking down the stairs and Tessa appeared decked out in a tight navy satin outfit. She looked drop dead gorgeous. Not that she didn't all the time, but with her hair up and makeup enhancing her already perfect features, she looked like a supermodel, not a mommy or a nurse.

"Hi, Taylor," she greeted him as she turned to make sure the door was locked. Turning to him, she took in the tall man before her. He had left his glorious hair down, brushing the top of broad shoulders. He wore a beautiful dark blue suit paired with a white shirt and pale blue tie. He looked yummy. Tessa get a hold of your glands, she scolded herself.

Taylor smiled at her, taking her hand to help her down the few steps and escorting her over to the Suburban. "Hi yourself," he responded. "You look great," he remarked as he opened the door so she could slide into the passenger seat.

When he took his place in the driver's seat, she answered him. "Thanks. You don't look too bad yourself."

"Well, I wanted to dress to impress," he chuckled, starting up the vehicle and turning on the GPS system.

Tessa's brows arched. "What is that little gadget?"

Taylor glanced over at her as he backed down the driveway. "It's a GPS system. It will give me directions to the restaurant so I don't get lost. Unlike you, I don't know where I'm going around here. It comes in handy."

Tessa frowned a bit. She really wasn't familiar with all the new hi-tech stuff coming out. She had a cell phone she always carried but that was about as hi-tech as she got.

As he headed out the main road, she cleared her throat, looking over at his perfect profile as he drove. The sun was just starting to set and the waning rays of the sun lit his golden hair up. He looked like a god! She shook off the thought and tried to make conversation. "Any problems with the reservation?"

"Nope. They didn't want to give me one of their choice tables, but I soon talked them into it. By the way, I made the reservation under your name. Patterson."

She chuckled. "That must have been a bit of a snag for you. Not getting a choice table when you asked for one, I mean."

"Yeah, a bit, but I talked them into it. Rose is with Andrew?"

Tessa frowned a bit. "Yes. He had a bit of an issue with me going out with you tonight."

Taylor turned to glance at her. "Oh really? Why is that, d'ya suppose?"

Tessa shrugged her shoulders. Taylor liked the way the movement lifted her breasts. "I don't know. I've gone on dates in the past and it was never a problem."

"My guess is he is a bit more familiar with me and that he might view me as encroaching on his territory."

This thought had never occurred to Tessa but it could very well be exactly what was happening and she was stunned that Taylor had figured something out about her own son that she never would have considered. She glanced over to study him more carefully as he drove. Sometimes Taylor surprised her with his insight.

They arrived at the restaurant and Tessa silently thanked the Gods the rain had stopped. It was hard enough walking in spike heels. Taylor came around and helped her down from the big beast that was his vehicle.

Escorting her inside, he gave his name to the hostess and they were shown directly to a table where windows extended the entire length of the area. The sun was setting further and the restaurant was located on a hill that looked down a slight valley. In the distance Taylor could see lights twinkling as night approached and assumed it must be Toronto.

He seated Tessa and moved to take his seat as his glance moved around the room. He could see why Tessa liked the place. It was romantic and elegant. The walls were painted a pale aqua and all of the round tables were covered with elegant linen. Wait staff moved quietly and unobtrusively around tables and the clink of crystal and quiet conversation hummed. It was classy and probably the food was great. Taylor had eaten in some of the most famous restaurants in the world but he thought Shamuses had a charming ambiance. A glass candle holder sat in the middle of their table and the light danced on the single rose placed in the center of the table.

Taylor took the linen napkin and put it in his lap as Tessa did the same. Before either of them could strike up a conversation, their waiter appeared with a wine list. Taylor arched a brow at Tessa. "Like champagne?" he questioned.

"Yes. I love it," she sighed.

"We'll have a bottle of the Perrier Jouie," the French words rolled off of his tongue smoothly, even with that Texan accent.

"Yes, of course, sir. I shall be right back." The waiter was very happy with this very extravagant choice and decided to take very good care of this couple. They were both extremely good looking and the man looked just like that movie star, Taylor Boudrain. No, it couldn't be, he decided as he moved off.

The waiter had left menus and they both perused them, finally laying them aside. "So, what's good here, Tessa?"

She hesitated, blushing a bit. She liked the lobster but it was the most expensive dish on the menu. Of course, that shouldn't be a problem for Taylor. "Well…I like the lobster," she finally answered.

Taylor noticed the blush and hesitation. "Tessa, have anything you want. Really. It's not an issue. This is your night. I want you to enjoy yourself."

Tessa's brown eyes studied Taylor. With the candlelight flickering on his face and the waning sun painting beautiful colors around the room, it was very romantic. Watch yourself Tessa, she warned. Only have *two* glasses of the expensive champagne.

It arrived shortly, the waiter displaying the beautiful green bottle with the white floral motif in a silver ice bucket draped with white linen. He made an elaborate show of opening the bottle and pouring a small portion in Taylor's flute. Taylor went through the ritual, testing the wine and nodded his approval. The waiter then filled Tessa's flute and topped off Taylor's.

"Are you folks ready to order, or would you like more time?"

Taylor glanced across the table. "Ready to order?"

"Sure."

Tessa ordered the lobster and Taylor ordered a surf and turf special they were running. He also ordered an appetizer of shrimp for the two of them, handing the bulky menus back to the waiter. The waiter placed the ice bucket on a stand very close to Taylor so he would have easy access to it and left them to chat.

"So, I can see why you like this place, Tessa. Veerryy classeee."

"I've been here before, you know, with Steve. The food is always terrific and I like the atmosphere." She played with her crystal flute, finally lifting it to take a sip. Ummmmmm, it tasted like liquid heaven.

Taylor also sipped his champagne, studying the lovely woman across from him. "Tell me about Steve, if you don't mind. I'm curious. How long were you married? How did you meet?"

Tessa's lovely brown eyes rose to his, hesitating a bit. Well, it was all in the past, why not talk about it? "Well, I met Steve at work. You know, at the hospital. He was a surgeon, a very renowned and respected doctor. He came from one of the old wealthy families in Lewiston. I met him in the ER one day and he— I guess you could say— pursued me. Eventually I relented and had dinner with him and we continued to date. We fell in love and married within a year. Andrew was born the next year. And Steve— well, he died when Andrew was about two. So we were only together a brief time. Three, four years." Her words dwindled into silence and she sipped at her champagne.

Taylor mulled over this information. "Did he have family in the area?" Tessa seemed to be so alone, with just Rose helping her out. And what about Tessa's family?

She snorted a bit. "Oh, yes. He has family in the area, but they want nothing to do with me. Or Andrew. And he happens to be their only grandchild. Steve was their only son also."

Taylor frowned. "Then I think they would want to see you and Andrew even more, considering their son is gone." Something here didn't make sense to Taylor.

Tessa considered Taylor. There were some things she just didn't talk about, Steve's family among them. But what could it hurt? Taylor did not know the Pattersons and he would be gone soon anyway. Why did that thought suddenly hurt her? She finally answered his question. "They pretty much disowned Steve and I when they found out Andrew had a disability. They could not accept the fact that their perfect son had an imperfect son. Mostly I think they blamed me for that. They never cared for me, thinking I was not good enough for Steve." She lapsed into silence, one elegant finger stroking her flute.

Taylor found this totally astounding. How could you not love and care for your grandson and daughter-in-law, especially when they were so in need of help and companionship? "Tessa, I'm really sorry to hear that. It's really too bad there are such ignorant people in the world. If they got to know Andrew, they would see what a special kid he is."

Tessa searched Taylor's eyes, trying to determine if he was this genuinely caring or if this was an act. This comment totally floored her. No one else besides his teachers and Rose had told her Andrew was special. Of course she knew her son was special, he was her entire world. She lived for Andrew. And now here was a man who FINALLY seemed to get it. Or was it an act?

Before she could muse further on it, their appetizers arrived.

Taylor changed the conversation to lighter subjects, asking her about her work and telling her some amusing stories about life on the sets. Tessa relaxed, enjoying her meal and Taylor's company. She could not remember the last time when she felt this relaxed and happy and tried not to think about the reasons why.

After their meal they relaxed with an after dinner cordial. Tessa chose Amaretto and Taylor had a brandy. The meal had been delicious and the service wonderful. Full evening had now arrived and you could see the lights of Toronto twinkling across the lake.

Taylor lazily studied Tessa. He would love to take her up to his carriage house and have hot sex with her, but he knew it would not happen. He knew Tessa was the type of woman who would not hop into the sack unless she was emotionally involved or in love and Taylor thought that pretty much left him nowhere. She wasn't in love with him and he still could not figure out what it was about her that so intrigued him. Yes, she was beautiful and that alone attracted him right from the start. But as he got to know her better, he found her even more attractive. Taylor had never been in love in his life so he could not recognize the signs when they were slapping him in the face. He figured all he wanted was sex and he knew he would not get it, at least not for a while. So why was he still hanging around? The million dollar question.

Well, there was still his bike to repair and in the mean time, who knew what could happen?

They finished their cocktails and Taylor paid the bill, leaving a generous tip.

He escorted Tessa out to his vehicle and they were both silent as he drove back to Tessa's home.

At the back door, Tessa fumbled in her clutch for her keys as Taylor stood behind her. She finally located them and shoved them in the lock. She had a little bit of a buzz going on from the champagne (and yes, she had limited herself to two) and the cocktail.

Taylor took her keys. "Here, let me." He inserted the key in smoothly and the door swung open.

Tessa turned to him. The balmy October night was beautiful and one could smell the roses growing next to the steps. The stars had appeared after the rain and everything was dewy and soft, as though waiting for magic. Magical, that is what the evening had been.

Tessa looked up at the handsome man in the lamp light. His wavy blond hair was a bit more mussed than the beginning of the evening, one blond lock falling on his forehead. Tessa was preparing to say good night and thank him for the evening but before she could speak Taylor leaned down and caught her lips with his own.

The kiss started out as light as a butterfly kiss. Soft, sweet, barely touching her lips. He moaned, wanting more of the honey she tasted like. He deepened the kiss and pulled her close, softly swirling his tongue, careful to do so gently, tenderly.

Tessa's head whirled as soon as Taylor started kissing her. She had never been kissed like this before. So sensuously and gently, as though she was fragile and might break. Moaning, she returned his kiss, ignoring the voice in the back of her mind that told her she was crazy, don't do this! She kissed him back passionately and she had never kissed anyone that way before, not even Steve. But it came so naturally with Taylor. She could feel him deepen the kiss, lazily exploring her mouth. Tessa's head was spinning away and she knew she had to stop this. *Now!*

She pushed gently at his chest, feeling the muscles under the expensive suit. He acquiesced immediately, stepping back.

Tenderly, he brushed tendrils of curls off of her face and cheeks and smiled softly. "Good night, Tessa. Sweet dreams."

And with that remark he strode down the stairs and disappeared into the entrance of his carriage house.

With flushed cheeks, Tessa quickly shut the door and locked it. She leaned against it, her breath quickened, breasts rising and falling.

Tessa you need to stay far, far away from Taylor!

Sighing, she moved up the stairs to go to Andrew and give him his good night kisses. She touched her lips softly, still feeling the heat of Taylor's lips.

Chapter

THIRTEEN

A SHRILL BUZZING NOISE woke Taylor. It seemed to be coming from his night stand. Oh damn! His cell phone. Groggily Taylor looked at his watch. It was nine a.m. He had slept in much later than normal. His brain tried to process events, not fully awake as his cell phone continued to make noise. What day was it? Oh yeah, Monday. He had spent Sunday driving around in the SUV because the weather was still too yucky to work on his bike. He had not seen hide nor hair of anyone from the bigger house and he spent Sunday evening reading, eventually stumbling to bed sometime around midnight.

Swearing to himself, he turned in the bed so he could reach his phone. Flipping it open, he flopped on his back.

"Yeah?" he answered abruptly.

"Taylor? Is that you? Christ, you finally answered your cell!"

Frank, and in his usual perky mood for a Monday morning. "Frank, what the hell? It must be like— six a.m. where you are?" he mumbled.

"Yeah and why are you still sleeping? You're half asleep, aren't you?" Frank accused.

"Yep, good buddy, you woke me from a sound sleep. What's up?" Taylor tried to wipe the sleep from his eyes and wake up enough to follow the conversation.

"What's up is you have to get your butt back to LA. How long are you planning on staying in that podunk town anyway?"

"Podunk...hmmmm...didn't know you even knew that Texan slang, buddy."

"Taylor, really, cut the shit. I need you back here. Remember that research hospital center that you and several other big donors are paying to build? Well all of the rest of the players can be here tomorrow, Tuesday, early a.m. and you need to be there too. You're the biggest donor and your ass *has* to be sitting in that meeting. And don't tell me to have the lawyers handle it! You have to sign papers, your signature, you!"

Taylor was getting another one of his damn headaches. He still got them on and off and this conversation, first damn thing in the morning, wasn't helping. "Can't I just email you a notary signature or something?" Taylor shook the sleep from his head, leaning up on an elbow. He really didn't want to fly to LA right now, not with things heating up between him and Tessa, although he had not seen her at all since Saturday.

"No, I have already been informed by your slew of lawyers that you have to physically be there. I can send the jet and the limo out today to pick you up. Can you be ready by two p.m.? The flight out of the private strip is around two thirty and you can be back in LA by around five or so. Does this work? And I don't want to hear again that you can't make it!" Frank said sternly.

"Ya know, sometimes you sound like my freakin' mother, Frank! Okay, okay. Send the limo, send the plane! I'll be ready!"

"Okay," Frank said, mollified. "And Taylor, for what it's worth, I do miss you." Frank hung up abruptly.

Taylor clicked off his phone, grinning wryly. He knew the son of a bitch actually liked him!

Taylor dressed in black jeans, a black shirt and boots for the trip back. He knew in LA it would still be warm, so he wouldn't need the black leather jacket. Since it was mid-day Monday, he knew both Tessa and Andrew would not be home. Rose would be. Taylor knew he really didn't need to tell his neighbors his comings and goings, but if he wasn't around for several days they would clearly wonder and he didn't want them to worry about him.

He walked over to the back door and rang the downstairs doorbell. He shivered a bit in his shirt. There was a chill in the air today and he could feel winter coming. He didn't much like the cold, being a Southern boy.

Soon his summons was answered and Rose looked up at him. She was wearing a pale pink sweater over one of her habitual dresses today and he didn't blame her.

She looked up in surprise. "Why, Taylor! How are you?"

He shivered a bit more. "Cold."

She waved him into the downstairs flat. "Come in, come. Would you like some hot tea? I have some brewing," she offered.

Taylor stepped into her warm cozy kitchen. Looking around, he could see it was very similar to Tessa's with that country look to it. However Rose's was decorated in the different manner that older people usually adopted—doilies here and there, ceramic figurines that probably dated from the fifties, way before he was born. She had a wide round table with padded chairs and she waved him into a seat but Taylor remained standing near the door.

"Thanks for the offer of tea, Rose, but no thanks. I just came by to give you some news. I'm leaving for LA today, probably will be gone several days. Something has come up and I need to go back. A limo is coming by in about an hour."

At this news, Rose's brows arched. "Oh really? You'll only be gone a few days?" She wanted to be assured he was not leaving for good.

"Yep. Just thought I'd let you and Tessa know why you won't be seeing me for a bit." Taylor smiled down at the older woman.

"Well, that was very nice of you to come by and let me know, Taylor. I'll be sure to tell Tessa. Do you know when you will be returning?"

"Hopefully by at least Thursday. This shouldn't take more than a couple of days. Well— take care of yourselves while I'm gone," he said awkwardly, backing up and turning to the door.

Rose came to him and gave him a brief hug. "God speed," she said.

"Thanks," Taylor mumbled, turning to go, not sure what to make of that.

The limo showed up right on time at two, a big black job. Frank never did anything in a small way, always the showy vehicles, the showy parties, glamorous Hollywood. And Taylor was on his way back.

He had packed a couple of business suits and casual clothes for several days.

The limo whisked him quickly to the private airstrip and Taylor found himself airborne shortly, heading back to California.

Taylor deplaned at a private VIP airstrip at LAX. Another limo (this one white) waited for him. He hopped in and gave the driver directions to his Beverly Hills mansion.

It was about six p.m. and still light out. Evening on the west coast wouldn't arrive for about an hour or so but already the neon signs of LA were lit up. Taylor passed by this whir of color hardly taking in any of the scenery, thinking of Tessa and Andrew and if Tessa would miss him or not.

Sighing, he laid his head back into the luxurious cushions and closed his eyes.

Taylor's business meetings lasted for two days. Frank, his attorneys and his business assistant were all at the meetings. They were able to wrap up the final details of the big project in a timely fashion. Taylor was thankful for that. He hated meetings and the whole corporate situation. That was why he was an actor. He acted because it was fun. Sitting in boardrooms was not. He only conceded to do these things because it would help people and Taylor was a big believer in giving back since he was now so wealthy. He always swore his business retinue to complete secrecy; he didn't want his bad boy Hollywood image tarnished. Taylor felt it was one of the reasons why he was so successful. Frank would have told him he was wrong. He was successful because he was talented and drop dead gorgeous.

Everyone shook hands all around and Taylor couldn't wait to head out. He had a date with a special friend.

The special friend was Marisa Maloy, an actress he had met at one of the many Hollywood parties. She had a successful television series and also lived in Beverly Hills, as he did. They met at the party, took one look at each other, said yes and went back to his place where they screwed their brains out all night. They remained good friends only, seeing each other in between relationships if either wanted sex. Taylor admitted he wanted sex—badly. Being around Tessa made him so horny and tonight he decided to do something about it. For a moment he felt a pang of guilt but squashed it. He and Tessa were not really in a relationship. Not at this point, anyway.

He took Marisa to a fashionable restaurant for dinner. Taylor made sure the table was far away from any paparazzi as he did not want their pictures splattered all over magazine covers. They finished up dinner and went to Marisa's place. It was a bit smaller than Taylor's and homier because she had bothered to decorate and furnish it. Taylor's was about as empty as a mausoleum because he was never there.

Marisa laughed at something Taylor had said about a colleague as the gates swung open to her estate. The limo pulled up her drive and Taylor dismissed the driver. He would just catch a cab out in the morning when he flew east again. He grabbed his luggage and hauled it into Marisa's place, setting it down in her elaborate foyer.

79

She went to her sunken living room to pour Taylor a bourbon since she knew it was his drink of choice. She opened her silver chased ice bucket to add a few rocks and fixed herself a martini. She brought the drinks over to her cushiony sofa where Taylor had settled in. He was wearing black dress slacks and a silk teal shirt that made his glorious eyes even brighter. Marisa had missed him. She had not seen him around town lately and she knew he wasn't working right now.

Taylor accepted his drink and as he sipped she settled next to him in the cushions, kicking off her black spike heels. She wore a sexy, low cut cocktail dress that showed off her divine cleavage. Marisa was blond (okay, like the rest of Hollywood, it wasn't her natural color) and had big brown eyes. She had a killer body and could have went the model route had she chose to but acting was her first love and by God, she was making it in Hollywood. She dated here and there, but Taylor was the only guy she met that she could be lovers with as well as friends. No strings attached on either side.

"So, Taylor. Where have you been? Haven't seen you around town lately." They had discussed mostly business at dinner and nothing really personal.

Taylor sighed. "Well, I went on a bit of a hiatus. Took my Harley and went cross country and fuck, wouldn't you know it! I get in an accident."

Marisa gasped and her eyes widened. "Are you okay?"

Taylor lifted the silk shirt, showing her the bandage that still encircled his middle. "Well, I have this little souvenir. Got a cracked rib. But I was very lucky. I was hit by a semi. Was in the hospital about a week. I'm still recuperating. Plan to go back east tomorrow for a while. Frank's not too happy, but oh well. Don't feel up to working quite yet."

"Taylor, I wish you would have told me! God—"

"Marisa, it's over and done with. Not a big deal. I'm gonna be fine."

"But still Taylor, we're friends. Friends look out for each other. I would have came right out." Marisa frowned a bit, sipping at her drink.

"See, that's what I didn't want. Even Frank didn't know where I was right away, didn't want my identity known. The people there were great and I didn't want the media descending like buzzing wasps."

"Well, I can understand that, but I still care Taylor. I know we're not exactly in a relationship, but we do keep up. I would figure something that important, you would tell me."

Taylor swallowed the rest of his bourbon. "I don't care to talk about it anymore, Marisa. Where is the bedroom again?"

Marisa laughed as she took his hand, leading him up the long circular staircase.

Taylor and Marisa fell on her fluffy white duvet, kissing passionately. Taylor peeled off Marisa's black dress. She was wearing a black garter belt with a lacy bra and thong to match.

"Ummm...always liked your taste in lingerie, baby," he murmured, placing soft kisses on her cleavage, working his way up her neck, chin and to her full lips. He kissed her as he removed her bra, releasing her full breasts. Marisa was proud of the fact that her size 38c's were real. Unlike most actresses, she did not have a boob job.

Taylor went to work on them, sucking vigorously at the nipples, making her gasp, grabbing at his blond hair. She moaned as he continued to nip and suck. Eventually his hands wandered down to her thong, removing it, leaving the garter belt in place. He moved his head down between her thighs and gently parted them, his full lips exploring everywhere. She bucked, moaning, wanting to feel his large penis inside her.

They usually took their time, but it had been a while for Taylor so he was humming and ready to go. He quickly removed his clothes and climbed back on top of her, shoving his penis into her abruptly.

Marisa gave a little scream and came immediately. Taylor grinned down at her as he rode her slowly, slowly. She moaned and moved her hips up and down and had another orgasm. With Taylor she always had multiples and that was unusual for her. He continued to fuck slowly, increasing the pace a bit more. Then more and more until he exploded inside her. Moaning he laid heavily on her, finally moving to the side.

They were both breathing heavily and after a few moments they slid under the sheets, Marisa removing her garter belt and stockings. Naked, they snuggled.

Marisa looked up at Taylor, snuggled against his chest. He had his eyes closed as though he would fall asleep. She knew that was not the case. He was always ready for round two very quickly.

"So, Taylor. Why are you heading back east tomorrow? Why aren't you staying in LA?" She stroked the hard muscles on his chest. He had the most magnificent body she had ever seen.

Taylor opened his teal eyes, sighing. "Because I need some R&R."

She shrugged. "You can get that here." She leaned up on an elbow.

"Yeah. But my bike is back there. I'm spending my recuperating time fixing it, working on it. I'll probably spend a few months there, at least."

"But you can do that here. Fix your Harley, that is." She continued to stroke as she looked up into his face.

He shrugged. "It's just a change of pace. It's quieter there, peaceful. I like it, for now."

She narrowed her eyes. "Where are you staying?"

"I found a pretty little carriage house someone rented out to me. Hell, the place is nicer than my mansion. Hired a decorator and I love the place. And the area is beautiful too; it's in Western New York."

She sat up, clasping the sheet to her breasts. "You're not telling me everything. What else is going on?"

Taylor glanced at her face and chuckled. "Never can hide anything from you, can I?"

"Nope."

"Weeelll—there is kind of a person I'm interested in—"

"A woman!" she gasped. "You met a woman you're interested in?!" She could hardly believe this. Taylor was the playboy type and didn't settle too long with any woman, even her.

"I don't know if the word is 'interested' but I'm living on her property and for now, she helps me out and stuff. She's a nurse."

"A nurse! I could never picture you with a nurse! Spill! Tell me everything!" Marisa was very excited by this news, but Taylor's expression closed up.

"I don't want to discuss her, Marisa. I really don't."

Marisa frowned. This woman was more important than Taylor was letting on. Before she could begin to question him again, Taylor rolled over on top of her.

"Enough talk. Time to fuck again."

And with that, he proceeded to screw her brains out.

When Rose gave Tessa the news that Taylor would be away in LA for several days on business, she frowned.

Tessa had been wrestling with her feelings for Taylor ever since Saturday evening and the kiss at the back door. He had been tender and passionate, a combination that totally melted Tessa's knees. She scolded herself. The *last* thing she needed was to get involved with a famous Hollywood movie star. She knew that she and Andrew would have no place in his life. Perhaps she had made a big mistake in letting him come here. On the other hand, she could see Andrew coming a bit more out of his shell when he was around Taylor and Taylor was very good with her son.

Her thoughts whirled. She just didn't know what to do about Taylor. She just didn't.

CHAPTER
FOURTEEN

THE SNOW FELL FROM the dark sky relentlessly. Tessa pressed her nose to her back kitchen window. She could barely see the outside lamp on the carriage house across the way. All she could see was swirling white snow, hurled around by the wind. It howled and slammed against the big Victorian house, like a ghostly intruder demanding entrance.

Tessa shivered in her robe. Andrew was in bed and that was certainly where she should be at this hour. She had to work tomorrow as it was Friday. Thankfully Andrew would not have school because of this storm but she still had to get out and to work. Hospitals did not close down for snow storms.

This was a very early storm, even for this area. It was only October fourth, tomorrow would be the fifth. The weather forecasted the storm to be around well into Saturday. Tessa was unprepared for this early storm. She had not even taken in her snow blower to the local hardware store to have it serviced and primed and ready to go. The way the snow was adding up, she would have a difficult time even using the thing if it *did* work. She didn't have a choice, though. Hopefully her red Blazer would get her down the drive and to work since it had four wheel drive. Still it would be very nasty driving. It looked like they were working on eight inches already and the total prediction was two feet of snow. Two feet!!

Tessa turned from the window and shut off the light in her kitchen, moving down the hallway to her room.

Where was Taylor when she needed him?

Sure enough, the next morning Tessa had to struggle with the snow blower. No matter how hard she pulled on the string to activate it all it did was sputter and die. Sputter and die. Sighing, she dug her shovel out of storage and went to work on the area around the stairs and her vehicle, which she had unwisely left outside. After scraping all of the ice and snow off of it, she shoveled around the SUV so she could at least back out a bit. She removed snow from the backstairs entrance so that if Rose decided to take Andrew out in the snow, they would not trip. Chances of that were very unlikely. It was still snowing hard. Tessa wore a knit hat to protect her head and for warmth from the blasts of wind and snow, but it did little good. Snow sprinkled her cap, lashes and clothes. She wore her bulky winter coat and boots over her uniform and she shivered as she worked away at the snow.

Finally she had the area cleared enough to try to attempt to move down the driveway. Making sure the vehicle was in four wheel drive, Tessa put the SUV in reverse. She had warmed it up for fifteen minutes so the windows were clear of snow and ice. She could see clearly behind her and the snow swirled madly. Carefully she backed up about fifteen feet, enough to turn the SUV to head down the driveway. She accomplished the feat and turned the vehicle down the driveway and to the main road carefully.

She prayed they did not lose power. At the hospital they had backup generators but not so for her house. She would have to make sure she checked on Rose and Andrew throughout the day. Sighing she wished the storm had arrived on Saturday, a non work day. She also secretly wished for Taylor's presence. He would have been a big help at this time.

Tessa scolded herself. She had done without a man for a long time and she could continue to. Where the hell was he anyway?

Taylor was asleep in Marisa's bed. Marisa was awake and had the early news on low so as not to wake Taylor. They had spent a good part of the evening making love and she knew he was tired and was planning to fly back to New York later on today. She did not have to work today as they had wrapped this week's filming yesterday on Thursday. So it was a nice break to have Friday off, especially with Taylor here.

Eventually he groaned and moved over onto his back, blinking sleepily. Marisa knew he was not a morning person and already had coffee brewed, hot and black. As he wiped sleep out of his eyes, she greeted him.

"Good morning, sleepyhead!" she chirped.

Taylor groaned. "God, what time is it?" He rubbed his hand over his forehead. He had another damn headache. What the fuck? Maybe that was exactly why. He had been fucking all night. Cripes! "Coffee," he croaked.

"Got ya covered!" She handed him a large ceramic mug containing hot strong coffee.

Taylor accepted it gratefully as he sat up in the bed, sheets wrapped around his waist as he sipped at it. Marisa was sitting at the end of the huge bed wearing a silk paisley robe. She had the early news on but Taylor ignored it, concentrating on his coffee. Thank the Lord somebody had invented the stuff!

"That is really amazing!" Marisa remarked, watching the screen across the room. "Can you believe New York and New England are getting blasted with a major snow storm out of Canada? It's only October fifth!" Marisa sipped at her own cup, taking in the action which showed cars abandoned in huge drifts of snow, highways shut down or with semis and cars just crawling along. One semi had actually jack knifed off of the highway.

Taylor immediately snapped awake and brought his attention to the screen. "What?!"

Marisa raised the volume and Taylor listened to some weather reporter who could barely be seen because of the vast snow and wind whipping around his head. He was bundled up in a parka and informed the viewing audience this storm was parked over the Great Lakes and probably would not move out until Saturday, but not before dumping two feet of snow on the area.

"Fuck!" Taylor jumped out of bed and reached for a pair of jeans, pulling them on commando style. He searched around and finally found his cell phone. He called the airline to check on the status of his flight and sure enough, no airlines were flying anywhere near the Western New York area. Taylor argued that he needed to get back, but to no avail. The airport was closed in the Buffalo/Niagara Falls area for Friday. Even Saturday was questionable.

Taylor threw the phone down on Marisa's bed in disgust, hands on his hips. "I can't get a flight out until at least tomorrow. Christ!" He ran his fingers through his hair.

Marisa studied him. "It's okay, baby. You can stay here, for as long as you like."

"You don't understand! Tessa…" His words dwindled off.

"Ah, so her name is Tessa. She lives in the middle of that?" She gestured to the screen with her mug.

Taylor sat on the bed sighing. He needed to get his butt back home to Tessa and Andrew. They needed him.

Taylor completely missed the fact that he considered home where Tessa and Andrew were.

Tessa made several phone calls to Rose during the day. The storm had not let up. Instead it seemed to be intensifying. Fortunately they had not lost power at the house. Tessa had made sure there was enough firewood and Rose had a fire going and she and Andrew were spending time in the living room together. Tessa was relieved they were both safe and warm.

As for herself, her day had started out bad and had not improved. Tessa loved being a nurse because she wanted to help others but every nurse had to deal with some patients that were testy, inconsiderate or downright mean. Today Tessa was dealing with an elderly woman that thought the nurse's button should be pressed every five minutes. After answering her summons five times and finding each time she needed only minor help, Tessa finally passed her to a PA. She was starting to develop a headache and could not wait for her shift to end. She was worried about Rose and Andrew, but she also dreaded driving back. It had taken her forty minutes to get in this morning for a trip that usually took fifteen, twenty minutes tops. She suspected it would be even worse when she left.

Tessa tried to put unpleasant thoughts from her mind and when she did inevitably thoughts of Taylor would return. He was in sunny LA and she was here struggling with the elements and her job. Did he have a girlfriend back in LA? No, he was the love them and leave them type. She needed to keep that foremost in her mind, too. Taylor was definitely not keeper material.

This thought made her sad. Sighing, Tessa went to answer a nurse's summons. This seemed to be the longest Friday of her life.

Tessa could barely see outside her windshield. The grey sky dumped more snow over Lewiston and traffic moved at a crawl. Thank God she did not need to use any major highways to get home. Back and side streets were not plowed too well yet and there was always some jerk with a bigass SUV who drove way too fast for the conditions. Tessa's Blazer was moderate size, not huge but it could get her around in bad weather if she drove carefully. Tessa always drove carefully. She had made it a habit ever since Andrew was born. She needed to make it home safely because her son needed her.

Tessa prayed fervently as the traffic inched along. She could see some cars in ditches, abandoned by drivers who had been careless or simply unlucky. Keeping her eyes firmly ahead she drove carefully and steadily, knuckles white as she gripped the wheel. The whole day had been so stressful and Tessa could feel tears prick her eyes.

Finally she pulled into the entrance of her drive and there was so much snow she really had to gun it to get up the drive. She managed to do it without getting stuck but she didn't bother to maneuver into her regular parking spot. She stopped the SUV in front of the garage, next to Taylor's Suburban. She used her automatic opener and carefully pulled into the garage, shutting down the motor.

She leaned her head on the steering wheel. She had made it. She was home.

Taylor hung out with Marisa on Friday. They again went to dinner and then directly back to Marisa's. Taylor tried to reach Tessa by cell phone, but kept getting a message service was down in the area.

Finally in frustration, he phoned Frank.

"Taylor? You still here? I thought you would have moved on by now, you seemed so eager to leave. What gives?" Frank was his usual succinct self.

"What gives is there is a snow storm back east. You haven't heard about it?"

"Oh, yeah. I heard something about that…oh yeah. That's where you were going, right? Well, staying with Marisa another night won't hurt you."

"No, Frank. You don't understand. I gotta get back. Charter me a private plane, do whatever you gotta do, but I want out of here tomorrow on Saturday. I know you can do it, Frank. You perform miracles all of the time!" Taylor insisted.

Frank sighed. "Taylor, I heard the storm isn't supposed to let up until sometime Saturday. I don't know if—"

"There has to be some private strip that will be open. Hell, I can take my private plane. Just make arrangements for me back east Saturday, early as you can."

"Taylor, why would you want to fly in such weather? It's damn dangerous. Why not wait until the weather clears and go back Sunday? Suppose to let up by then."

"Because I need to get back *now*. I know I can't get out today, but Saturday should be feasible. Make it happen, Frank!" Taylor warned.

Frank sighed. "Okay, Taylor. It's your life you are playing with, not to mention my livelihood."

"Yeah, my heart's breakin', Frank. Call me when you have the deets." Taylor disconnected.

"Wow. You're really worried about this woman, Taylor. Is she so special?" Marisa arched a brow as she contemplated Taylor. She had never seen him this worried.

Taylor sighed. "There is a little boy and a young woman back there that I've grown close to. They need me and I have to get back to them."

"Why, Taylor! You surprise me!"

Taylor frowned. Yeah, he surprised himself too sometimes.

CHAPTER
FIFTEEN

FRANK CAME THROUGH FOR Taylor. The airport in the Buffalo area actually had a few runways cleared Saturday morning and Frank was able to bribe someone he knew to get Taylor on a commercial jet flying into the area. He felt that would be much safer than Taylor flying in a smaller private plane. Frank called up Taylor and gave him all of the details. His plane would leave LAX, stop over at O'Hare then continue on to Buffalo, arriving about three p.m. eastern time. Taylor figured that wouldn't put him back in Lewiston until about dinner time, but it was the best he could do.

Taylor and Marisa had shopped on Friday so that Taylor would have appropriate apparel. It was hard on Rodeo Drive to find a store that sold cold weather clothing but they finally found a little boutique that specialized in it. Taylor was able to obtain a black Sherpa lined parka with a generous hood. He added black lace up winter boots and warm gloves. They had some warm cashmere sweaters so he picked up a variety of colors and warm socks. He already had some thermals back east so he didn't bother with that.

Sighing, he packed his new apparel into his luggage and placed it in the foyer, looking up at Marisa who watched him from the living room.

He joined her, sinking into the comfortable cushions as she made room for him.

She studied his face as he laid his head back, eyes closed. He looked tired and most of all, worried. This woman obviously meant more to Taylor than he was letting on. A limo was picking him up at nine a.m. to take him to the airport. She had insisted on coming along to see him off, even though he told her it wasn't necessary.

She had a feeling she might not be seeing him for a long time.

The limo arrived right on time and Taylor helped the driver heave the luggage in. He joined Marisa in the back seat and the limo smoothly pulled into traffic.

Taylor wore black jeans with a black turtleneck under a black cashmere sweater, the winter boots on his feet. A black knit cap was pulled down over his long blond locks. The parka lay next to him on the seat, since it was too warm here in LA to wear it. That would be a different story when he reached O'Hare.

"So, Taylor. Are you happy to be going back east?" Marisa questioned as she took in the scenery whizzing by.

Taylor sighed. "Yeah. I need to get back."

Marisa turned to study him. "This is the last time we'll ever make love, isn't it?"

Taylor was startled by that remark, turning to study her, crossing his arms over his chest. "What makes you say that?"

"This woman. Once you become intimate with her that will be it. You're already falling in love with her." Marisa studied his eyes but Taylor was adept at hiding his feelings, even from her. His expression was bland and neutral.

"I don't know why you think that, Marisa. Like you, she's a friend."

"For now. She's a friend for now. But you would like it to be much more. Am I right?" She arched a brow.

Taylor sighed. "Yeah, I guess so. I'm not running back into a snow storm because I'm indifferent. But I'm hardly in love," he insisted.

Marisa snorted. "If you say so, Taylor." She turned her attention to the crowds on the sidewalks as they continued on to the airport.

Taylor's layover at O'Hare wasn't too bad, considering the weather. It was snowing lightly but nothing as bad as further east. He boarded the plane and settled in first class. He was now wearing his parka over his black clothes and the knit cap kept people from checking him out too directly. He was trying to fly under the radar (ha!) so people would not recognize him. So far, it had worked.

When they landed in Buffalo and Taylor looked out the window, he could not believe what he saw. It looked like the tundra or Antarctica, not upstate New York. There were huge mounds of snow shoved to the side off the runway that had to be as high as houses. It was still snowing, the wind whirling the flakes around the tarmac and the airplanes. Considering the weather, the flight had been smooth and without incident.

Taylor deplaned with the other passengers, carrying his luggage with him. Frank had promised to have a driver with a SUV waiting for him.

Taylor entered the terminal and right away a tall man with black hair approached him.

"Mr. Boudrain?" he said in a low discreet voice.

"Yep." Taylor answered.

"Right this way. Do you have any other luggage?" the driver asked as he divested Taylor of the two bags he was carrying.

"This is it, hoss."

"Then we can be on our way."

"How bad out there is it? How are the roads?"

"Bad. Very bad. It will take quite some time to drive up to the Lewiston area. They got hit very hard."

Taylor groaned, thinking of Tessa alone in this mess.

Tessa gave up on trying to shovel a short path from the garage to the back door. There was just too much snow. It was Saturday morning and she had dressed in her warmest clothes, hat, gloves and boots. The snow still was swirling down, not as hard, but it was still steady and had not let up. They had two feet already and it was forecasted to continue to snow throughout the day. Total accumulation could reach almost three feet. She could not believe this was happening at the beginning of October.

She put the shovel away in the garage and closed the door. Fortunately Taylor had stored his bike in the garage and had not left it outdoors. It would be buried, probably never to be seen until spring, if then. Ha! Taylor's bike was the least of her worries. She needed to get out to obtain supplies and grocery shop but it wasn't possible in this weather. It just wasn't worth the risk.

She shook off the snow in the back hallway and tried to wipe down her clothes before going downstairs to Rose's place where she and Andrew were watching a movie.

She joined them shortly, watching the snow from the living room windows. On days like this it was best just to stay inside. She curled up on the couch with a cup of tea Rose gave her to chase away the shivers.

Taylor stared in disbelief the closer they got to Lewiston. It looked like a barren moonscape with everything buried in white. Houses, cars, parking lots, roads, everywhere you looked everything was buried in snow. Taylor had never seen so much snow. Being southern, he had never even seen snow until he started traveling more for his acting career. Even then he had never seen anything like this. The place was practically *buried* in it.

Eventually the driver pulled into Tessa's drive. Taylor could see his Suburban was half buried in snow. He wondered immediately if Tessa had a snow blower. If she did, there was no evidence she had used it. He could see someone had attempted to shovel a bit and then gave up. He could understand that with the massive mounds of snow all around. It would take a tractor with a plow to blow this mess away. Thank God it was Saturday and she didn't have to go out in this storm today but she must have yesterday. He prayed to the Gods they were all safe.

The driver helped Taylor wade through the snow with his luggage. Taylor quickly unlocked the door to the carriage house and they both carried luggage upstairs. Taylor's cap, coat and boots were crusted with snow. Christ, it was only October sixth, how could there be this much snow?

Taylor offered the driver a warm drink but he politely declined, saying he wanted to be on his way. Taylor tipped him generously and then shortly Taylor heard the SUV backing down the driveway.

Sighing, he moved to his bedroom to dump his luggage on the bed. He had to get over to the main house to see how things were going.

Tessa was astonished to see a navy blue Suburban pulling up her driveway and when Taylor emerged with another guy, her heart sang. He was back! Careful Tessa, she warned herself. Don't go off the deep end. But she could feel total relief sweep over her as she recognized Taylor even though he was wearing a black knit cap over his blond hair.

Rose joined Tessa at the dining room windows which overlooked the drive. "Was that a car that just drove in?"

Tessa smiled and turned to Rose. "Yes. It's Taylor. He's back!"

Rose gasped. "Oh, my Lord! How did he ever get back in this storm?"

Tessa shrugged, watching as the two men disappeared into Taylor's carriage house. "I don't know, Rose. But I'm glad he's back." The words slipped out before Tessa could stop them.

"Me too, Tessa. Me too."

Shortly Tessa heard a knock on the back door and opened the door to Taylor. She gave him a huge smile and motioned him inside.

He stood in the hallway, stamping snow from his boots. "I don't want to come in any further. I'm full of snow."

The tall man before her was still wearing the black knit hat. He was dressed in a warm black parka, black jeans and black winter boots. Obviously he had picked up winter clothes somewhere. He took off the cap and shook out his blond hair a bit, shaking snow from it.

"I just wanted to check on ya'll and see if you're all okay."

Tessa was wearing a warm red sweater and jeans, thick socks and slippers on her feet. Her beautiful hair swept her shoulders and back and she looked lovely and sweet. She smiled up at him.

"Yes, we're making it okay. I tried to shovel a bit. My snow blower is kaput. I tried to get it started, but to no avail. It isn't even big enough to handle a job of this size even if it *did* work. For now, we're stuck. House bound." She waved her hand behind her. "Rose and Andrew are watching a movie."

Taylor replaced his cap, clapping his gloved hands together. "Well, something has to be done about that. I'm gonna clear off the Suburban and then go down to the local Home Depot. I'm gonna purchase a plow to put on front of the thing and I'll have us dug out in no time. Another time, perhaps I can take a look at your snow blower and get it working for you." He paused, gazing into her lovely brown eyes. God, he had missed her. "I just wanted to make sure you guys were safe."

Tessa blushed. "I appreciate that, Taylor. But you really should not have flown back until the storm was over. It must have been dangerous flying."

"Not really. Once we got above the storm, it wasn't bad. I just couldn't believe it when I deplaned and saw all of this white crap. Does it always snow this early? Cripes!"

Tessa laughed. "No. Never quite this early. You got an early taste of what it can be like around here and usually it's not this bad. This was a very unseasonal storm."

Taylor turned to go. "Well, to work! I'll get the drive cleared out for you."

Tessa felt bad he was doing all the work. "Let me help you, Taylor. I can—"

"Nope. Its gonna be a cinch for me, Tessa. Don't worry about it. Once I have the necessary equipment, it will go quickly. I'll see ya later on."

Tessa sighed as she closed the door. She was so glad he was back and she refused to examine the reasons why.

True to his word, within a few hours Taylor had the drive totally cleared. He had purchased a huge plow that he attached to the front of the behemoth beast he drove. The snow was no match for the big Suburban and plow and Taylor carefully cleared all areas around the drive, house and garage. He used a shovel around doors and entrances and it was magically cleared, as though a giant fist had reached down from the heavens and threw all the snow away. Tessa was amazed. There really were good reasons to have a man around sometimes. Tessa recalled their kiss. Maybe for more than just removing snow too.

She came out to help him with the shoveling, even though he insisted he could handle it. She ignored his protests, shoveling across from him and as they worked together she felt comfortable and safe, as though they were a couple. How absurd! That was the *last* thing they were. They were just good friends.

Yeah, Tessa. You keep telling yourself that.

CHAPTER
SIXTEEN

ROSE MADE DINNER FOR everyone and Taylor was invited. He accepted gratefully. Clearing the driveway of snow had chilled him to the bone. He wasn't used to such frigid weather. Rose informed him she had made beef stew in her slow cooker and that sounded wonderful to Taylor.

He settled with Tessa, Andrew and Rose around Rose's dining table. The stew was tasty and hot and Rose served it with crusty bread. It was the most delicious meal Taylor had ever eaten and he was accustomed to eating in the finest, trendiest restaurants in the world. Nothing could compare to good home cooking. Absolutely nothing. Taylor complimented Rose on the meal and how much he enjoyed it. Rose blushed, thanking him.

"If you think Rose's stew is great, just wait until you taste her apple pie, Taylor. It is heaven," Tessa remarked, spooning up stew.

"I'll make a special pie just for you, Taylor. What kind do you like?" Rose remarked.

"I like any kinda pie, but apple and blueberry are my favorites," Taylor answered. He accepted a second helping of stew from Rose.

"Pie?" Andrew said, a wary expression on his face.

Tessa immediately picked up on Andrew's mood, glancing uneasily at Rose.

Taylor answered the boy. "Yep, pie buddy. If Rose makes me one, I'll share it with you." Taylor grinned at Andrew and the little boy slowly grinned in response.

"Share?"

"Yes, Andrew. Taylor will share with you. Just like your friends at school share." Tessa knew they had been teaching this concept to the children and was silently relieved Taylor had diffused the situation, and very easily at that.

She studied him discreetly under her lashes as he ate his dinner. He had removed his knit cap, but his long golden locks were wavy and a bit unruly from the dampness of the snow. It only made him look sexier, as did the black clothes. The contrast between his light hair and the dark clothes was stunning and sighing, Tessa looked away. Forget it, Tessa. Even though he had been a big help today, Taylor had "danger" written all over him.

After the meal, Taylor offered to help clean up but was shooed into the living room by Tessa and Rose. They insisted they could handle it so Taylor went into the living room with Andrew. He could see through the windows it was still snowing lightly, but it looked like it would stop soon. Since tomorrow was Sunday, he could help Tessa out with her snow blower. Hopefully since it was still October, this white crap would not last too long.

Taylor was a bit uncomfortable as he sat on Rose's sofa, watching as Andrew went to the television set to click it on. He had never been alone with the boy except for the times when Andrew would watch him working on his motorcycle. At those times he had been occupied and it was easier to talk casually. Now they were together for the first time in a different situation. Well Taylor, just treat him as a kid. He's a kid, right?

As Andrew flicked on the television, Taylor directed a question to him. "What's your favorite show, buddy?"

Andrew turned to him, his brow quirked in puzzlement. He still held the remote, but was ignoring the TV, his attention on the man across from him.

Taylor leaned forward a bit, clasping his hands together and studying Andrew carefully. "What do you like to watch on TV?" Taylor waved at the television on a wooden stand Rose had placed it on.

Then Andrew's face lit up. The change was remarkable and he looked so much like Tessa when he smiled. Taylor could feel a strange emotion at this reaction and quickly damped it down.

"Barney!" Andrew declared.

Taylor frowned. Then a memory came back to him. One of his married friends had younger kids and there was a show with a purple dinosaur they were all enthralled with. "Barney? The dinosaur?"

"Yes, yes!" Andrew was practically jumping up and down, the smile as big as ever. He turned to activate the DVD player and magically a big goofy looking purple dinosaur greeted his television audience and started singing sappy songs.

Taylor rolled his eyes. He would watch for Andrew's sake but he hoped Tessa rescued him soon. He could see he would not have to worry about further conversation as Andrew's total focus was on the tube, as though Taylor did not exist.

Shortly the two women joined him and Tessa offered him a glass of Merlot. He accepted it gratefully. Barney was starting to get to him. She had a glass of chardonnay for herself and Rose sipped a sherry. They both settled in wing chairs Rose had placed opposite her sofa. Andrew had not joined Taylor on the sofa. He was watching his show sitting on the floor in front of the television.

Tessa chuckled. "Thought you could use a libation after putting up with Barney." She smiled, sipping her wine as Rose chuckled also.

Taylor raised his wineglass in a toast. "To you, God bless you!" He drank a big gulp, underlining his words.

"Barney is very entertaining to kids. Adults find him tedious, but what can I say?" She shrugged her shoulders. "It makes him happy. He'll be going to bed in an hour or so, so you and Rose will then have relief from the dinosaur."

"I don't mind watching Andrew's shows. Sometimes they are fun. Of course, I *have* seen them many times! I am trying to get him to watch different things too. Nickelodeon or Disney. We're working on that," Rose commented.

"I can see he really enjoys it. As soon as I mentioned Barney, he got very excited."

Tessa arched a brow. "How do you know about Barney, Taylor?" She figured that would be the *last* show he would know anything about, particularly because he didn't watch TV. Maybe he had a girlfriend or two with younger kids?

"Andrew told me. I asked him his favorite show and he told me it was Barney. I seem to recall some friends' kids watching once. And you're right. It *is* a tedious show!" Taylor glanced down at the child on the floor. "But I can see why you put up with it," he said quietly.

Tessa was again surprised by Taylor's remarks. He was the only man she had ever met who treated Andrew like a person and actually tried to converse with him. The amazing thing was Andrew *did* converse with Taylor. That had never happened in the past. Andrew would just ignore men she chose to date.

"He told you he likes Barney?"

"Yep. I asked him his favorite TV show. He seemed puzzled at first but when I phrased it differently, he answered me." Taylor sipped at his wine, studying Tessa over the rim. She was snuggled in the wing chair opposite him, long jean clad legs tucked underneath her, slowly sipping her wine. She looked lovely in the low light. Rose had a few lamps lit on low and Taylor let his thoughts roam, wondering what Tessa would look like naked. He silently berated himself. Stop it, Taylor.

He finished his wine in a gulp and placed the glass aside. He glanced up at a clock Rose had on the wall. It was going on nine o'clock. He stood, looking down at the women.

"I'm gonna go. It's getting late and I'm pretty beat from traveling and stuff."

Rose smiled as Tessa rose. "Not to mention shoving around a ton of snow," she said sardonically.

"Yeah, that too. But no big deal. Tomorrow I'll fix your snow blower for you. G'night."

Tessa walked Taylor over to the back door and watched as he put his boots back on. "Thank you again Taylor for all you've done today. It really isn't your responsibility to clear the drive," she said quietly.

Taylor rose to full height, looking down at her as he clapped his knit cap back on. "It wasn't a problem, Tessa. Really. Glad to help. I'll see you tomorrow." He turned to go, opening the back door and closing it snugly and Tessa watched his tall form as he moved over to the carriage house door.

Sighing, she returned to the living room to join Andrew and Rose.

In the morning Taylor came over and knocked on the back door and Tessa left Andrew with Rose for a bit as she showed Taylor the snow blower in the garage. Both of their vehicles were parked inside and Tessa carefully stepped around and found the red and black machine tucked into a far corner.

Taylor hauled it out and pulled on the starter string and it sputtered and stopped, just as it had when Tessa tried it.

"Hmmmm. Got any starting fluid around here? I think it's just a matter of spraying the carburetor a bit." Taylor looked up at Tessa who was wearing a berry colored parka with the hood over her hair.

"I don't know." She turned to the shelves. "I know the repairman said I should purchase some. There may be some here somewhere." She searched shelves and Taylor joined her.

"Nope. Looks like I'll have to go down to the local hardware store. It needs cleaned up a bit too. I'll get some stuff and be right back. This isn't going to be a hard thing to fix."

"Taylor I can go to the store and get everything! You really don't have to—"

"I know what to purchase, Tessa. It's just easier. I won't be gone long."

He grabbed the keys for his Suburban and he was gone.

True to his word, Taylor had Tessa's snow blower running in top condition, almost like it was new. Tessa was amazed! She stored it close to the front of the garage so it would be handy when she needed it. She expected the snow to melt within the week. They were calling for much warmer temperatures and most of this snow should be gone.

Tessa watched as Taylor tinkered with the machine, trying to remember what he was doing. Try as she might, she just could not follow what he was doing. She was not in the least bit mechanical. She could fix very easy things in her home, but anything complicated she always called a repairman for. It was handy having a man around.

Don't get too used to it Tessa, she warned herself.

CHAPTER
SEVENTEEN

THE WEATHER IMPROVED AS the week progressed. The temperatures soared back up into the mid sixties by Wednesday and most of the snow was melting. There were a few patches of it here and there from the huge piles but four days after the storm you could hardly tell there had been a major snow storm. Taylor was relieved to see the snow go so quickly. Since it was October the temperatures could rebound. That would definitely not be the case in January or December. Would he still be here then? He knew he definitely did not care for snow after dealing with this early storm and in this area of the country they received quite a bit of it.

Taylor had purchased a big space heater he had placed in the garage so he could work on his motorcycle. By the end of the week it was unnecessary to be inside and he again moved the mangled bike outside where he could work on it in the sun. He wanted to take advantage of the good weather while it lasted.

Again Taylor did not see anybody from the bigger house too often. When Andrew arrived back from school he seemed to be spending most of his time in the house and Taylor concentrated on his bike. He had received the custom made parts he needed to get the Harley back in top condition and he intently worked on it, trying to keep thoughts of Tessa at bay.

Friday afternoon Andrew finally came out on his bike to ride. Rose asked him if he could keep an eye on Andrew as he worked, as she was busy in the kitchen baking. It was very warm and sunny— the temps approaching seventy— and Taylor was amazed at the abrupt swings in the weather in the area. Today he wore cut-off denim jeans and a white muscle tee. He had tied a navy and white bandana around his hair to keep it off of his face and wore his ubiquitous sunglasses. He assured Rose it would not be a problem and kept a casual eye on Andrew as he tinkered with his bike.

Finally Andrew approached closer to watch Taylor work. Taylor remembered to always keep the garage doors closed when Andrew was around. He had all of his tools and equipment outside and he casually said hello to Andrew as he worked. Andrew did not answer him, continuing to watch Taylor work.

The boy inched his bike closer, his brow puckered in thought. He was frowning and again did not seem happy with Taylor's presence but Taylor ignored this, continuing to work on the Harley, silent. He figured if Andrew wanted to speak, he would. For now he was intently working. He had to use a hammer to bang out one of the metal fenders and as soon as he started, Andrew put his hands up to his ears and started to scream. Taylor immediately stopped with the hammer, angry at himself for forgetting that noise bothered Andrew.

Rising from underneath the bike, he placed the hammer aside and started to reassure Andrew the noise had stopped, but the screaming continued unabated as the boy sat on his bike and just wailed.

Great. Just great, Taylor thought. What do I do now? Perhaps Rose would hear and come to his rescue? But as Andrew continued to scream, Rose did not appear. It was just he and the boy.

Okay. His first challenge with Andrew.

He stooped down to the boy's level and carefully removed Andrew's hands from his ears. He tipped the boy's chin up to look directly into the brown eyes and spoke loudly and firmly over the caterwauling. "Andrew, the noise has stopped. I am *all done*," he emphasized.

Andrew continued to scream as though he had not heard the words and Taylor knew he had. He sighed. What next? He spied a big red ball on the grass over in the yard that Andrew occasionally played with. He moved over to pick it up and presented it to Andrew. The screaming had not ceased.

"Hey, buddy. Want to play ball with me? I'll toss it to you and we can play catch? How does that sound?" Taylor entreated. He removed his sunglasses so the boy could see his eyes.

Andrew abruptly stopped screaming, looking up into teal eyes with entreaty in them. Andrew searched the man's eyes and saw kindness, not really knowing what this meant but it instantly calmed him. He could feel the man was no threat to him and magically the noise had stopped. Andrew looked over at the hammer and then back at the ball.

"No more?" he pointed at the hammer.

"No more, Andrew. I'm sorry I scared you. Do you want to play ball with me?"

Andrew moved off of his bicycle. "Yes, yes!" he responded eagerly.

Taylor and Andrew moved to the lawn to throw the ball back and forth and Taylor sighed inwardly. Another incident averted.

Where was Rose?

Rose came out about a half hour later to collect Andrew and take him into the house. Taylor motioned her to the side to speak with her as Andrew put his bicycle away.

"I just wanted to tell you we had a problem earlier," Taylor informed her in a low voice.

Rose's brows arched. "Oh?" Her brown eyes studied his.

Taylor met her eyes. "Didn't you hear him screaming earlier?"

Rose was perplexed. "No. What happened?" she asked anxiously, her gaze turning toward the little boy storing his bike away in the garage. Andrew seemed fine and in a good mood.

Taylor sighed, then answered her. "I forgot about his sensory for some reason. I started banging away at my cycle with a hammer and he started screaming like the world was ending. Quite frankly, I was at a loss," Taylor began.

Rose was surprised. "I always keep an ear out for Andrew. I was preoccupied in the kitchen and I knew you were with him. I didn't hear him—"

"It's okay," Taylor assured her. "I was able to calm him down after a bit by distracting him by playing ball." He gestured to the red ball on the lawn. "But it took me a good five minutes to figure out what to do and he screamed the whole time. I just want you to know this happened."

Andrew went into the back door of the house, ignoring Rose and Taylor as they conversed. Rose moved toward the house also, not wanting to leave Andrew out of her sight. "You did the right thing, Taylor. Next time, please come and get me." She disappeared into the house as Taylor sighed.

It was early evening and Taylor had finished up dinner and was reading. The buzzer sounded downstairs and Taylor was not really surprised by that. He figured Tessa would be coming by at some point to discuss today's events.

Taylor went down the stairs to answer the door. He was clad in his faded jeans and a navy tee shirt. He opened the door to Tessa who looked up at him warily. Oh just great. She didn't look too happy but she looked gorgeous as usual. She was wearing a summer gauzy yellow dress that flowed around her perfect figure and flat white sandals. He motioned her up the steps and she followed him silently.

Taylor arched a brow. "Can I get you anything? Coffee, wine?"

"No thanks, Taylor. This isn't a social visit."

Taylor waved her to his sectional. "Well, at least sit down, be comfortable."

She moved to his sectional, sitting gracefully on the edge of the comfy cushions. He settled a little further down from her and waited for the barrage to come. She was silent, studying his face for several minutes.

The silence spun out and Taylor was getting uncomfortable to say the least. "Well? Did you come to ream my ass out or what?" he finally demanded.

"No. Of course not, Taylor. I just want to hear your version of what happened with Andrew this afternoon," she replied calmly, her brown eyes steady on his.

Taylor was a bit surprised by this remark. He figured she would be jumping his case right away but she was giving him the chance to explain. He sighed deeply, then met her eyes. "Basically I forgot about Andrew's sensory issues. I was so into what I was working on that I forgot about Andrew's issues. I started banging away at the bike with a hammer and Andrew started screaming. It took me a good five minutes to calm him down. I was at a loss." He shrugged broad shoulders. "Finally I diverted his attention by suggesting we play ball. That did the trick and he was fine after that. I feel really lousy for upsetting him," he ended quietly, looking away, not meeting her eyes.

Tessa took in all of this information and could see Taylor was genuinely sorry and concerned about her son. Still, he should have known better and remembered anytime Andrew was around to be careful of anything that might upset him. There would be times in the future where he might forget or Andrew would inadvertently have an issue that no one would know what precipitated it. That was just the nature of his disability. Even *she*, his mother, could upset Andrew without meaning to. It was all a process of learning so she could not really blame Taylor or Andrew. She didn't however want her son upset or screaming. It broke her heart to think about that.

Sighing, she finally replied. "I know you try around Andrew, Taylor. I know you really do," she began carefully. "The thing is you always have to be vigilant. Anything or anyone can set him off at anytime. I thought you understood that."

Teal eyes turned back to her. "I DO understand that. I can assure you, I'll be more careful in the future."

Tessa stood. "Let's hope so, Taylor. For all of our sakes. Otherwise, I will have to ask you to leave."

Taylor stood too. "Don't you think that is a bit unfair, Tessa? This is the first time there has been a problem and I handled it. Don't I get points for that?"

Tessa headed to the stairs. "This isn't a contest where you get points, Taylor. This is my son's life." With that, she headed down his stairs and out the door.

Taylor stood at the top of his stairs as she exited, shaking his head.

Taylor spent that evening reviewing the events of the day and the best way to proceed from here. Maybe if he spent more one on one time with Andrew it would help their relationship, help the boy become more comfortable around him. Tessa had mentioned he didn't have male role models and Taylor could fulfill that particular role. Maybe he should suggest to her that he take Andrew on an outing, maybe camping or something.

Did he really want to do that? If there was an issue while they were alone together, could he handle it? He felt fairly confident he could. He had read up on autism and knew the signs of anxiety and what to do. Would Tessa let him take her son?

All of these thoughts flew through his head but the underlying theme that teased his brain was: why are you even trying or concerned, Taylor? Move on, go back to your old life, partying and making movies.

Then he remembered two pairs of beautiful brown eyes and knew he wouldn't be doing that anytime soon.

CHAPTER
EIGHTEEN

TAYLOR SPENT SEVERAL DAYS working on his motorcycle. He didn't see any one at all from the bigger house. He didn't even see Andrew coming and going in the afternoon because for some reason he was always in his own place around the time Andrew returned. During this time Taylor ruminated on how to approach Tessa about taking Andrew on an outing. He really felt it would make everyone feel more comfortable with his presence and it would help Taylor learn more about Andrew. He decided to phone her and ask her to come up to his place to discuss his idea. He wanted to do it away from Andrew.

Tessa was surprised when she received his call but she agreed to come over and meet with him when he told her he wanted to discuss Andrew. She came by after dinner mid week and Taylor led her up to his sectional and they both took seats facing each other.

As usual, she looked scrumptious. Even in her jeans and coral sweater with her hair sweeping her shoulders she was just as gorgeous as the evening they went to dinner. Taylor tried to tamp down these thoughts as Tessa's brown eyes studied him. He had a very important point to make and he didn't need his lust interfering.

"I've been thinking a lot about what happened last weekend and I have an idea I want to run by you," he began, watching her face closely.

Tessa's brows arched. "Oh? What idea would that be?"

Taylor ran his hands through his hair, pushing it back. Tessa had noted he did this when he was nervous and watched him intently.

Sighing, he met her eyes. "I've been thinking it might be a good idea for Andrew and I to spend more time together. Ya know, one on one. I could take him on an outing for a few days or something. I was thinking maybe camping." He paused. "What do you think of this?"

Tessa's reaction was one of immense surprise. No one had *ever* offered to take Andrew anywhere. All of his social outings were with her, Rose or school outings. Tessa was very uncomfortable with this idea for several reasons, mostly because Andrew could be a handful and Taylor and her son had only spent moments together here and there. She finally answered him. "I don't think that is a very good idea, Taylor. I appreciate the sentiment behind it, but Andrew is quite a handful. And he is a runner too. What that means is he needs *constant* adult supervision or he will just take off," she gestured with her hand in an upward wave. "I just can't take that kind of a chance."

Taylor sighed. "Tessa, hear me out, okay?" At her silence, he continued. "Andrew is a kid. Yes I know he has autism and I realize all of the ramifications of that. I've read up on it thoroughly and know what to expect. I think I can handle that. Believe me he will not be out of my sight, not for one second. I also have a cell phone and if I need to call you for help of any kind, it's a phone call away." He paused, studying her. "Tess— sometimes I don't think you look at Andrew as just a kid. He needs to be a kid and just have fun. Has Andrew ever been camping, to the movies, bowling or on a picnic or a playground with other kids?" At the negative shake of her head, he continued. "He needs to be. You need to always remember that he is a child first. Yes one with a disability, but a child. And all kids need to have fun." Taylor thought if this didn't convince her, nothing would. He waited for her response.

Tessa's mind whirled with many different thoughts. She knew Taylor had a point. Andrew needed male companionship also. The tutor she had hired was a female. Try as hard as she could, she could not find a male tutor appropriate for Andrew's needs. He was exposed to other little boys at school and she had tried to arrange play dates but they never went over too well and finally she had given up. She felt she and Rose could provide whatever outings and entertainment Andrew needed and they had. Andrew was a happy and well adjusted child, even considering his disability. But Taylor had a point too. Andrew needed to have fun, like any other kid. Could she trust her son with Taylor? That was the big issue. After hearing him plead his case, she knew she could. This outing also could either solidify Taylor's relationship with her son or make him turn tail and run, like most men she had known had done.

Finally she answered him. "Okay, Taylor. I have some reservations, but I agree this might be a good idea. This upcoming weekend is Columbus Day and Andrew has a three day weekend. If you want to take him camping, there is a state park very close by. I'll have to write up a list of instructions for you because his diet is limited and other rituals that are important." She paused as she stood, crossing her arms over her breasts. "I am very nervous about this, Taylor."

Taylor looked her directly in the eyes. "Tessa, I will care for your son as if he were my own. I swear on my life he will be safe with me."

"Thank you, Taylor. I appreciate that. I'll have to speak to Andrew over the next several days to prepare him. When do you want to take him? Friday evening?"

"Yep. We can get a start. The few days in between will allow me to buy the gear we'll need."

Tessa turned to go. "Okay, Taylor. I'll make sure I do everything I can to prepare Andrew for this. And thank you." She descended his stairs and disappeared through his door.

Taylor picked up sleeping bags, lanterns, a big tent, coolers and snacks and food he thought Andrew would enjoy, specifically marshmallows and chocolate with graham crackers in case they made s'mores. Taylor remembered the many camping trips he had taken as a kid and they were the only really good memories he had of his childhood. Hopefully he could give Andrew some good memories also.

Taylor had the SUV packed and ready to go Friday afternoon. Taylor wore jeans and hiking boots paired with a warm flannel shirt and his leather jacket was tossed in the back. He knew the evenings could get chilly and he wore thin thermals under his clothes.

He headed over to the big house to collect Andrew. Taylor prayed the weekend would go okay. There was never any sure way of knowing with Andrew. Well, he would take things as they came. He wasn't afraid of no six year old!

Tessa gave him instructions and Taylor listened intently, committing everything to memory. Everything she told him he felt could be handled easily. She handed him Andrew's bags and he packed them away as she turned to get Andrew.

The little boy appeared in the doorway and came hesitantly down the steps, looking up at the big man in front of him. Tessa had him dressed in warm clothes also. Jeans, hiking boots, a warm sweater with a quilted red vest over it and a Buffalo Bills blue ball cap. Taylor grinned at that.

"Hey, buddy! You ready for our camping trip?" Taylor greeted the boy, hunkering down, smiling broadly.

Andrew smiled tentatively then looked in the back of the SUV where he could see their gear stored. Looking back up at Taylor he simply said "We go?"

Taylor rose, glancing over at Tessa. "Yep. Do you want to say goodbye to your mommy and Mrs. H?" Rose was standing next to Tessa and they both looked nervous. Cripes!

Andrew ran to his mommy to throw his arms around her waist and she leaned down to cover his face with kisses. He giggled and then turned to Rose for the same treatment. Rose sniffed, tears pricking her eyes. Taylor could see Tessa was trying to hold back tears too. Well, this was a big deal to them, the first time Andrew had ever been away from them.

"I promise I'll take good care of him," he told them both solemnly.

"Yes, okay. Have a good time!" She waved as Taylor buckled Andrew in the back seat. It was safer for him to be in the back than the front.

Taylor took his place in the driver's seat and carefully backed down the driveway, waving to the women who watched until the vehicle pulled out of sight.

Andrew had a book he was perusing as Taylor drove to the state park. It was located in Niagara Falls and was only about a twenty minute or so drive from Tessa's place. Andrew was silent during the ride as he looked through his book. Taylor found the park easily and drove around, following the arrows directing him to the camping area.

Once there, Taylor drove slowly, looking for a spot that would not be near water. He just didn't want to chance that with Andrew. He finally found an open knoll with several evergreen trees growing on it and thought that would be a perfect spot to pitch the tent. He drove onto the knoll and parked nearby the trees.

He turned in his seat to address Andrew. "We're here, bud. We need to unload our stuff and get our tent set up. Then we'll build a campfire. How does that sound?"

Big brown eyes moved to Taylor under the brim of his ball cap. Andrew was silent and just watched Taylor.

Taylor exited the vehicle, helping Andrew out of his seat belt and picking him up gently to set him down next to him. He closed the door and turned to the boy. "Wanna help me unpack?"

He indicated the back of the SUV, taking the book from Andrew's hands.

Andrew went to the back of the black SUV, waiting for further instructions.

The next half hour was spent getting their campsite set up. Taylor tried to make casual conversation but so far, Andrew remained silent. But at least he had not tried to run off.

Taylor assigned Andrew the task of getting sticks for their campfire. He kept a watchful eye on Andrew as he went around the area and collected small sticks. When he returned, Taylor could see they were too small to use but he grinned and high fived Andrew, telling him how proud he was of him. Andrew grinned back.

Right now they were in the process of toasting marshmallows. Andrew did not want s'mores so the sticks contained only the white gooey stuff. Taylor carefully toasted a marshmallow and let it cool. Presenting the stick to Andrew he let him remove the marshmallow. Andrew did so warily, looking to Taylor for approval. Taylor nodded and Andrew took the gooey mess and Taylor told him to eat it, that he would like it. Andrew felt the gushy texture and wiped it on his jeans, making a smeary gooey mess. Taylor sighed. Obviously toasted marshmallows were out too.

He helped Andrew clean up his jeans and decided to tell Andrew a story. Campfires were for stories too. He told a scary ghost story, not knowing if the boy would understand or not, but heck, he would try. Andrew listened intently and for the first time, Taylor could see he had the boy's complete attention. Then Taylor launched into a version of "Old MacDonald" and "Bingo" and Andrew was delighted, actually singing along. Taylor figured they sang such songs in school so he scraped his memory for all kids songs he could remember and they sang together for a while, both relaxed and happy. Taylor hoped this continued.

When it was time to retire for the evening, Taylor helped Andrew change into thermal pajamas and warm socks Tessa had sent along. Taylor planned to sleep in his clothes. They snuggled in their sleeping bags, Barney by Andrew's side. Tessa explained this was a ritual and he always slept with the toy. The coals from the fire were low and provided minimal light, but Taylor had a lantern on a very low setting. Tessa had also explained Andrew always had a night light. Taylor had his hands crossed behind his head as he laid back in his warm bedding. The weather had cooperated and it was probably only in the fifties and with their warm clothes, tent and bedding, they were comfortable and warm. Taylor ruminated that the first evening had gone quite well, but there were still two more days to get through. He glanced over at Andrew and could see the boy was still awake, his brown eyes staring at Taylor.

"Did you have fun today, buddy?"

Andrew was silent. Then he made a request. "Story?"

Taylor was surprised. Okay, he wanted a bed time story. Wracking his brain, Taylor finally came up with an appropriate story. As he told it, he could see the brown eyes flutter and eventually shut. Soon the boy was sleeping peacefully, his little chest rising and falling. Taylor felt an overwhelming feeling of affection well up and had no idea where it came from. He leaned over and gently kissed Andrew's cheek.

"Good night, little guy." He rolled over and closed his eyes. Soon he was asleep also.

When Taylor woke in the morning, the first thing he did was glance over at Andrew only to find an empty sleeping bag.

Taylor shot up at once. Oh my God! Where was the kid?

Taylor hopped into his boots and flung the tent entrance back, his glance wildly going around the area. He felt immediate relief when he saw Andrew sitting in his pj's by the burnt out campfire. Taylor's racing heart calmed a bit and he approached the boy who looked back at him, clutching Barney.

Taylor sat next to Andrew and could see he was shivering. "Andrew, buddy. What are you doing out here? You must always stay with me!" Taylor said sternly. "And you're freezing!"

"Mommy. Where is mommy?" His brown eyes were confused and sad.

Taylor picked up the little boy and took him into the relative warmth of the tent. "Your mommy is home, little buddy. We're camping, remember? And you're cold. Let's get dressed for the day, have something to eat, then we'll go for a walk. You like to walk, don't you?" Taylor asked as he rummaged in Andrew's bags for warm clothes.

Andrew perked up. "Yes, yes! Walk!"

"Good, good. Let's get dressed and stuff and we'll get started. And buddy," he caught the boy's eyes to make sure he was listening, "don't ever leave me again. Always stay with me just like you would your mommy."

Andrew nodded solemnly.

The rest of the day passed without incident and Andrew was even willing to try a s'more at the campsite that night. They sang songs again. Taylor had already figured out this was a favorite activity for Andrew.

Taylor rigged the opening of the tent with cans that would crash if the entrance was breached and wake him. He didn't want a repeat of the almost heart attack he had had this morning.

When he woke Sunday morning, Andrew was just where he was supposed to be, snuggled up with Barney in his sleeping bag. Taylor's heart turned over. There was something so very sweet about this kid, even though his total number of words this weekend toward Taylor had been about ten. It just didn't matter.

Taylor again leaned down to kiss Andrew's cheek and this time he saw a tiny smile.

Monday afternoon Taylor packed up their gear and they headed back to Tessa's. He told her they would be returning mid-afternoon and glancing at his watch, he could see it was about two thirty. He had taken Andrew fishing this morning at a small pond they found and Andrew loved it. He couldn't wait to tell Tessa all of the details of their trip. He glanced back at Andrew in the backseat and once again he was engrossed in a book, Barney by his side. Except for that one incident Saturday morning, the trip had gone very well. Andrew missed his mom the most in the morning and evenings, but Taylor was able to reassure him he would see his mommy real soon. In the meantime, they were gonna have fun.

He pulled up the drive and could see Tessa in the back, raking some leaves. She had her hair up in a high ponytail and wore a quilted aqua vest over a warm white sweater and jeans. She looked lovely. As soon as she spied his SUV, she dropped the rake and came running.

Tessa had missed her son immensely and hoped the weekend had gone well. She waited impatiently for Taylor to park so she could remove her son from the vehicle. As soon as it halted, she ran to Andrew's door and unstrapped him, smiling and hugging him tightly.

"Oh, Andrew! I missed you so much!" she exclaimed.

Taylor emerged from the SUV, smiling down as mother and son were reunited.

Tessa covered Andrew's face with kisses and he giggled and hugged her back, clearly glad to see her again. Then he looked up at Taylor and pointed to the back of the SUV. "Help?"

Taylor's gaze went to the gear. "That's okay, buddy. I'll take care of unpacking. Your mommy missed you. You go spend some time with her."

Andrew laughed and ran into the house where Rose waited to greet him.

Tessa followed Taylor around to the back of the SUV. "So, how did it go?" she asked in a low voice.

Taylor grinned. "It went fine. That's a great kid you got there. We sang lots of songs around the campfire. He loved that! And I taught him to fish this morning. He didn't want to touch it, but he was so proud of himself when he caught a little one. I threw it back," he ended casually.

"So—there were no— incidents?" she asked anxiously.

Taylor had debated about telling Tessa about Saturday morning. He didn't want her to worry, but he decided she deserved to know the truth. "Wee-ll, one little incident on Saturday morning. Nothing to worry about, though. I woke and he wasn't beside me. When I checked the campsite, he was sitting right there. He was missing you. I quickly got him dressed and we hiked. And the rest of the weekend went fine."

Tessa had gasped and her eyes had widened when he mentioned Andrew was gone from the tent. Tears welled in her eyes.

Taylor saw them and tried to reassure her. "Really, Tessa. That was as close as we came to a problem. Fortunately he was there and didn't run. I rigged the tent entrance after that so that if he tried to leave, I would hear him. But he didn't. I had a talk with him about it and it didn't happen again. And we both had fun." He could see she was still worried by his words. He laid both of his hands on her shoulders and squeezed. "Tessa, your son was fine all weekend. He had a good time. He did miss you, but that would be normal."

Tessa swallowed her tears. Her son was home safe and sound and that was all that mattered. "Okay, Taylor," she said in a subdued voice. "Thank you for taking him."

She turned to walk back into her house and suddenly Taylor felt very deflated.

CHAPTER
NINETEEN

TESSA SPENT THE WEEK working, taking care of her patients, trying to keep her mind off of Taylor but it was hard. She kept replaying in her mind his comments about Andrew being missing and outside the tent. This thought terrorized her but Taylor had been nonchalant, like it was no big deal. It was a HUGE deal but he had taken very good care of her son. Andrew was back safe and he chattered away about fishing and singing songs. He had obviously enjoyed himself and it was so rare for Andrew to get away and just "be a kid" as Taylor phrased it.

She decided to ask him over for dinner Saturday evening to thank him for taking Andrew. It was the least she could do to show her appreciation. Taylor did not need to make an effort with her son but he was and that was important to Tessa.

She called him later that evening when she returned home.

Taylor could hear his phone chirping over on the cocktail table. He had left it there while he ate a small dinner at the kitchen bar. His day as usual had been spent working on his bike and it was finally becoming recognizable as a motorcycle and not a tangled mass of steel. He still had quite a bit of work to do on it mechanically. Once that was finished, he would ship it back west for a custom paint job.

He moved over to the table to click his phone on. "Yep?" he answered.

"Hi, Taylor." Tessa's soft voice on the phone.

Taylor was surprised to hear from her. It seemed she had been avoiding him all week. Today was Friday, about a week after their camping trip and

113

he really had not seen anyone around. They were well into October and the weather was definitely getting chillier but it was still seasonal enough to work outside.

"Hey, Tessa," he answered.

"I just wanted to ask you if you have any plans tomorrow evening on Saturday. If not, I wanted to know if you would like to come over for dinner. I'd kinda of like to thank you for taking Andrew and I thought—" she hesitated and her words dwindled off.

"I wanted to take him, Tessa. You don't have to thank me, but dinner would be great," he said hurriedly. He wanted to see her again and Andrew too.

"Do you like spaghetti and meatballs?"

"Italian food? You bet! Sounds great."

"Okay. How is six p.m.? Can you come over then? And Rose will be with us, I always include her as she is like part of the family. Is that okay with you?" She sounded tentative and unsure.

"Of course! I'd love to see Rose too. And six is fine. Do you need me to bring anything?" he offered.

"No, no. I have everything covered. See ya then, okay?"

"Sure. And thanks for inviting me."

He clicked off. Hot damn! Dinner with Tessa. He couldn't wait!

Taylor decided to go for black clothes again. He wore black jeans with a black cashmere vee neck sweater, black suede oxfords on his feet. He brushed his blond locks off of his face and shaved carefully.

He pushed the bell on the back door right on the dot, six p.m. Shortly he heard footsteps descend and Tessa opened the door to him. She literally took his breath away. She was wearing a fitted sheath dress, navy blue in color with long sleeves and black pumps. Her beautiful hair was down, tumbling around her shoulders. She motioned him inside and he tried hard to keep his eyes from wandering to the splendid curves displayed. He noticed as he followed her up the stairs she had gorgeous legs too, long and shapely.

He entered her kitchen with her and right away the delicious aroma of spaghetti sauce hit his nostrils. Ummmm— it smelled delicious.

Tawny eyes met his. "Everything is ready. Rose and Andrew are in the front room and the dining table is set. Would you like a glass of wine?" she offered.

Taylor cleared his throat. "Sure. Got red?"

"I know you like Merlot, I have that."

"That's fine."

He watched as she went to a cupboard and removed a balloon wine glass, filling it half full of the purple liquid. Silently she handed it to him. He accepted it and arched a brow. "Not joining me?"

"No, not tonight. If you want, we can go right in to the dining room. Everything is ready. I'll get Rose and Andrew."

She motioned him down a short hallway from the kitchen and Taylor finally got his first look at her home. The dining table and buffet were large and looked like an antique Victorian style. Tessa had updated the look with a lacy ivory table cloth and ivory cushions for the large chairs. He could see an ivory and crimson Aubusson rug underneath. There were beautiful gleaming hardwood floors throughout the apartment. Double French doors led into the front living room where he could see a comfortable sofa and a huge entertainment unit where Rose and Andrew were watching television. Looking further, he could see another pair of French doors that opened onto a porch and afforded a beautiful view of autumn colored trees. The overall effect was cozy, comfortable and classy.

He could see she had the table set with china and silver with a big bowl of steaming sauce placed in the middle of the table.

After summoning Rose and Andrew, Tessa headed to the kitchen to bring out the steaming pot of pasta which she placed on a warmer mat. Bread and all other items were already waiting for the diners.

Rose greeted Taylor and he smiled. "Hi, Rose. Good to see you again."

"Thank you. I know you'll love Tessa's homemade sauce. It's delicious."

Tessa laughed as she brought in a special sandwich and an apple for Andrew, seating him at the table. "It is one of the only things I really cook well. I can't compare to you, Rose."

Rose waved this away as she took her seat. "Nonsense. You do just fine."

Tessa waved him to a seat and Taylor sat, placing his wineglass down. He watched as she fussed with Andrew and soon he was eating his dinner, occasionally looking up at Taylor who sat across from him. Rose sat at one end of the table and Tessa sat down at the other. Spaghetti, sauce and bread were passed around and soon everyone was enjoying the meal.

Tessa and Rose spoke casually about Andrew's school week. Taylor caught snatches of how speech therapy and occupational therapy were going. Mostly his attention was on Tessa. She could make mean spaghetti sauce, it was awesome. She had the chandelier light on low and the light picked out golden strands among her brown hair. Taylor averted his attention, trying to concentrate on his food but it was damn hard when all he could think about was how much he wanted to jump Tessa.

The two women politely included him in the conversation, asking about their camping trip. Taylor filled them in on little tidbits he had not told them yet and even coaxed a smile and a reaction from Andrew, who got very excited when fishing was mentioned. It was a very pleasant meal and Taylor was enjoying himself. This sure beat eating at his bar kitchen alone.

After the meal, Taylor insisted he would help clean up. He shooed Rose into the living room with Andrew and helped Tessa carry dishes into the kitchen. He helped her rinse and load the dishwasher and even scrubbed pots.

"Taylor, you really don't need to do this. You're a guest," Tessa remarked, eyeing the tall man bent over the sink. The black clothes again brought out the light hair and the darker honey streaks. His tall lean body looked delicious in his dark clothes. Stop it, Tessa! Don't be lusting after a movie star. It will never work!

Taylor flashed her a grin and just that motion made her heart turn over.

"Don't worry, sweetheart. I've done my share of dishes in my day. This will hardly kill me and it's the least I can do for dinner. Which by the way was wonderful! Your spaghetti was great!"

She dried pots as he washed them and the domestic tranquility of the moment made her a bit uncomfortable. What was she doing here with him? *Why* was he here with them?

They both put dishes and pots away in cupboards. It was around eight o'clock and Andrew's bed time. Rose came into the kitchen and told Tessa she would get Andrew into bed. Tessa thanked her and sat down at her kitchen table after pouring herself and Taylor a glass of wine.

Taylor accepted it, sipping slowly, smiling slightly as he studied her. This made Tessa uncomfortable, but dinner had been her idea so she had to at least make an effort.

"So, how are things going with the motorcycle?" she said to make conversation.

He shrugged broad shoulders as he turned his balloon glass slightly. "Okay. It's getting there. About another month it will be ready for custom painting and to have some chrome fittings put on. I'll send it back to LA for that."

"LA?" Tessa arched a brow. "And when are you returning to LA?" This thought was never too far from Tessa's mind.

Teal eyes speared her. "I don't have any plans to go back any time soon. My agent Frank keeps bugging me to come back. He wants me to work, but I'm not quite ready."

"Your bandage is now off. You seem to be pain free for the most part. You can probably return whenever you want. Your rib is most likely just about healed." Tessa sipped her wine, contemplating him.

Taylor pushed his blond locks off of his face. "That's true. I have residual pain here and there, but nothing major."

Rose entered the kitchen with her sweater on. "Andrew is all settled for the night. He just needs his goodnight kisses. I'm going to go now. There's a program I want to catch on TV." What she didn't say was she wanted to leave the two of them alone.

Tessa stood to hug Rose. "Thank you, Rose. I'll see you tomorrow."

Taylor also said goodnight as Rose descended the stairs to her flat.

"Excuse me, Taylor. I have to give Andrew his kisses. I'll be right back."

"Sure. Okay," Taylor responded, wondering if he would get any goodnight kisses. He sure hoped so.

She was back within five minutes and Taylor sipped at his wine while she was gone. She took her seat across from him and picked up her wine goblet, sipping slowly, brown eyes watching the man across from her.

Taylor sighed. He was tired of this cat and mouse scenario. Time to take matters into hand. He rose and pulled Tessa out of her chair gently and pressed her against the kitchen wall, his body snug against hers.

"Taylor— what—"

He lowered his head, taking her lips, silencing her. He kissed her slowly and deeply, running his big hands through her thick silky mane. He pulled her closer so he could feel her curves, her breasts and hips pressing into his lean frame. His penis swelled, pressing into her stomach and he deepened the kiss, kissing her passionately. This was not sweet and tender like their first kiss. This was wild and animalistic and he groaned, feathering kisses down her throat and neck.

"Oh God, Tessa. I want you so much, baby." His lips returned to hers before she could utter a word.

Tessa's head whirled with the suddenness of all of this. They had been sipping wine, quietly talking and now they were making out like they were going to do it on her kitchen floor! Helplessly Tessa kissed him back, grabbing handfuls of thick blond waves. She knew this was wrong, she knew she had to stop this but the sensible Tessa was not in control, the sensual woman who had not had sex in five years was. And Taylor *really* knew how to kiss, knowing when to tease and when to force. Oh God, she had to stop this! Gasping, she pushed him away.

Taylor took a step backward, breathing heavily, chest heaving. Tessa's lips were slightly swollen from being kissed, her beautiful hair mussed. "Tessa—"

She moved away from him, across the kitchen, holding one hand up in a stop gesture. She also was breathing heavily and needed to catch her breath. When she was calm enough, she turned to him.

"We can't do this, Taylor. We just can't."

Taylor crossed his arms over his chest. "Why not, Tessa? We are very attracted to each other. We are both single, we are adults, so why not?"

Tessa finally met his eyes. "You know why not. I have a son and a life here." He started to interrupt but she said "Let me continue. I have a life here. Your life is not here, it is back in California and someday you will be leaving again to make a movie. That is what you do, you are a movie star." She laughed sardonically. "You will move on because that is what you do. And I don't want my son hurt, or Rose hurt or myself because we got too close to you. I can't let that happen. Taylor, if the real reason you are still here is because you think I will sleep with you, I'm telling you right now, *it will not happen.*"

He snorted shortly. "After the way you just kissed me baby, I think it very possibly could. You're right, though. Someday I will be moving on, but not yet. There is still too much unsettled between us. You think about that, Tessa. Good night."

He opened the door and descended the stairs as Tessa still tried to catch her breath.

Taylor spoke to Frank Sunday on the phone. As usual, Frank was urging him to come back. After what had happened yesterday at Tessa's, Taylor was considering going back again for a few days. Maybe they needed to cool things off a bit.

"I've got scripts galore here for you kid that producers and directors want you to read. I can fax 'em to you but it would be best if you came back and you and I discussed things. How long are you gonna stay in New York, anyway?"

Taylor sighed. "I don't know, Frank. Things are pretty much up in the air." He paused. "I may come back for a few days. I'm healed up enough to fly. If you want to send the jet out tomorrow on Monday, I'll head back for a few days."

Frank was happy with this news. "Now you're finally showing some sense, kid. You gotta make another movie within the next few months so you stay on top. That is crucial."

"Not worried about that, Frank. But I'll be back. Send the jet to Buffalo/ Niagara airport Monday. I'll see ya sometime tomorrow."

"Okay, great!" Frank clicked off.

Taylor threw the phone down. How would Tessa react to his absence? Would she be happy? The end of October was approaching and thankfully they had not had any more snow. He checked the five day forecast. No snow at all, some chilly temps which was normal here for October twenty fifth.

Taylor decided to leave a voice mail on Tessa's machine so she would know he was gone for a bit. He figured she deserved that consideration.

CHAPTER
TWENTY

"TESSA, ITS TAYLOR. JUST wanted to let you know I have to head out to LA for a while on business. Probably four or five days, then I'll be back." Pause. "Talk to ya soon." Click.

Tessa sighed as she played back Taylor's message. So, he was gone again. Fortunately the forecast was clear and snow was not expected. Halloween was in a few nights and they were calling for clear and chilly temps. Andrew had already decided he wanted to be Spiderman for Halloween. Thank God he had not picked one of the characters Taylor had portrayed in any of his many movies. She wanted Taylor to remain just the neighbor across the way to Andrew.

Tessa dressed for work, ruminating about Taylor and what "business" had suddenly called him to California.

Taylor met with Frank in his business office. Since Frank was a hot shot, his office was actually a suite. Tastefully decorated in a masculine style, with a formal bar, fancy globe, shelves of books/scripts and the requisite leather burgundy wing chairs. Taylor settled across from Frank in one of the chairs as Frank settled behind his massive desk. It was shiny and clear except for a pile of scripts Frank had placed front and center. Frank was dressed in one of his many expensive business suits, this one light grey with thin stripes paired with a white shirt and a silky red tie.

Taylor lounged across from him, steepling his fingers as he studied his agent/manager. Taylor had opted for his usual casual wear, jeans and a white cotton shirt, paired with dark cowboy boots. Taylor had just washed his hair and it waved to his shoulders. Taylor idly thought about cutting it a bit, it was getting a bit long.

"So, Taylor," Frank began, "I have quite a few scripts for you to peruse. I picked the top five I thought you would have the most interest in, but I have about thirty here." Frank arched a dark brow. "As you know, you've received hundreds but I culled only the ones we normally do business with. If you want, you can read them at your leisure."

"I'll do that, hoss. Got lots of leisure time these days," Taylor remarked, placing one booted foot across his thigh and settling back into the comfortable leather cushions. "Let's hear what ya got."

"The biggest one is from Weinberg. He has an action adventure thriller you would be perfect for. There are several drama thrillers and they look interesting also. Plus the usual comedy/romance/chick flick kinda stuff women love to see you in. Since you last did sci fi, I thought you might want to go for more of an adventure type flick this time and Weinberg has submitted a very good script. It is not yet complete because they want to know if you have a serious interest before they go ahead."

"Time to film? Location? Director? Co-stars?" Taylor fired his questions. He always got right to the point.

"They want to begin filming early summer, about mid May. The location is," he flipped some paperwork over, "Edmonton, Canada. Weinberg is directing himself. Co-stars— undecided at this point." Frank looked up to catch Taylor's reaction.

"Sounds okay. What else caught your eye?" Teal eyes studied Frank.

Frank met his eyes. "I know you don't usually like to do romantic comedies but I have a good one. Submitted by the person who did the screenplay for *Notebook*. Scarlett Johansen would be your co-star for that one."

Taylor shrugged broad shoulders. "Keep going."

Frank rearranged his bundle and looked down. "Okay, new action adventure hero with really cool skills. Makes Spiderman and Batman look like amateurs. This has box office smash written all over it, especially if you take it on. Movie goers love it when real stars take these kinds of roles." Frank looked up. "What say you so far?"

"Like the first one you mentioned. I'll take a look at all of them, all thirty. I have time to read through all of them. Winter is coming to Western New York." Taylor stood to accept the large bundle from Frank.

Frank stood too. "Taylor, you aren't seriously thinking of staying there through the winter, are you? That's lunacy. You'll get buried in snow again. Thought you southern boys don't care for snow." Frank handed over the bundle as he spoke.

Taylor accepted it, arching a golden brow. "Let's just say things are interesting there right now."

"Taylor don't get involved with some woman there. You are not the type to get romantically involved. You are young, making movies and having fun. Where does a woman from western New York fit into that scenario?"

Taylor shrugged as he reached across to shake Frank's hand. "I don't know if she does or not, hoss. The fun is in the mystery of finding out." Taylor tipped his finger to his forehead, saluting Frank, gave his famous grin and left through the massive double doors.

Frank sighed as he sat back down at his desk. He hoped vehemently that Taylor forgot about this woman and got his ass back to work.

Taylor spent time at his mansion reading scripts, swimming in his pool— it was great to see sunshine again— and he actually managed to get a bit more of a tan which complimented his teal eyes and golden hair.

Evenings were spent partying. Taylor had made many friends from filming movies and he was well known in Hollywood. One of his ex-co stars was throwing a big bash at her Bel Aire home and Taylor attended. She was all over him all evening and though he had slept with her in the past, he had no desire to do so again. He avoided her and spoke to other friends there. He looked around for Marisa but she was not there. Since it was mid week she was probably home sleeping after filming all day.

Several days passed and Taylor decided to wrap up his trip and head back east. He would take all of the voluminous scripts Frank had given him and read them in the evenings. He wondered if Tessa had missed him.

Halloween night arrived and Tessa took Andrew trick or treating in the neighborhood. They never did too many houses because Andrew would become tired quickly. Rose was at the house to give out candy to children that came to Tessa's house while they were out. The weather had cooperated. Although it was chilly, in the mid forties, that was pretty balmy for the end of October.

Andrew was quite happy as they skipped from house to house, holding up his orange pumpkin candy container hopefully when they stopped at the various neighbors. They had to walk because houses in the area were not close together, with many trees in between properties. This was why Andrew tired easily but he was usually game for at least six or seven houses. He did not eat the candy. He was only interested in the dressing up part. Tessa did have to prompt him to say "Trick or Treat" as he did not say it, silently offering the pumpkin as doors were opened. After two houses, he caught on and happily said it for the remainder. Soon Tessa could see his walk getting slower and his shoulders slumping.

She bent down so she was eye level with Spiderman. "Getting tired, buddy? Want to head back?"

Andrew shook his head in a positive gesture and Tessa picked up her son, carrying him the block to her house and her Spiderman snuggled on her shoulder, his candy pumpkin holder clutched close.

As Tessa walked up their drive (she had finally put Andrew back on his feet and he held her hand as they walked up) Tessa saw Taylor's black SUV parked in his normal space. Her heart raced a bit. So, he was back! She could feel happiness swell in her chest and scolded herself.

Taylor had a life in Hollywood. She had a life in Lewiston. The two would never mesh and she needed to remember that, no matter how much she was attracted to him.

Sighing, she and Andrew headed upstairs so she could help him bathe and put him into bed.

CHAPTER
TWENTY ONE

TAYLOR ARRIVED BACK IN Lewiston Halloween evening. As he pulled into the drive he could see porch lights on downstairs and two jack 'o lanterns lit up. The pumpkins both sported orange smiles. Taylor grinned to himself. The upstairs flat was dark, no lights were lit so Taylor surmised Tessa had Andrew out trick or treating and Rose was giving out candy. Since Taylor did not have any candy at his place he would have to leave the outdoors light off.

He hauled his luggage out of the SUV, making a second trip down to get the bundle that contained all of the scripts Frank had loaded him down with. Since the evenings were longer now with the advent of winter, he would have quite a bit of time to review them to decide on his next project. He still had his bike to work on, but most of the basic work was done on it and in a few weeks it would be ready to be shipped back west for the remaining work. What then?

Taylor threw his luggage on his bed and proceeded to put away articles of clothing and throwing dirty laundry in the hamper. He had bit the bullet and cut his hair, quite a bit. Now it was just a bit longer than his collar. As a result his wavy hair was thick and full and the new style fell over his forehead a bit. He wondered idly if Tessa would like the new look.

November arrived and Taylor did most of the restoration of the motorcycle inside the garage. On sunnier days he would work outside but with November upon them it was colder. Taylor would bundle up in a quilted vest worn over his jeans and flannel shirts. He always wore sturdy work boots and was careful to have the garage doors down if he was working outside.

124

He saw his neighbors now and then, but mostly to wave in passing. He saw more of Rose and Andrew than Tessa. She usually arrived home when Taylor was upstairs eating dinner or running errands or at the gym. Taylor had joined a local gym several weeks ago to get back into shape. He also ran five miles every morning if the weather cooperated. If not, he ran on the treadmill at the gym and lifted there. As a result he could feel his strength returning and he was starting to feel like his old self again. He rarely had any pain in his ribs. Once in a while he would get a slight headache, but nothing simple Advil could not handle.

Today Taylor worked outside in the sunshine. It was late afternoon, going on four thirty and he was thinking of quitting for the day. Maybe order a pizza for dinner. It was Friday evening and he was sure there were probably restaurants around, but he did not want to eat alone. It seemed Tessa had been avoiding him like the plague. Taylor sighed as he tightened a bolt on the bike. Andrew had arrived home about an hour ago. Rose met the bus, waving as she usually did. She murmured something to Andrew and then the boy waved also. Taylor waved, grinning at the two of them.

Taylor's attention was totally on his bike. He was lying underneath the thing, trying to get a stubborn bolt in. It was halfway out and Taylor grunted as he used his wrench to get the damn thing tightened properly. Suddenly Taylor heard someone screaming his name. It sounded like Rose!

Taylor jumped up and ran toward the back door where he could definitely now hear the woman screaming frantically.

He found her on her kitchen floor and she was grimacing in pain.

He went to her, trying to help her to sit up but she shooed this gesture away. "Quick! Andrew! You must go after him and find him Taylor. I fell trying to follow him outside. I think it's my ankle— but Andrew! You must find Andrew!"

Taylor quickly took his cell phone out and called 911 to come out to help Rose. Flipping it shut, he carefully helped her to sit in a chair.

"Rose, where would he go? Which direction should I look in?" Taylor asked urgently.

Rose tried to think through the pain and finally remembered. "Oh, no! The railroad tracks! They are about a half a mile away and Andrew is attracted to the sound of the train whistle. He might of— Oh God!"

Taylor sprinted to the door. "Medical personnel will be here shortly to help you Rose. Don't worry! I'll find him!"

Taylor jumped into his SUV and backed down the drive. As he hit the main road, he could hear the sound of sirens approaching.

Taylor drove directly to the railroad tracks. He had passed them many times coming and going. The trains that came through were usually higher speed passenger trains and he prayed Andrew had not wandered onto the tracks.

Taylor arrived within minutes and parked the SUV, hopping out. Christ, the gates were down and red lights were flashing. There was definitely a train coming, Taylor could hear the rumble of the engines. He looked frantically around for Andrew and sure enough, there he was, right in the middle of the tracks! He was throwing stones idly toward the far side and as Taylor loped closer, he could see if he tried to call to Andrew it would distract him and maybe make him run closer toward the train. Taylor looked down the track and the train was approaching quickly, much too quickly. The engineer had seen the child on the tracks and was tooting his horn and Taylor heard the squeal of brakes but he knew instinctively the train would not be able to stop before reaching Andrew.

Taylor leaped onto the tracks, tackling Andrew and lifting himself and the boy and rolling, rolling to the far side off of the tracks where there was a grassy area. The train whizzed by seconds later so fast that Taylor could feel his hair and clothes whipped by the speed. God, if he had not been in time, Andrew could have died!

Taylor was breathing hard and carefully rolled off of the child, checking to see if he was hurt.

"Andrew, buddy! Are you okay? Anything hurt?" Taylor ran his hands up and down the boy's sides, checking his legs and head.

Andrew's wide brown eyes looked up at Taylor in wonder, barely comprehending what had just happened. He saw the big train go by and suddenly there was Taylor.

Taylor repeated his question urgently. "Andrew? Are you hurt?"

Andrew shook his head in a negative gesture and Taylor clutched him close.

"Thank God you're okay, buddy."

The two knelt by the side of the tracks, listening as the eerie sound of the train whistle faded away.

Taylor returned to the house to see the medics were attending Rose. They had wrapped her ankle tightly in a bandage and a medic was instructing her to have a doctor look at it tomorrow and to keep it elevated.

Rose ignored him as soon as she saw Taylor at her door with Andrew. "Oh, thank God, you found him! Where was he?" The medics continued to fuss around her as Andrew came over to hug her.

"Boo boo?" he asked, pointing to her foot.

"Yes, Andrew, but I'll be fine. You can go in to watch TV for now, okay?"

Andrew did something very rare. He kissed Rose softly on her cheek and silently went into the living room.

Taylor could see Rose was in tears, seemingly oblivious of her own situation, worried sick about Andrew.

He had to tell her the truth. She and Tessa needed to make sure Andrew never got close to the train tracks again.

"I found him right where you said he might be. He was right in the middle of the train tracks and a fast train was coming. I didn't have time to think, I just reacted. I jumped onto the tracks and rolled us both to the far side as the thing whizzed by. Rose, he could have been killed." Taylor had tears in his own eyes.

"Oh, my God! All because I am a silly old woman who can't keep up with him and fell! I feel just horrible!" She started to really cry now and the medics were looking more concerned but Taylor knelt down by her chair, careful not to bump her injured foot.

"Rose, it is not your fault. You take wonderful care of Andrew day after day. It was an accident that you tripped and fell and got hurt. The important thing is Andrew is all right. You have to take care of yourself now." He leaned down to hug her tightly. "Rose, don't cry. Everything is okay."

"Yes, because you are here, Taylor." She sobbed. "What would we do without you?"

Taylor stepped back and could see it was almost five. "Does Tessa know about any of this?"

"No, no. I haven't been able to call her yet. She will be home any minute. I feel like I let her down so much…" Rose still was crying slightly.

"Don't worry. I'll call her. Please listen to the medics. They need to give you some pain medication and advice."

He moved to another part of her kitchen as the medics once again swarmed around the older woman, having no idea of the true tragedy that had narrowly been averted. Oh Christ! What was he to tell Tessa?

He dialed her number and she picked up right away. "Hello?"

"Hi, Tessa. It's Taylor. We have a situation here at your house and I thought I better give you a call before you get home."

"I'm on my way. I'm about five minutes away. What has happened?"

He could hear the sound of traffic so she must be in her vehicle headed home. "Rose fell and fractured her ankle." He could hear her gasp. "She's okay," he reassured her right away. "I called 911 and the medics are here and wrapped her foot and she is getting medical attention."

He could hear her relieved sigh. "Oh, thank God!" Then she realized the implications of this accident. "Andrew! Is Andrew okay? Are you there with him?" she asked anxiously.

"Yes, yes. I'm here with them both. But Tessa, something else happened and we need to talk about it. I don't want to do it over the phone."

"Okay. I'll be there in two minutes." She clicked off.

True to her word, two minutes later he could see Tessa's red Blazer pulling into the driveway. She parked hurriedly and jumped down from the vehicle. She was still wearing her nurse's uniform, her beautiful hair cascading around her shoulders. She ran into the back door. Most of the medic vans had departed; however, there was still one parked outside. Taylor met her at the door. Immediately Tessa's eyes went to Rose and she hurried to her side.

"Rose— my God! What happened?" She looked at Rose's bound foot. "Your foot—"

Rose waved away her concern. "I'm fine, Tessa. Taylor called the medics and they have taken care of me. I guess I fractured my ankle when I fell. I'll heal up." She choked up with tears. "Andrew— it is Andrew—"

Tessa gasped, her gaze swinging to Taylor. "I thought you said he was all right!" she remarked in an angry tone.

"Tessa, Tessa, no! Taylor— Andrew ran away when I fell. I screamed for Taylor and fortunately he was working outside on his bike. He—" she was obviously overwrought and very upset.

Taylor came over and led Tessa away from Rose. "Tessa, she needs a moment. Let the medic give her final instructions. I'll fill you in on what happened. And Andrew is safe. He is in the front living room watching TV."

Relief spread through Tessa's body. "Oh, thank God!" She put her purse down on the counter and removed her jacket, watching as the medic helped place a pillow under Rose's foot. She turned back to Taylor. "Something else happened having to do with Andrew?" she asked.

"Can we step outside a minute? Put your jacket back on." He handed it to her and motioned her out the door. Since Tessa could see Rose was in good hands for now, she followed Taylor down the several steps and outside.

"Taylor, what's up? Really, I should be inside with Rose—"

"Tessa, when Rose fell, Andrew ran away." As soon as these words were out, Tessa gasped and her hands flew to her mouth, eyes wide. She was silent, waiting for him to continue. "I called the medics for Rose and then asked her where would be the most likely place he would go. She mentioned the nearby railroad tracks." At these words he could see tears prick the beautiful brown eyes. He continued. "I jumped into my SUV and headed straight there and sure enough he was there." He paused uncomfortably. "He was right in the middle of the tracks and the gates were down and the lights were flashing. I could hear the train coming. I just reacted. I jumped onto the tracks and rolled and rolled. We made it to the far side safely." He could see she was openly crying now, tears tracking down her cheeks. "Oh baby." He pulled her into his arms. "Don't cry, baby. Your son is safe."

She cried for several minutes and Taylor held her tightly, rocking her gently. Finally she pushed back a bit.

Moisture clung to her long lashes as she looked up at him. "You saved his life. You saved my son's life," she choked.

Taylor touched her cheek gently. "Tess— he is safe. I wanted you to know everything so that you and Rose are careful about the proximity of the trains. He seems to have a fascination with them." He shrugged broad shoulders. "I'm glad I heard Rose screaming. I didn't see him leave, I was working. But he is okay. He is in the living room in Rose's flat if you want to see him."

"Yes. Yes I do." She turned to go, then turned back to the man standing at the end of the steps. "Thank you, Taylor. There is no way I can ever repay you." Her brown eyes were sad and worried.

"Go to your son, Tessa. I would do the same thing in a heart beat."

She disappeared into the house and Taylor sighed.

Finally the medic left and Taylor checked on his neighbors. Tessa informed him she would be staying with Rose in her flat to care for her over the weekend. She was in the process of hiring a visiting nurse to come be with Rose during the days.

"If you like Tessa, I can get Andrew off of the bus every day. I can keep an eye on him until you return as Rose recuperates."

Tessa hesitated. "I hate to ask you Taylor. You've done so much already. But if you could, that would help so much. I—"

"Consider it done. I'll be down there everyday, three thirty like clockwork. You don't need to worry."

Tessa looked deep into Taylor's eyes. "No, Taylor. With you here, I don't need to worry."

Taylor returned to his own place, ruminating about the events of the day. He was exhausted and stressed out. A little wine might be in order.

CHAPTER
TWENTY TWO

FRIDAY EVENING TESSA STAYED at Rose's apartment. She made sure Rose was comfortable in her bed and administered pain medication. On Monday Rose would need to see a doctor to see if her foot would need to be casted. Tessa had already called her supervisor to ask for a half day off, explaining what happened. In the meantime during the week a nurse Tessa had hired would care for Rose.

After making sure Rose was set for the evening, Tessa bathed her son and put warm pajamas on him. She and Andrew were staying in Rose's second bedroom which had a full size bed. Tessa told him a bedtime story and soon her son drifted to sleep, Barney clutched close. As Tessa gazed down at her son she recalled how close she had come to losing him today. She gently moved Andrew closer to her, careful not to wake him and hugged him close. Tears streamed down Tessa's face and she cried and cried. If not for Taylor...

He had also offered to help care for her son while she was at work. Rose would be in no condition to care for him for at least a month, maybe longer. If she did need a cast, she would probably have it on for six weeks or longer. So having Taylor here was a real God send.

As Tessa silently cried, holding her son, she thought about Taylor and all of her conflicting emotions. Taylor was always there when she needed him— be it for snow storms, caring for and entertaining her son, or simply taking her out to dinner, simple companionship. He seemed to be quickly becoming part of their lives and Tessa was happy but also sad. Taylor would someday leave them and she knew neither she nor Rose and possibly even Andrew would ever forget him.

Tessa fell asleep with her son in her arms, Taylor's face in her dreams.

Taylor checked on his neighbors on Saturday and Tessa informed him Rose was still in a lot of pain. They were planning on staying indoors. The new nurse was coming later to speak to Rose and do an evaluation. Tessa informed Taylor they would be staying indoors for the remainder of the weekend.

Tessa gave Taylor instructions on getting Andrew off of the bus on Monday and what his typical routine was. She also gave him a key to her apartment so that he could care for Andrew upstairs so he would not disturb Rose. Rose protested over this but Tessa insisted. Andrew could be a handful and Rose needed to recover. Taylor promised Rose he would bring Andrew down to visit occasionally and this cheered her up.

Taylor did not stay long. He could see Tessa had her hands full caring for both Rose and Andrew. He offered to help but Tessa assured him she could handle things.

Tessa thanked Taylor once again and he left to go to his own place.

Monday afternoon he would begin his caretaker duties for Andrew.

Three thirty Taylor was down at the end of the drive to meet Andrew's bus. He arrived right on time and Taylor introduced himself to the driver and aide, explaining why he would be getting Andrew off of the bus. Tessa had already called the transportation company so they would know that Taylor was not a stranger and had her permission to take Andrew.

The driver and aide smiled at him and he watched as the aide removed Andrew's seat belt and Andrew grabbed his backpack, putting it on and moving to the steps. When he saw Taylor he hesitated briefly, then he gave Taylor a sunny smile. Taylor's heart turned over.

"Hi, buddy! Did you have a good day at school?" Taylor questioned as they moved up the driveway and the little bus went on its way.

Andrew looked up into Taylor's face and the brown eyes widened. "Hair?" he motioned to Taylor's golden locks.

Taylor ran a hand through his shorter hair. "Yeah, I got it cut. What do you think of it? Like it?"

As they moved into the back of the house and up the stairs Andrew continued to study him, but he did not answer Taylor's questions.

Taylor knew Andrew would now have a snack after checking on Barney. He prepared the snack (Tessa left a list where everything in the kitchen was located) and placed it on the table. Soon Andrew was back to eat his snack and glanced silently up at Taylor.

Taylor knew it was important to get Andrew to speak, so he kept asking questions about his day. Eventually he wormed a little information out of Andrew but it was slow going. However they were getting along just fine and Taylor thought this was definite progress.

As Andrew watched his favorite show, Taylor read through scripts Frank had sent him. This would keep him occupied until Tessa returned at five. The little boy and the famous movie star spent their time in comfortable silence as they waited for Tessa.

Taylor ordered a pizza to be delivered at five fifteen. He knew Tessa probably would not want to cook after being on her feet all day and he knew she would be worrying about both Andrew and Rose.

He heard her car door slam at exactly five ten but she went downstairs first to check on Rose. The visiting nurses had shifts she had explained, so someone was always with Rose and they also prepared meals for her.

Five minutes later he could hear her footsteps on the stairs and she appeared in the kitchen doorway holding a large pizza.

"Hi! I met a pizza guy outside and he said we ordered pizza. Yum!" She smiled and placed it on the table.

"Tessa, you should have let me pay for—"

"It's no problem, Taylor. Thanks for ordering dinner." She turned to her son who came running from the living room. "Hi, Andrew! How are you? Mommy missed you *so* much today!"

Andrew giggled as he received hugs from his mommy.

Taylor shoved his hands in his jean pockets. "I wasn't sure if Andrew liked pizza or not. I was hoping it was a safe bet."

Tessa straightened and looked at Taylor. He looked marvelous with his new hair cut. Today he was wearing a teal sweater with his jeans that made his eyes brighter. His wavy blond locks fell slightly over his forehead and as Tessa studied him her heart did flip flops. Careful, down girl!

She gave Taylor a dazzling smile. "Pizza is great! I'll get plates and we can all eat!"

The three of them settled around the table and enjoyed pizza and casual conversation.

Taylor helped clean up and visited for about an hour and then left. He checked on Rose and chatted for a bit, then went over to his own place.

The week passed by and the routine was pretty much the same everyday. Sometimes Taylor cooked (yeah, he had to learn when he was a kid or he didn't eat) or they ordered out.

What disturbed Taylor and scared the hell out of him was he was actually starting to feel like part of a family.

Tessa had been doing quite a bit of thinking about Taylor, especially during the day when she should be concentrating on her job. She ruminated about his relationship with her son. He was taking excellent care of Andrew and she did not have to cook all week! She was astounded to learn he was a good cook. She knew she was very attracted to Taylor and she was so very grateful for all he had done for them.

He had saved her son's life. If fate had not sent Taylor here to Lewiston, would her son have died on that Friday afternoon? This horrible thought kept looping through her mind. She tried to just be grateful her son was safe and Rose was on the mend but she felt she somehow owed Taylor something more than a simple "thank you very much." It just did not convey the depth of her total gratitude. Her son was her life and if she had lost him, she was not sure if she could go on. But because of Taylor, Andrew was safe.

Thoughts and emotions chased themselves through Tessa's head all week. What was she to do about Taylor?

Saturday evening arrived and Taylor was relaxing on his sectional reading through some scripts. Since it was the weekend Tessa had resumed care of both Andrew and Rose. Rose did not need to have her foot casted, but she had to wear one of those fluky boot shoes they strapped to your foot to keep it from moving a lot. Her recovery would be quicker, which was a good thing. He usually stopped over a couple of times a week just to chat and help out a bit; he did this before Andrew returned because he had time then.

Sighing, he turned the page of the script when suddenly his buzzer sounded downstairs. Puzzled, he threw the script on his table and stood. He wasn't expecting anybody and was dressed casually in jeans and a black sweater.

He descended his stairs to open the door to Tessa.

Oh – my— God! She looked stunning. She had a tight red dress on, red heels and her hair was pinned up in a sexy style, curls cascading. Full makeup enhanced her gorgeous features and she was holding a bottle of champagne.

She smiled teasingly. "May I come in?"

Silently, Taylor stepped back, opening the door further, ushering her up the stairs. She ascended them as he closed the door and followed closely, never taking his eyes off of the sexy legs in red heels.

When they reached the main room, Tessa looked around, noticing the script on the table. "I'm not interrupting anything, am I?" She arched a brow, turning to him.

Taylor cleared his throat. It took several attempts to get coherent words out. She was so drop dead sexy. "No— no. I was just reading some scripts my agent sent me."

"Good." She proceeded further into the room, placing the champagne on his bar. "I hope you have some champagne flutes around here somewhere?" Tawny eyes chased to Taylor who was still standing at the top of the stairs.

"Ah, yeah. Under the bar." He moved behind the bar and searched around for flutes, finally finding two crystal flutes he had tucked away. He produced them and set them on the bar. "To what do I owe this occasion?" he asked as Tessa popped the cork and poured fizzy gold liquid in the flutes.

She smiled saucily. "Always with the questions, Taylor." She picked up her flute and clicked it against his. "Let's go relax and enjoy our champagne." She moved toward his sectional and he followed her.

"Of course I have questions when you show up at my door looking like you're ready to party for New Year's Eve or something." He settled on the sectional also, sipping champagne, teal eyes studying the beautiful woman opposite him. "I take it Rose is with Andrew?"

"Yes, she felt up to watching him for a little while. I explained I would be here and she could reach me here if she needed me. As to your other comment, I thought you liked women dressed 'ready to party' as you remarked." She arched a brow, sipping champagne.

Taylor was totally at a loss. Except for their dinner date, Tessa always wore either her uniform or casual clothes. He tried to figure out what she was up to and then damn! It dawned on him. She was trying to seduce him. He had had many women in the past trying to do that exact same thing and recognized the signs. But Tessa?! This was totally out of character.

Taylor sipped some more champagne, silent. His eyes moved over the luscious curves displayed in the dress, moving to her long sexy legs and back up again to her face. Tessa was silent, blushing a bit, also sipping champagne.

"Tessa, what are you up to?" Taylor finally spoke.

Tessa waved an elegant hand. "Isn't it obvious? Champagne, sexy dress, alone together…" her words trailed off.

"Tessa, are you trying to tell me you are here to have sex with me?" Taylor arched a brow, setting his champagne aside and studying her closely.

Now Tessa was really blushing, but then she met his eyes directly. "Yes."

At this response, Taylor's brows rose. What the hell was going on? She had made it quite clear in the past that she would never sleep with him. What had changed?

Then Taylor remembered the events of the week. How he had saved her son's life and cared for him this week and this was her way of thanking him— sleeping with him. Although he badly wanted to have sex with Tessa he did not want it to be this way. Her bartering her body because he had done a simple kindness that any decent person would. Okay, so maybe a lot of people would not jump on train tracks but Taylor cared enough about Tessa and Andrew to risk his life for them. What does that say about you Taylor? He didn't want to figure that out right now.

"Tess— I don't want to do this. I don't want you thinking you have to somehow repay me for anything I have done for you or your son by offering to have sex with me. I would do those things anyway. Yes, I do want to have sex with you and eventually I think it will happen, but not this way Tessa. Not this way."

She put her champagne glass down on his table and then burst into tears. Taylor was alarmed and moved over to her. "Tessa— what's wrong? What— did I say something wrong? What—"

"Hold me," she sobbed through her tears. "Just hold me."

Taylor took her into his arms, first flinging off her heels. He laid back on the sectional with the crying woman in his arms and soothed her, hugging her close to his chest. "It's okay, baby. It's okay," he murmured.

Tessa cried for several minutes and Taylor rubbed his hands up and down her back, soothing her and murmuring sweet words to her.

Finally she pushed back and rubbed under her eyes, wiping away mascara and tears. She tried to fix her appearance, pulling her dress down, wiping tendrils of curls off of her face. As she reached for her heels, she addressed him. "You must think I am such a fool." She avoided his eyes as she put on her shoes.

"No, Tessa," he said seriously. "I believe you are a woman who fiercely loves her son and wanted to show me just how much by doing something for me you thought would make me happy. I appreciate the thought, I really do," he grinned. "But our time and place will come. I am sure of that. And I don't want to take advantage of your sorrow over what happened."

Tessa's tawny eyes were moist from her tears. She met his eyes. "Taylor, you totally amaze me."

"Yeah, I've been told that by women a lot, darlin'," he said, trying to lighten the mood. "I must say, you're one of the few I've turned down."

She chuckled. "I just bet!"

Grinning, he poured more champagne. "Let's enjoy this excellent champagne you brought. Then I'd like your opinion on some scripts I've got here."

Tessa removed her heels again, tucking her legs underneath her, relaxing back into the cushions. A soft smile touched her face. "Sounds great, Taylor."

CHAPTER
TWENTY THREE

TESSA'S ALARM CLOCK WOKE her a bit later than usual and glancing sleepily at the clock she remembered why. She had to get Andrew on the bus in the mornings and she now went into work an hour and a half later than normal. The night shift nurse, Cathy Wilson, had offered to stay the extra time so Tessa could get her son off to school. Tessa did not want to ask Taylor to wake early because she knew he was not really a morning person and he had done so much for them already.

Sighing, Tessa moved to her bathroom to take a quick shower and then wake Andrew, dress him, feed him breakfast and pack his lunch and backpack. There was quite a bit to do in the morning to get the little guy off to school and usually it was Rose that attended to all of this. Tessa could really appreciate Rose even more after going through the morning routine every day. Tessa just usually showered, threw on her uniform, grabbed coffee and headed out the door after softly kissing her son. The reward to all of this was she got to see him in the morning and had the opportunity to kiss him goodbye.

Tessa threw back her coverlet and headed to the shower. She shivered as she did so. It was now close to mid November and the days and evenings were chillier. She would have to bundle Andrew up today and put his new winter coat on him.

Tessa hugged and kissed Andrew as he boarded the steps of the bus. As usual, she chatted briefly with the driver and watched as the doors hissed closed and the yellow bus moved off. She blew kisses to Andrew who was watching her out of a window. She saw him smile at her and then the bus moved away down the street.

Tessa moved to her SUV, shivering a bit. She also had finally dragged her winter coat out and wore gloves to keep her hands warm. She looked up at the carriage house as she moved up the driveway. All of the shades were securely down and there was no movement or sign of Taylor. Since it was seven thirty in the morning, she did not expect any activity. Entering her SUV, she turned the heat up to full blast and backed down her driveway carefully.

Another day of nursing would begin.

As Tessa worked her shift, she kept recalling the events of last Saturday evening. She was shocked and surprised (and secretly relieved for reasons she did not want to examine) that Taylor had turned down her offer of sex. She had not had sex in five years and was not even sure of her moves anymore. Somehow she did not think that would be a problem with Taylor. She was sure that he would be very experienced which would balance out her inexperience and she knew he would be a good lover. It was just something that sensual women could sense by the way a man moved, talked and dressed. She felt embarrassment that he had turned her down too. Her emotions were a mixture of hope and frustration, trust and wariness. She also knew they were all growing very close to Taylor and this made her uneasy.

Tessa tried to forget Taylor as the head nurse asked her a question. She had a job to do and could not let the golden stud distract her.

Taylor woke at his usual time on Monday morning, eight a.m. Shaking the sleep from his eyes, he stumbled to his kitchen to put coffee on. That accomplished, he checked the weather. It was cold but if he bundled up, he should still be able to run. A quick hot shower after that, then he usually checked on Rose. The rest of the day was spent *inside* the garage working on his bike. With mid November upon them it was too cold to work outdoors. He worked until about three in the afternoon. That gave him some time to clean up and grab a sandwich or something before meeting Andrew's bus. Thus, Taylor's routine for the day. Evenings were spent reviewing scripts and conferencing with Frank and his publicist on the phone. Both were still urging him to return to California but Thanksgiving was coming up soon and Taylor wanted to stay at least until then. At least until he could figure out what to do about Tessa.

Bundling up, Taylor left to go for his run, trying to forget about the beautiful brunette who drove him crazy.

As the weeks passed by, Taylor and Andrew were forging a closer relationship. Andrew would now answer simple questions Taylor asked him and Taylor spoke to Tessa about taking Andrew on little outings. Taylor took Andrew bowling. He could see the noise bothered the boy so he purchased ear plugs and tried again and that worked. Andrew was willing to try bowling. Taylor patiently taught him how to handle and throw the ball, his large hands curling around the smaller ones. They had to use a very small ball for Andrew but Andrew was so proud of himself when he knocked down some pins. Taylor made sure he gave Andrew lots of verbal praise. He knew from his reading on Andrew's disability that this was an integral piece to build self confidence and Andrew responded well to verbal praise. His smile melted Taylor's heart. He knew he was falling in love with this boy. As for his mom… Taylor was not so sure what was going on there. He saw Tessa everyday after work but lately she had been a bit more remote and Taylor could not figure out why.

He enjoyed the time he spent with Andrew and decided to take each day as it came. He had been told by both Tessa and Rose that Rose would probably be ready to start taking care of Andrew again in several weeks. Her booted shoe would be coming off next week and she would be more mobile. Then what would happen? Taylor would miss the time he spent with Andrew.

Thanksgiving arrived and Tessa and Rose invited him to Rose's place for dinner. Tessa was cooking the meal and Taylor was invited over. He spent the time before dinner watching football and making a key lime pie. It was a recipe his mom had taught him long ago and he did not want to arrive empty handed.

He chose a pair of charcoal grey slacks to wear with a lighter grey ribbed sweater, grey suede shoes on his feet. He washed and styled his hair. When the pie was ready, he flung on a grey leather jacket and headed over to the big house.

Ringing the bell, he held the pie and shivered in the wind. They had not had anymore snow but it was forecasted for next week and Taylor was not looking forward to that.

Rose answered his summons and he noticed right away she was wearing her normal regular comfortable shoes. She wore a brown dress with golden leaves scattered over it and her thick hair up in a golden clip. Her brown eyes smiled up at him. "Come in, Taylor," she motioned him inside. "Dinner is just about ready."

Taylor stepped into the warmth of the kitchen. "Thanks."

Rose looked down at the pie he was holding. "What do we have here?"

"It's a key lime pie. My mama taught me how to make them and they are killer good. I know you probably already have some pies, but I wanted to bring something..." his words drifted off as he noticed Tessa basting a turkey in a huge pan at one of the counters.

She wore an emerald green corduroy dress with her hair pinned up and swirled, golden earrings hanging from delicate earlobes. The fashionable outfit was complete with a pair of tall leather brown boots that hid her gorgeous legs. She looked up and smiled when she heard him conversing with Rose.

"Yes, Rose made her famous apple and pumpkin pies. Even though she should be resting," Tessa scolded lightly.

The smells emanating from the kitchen made Taylor even hungrier. He handed Rose the pie as he remarked "Ummmm...something smells delicious!"

Rose also accepted his grey jacket as he removed it and carried the pie over to a counter, putting his jacket over a kitchen chair. "I'm just fine," she insisted. "She doesn't let me do enough. All of my pain is gone and I am walking normally."

Tessa smiled again as she started to carve the turkey. "I know, Rose. I just don't want you to push it."

"What can I do to help?" Taylor offered.

Tessa looked up from her chore. "Everything is already on the table. I just have to finish carving the turkey and we can start right in." She placed large slices of white breast meat on an autumn turkey platter. Finishing, she carried the platter and placed it in the middle of the dining table.

Taylor and Rose followed her into Rose's dining room and Taylor could see a complete feast laid out. Sweet potatoes, stuffing, biscuits, cranberry sauce, green bean casserole and several other dishes. The china and silver gleamed, waiting for diners. Taylor noticed Andrew sitting on the couch in Rose's living room, watching a parade on TV. He smiled as Tessa called her son for dinner.

Andrew turned off the set and sat down at the seat his mommy indicated. As usual, she had a special plate of food all set for him. He was dressed in a plaid teal and hunter green shirt with grey slacks and the colors brought out his brown eyes. He looked up at Taylor and smiled. "'lo, Taylor."

Taylor grinned back. "Hello, Andrew. Happy Thanksgiving!"

Tessa motioned him to sit and Taylor sat after Rose did. Tessa finally took her seat and food was passed around.

"Boy, Tessa! You made enough food for an army!"

Rose chuckled at this remark as Tessa answered him. "I wasn't sure how much to make. Usually Rose does Thanksgiving. I hope everything turned out okay. And it will mean plenty of leftovers for you to take home." Tawny eyes rose to teal.

Taylor piled food on his plate, grinning. "Yeah, I can tuck it away. But I want to save room for some of that famous apple pie."

Andrew looked up from his dinner. "Pie good."

"Yep! Pie is the best, buddy!"

"Taylor actually brought a special pie, Andrew. It is called key lime pie. You can try it if you like," Rose said.

Andrew made a sour face and shook his head in a negative gesture. "Pumpkin!" he insisted.

Taylor laughed as Tessa answered her son. "You may have your pumpkin pie, Andrew. And mommy has ice cream to go with it."

Andrew perked up at this news and happily ate his Thanksgiving dinner.

Taylor helped Tessa clean up, insisting Rose rest her foot. She and Andrew were in the front room watching football, which surprised Taylor. Football was sort of a Thanksgiving tradition as well as turkey, he supposed.

He and Tessa worked together, making small talk. He complimented her on the meal and she thanked him. They discussed Andrew a bit and she also informed him that after the Thanksgiving school break, Rose would be ready to resume her duties of caring for Andrew. Taylor was sad to hear this but he also had expected it.

Now things would change again. Taylor could not help but feel a bit let down. He enjoyed the time he spent with Andrew.

Tessa could see that Taylor was disappointed by this news and assured him if he wanted to take Andrew on outings on weekends that would be fine.

This news cheered Taylor a bit but winter was coming and he was unsure how much longer he would be around.

Finishing cleanup, Taylor stayed a bit to watch football and then returned to his carriage house. All of the food made him drowsy and he fell asleep in the middle of a football game.

Just before he nodded off, he thought today was the best Thanksgiving he had ever had.

CHAPTER
TWENTY FOUR

"How was your Thanksgiving, Taylor? Did you have a blizzard?" Frank joked.

Taylor was speaking to his agent several days after the holiday. Rose had resumed caretaking duties and Taylor was just about finished up with the work on his motorcycle. Winter was coming and he was seriously debating what to do next.

He chuckled at his agent's remarks. "My Thanksgiving was just fine, Frank. I hope yours and Lila's was too," Taylor referred to Frank's wife. "And no, no blizzards. We do have several inches lying around but nothing a snow blower and plow can't take care of." Taylor said the words casually as though he was used to dealing with snow all of the time. Nothing could be further from the truth. Ha!

"Well, Taylor. Made any decisions about the scripts I loaded you down with?"

"I've read through them all, most of them anyway. I've got it kinda narrowed down to five."

"Oh?" Frank answered. "Which five, can we be more specific? And Taylor, I do need you to come into town for some business meetings again. Unfortunately I know how you hate them but the Foundation is insisting again. Personally I think they want more of your money, buddy."

Taylor sighed. "Can't the lawyers handle that aspect, Frank?"

"I think it is in your best interests to be present. Just sayin'. And while you're here, we can discuss your next project. Unless something of vital importance is happening in Western New York," he said sarcastically.

Taylor sighed, recalling his earlier thoughts. "No, nothing earth shattering that I can't take a few days to fly west for. When do you want me?"

"As soon as possible would be good."

"All right. But send a limo or SUV. I plan to leave my personal vehicle here." Taylor wanted Tessa to have access to it if another storm blasted the area.

"Will do, buddy. You can expect the limo later this afternoon, around two."

"Yeah, okay. See ya soon, Frank."

Taylor clicked off. Now he had to leave a message for Tessa again and leave the keys to his SUV for her use, just in case.

Taylor left a message on Tessa's machine explaining his absence and informing her he left the keys to his SUV in his mailbox. He had detached the plow after the big storm in October because there had since not been a need for it but she could take the larger vehicle back and forth to work and the snow plow was up and running. Taylor made arrangements for a local company to come out and plow for Tessa so she would not need to worry about it. He hired them for the entire winter season and also left Tessa that news. He didn't want her stranded or having to worry about getting to work in dangerous conditions.

Having settled all of these things, he threw some clothes in luggage and waited for the limo, which showed up right on time at two p.m.

"Hey, Marisa! It's Taylor. I'm back in town again for some business meetings. You busy tonight, honey?" Taylor was calling Marisa on his cell phone.

"Taylor!" She was very happy to hear from him again. "That is so great that you're here! I have to film until six or so, then I'm free. Wanna do dinner?"

"Sounds good. How about I pick you up at your place at seven?"

"Cool."

"And dress casual. I wanna relax."

"Casual it is! See ya then, baby!"

Taylor took Marisa to a terrific Mexican restaurant in downtown LA. It was tucked away in a little back street and the media had not caught on to the fact yet that many celebs dined there to avoid the spotlight. Many stars courted the media and Taylor used to be one of them, but now he wanted his privacy. The place was intimate and decorated in the traditional Latin manner, bright colors and tiles, fountains and plants everywhere. Cozy booths shielded one from fellow diners and it was a great place to relax and the margaritas were out of this world.

Taylor and Marisa settled in a booth together and Marisa smiled at the handsome man opposite her. She had opted for a gauzy white skirt which she paired with a white eyelet blouse, wrapped sandals on her feet. Here in LA the temps at the end of November hovered in the seventies, unlike back east where Taylor was staying. She was very surprised he was still there with winter coming up. This evening he looked delicious in the sapphire blue shirt he wore with his jeans and cowboy boots. She noticed he had cut his hair and although she had liked the longer sexy length, this cut looked good on him too. Of course, nothing could make Taylor look bad. These thoughts flew through her head as they perused menus and then ordered dinner.

"So, Taylor. Why are you back in town? Are you staying?" she asked as she sipped at her margarita.

Taylor sighed, settling back in the booth. "Frank called me up about business meetings I have to attend. My first one is tomorrow and hopefully the next day we can wrap up. Also have to meet with Frank about my next project. Thinking of going back to work in the spring."

Marisa arched a brow. "Does that mean you are staying in Western New York for the winter?"

Taylor crossed his arms over his chest, teal eyes studying her. "Probably. Right now I don't have plans to move on and we're almost into December. I'm actually getting used to snow!" he laughed.

She grinned wickedly. "Why Taylor, you southern boy, you! I *never* thought I would hear those words coming from you," she teased.

Taylor shrugged broad shoulders. "It really isn't all that bad once you get used to it. And I do hear it does eventually melt!"

Her brown eyes lifted to his. "So Taylor, tell me more about this woman Tessa. She must really be something for you to stay in tundra land through the winter."

The waiter showed up with their meals and Taylor waited until he had departed before answering Marisa. "Let's just say she intrigues me and I'd like to see what happens."

Her brows arched. "You haven't slept with her yet? Taylor, you're slacking!"

He met her eyes, chuckling as he cut his burrito. "Let's just say she is a very different type of woman than those I am used to. Stubborn, beautiful, caring and petulant all at the same time. And her little boy is adorable!"

Again Marisa was stunned. "She has a child?"

"Yeah, she does. A little boy, six years old. He has autism."

She frowned. "Explain."

"Autism is a developmental disorder, usually manifests around eighteen months or so. It impairs the ability for an individual to socialize normally, speak normally and many are sensitive to sensory issues. Loud crowds, fireworks, things like that." He continued to eat his dinner as Marisa frowned.

"Taylor, this sounds like a lot to take on. Are you close with this boy?"

"Andrew. His name is Andrew, and yes, I guess I am. I take him on outings and took care of him for a while when his caretaker was injured. Tessa has to work so she needed help and I was there," he shrugged.

"Careful, Taylor. If you get too involved and then leave, you could hurt this family and yourself. Maybe you should consider coming back before winter," she suggested.

Taylor sighed. "Marisa, no matter what happens, if I leave tomorrow or leave in May, I will miss them and I am pretty sure they will miss me. So either way— I just don't know…"

Marisa leaned forward, catching his eyes. "Taylor, you are a movie star. There is no place in your life for a woman who has a child with a disability. You travel, you are never around. Yes, you can be there for them now, but not when you return to work. And them's the facts!" she emphasized, sipping at her drink.

"Marisa, don't you think those same exact thoughts have not been in my head? I can't help it though. I just can't leave them. Not now, maybe—"

"Maybe not ever? Are you planning to stay there?!" Marisa was aghast.

Taylor sighed, looking down at his food. Then his beautiful eyes rose to hers. "I don't know. I don't think so, but I just don't know."

Marisa was silent, eating her dinner, studying the man opposite her. Finally she asked a question. "Are you in love with her? Tessa?"

Taylor was startled by this question. "In love? No, I'm not in love with her."

"Don't kid yourself, Taylor. You wouldn't still be there if you didn't have some type of feelings for her."

"I do have feelings for her. I like her. I like her kid and the caretaker too. She's an elderly woman who is very sweet and they have allowed me to be part of their family." He paused. "I never really felt a part of my own family, as you know. I don't know, Marisa. I have very mixed feelings about everything. Time will tell, I guess."

They finished up their dinners and Marisa invited him back to her place. "I want to jump your bones, Taylor."

He laughed. "Sorry, I'm in a relationship."

"So you say, so you don't say. Make up your mind."

Taylor could not quite figure out what had changed since his last visit when he spent quite a bit of time nailing Marisa. This time it would feel like cheating, even though he and Tessa were not intimate yet. But he planned to be and very soon.

Taylor smiled at Marisa. "I'll be happy to come by for a drink. Then I gotta get ready for my meetings."

Marisa sighed. She and Taylor were friends and she would always value their friendship, but she would miss the sex.

Taylor was able to wrap up his meetings in a timely fashion. He met with Frank about his next project and told him he was leaning toward doing Weinberg's action/adventure flick but that he did not want to sign anything formally yet. He planned to take the script back east with him and look it over more thoroughly over the winter. If he chose to go ahead with the project he had plenty of time to fly back and sign on as they were not starting filming until mid May. Taylor figured by then he would have things settled and figured out in Western New York. And Tessa.

Tessa. He had missed her a lot although he had only been gone three days. As he flew back east and looked out at the clouds, her beautiful face was always in his mind. No, he wasn't in love. He was just in lust. He was sure of it.

Closing his eyes, he relaxed back into the cushions as the jet carried him back to the little family he had left behind.

CHAPTER
TWENTY FIVE

TESSA LISTENED TO TAYLOR'S message mid week. So, he would be going to California again on business. He had made arrangements for snow plowing to begin and left the name and number of the company. Tessa jotted down the information in case she had need of it while he was gone. According to the message, he would be returning by the weekend.

Tessa's week was spent working and caring for Andrew and Rose. Rose was definitely on the mend but Tessa always took time to visit with her and make sure she could handle her routine. Rose always blustered about this but Tessa ignored that. Rose was very important to Tessa and Andrew and she wanted to make sure Rose could move about comfortably and handle caretaking duties for Andrew.

As the weekend approached she wondered when Taylor would be returning. She then reminded herself that some day he would not be returning at all. She had to keep that foremost in her mind.

Tessa saw a limo pull into the driveway early Saturday morning, about nine a.m. She was sitting at her kitchen table sipping coffee as Andrew occupied himself drawing pictures at the dining table. She was contemplating the errands she had to run for the day when the long white vehicle pulled up. She saw Taylor emerge wearing a denim jacket over his jeans, a black knit cap pulled over his blond hair. He pulled some luggage out of the back and the driver said a few words to him and Taylor shook his head negatively, heading to the door of his carriage house with his luggage. He dropped the luggage, checking his mailbox to see if the SUV keys were there. She had not taken his vehicle because the weather had not been bad and she really felt a bit uncomfortable driving his fancy big SUV, so the keys were right where he left them. She saw him frown a bit, collect the keys, unlock his door and hefting his luggage, he disappeared inside.

So, he was back. Sometimes she really believed that when he left, he would not return. The thought made her sad for all of them. She knew someday it would actually happen.

Sighing, she dumped out her coffee and prepared for the day. She and Andrew were going grocery shopping and then she planned to take him to lunch at McDonald's, his favorite eatery. Life would go on in Lewiston with or without Taylor Boudrain.

Taylor put away his luggage and decided to go out for groceries. He did not have any food at his place and he needed some of the basics, especially bread, milk, eggs, coffee and juice.

He took a quick shower and changed his clothes, choosing a black turtleneck sweater to wear over faded Levis, lacing up black work boots. When he returned, he would work on the bike for a while. Since it was quite cold out (it was now December first) he did not know if he would see any of his neighbors. Probably not.

He grabbed the keys that Tessa had not bothered to use and headed out to the nearest grocery store.

As Taylor pushed his cart down the aisle looking for the brand of coffee he preferred, he heard a little boy calling his name. Turning, Taylor saw Tessa and Andrew behind him and Andrew was walking quickly toward him, smiling, repeating his name over and over. When he reached Taylor, he raised his arms and Taylor picked him up, hugging him close, eyes closed. God, he had missed this boy!

As Tessa watched her son and Taylor embrace in the middle of the grocery aisle, her heart turned over. Andrew had recognized Taylor right away and moved as quickly as his little legs would take him over to the tall blond man. Tessa noticed he had changed clothes and was now wearing black. She reached for some diet soda they needed as she watched her son converse with Taylor and as he did so, Taylor gently wiped Andrew's hair back, smiling down into her child's face. The two had obviously become closer than even Tessa suspected and she was really worried now. What if Taylor left for good? Her son would be heart broken.

Finally Taylor set Andrew down and Andrew gestured toward his mommy at the end of the lane. Taylor looked up and waved and she returned the wave, watching as Taylor took Andrew's hand and moved toward her with his cart and Andrew in tow.

"Hi, Tessa!" Taylor greeted, his white teeth gleaming as he smiled down at her.

"Hello, Taylor. I see you made it back from California safe and sound."

"You bet! Needed groceries since I've been away. Guess you did too."

Andrew piped up. "Taylor, McDonald's! McDonald's! You— come!"

Again Tessa was concerned and aghast. Andrew had *never* invited anyone to share their habitual Saturday lunch, not even Rose. That was strictly time that mother and son spent together and now here he was inviting Taylor. Her brown eyes rose to Taylor's as teal eyes studied her.

"Well, I don't know, buddy. That's kinda up to your mom."

"No, no! You come!" Andrew insisted.

Taylor arched a brow, waiting for Tessa's reaction.

"Do you really want to go to McDonald's, Taylor?" She figured that was probably the last place he would want to eat.

"Sure. If I'm invited."

"Well, consider yourself invited. We're just about through here. You?"

"I just gotta grab o.j. then I'm finished too. I can meet you at Micky D's. Are you going to the one down the street?"

"Yep. It's closest. That is where we always go."

"Okay. I'll meet you there in about ten minutes."

"Fine, okay." She leaned down to her son who still clutched Taylor's hand, not wanting to let go. "Taylor will come to McDonald's with us, Andrew. We need to finish our shopping and then we'll see Taylor there." She held out her own hand for Andrew to take it.

Reluctantly Andrew dropped his grip on Taylor and took his mommy's hand. "Taylor come?" Brown eyes looked up at her hopefully.

"Yes, honey. Taylor will come."

"Yaaaaeah!"

Tessa moved her cart down the aisle and Taylor high tailed it to the juice aisle. He wanted to get there first so he could buy the two of them lunch.

As Tessa pulled her Blazer up to the restaurant she could see Taylor's Suburban already parked there. She pulled into the vacant space next to him and turned to Andrew.

"We're here, bud. And it looks like Taylor is here already."

Andrew looked around for the tall blond man, not seeing him anywhere.

At this action, Tessa clarified for him. "He is inside, honey. We'll go in and order your special meal and Taylor will join us." Oh boy, how would this go?

Andrew was all smiles as they walked into the restaurant. Tessa held his hand and when they entered, Taylor was standing casually against the nearest wall, arms crossed over his chest. He smiled as they entered and moved toward them.

"Hey guys!"

Andrew grinned. "Taylor!"

"Yep, I'm here to have lunch with you." He turned to Tessa. "What do you guys normally get? I'm buying."

Tessa moved toward the line. "That's okay, Taylor. I can get our lunch."

Taylor gently restrained her. "Come on, Tessa. Why don't you and Andrew find seats and I'll order our lunch? Now, what does he like?"

Tessa could see he wasn't going to back down so she told him what they ordered and went to find a roomy booth. She and Andrew removed their winter coats and waited for Taylor to join them.

Soon he was back with hot steaming food. Andrew especially enjoyed the French fries and Taylor removed his jacket as Tessa distributed the food. Taylor settled across from mother and son and they all dug in. Andrew had a big smile on his face and Tessa could see having lunch with Taylor had made his day and she felt a tiny twinge of jealousy. God, where had that thought come from? She ate her lunch in silence as Andrew chattered away to Taylor. Some of his words did not make sense or were hard to understand but he told Taylor details about school, Rose and mommy.

Taylor grinned as he listened to Andrew chatter, noticing Tessa's silence. For some reason, she wasn't too happy with him. Maybe because he had intruded on a ritual? Hmmmmm...

After twenty minutes or so, they finished up and each returned to their own vehicles, heading back out to Tessa's place.

Since they both pulled up at the same time, Taylor insisted on carrying in groceries for Tessa. She again insisted she could handle it, but Taylor ignored that, grabbing most of her bags and following Andrew upstairs. Sighing, Tessa picked up the two remaining bags and carried them upstairs to her kitchen.

Taylor had placed the bags on the table and Andrew ran to the dining room, soon returning with the drawings he had made. As Taylor inspected them, praising Andrew, Tessa put away groceries. Since it was very chilly today, she intended to make a fire in the fireplace. But first she had to get rid of Taylor.

After putting everything away, she turned to the man who was standing near the kitchen table with her son.

"Well, Taylor. I'm sure you should put your own groceries away. I plan to go make a fire."

"I can do that for you, Tessa."

"No, really, I can handle that, Taylor. I do it all of the time," she said in exasperation. He acted like she was some helpless female. She had been taking care of things quite well for years. She completely forgot at the moment how helpful it had been to have Taylor around the last two and a half months. For some reason, right now, she was peeved at him and even she did not know why. She crossed her arms over her breasts, waiting for him to leave.

Taylor could tell that Tessa wanted him gone, even though Andrew was quite happy to see him. Okay, so be it.

"Okay. Yeah, good idea. I'll see ya around." Taylor disappeared through the kitchen door and descended the stairs.

"Why Taylor go?" Andrew asked.

"Mommy is going to make a fire for the two of us and then we'll read some of your favorite books. Doesn't that sound fun?"

Andrew frowned up at his mommy, then turned and marched off to his bedroom.

Tessa was totally confused by this reaction.

After Andrew spent the day moping because Taylor was not around, Tessa decided it was time to have a serious chat with Taylor. She asked Rose if she could come up and watch Andrew for a while because she planned to spend some time at Taylor's. Rose immediately acquiesced and she and Andrew played checkers and watched TV.

Tessa threw a parka on over her jeans and sweater and went over to the carriage house to ring the bell. She shivered in the cold as she waited for Taylor to answer the summons. She had to wait about five minutes and she was seriously thinking about ringing again when the door was opened by Taylor.

Tessa gulped. He wore only jeans, feet bare and his magnificent torso bare also. Changing his bandage through the fall Tessa had not received a really good look at his gorgeous body as it was bound up by bandages. Now she got a good look and she gulped. He had a perfect body, washboard abs, strong muscular pecs and arms, but he was long and lean also. His hair was slightly mussed and she surmised she might have just woke him from a nap.

Taylor shivered from the cold and could see Tessa was cold too. He motioned her in up the stairs and closed the door against the icy blasts.

She moved up his stairs, careful to take off her snowy boots at the top. Turning to him, she tried to keep her eyes off of his chest. God, he even had a tan, something one never saw in Lewiston in December but his California trips afforded him sun. Shaking off these thoughts, she looked up at him.

"I was wondering if I could speak to you about something," she began.

Silently, he waved her over to his sectional and Tessa removed her parka, sitting on the cushions. Taylor settled across from her a little ways and she waited for him to put some clothes on. Seeing him half naked was totally distracting her. However he did not, merely settling back and waiting for her to begin.

She cleared her throat and then turned to him. "I'm sorry if I woke you from a nap. Maybe you want to go put a sweater or something on—" she waved her hand casually.

"No, I'm fine," he answered.

Well I'm not, Tessa thought. In fact she was starting to feel sexually aroused and this amazed Tessa too. God, she had to get this over with and get the hell outta here.

"I wanted to speak to you about Andrew and what happened today..." she began.

He shrugged his broad shoulders and she tried not to notice how it made his muscles ripple. "What's to talk about? We had lunch, came back. Problem?" He arched a golden brow.

"Well yes, maybe. He hasn't been himself all day—" she tried to explain.

Teal eyes studied her. "What do you mean, he hasn't been himself?"

"Well, he's just been— I don't know— mopey, like the world ended when you left earlier. He's— I don't know—"

"Ever think he might care for me, Tessa? We DID spend a lot of time together recently. He's a great kid and we had some good times. He remembers that, what's wrong with that?" Taylor honestly could not see the problem.

Tessa struggled to make him understand that this behavior was totally bizarre for her son and out of character. Yes, she knew her son liked Taylor but after seeing the two of them embrace in the store she knew her son *loved* Taylor and that greatly upset her because she knew some day, some how,

Taylor would be leaving them. She tried to find the words to explain this to the man opposite her and when she turned, she saw he had moved very close to her on the sectional.

He reached out a hand to gently smooth her thick brown hair. "You worry too much, baby," he said quietly. His hand moved from her hair to her neck and he pulled her close.

Before Tessa had a chance to react Taylor's lips closed over hers, kissing her deeply, his tongue swirling and coaxing a moan from Tessa. When she tried to push him away, she felt his hard bare chest and instead rubbed her palms in small circles against his skin.

Taylor deepened the kiss as he pushed Tessa back against the cushions, lying on top of her. His big hands dove into her hair and he slanted her face up so that he could kiss her thoroughly. Finally he came up for air and looked deep into tawny eyes. "It's time," he whispered.

Tessa was still hazed out from the blistering kiss. "Time? Time for what—"

The next thing she knew Taylor was lifting her up in his arms and carrying her into his bedroom. He laid her gently on his big bed and again resumed the kisses that drove her wild even as she tried to protest.

Finally she freed her mouth and spoke. "No, Taylor! We are *not* doing this!"

"Oh yes, we are."

He took her red sweater and removed it, throwing it behind him. She was wearing a lacy white bra that showed off divine cleavage. He knew instinctively she would have lovely breasts. His lips searched the cleavage, licking and kissing gently and Tessa's head spun away. Oh God, it had been so long for her, so long. And yes, she did want to have sex with Taylor but she knew it wasn't wise. It would complicate everything.

"No, no— really, we can't—"

"Sorry. I'm tired of waiting and I think you are too," he said between soft kisses.

Abruptly he got up and drew back the satin duvet, placing her in the middle of his bed. He went to work on her jeans, removing them and revealing lacy panties that matched her bra. He quickly removed her thick socks and then started kissing her stomach. Softly, barely touching her, nipping gently.

Tessa could feel her hips buck up as she fell into sensual delirium. Tessa was a very sensual woman and Taylor knew just what to do to drive a woman mad.

Soon her bra and panties joined her clothes and she lay totally naked. Taylor took his time studying her body, running his hands gently over her skin as Tessa tossed her head from side to side, moaning.

"Oh baby. I knew you would be beautiful but you've exceeded my expectations. You are so— perfect!"

He nudged her thighs apart and his blond head descended, gently parting petal soft lips that were slick, wet and ready. Swollen for him. He leisurely ate her, taking his time, not knowing if he would ever have another opportunity to do this. She allowed him total access to her body, moaning softly. Taylor still wore his jeans. He moved up her body to give her breasts the same treatment, taking the nipples into his mouth and sipping, sucking, nipping, driving her totally mad.

Grunting, he removed his jeans and his giant penis sprang free. Tessa's eyes widened at the size of his penis nestled in blond curls. Oh my God, the man was sexy! But she had only been with Steve and he wasn't nearly as—

Tessa had no more time to ruminate as he shoved his penis into her abruptly. Tessa moaned and felt his stabbing penis stretch her vagina a bit. Her female body accommodated the large organ and she almost exploded when she felt him take his fingertip and rub at her clitoris as he slowly moved his penis in and out, fucking slowly, making it last. Tessa had an orgasm and screamed. It had been years and years since she had had one and she immediately had another.

Taylor grinned down at her, the beautiful blonde man working her body, making her see stars, making her feel things she had never felt before. Sheer paradise.

Finally, with one final grunt, he emptied himself inside her. Groaning, he moved to her side to take her into his arms, snuggling them both under the duvet.

Round two came very soon and Tessa protested that she had to get back to Andrew and Rose. Taylor ignored that, doing everything to the lovely brunette that he had spent nights dreaming about. He showed her several positions, including the back position and Tessa was going wild. This could not be happening, this was not *her*! But they rutted like animals in heat. The first time had been sensual and slow, this time was wild, wet, sweaty. The kind of sex every woman dreams of and rarely gets. Oh— my— God!

After that, no matter how much Taylor insisted, Tessa quickly dressed and practically *ran* back to her own place.

Taylor watched her go with regret but now finally maybe she would figure out that they had something together. They were great in the sack together and he was hoping she would want it again.

Sighing, he flopped over on his back and went to sleep.

CHAPTER
TWENTY SIX

TESSA SPENT THE UPCOMING week avoiding Taylor. She was so embarrassed about what had occurred at his carriage house Saturday. She had avoided Rose's questions and put Andrew to bed and had taken a very long hot shower, trying to erase the memories as she watched suds swirl down the drain. She wished she could forget everything that easily— just let the thoughts drift away into obscurity but that was impossible. She and Taylor had become lovers and it totally changed the tempo of their relationship. Maybe since he now had received what he claimed he wanted from her he would go back to LA. Her heart ached at that thought. She was doing something she told herself over and over she should never do. She was falling for Taylor. Big time. Overboard. Unquestionably. Unequivocally. She did not want to. She would get hurt and so would her son and Tessa fiercely wanted to protect Andrew from being hurt. Should she ask Taylor to leave? She recalled the embrace her son had shared with Taylor in the grocery store. It was quite apparent the two had become very close and if she asked Taylor to leave that would break Andrew's heart and she did not want to be the one responsible for that. If Taylor left on his own that would be one less thing to feel guilt over.

Sighing, Tessa wrapped herself in her robe and curled up in a fetal position on her bed. She didn't know what to do about Taylor and so for now she would simply do nothing. Avoid him, pretend he didn't exist.

Taylor spent his days finishing up the motorcycle in the garage. He could see it would only take about another week for the bike to be ready to be sent back to LA to be detailed. December had arrived and it was snowy and cold.

Frigid blasts of wind rattled the windows outside of the garage as the snow was swirled around by gusts. Taylor always dressed warmly and he had the space heater always going full blast but he still shivered. He was not used to this Arctic weather. LA would be sunny and warm right about now and he knew he could leave anytime his bike was ready to be shipped back.

Leave. He contemplated that thought. That meant he would be leaving behind three people (especially two) that he had very deep strong feelings for. Taylor was not quite sure what those feelings were, he had not sorted it out all yet. But he knew leaving would put a hole in his life and he was not yet ready to leave. He and Tessa still had some unfinished business and she was a phenomenal sexual partner and he could not wait to have sex with her again. But the way she had been avoiding him, he was unsure at this point what would happen. Christmas was coming up very soon too, within weeks.

Taylor went Christmas shopping for the small family he now felt a part of. He did not know if he would be here for the holiday or if Tessa would kick him out before then but he intended to at least leave gifts for them. It was the least he could do.

Tessa and Rose prepared for Christmas in the usual manner with some help from Andrew. They strung white lights on the evergreens growing along the drive and also added white lights to Rose's porch. A big evergreen wreath adorned with a huge red bow hung from the door. Tessa helped Rose assemble her Christmas tree and the three of them decorated it. Tessa always went the natural route, buying a real tree. It was a real pain to clean up afterwards but she loved the piney smell and Andrew loved to go look at trees on the lots. Tessa also decorated her flat putting pine boughs interspersed with lights on her fireplace mantel and adding holiday candles and decorations all around. Andrew always got so excited at this time of year and Tessa read him a Christmas story every evening leading up to the big night. His belief that Santa Claus would be bringing him presents kept the holiday magical for Tessa. When she was a child, Christmases were rarely celebrated, if at all. So she loved to go all out for her son.

As they were baking cookies one Saturday afternoon, Tessa heard the downstairs buzzer and knew it was Taylor. Rose would just come upstairs. She sighed. She had not seen him in two weeks and that was the way she wanted to keep it.

"Andrew, can you go into the living room and find mommy the special spoon I need? I think I left it in there somewhere." She knew the spoon was right in the drawer where it belonged but it would keep Andrew occupied as she spoke to Taylor.

Andrew happily went on his quest and Tessa descended the stairs to open the door to Taylor. It was snowing lightly and white droplets clung to his blond hair. He was wearing his black parka and jeans. He shook his hair out a bit, looking down at her.

"Hi," he addressed her. "I'd like to talk to you about something."

Tessa crossed her arms over her breasts. "Yes?"

Taylor arched a brow. "Can we do it inside? It is kinda cold out here."

"Okay. But this better be quick. Andrew and I are a bit occupied in the kitchen."

She motioned him to follow her up the stairs as Taylor stamped snow from his boots. He entered her kitchen and could smell the delicious aroma of cookies baking. He noticed Christmas decorations and red bows on the cupboards and smiled. He hoped she had not put her tree up yet. He could see Andrew was not in the kitchen at the moment.

Tessa went to her oven and removed a sheet of what looked like chocolate chip cookies. He could see some already cooling on wire racks on the counter. She wore a red sweater adorned with beads shaped into a rose across her breasts and jeans. He quickly looked away from her breasts, not wanting to be caught ogling her chest.

She was silent, obviously waiting for him to begin. She did not invite him to sit and she did not offer him a cookie. Okay. Get to the point, Taylor.

"I was wondering if you have your Christmas tree up yet, Tessa."

Tessa turned to the man behind her, totally flabbergasted by this question. This was the last thing she expected him to discuss. Tawny eyes chased to teal. "No, not yet. Everything else is up and as you can see we are baking cookies. I usually save the tree for last."

Taylor shoved his hands in his pockets and studied her. "I was wondering if you would let me take Andrew to a Christmas farm nearby and cut a tree down for you guys. I thought it might be a fun outing for him."

To Tessa's dismay, Andrew chose that moment to enter the kitchen. "No spoon," he reported. Then he noticed Taylor's presence and his whole face lit up. He had not seen Taylor for a while. "Taylor!"

He ran to the tall man to give him a hug and Taylor chuckled and lifted him, squeezing him tightly. "Hey, bud! How are you? Merry Christmas!"

He placed the boy back down as Andrew smiled up at him. "Santa Claus! Toys!" The beautiful brown eyes, so much like Tessa's, smiled up at him and Taylor's heart ached.

"I can see you are looking forward to the big night, Christmas Eve. Where does Santa Claus come down from?" Taylor arched a brow, waiting to see if Andrew could answer this question.

Andrew frowned for a moment, then remembered a Christmas story his mommy had read. "Fire?" He pointed toward the living room.

Taylor grinned. "High five, buddy! Down the chimney! You got it!"

Andrew fived him back and then pointed to the cookies. "Taylor, cookie?" he offered.

Taylor's eyes rose to Tessa's and he could see she was not pleased by his presence. He did not want to piss her off because he wanted her to agree to his request. "I don't know, buddy. Let's ask mom."

Andrew turned eagerly to his mother and Tessa addressed her son. "Yes, Andrew. You may give Taylor a cookie. Then can you go watch some TV? I need to talk to Taylor."

The little boy frowned at that but he scooped up a big cookie, offering it to Taylor with a huge smile. Taylor stooped down to Andrew's level to accept it and to look directly into Andrew's eyes. "Thank you, Andrew. I bet it is the best one of them all!" Taylor took a big bite to emphasize his point.

Giggling, Andrew left them for the front room.

Taylor stood to full height, looking over at Tessa as he munched the cookie. "So? What do you think of my request?"

Tessa leaned back against a counter, crossing her arms. "Well, Taylor. That is one of our many Christmas rituals together. Andrew and I go shop for a tree on the lots and he loves to do that. It is a special thing he and I do together at the holiday."

"Well, you're invited too, if you'd like to come along."

"No, I think he would really prefer to purchase a tree with me. Not traipse through woods in the snow and cold with you to get a tree."

Andrew piped up. Neither of the adults had noticed he had returned from the living room. "Get tree, Taylor!" he insisted, frowning up at his mommy.

Tessa was totally taken aback. This was the first time Andrew had ever argued or disagreed with anything his mommy suggested and Tessa was upset and felt tears prick her eyes.

Taylor immediately saw that he was causing tension between mother and son. Looking over at Tessa, he could see she was practically in tears. Turning to the boy, Taylor spoke. "Maybe it would be more fun for you to go with your mommy, Andrew. I know you like to do that every year. You have fun doing that."

"No, Taylor! Go you!" Andrew was not aware he was upsetting his mother by this insistence.

Before things could get really out of hand, Tessa spoke. "That is fine, Andrew. You and Taylor can go chop down a special tree for us. I think it will be just as much fun for you to do that too." She wiped her tears away, hoping nobody had noticed them.

"Hooray!" Andrew shouted, disappearing into the other room.

Taylor turned back reluctantly to the woman behind him. "Look, I'm sorry. I didn't mean to cause a problem."

Tessa turned back to her cookies, using a spatula to remove them from the baking sheet. "It's not a problem," she said off handedly.

Taylor approached her from behind, putting his arms around her and pulling her against his body. Her shoulders were shaking and he could see she was crying. "Sssssh. Sssh, baby. It's okay. He didn't mean to hurt you. You know that."

She turned to him and cried silently, weeping on his chest. Finally she pushed away, wiping at her tears. "I know."

"Please come with us, I would really like you to and Andrew would too," he entreated.

Tessa's beautiful brown eyes looked up into his face. "No, Taylor. You are right. He needs to be with you and have some Christmas memories with you. It was selfish of me to deny him that. I will stay here and when you return, we can all decorate the tree together. He would love that."

"Tess, baby. I'm so sorry I upset you. Christ— I—"

"Forget it, Taylor. When do you want to do this?"

"Tomorrow is Sunday. I thought that would be a good day. Okay with you?"

"Yep. I'll have him ready to go. What— ten or so in the morning?"

"Yeah, that would work. The farm isn't that far away and we should be able to find a tree fairly quickly. I don't want him to freeze to death and I don't want to either!"

Tessa turned back to her baking. "Fine. I'll make sure he is ready."

It was quite apparent he was dismissed. He stood for a few more minutes watching her, wondering what to say, but the words would not come. He was not in the habit of consoling women and felt at a complete loss.

Finally he turned to go, feeling both sad but also happy that she had agreed to the outing.

Sunday morning arrived and Taylor picked up Andrew at the back door. Tessa was with him but said little to Taylor. She had him bundled up in his winter parka with a red knit hat and his hood over the hat, warm winter boots, scarf and thermal gloves. Taylor was dressed in a similar manner with his black winter coat and sturdy black boots. It was snowing lightly but it was in the low thirties, so it wasn't too cold. Tessa gave her son kisses and then stood to look at Taylor.

"We should be back soon. I'd estimate an hour or so. Okay if I take him to lunch at Micky D's too?"

Andrew danced in place at this news and Tessa acquiesced.

"Okay. We'll be back soon. Say goodbye to your mommy, Andrew," Taylor instructed him.

Andrew waved a gloved hand. "Bye, mommy! Bye!"

Tessa waved goodbye as she watched Taylor put her son's seat belt on. Then he carefully backed his SUV down the driveway. Sighing, Tessa closed the door.

Taylor and Andrew enjoyed themselves stomping through snow between carefully planted columns of evergreens. They even had a snow fight, giggling and playing. Taylor felt like a kid again and it was a good feeling.

Finally they found a tree they both agreed would be perfect. Taylor took out his saw and instructed Andrew to keep at a safe distance. The boy obeyed him and watched intently as Taylor sawed down the evergreen. It was about seven feet high and should be just about the perfect size for Tessa's front room.

As the tree fell to the ground, Andrew giggled with delight, coming over to softly touch the needles with his glove. "Christmas tree!" he screamed in delight.

"Yep, buddy. Now I gotta drag this baby back to my car and rope it to the roof. Then lunch time. Us hard working men deserve good fast food at Micky D's, don't ya think?" Taylor glanced down at the little boy who followed him by his side.

Andrew looked up at Taylor with adoration in his brown eyes and Taylor had never seen anyone look at him like that in his life, not even Tessa. Oh God, what was he going to do? He loved this little kid.

"Yes! Micky D's!"

Taylor roped the tree to the roof of the Suburban then it was off to McDonald's for lunch.

Andrew and Taylor returned to Tessa's several hours later, Christmas tree in tow. Andrew ran into the house to tell his mother the good news as Taylor wrestled with unroping the tree. He finally accomplished that as

Tessa appeared in the doorway with Andrew. Today she was wearing an emerald green cashmere sweater and taupe corduroy jeans. She helped Taylor maneuver the tree up the stairs as Andrew waited breathlessly at the top. He was so excited he was dancing.

Finally Taylor had the tree moved into the front room where Tessa already had the stand ready. The tree was to be placed in front of the outside porch French doors.

Taylor securely fastened the tree in the stand and stood back. It looked perfect where it was and he was very satisfied.

"Decorate!" Andrew chirped.

Looking around on tables and chairs, Taylor could see Tessa had lights out and various Christmas decorations, as well as a star for the top.

Turning to her, Taylor arched a brow. "Would you like me to do the star and then the lights?"

"Sure Taylor. That would be good," she was rummaging in boxes as she spoke, her back to him.

Sighing, Taylor removed his parka and went to work. Soon the star was twinkling at the top and the multi colored lights decorated the beautiful evergreen. The two of them had chosen well. The tree was full and nicely shaped and once decorations were added it would be absolutely stunning.

Taylor wiped his hands together, reaching for his parka. "Well, now that that's done, I'll leave the rest to you two." He donned his parka as Tessa turned to him.

"You're not going to help finish decorating?" She arched a dark brow.

"Nope. I think you and Andrew can handle that." Taylor wanted Tessa to have this special time with her son today. He knew she had really missed getting the tree with her son and he wanted her to have the joy of doing the fun part with just Andrew.

Tessa studied him for a moment. "I see," she finally said. "Well, thank you for taking Andrew today. I know he had a terrific time."

Andrew was ignoring them as he placed ornaments on the tree.

"Yep. He did. We both did. Thank *you* for letting me take him. No matter what happens in the future, it is a memory I will always treasure. Goodbye, Tessa."

Taylor moved into the kitchen and down the stairs and Tessa turned to the tree to help decorate it, wondering about the movie star and whether he would be around for Christmas or not. She intended to take Andrew Christmas shopping so he could purchase gifts for Taylor, Rose and his teacher.

The tree was lovely and she spent an enjoyable day decorating and spending time with her son.

CHAPTER
TWENTY SEVEN

TESSA TOOK ANDREW CHRISTMAS shopping at a local mall. The large shopping center was decorated for the holiday with twinkling stars hung from the ceiling and holiday trees and poinsettias placed about. It was beautiful and Macy's had a big animated Christmas display Andrew loved to watch. Tessa always brought her camera and took photos of her son in front of the displays and decorations. She always took a special photo and framed it every Christmas. This would be her sixth framed picture to add to her collection. Andrew was quite excited visiting all of the stores.

Andrew usually always picked out his gifts for others with help from his mommy. This year he was doing quite well, actually finding items on his own and pointing to them. He found a crystal vase decorated with blue roses and pointed to it. "Mrs. H," he remarked, looking back at his mommy. "Mrs. C," he said, referring to his teacher, pointing to a tote that had "Teacher" inscribed across it. He looked long and hard for his mommy and finally pointed to a soft blue sweater. Smiling, he rubbed his hand over the smooth material. "Mommy?" he asked, unsure.

Tessa leaned down to hug her son. "It's beautiful, Andrew! I love it!"

Andrew also picked out candy for her and several other smaller gifts. The presents Tessa really loved were the ones he made for her at school. He had made several ornaments and they were all hung on their tree every year.

Finally Andrew turned to his mother with a question. "Taylor?"

That was a conundrum. Tessa had no idea what Taylor would like. They walked around for a bit and finally found a country/western store. The place sold cowboy boots, all kinds of leather belts and western shirts. Andrew pulled his mommy into the store and wonder of wonders, he pointed at a beautiful black Stetson hat. "Taylor?"

Tessa picked it up to inspect it. It was the real mc-coy, a black Stetson shaped as she recalled all of the country stars wore them. It had one thin leather band around the cropped crown and Tessa knew instinctively it would look great on Taylor with his blond hair. Looking at the price, she gulped a bit. It was one hundred dollars but Tessa decided to splurge and get it. Andrew had actually picked it out himself and that would mean a lot to Taylor.

Andrew proudly carried the hat to the counter and the older man sitting by the cash register smiled down at the little boy.

"You've chosen well, son. That is a beautiful Stetson! Got one myself, only grey." He took the hat and started ringing it up as Tessa got out her charge card (again!).

Andrew smiled at the man. "For Taylor," he informed him.

"Taylor, huh? That sounds like a good southern name," the man remarked.

Tessa smiled as she handed him her card. "Yes. Taylor is from Texas. So this should be a very appropriate gift."

The man's brows arched. "From Texas, you say? Well for such a fine customer, I must make sure the hat is perfectly shaped." He took the Stetson and placed it on a weird machine that Tessa had never seen in her life. He worked and fussed with the hat as the machine whirred a bit. It wasn't loud enough to bother Andrew and soon he came back to show off the Stetson to the two of them. Tessa could now see the shape was more sharply pointed and curved and would fit perfectly.

She smiled. "Thank you very much. I've never seen that process before."

He smiled back as he placed it in a box with tissue tucked around it. "I'm from Texas myself originally and this is how we Texans wear them. Glad to be of service, ma'm. Hope your man likes his Stetson." He handed her the bag containing the hat which Tessa gave to Andrew so he could proudly carry Taylor's present.

They left the store but the man's words kept ringing in Tessa's ears. "Your man..."

Tessa and Andrew wrapped gifts together as Christmas carols softly played in the background. Christmas was only a few days away and she thought about how to approach Taylor to invite him for Christmas. She planned to spend Christmas Eve with Andrew; that was a tradition. They would put out cookies and milk for Santa, Tessa would build a fire and read several Christmas stories to her son, then she would tuck him in bed, telling him to make sure to sleep tight so Santa could bring him presents. Andrew usually complied. When Tessa checked an hour or so later, Andrew was asleep. Tessa assumed her Santa Claus duties, placing all of the gifts under the tree. Rose always came up Christmas morning and she and Tessa prepared Christmas dinner after presents were opened. Tessa was unsure how to approach Taylor about Christmas.

Christmas Eve arrived and Tessa finally tucked Andrew in bed about eight thirty. She decided to treat herself to a glass of wine as she watched the fire before placing the gifts out. Tessa had found a beautiful cashmere sweater for Taylor and a silk teal shirt that would look great on him. She also bought him a navy velour bathrobe. She had not purchased gifts for a man in a long time and was not quite sure what to get him. She figured everyone could use clothes.

As she settled into the cushions of her sofa with her wine, she heard the downstairs buzzer. She was puzzled. She knew Rose would not be coming up until tomorrow. Taylor perhaps?

Warily she descended the stairs and looked out the back door window. Taylor stood on the steps, snow lightly showering down on him.

She unlocked the door and stepped back a bit. "Taylor?"

"Hi. Are you doing anything?" he asked.

"No. Just relaxing a bit. I just put Andrew into bed. Why? What's up?" She motioned him into the hallway out of the cold and he complied, stepping in.

He looked down at her. "It's Christmas Eve and I'm lonely. Want some company?"

Tessa's heart turned over. No one should be alone on Christmas Eve. She smiled. "Come in. I was just having a glass of wine in front of the fire. You can join me."

He grinned. "That sounds great."

He followed her up the stairs and removed his snowy boots at the top. Tessa went to get another wine glass and poured him a glass of Merlot.

She handed it to him, taking in his appearance. As usual he looked gorgeous without even trying. He was dressed in black cords and a black turtleneck. She knew he preferred black clothes and they always looked marvelous on him.

She led the way into her living room and Taylor could see the fire needed a bit of attention. Placing his glass down on her cocktail table, he went to the fire to poke it and add several logs. It blazed up pleasantly and crackled and popped. Taylor closed the doors and joined Tessa on the sofa, picking up his wine glass.

"Merry Christmas, Tessa," he clinked his glass against hers.

"Merry Christmas to you too, Taylor."

"The little guy is asleep?"

Tessa tucked her jean clad legs underneath her as she settled back into the cushions. "Yep. About a half hour ago he went. In another hour or so, I'll have to play Santa and put the gifts under the tree." She paused. "Speaking of Christmas, what are your plans for tomorrow?" Now that he was here it was a perfect opportunity to ask him to come for the holiday.

He shrugged. "No plans, really. I do have some presents for you guys I'd like to bring by at some point."

"Well, I was going to invite you over for Christmas. Ya know, for gifts and dinner and such. If you come over around noon, that would be good. Andrew will already have opened all of his gifts from Santa and Rose and we'll be starting on cooking dinner. That way, you can spend some time with Andrew and have dinner with us if you'd like."

Taylor grinned. "That sounds great, Tessa. Thank you for inviting me."

Tessa's brown eyes moved to Taylor's. "Andrew will love to see you. It will make the holiday complete for him. He did buy you a special present he picked out all on his own," she informed the man across from her.

Taylor's blond brows rose. "Really? He picked it out all by himself?"

"Yep. As soon as he saw it, he pointed to it and said your name." She sipped at her wine, contemplating Taylor. How did he usually spend Christmas? With a girlfriend? She had no idea and of course it wasn't her business.

There was a pause in the conversation and Tessa decided to fill the silence. "Have you made any decisions on the scripts you've read?"

Taylor sighed, closing his eyes for a moment. "Yeah, I got it narrowed down to one or two. Going to spend some time over the New Year reading and deciding. I sent my bike back west. All repairs have been completed so it just now needs things like a good paint job and stuff like that."

Tessa was surprised by this news. "I didn't know you sent it back. I didn't see anyone here to pick it up."

Taylor met her eyes. "They came by one day when you were at work about mid day last week. They had to crate it up pretty good and strap it down so it wouldn't get bounced around on the trip back."

"Were they driving it in a truck or something?"

"No, no. It will be flown back." Taylor sipped at his wine. He was enjoying himself. Quiet conversation, a cozy fire and a beautiful woman to spend Christmas Eve with. What could be better? He was really looking forward to seeing Andrew tomorrow too. He had bought him many special gifts that he hoped he liked. He had also been extravagant with Tessa and he already knew she would object but since it was Christmas she could not give it back.

Taylor helped Tessa bring out gifts and place them around the tree.

He munched a few cookies and drank a bit of the milk, playing Santa for Andrew.

Afterwards he prepared to leave, assuring Tessa he would be by around noon on Christmas day.

Sighing, Tessa closed the back door and locked it. She moved back upstairs to close the doors of the fireplace and ruminated about the man that had just left. Taylor was an enigma she still had not figured out. She was glad he was coming over for Christmas for her son's sake. She tried to ignore her own happiness that he would be here to share the holiday with them.

As she moved to her bedroom, turning off lights, she reminded herself for the umpteenth time that someday he would be gone.

CHAPTER
TWENTY EIGHT

CHRISTMAS DAY DAWNED AND there was complete pandemonium in the Patterson household. Rose always came up early to make sure she was there to see Andrew open his gifts and also to give her gifts to the Pattersons. Christmas wrapping paper flew as Andrew opened his many presents. Carols played softly in the background, the beautiful tree was lit and Tessa had a fire going. Both women were still in their warm robes and Andrew was wearing flannel Barney pj's. Tessa always went all out at Christmas (her card was maxed out for months but she didn't care). He received many Barney toys, Disney DVDs, some stuffed dinosaurs and also many other toys to address sensory needs. Rose bought him toys she knew he liked too and Andrew had a wonderful time playing with his many gifts on the floor as Rose and Tessa exchanged gifts. It was a merry and happy time for them all and Tessa was so thankful to have her loved ones close by for the holiday.

There was a little pile of presents waiting for Taylor when he would be by around noon. Tessa made sure Andrew and she were showered up and dressed by then. Rose went down to her place for the same purpose and returned shortly before noon.

She helped Tessa prepare the ham for dinner and make special peach glaze for it. Both women were chatting and in the process of preparing the meal in the kitchen. Andrew was eagerly awaiting Taylor's arrival, watching a new Barney DVD in the living room.

Suddenly both women looked up as they heard a loud and hearty "Ho, ho, ho!" from the doorway.

Santa stood in the doorway, a tall Santa, carrying a sack over his shoulder and patting his padded belly. Blue eyes twinkled down at the women.

"Taylor?" Tessa asked in a low voice.

Santa looked around. "Don't see no Taylor here. I'm Santa Claus and I have come to visit a special little boy named Andrew Patterson. Santa forgot to drop off some gifts last night. Where is the little guy?" Santa looked around as he spoke.

Tessa wiped her hands on a kitchen towel, approaching 'Santa.' Looking into the features, she could clearly see now it was Taylor. But how had he changed the color of his eyes? Then it hit her. Contacts, of course. He was wearing colored contacts so his teal eyes would not give him away. Smart, Tessa decided.

"Well, Santa, Andrew is in the front room. Let me show you," she proceeded to the front room with Santa behind her and Rose following, chuckling.

"Ho, ho, ho!" Santa boomed again, making his belly shake, looking around the apartment. "I'm looking for a boy named Andrew— yep! There he is!" Santa declared, moving over to the little boy who had jumped up as Santa entered.

Andrew's eyes were wide as saucers as he looked up and gulped. He knew Santa had already visited him and he had never had a special visit. He was clearly bewildered.

Santa leaned down to Andrew, the twinkling blue eyes looking directly into Andrew's. "Do you know why I am here, Andrew Patterson?"

Andrew shook his head in a negative gesture.

"Why, to give you presents I forgot to leave last night! Rudolph was getting antsy, something about his nose not blinking right. But I remembered I had more presents for a special little boy named Andrew." Santa removed the sack from his shoulder. "Okay, let's see what we have here." Santa rummaged in his pack as Tessa and Rose took in all of this action, smiling.

"Hmmm...yes, this is for Andrew, and this one," Santa unloaded about a dozen presents placing them next to Andrew on the floor. Then Santa turned to the ladies. "And oh look, Santa even remembered someone named 'Tessa' and 'Rose'." He took two gaily wrapped presents out and gave them to the two women, who graciously thanked Santa.

Santa stood to full height. "Well, my work here is done." He patted Andrew on the head. "You be a good boy Andrew and Santa will see you next year. Ho, ho, ho! Merry Christmas!" He waved a white gloved hand and ho ho hoed all the way out of the door.

The first thing Andrew said was "Fire?" and pointed to the fireplace. He expected Santa to come from that direction.

Tessa quickly gave an explanation. "Santa could not come down the chimney sweetheart because we have a fire going in there. See the fire? That would hurt Santa. At night there is no fire." She paused. "Open your gifts from Santa, sweetheart."

"Did someone say Santa was here?" Taylor entered the room. He wore dark green cords with a teal patterned sweater and his blond hair waved down his neck. He looked luscious in Tessa's opinion.

"Taylor!" Andrew ran to him to throw his arms around him. "Santa was here! Santa! Here!" He pointed to all of the gifts Santa had left them.

"Wow! Way cool, buddy. I say let's see you open them!"

Andrew tore into the wrappings and Santa had brought him a beautiful Brio train set complete with the table and all of the extra components for Andrew to set it up in his room. Also included were Christmas books, Christmas squishy figurines and a very large box containing a totally assembled new bicycle, slightly larger than the one he had. Andrew was dancing in joy, showing all his toys off to Taylor.

"I do have to confess the bicycle is from me, buddy. I snuck it in when Santa wasn't looking," Taylor said.

He was sitting on the floor with Andrew. The boy jumped up and gave him a huge hug, a wide smile on his face and Tessa's heart flipped over as she watched them embrace.

Finally Taylor turned to the ladies. "Your turn, ladies. Santa brought you gifts too, right?"

Smiling, Tessa and Rose went to the sofa and opened their gifts.

Rose gasped when she saw what Taylor had purchased for her. It was a black velvet cloche with a gleaming diamond brooch pinned to it. The diamonds were shaped into a floral design and flashed and gleamed. Rose looked up at Taylor, eyes wide. "Oh Taylor, I mean Santa— I—" she was overwhelmed and could not say anything further. She placed the cloche on her hair and modeled it for them, striking a saucy pose. Taylor and Tessa laughed as Andrew clapped, smiling.

"Prettee, preteee!" he exclaimed.

Tessa carefully unwrapped her present. A royal blue velvet box was displayed and glancing warily up at Taylor, who just grinned back, she opened the box and her brown eyes widened. On a bed of blue velvet rested the most beautiful pearl necklace and earring set she had ever seen. The pearls were long and lustrous and interspersed with golden strands, twisted into the pearls to gleam and spark. The earrings matched perfectly, pearl drops with golden strands twisted throughout. It was a very unusual combination and the set was just stunning. Tessa had always loved pearls so he chose the perfect gift for her.

"Santa?" Andrew asked, looking at the gift.

"No, honey. Taylor snuck gifts for Rose and I in Santa's sack too. This is from Taylor." Andrew swung his gaze to Taylor and smiled hugely.

Tessa closed the box gently and approached Taylor. "Thank you," she whispered, kissing his cheek. "They are just beautiful. But you shouldn't have—"

Taylor held up a hand. "It's Christmas and I wanted to. Please just accept them."

Tessa wiped a small tear away, nodding. She placed the velvet box with her other gifts.

"I must say, you have excellent taste, Taylor," Rose remarked. She had not removed her cloche, preferring to wear it for now. She was wearing a black dress with lace on the bodice and the cloche matched her outfit perfectly.

"Nothing is too good for my two ladies. Or my little lad. Come on, bud," he said to Andrew. "Let's put that train set together while mommy and Mrs. H make dinner."

"Yaaaah!" Andrew went to get the box and Taylor helped him open it as the women moved out of the room.

After they all enjoyed a delicious Christmas ham dinner, they retired to the front room where Andrew could not wait for Taylor to open his gifts. He had not had a chance to get to them because he had spent the afternoon assembling the train set and then showing Andrew how to play with the various pieces and how they fit together.

Taylor stoked the fire a bit and smiled as he settled into a comfortable wing chair near the fire and Andrew handed him a fairly large square wrapped present. "From me," the little boy said proudly.

Taylor shook the box, placing it close to his ear, pretending he was trying to guess what it was, eyes squinted a bit. "Hmmmmm…got me stumped, buddy."

"Open, open!" Andrew insisted.

Taylor did so, opening the box to see tissue paper nestled around. He recalled Tessa saying Andrew had picked out his gift all by himself and Taylor totally did not know what to expect. When he removed the tissue paper, he let out a genuine gasp of surprise. A beautiful black Stetson was nestled in the tissue and as Taylor lifted it out, he could see it was the genuine article, it could have been made in Texas. Taylor had several of his own, but not one this special or this color. He was so touched that Andrew had picked such a perfect gift for him. He placed it on his head, adjusting the crown to just the right angle and looked down at Andrew. "Well, pardner, ya done real good.

This is the best rootinest tootinest cowboy hat here in the east! C'mere!" He grabbed Andrew and gave him a big hug and a kiss on the cheek. Andrew giggled, snuggling in Taylor's lap.

"You like?"

"No, I love! I love it, bud! You are the best!"

Andrew was all smiles, so happy he could please Taylor and Tessa was so proud of her son. What a kind heart he had. This was the happiest she had seen him all day, even though he had thoroughly enjoyed opening all of his gifts this morning. She was so happy she had decided to invite Taylor. He really had made Christmas special for them all.

Tessa and Rose offered Taylor their gifts and he opened them, particularly taken with the soft velour robe Tessa had bought him. "Oh man, this is nice. It will keep me warm this winter. I don't have one. Thanks!" Teal eyes looked up at Tessa and he came over to kiss her cheek.

She blushed as he opened his gifts from Rose. She had bought him a motorcycle helmet that was black with blazing turquoise, azure and white stars streaking across it. It was unusual and very nice. "To keep you safe," she said simply.

Taylor smiled wistfully, coming over to kiss her also. "Thank you, Rose. I now have reasons to stay safe."

He tucked his gifts away in a corner as they all conversed, the adults enjoying a libation as Andrew played with his train. Taylor did not remove the Stetson, wearing it for the remainder of the evening.

Finally at nine o'clock Rose declared herself tired. Taylor offered to help her carry her gifts downstairs as Tessa got Andrew ready for bed.

When he returned upstairs, she still was not in the living room. He attended to the fire a bit and poured himself another glass of wine, then topped off Tessa's.

He settled on the sofa with his wine to watch the sparkling lights on the tree and the flames in the fire. Finally he heard her coming down the hallway and smiled, offering her the glass of wine.

Tessa accepted it, sitting next to him on the sofa. She was wearing a dark burgundy velour pant set and sighing she removed her low black heels. She wore gold hoops in her ears that caught the lights from the tree and the glow from the fire and refracted it back. In fact, he thought she was glowing just looking at her. She seemed happy and relaxed and he hoped he had had something to do with that.

"How long does it take him to go to sleep?" he asked, one finger reaching out to play with a brunette strand dangling on her shoulder.

She smiled, sipping her wine. "Why? Are you feeling playful tonight?" She tossed her head, making her beautiful hair fly a bit.

"Uhhmmm hmmmm. You?"

She moved over closer to him on the sofa, snuggling next to him. "My son had a wonderful Christmas because of you. Thank you."

"And you? Did you have a wonderful holiday?"

"Yes I did and so did Rose. You made us all very happy today. It is a Christmas none of us will ever forget. And that was a very cool idea being Santa for Andrew."

"Hey, I'm an actor. I like to act. This time I did it for a good purpose instead of a selfish purpose." He continued to play with her hair softly.

She pulled back a bit. "What do you mean it is usually for a selfish reason? You're an actor, that's what you do. Why is that selfish?"

Taylor sighed. "Because I get paid big bucks for something I like to do anyway. When I first became an actor, that was great to me. As you know, I came from a poor background so when the money started rolling in, man that was great! Now," he shrugged, "not so much."

"Taylor, are you telling me you are tired of acting? You *love* to act!" Tessa sipped her wine, brown eyes studying him carefully.

Taylor shrugged. "Yeah, I still like to act and all of that but my perspective or reasons for doing it have changed. Before it was for the money. Now it is more for the artistic end of it. Movies are fascinating and fun to make. But you also have to make a commitment of several months of your life each time. As a single young guy, yeah okay fine. Now," he met her eyes, "I don't know. I still want to act, but I'm torn. It's hard to explain."

Tessa took in this information and was truly surprised by what he said. If he was in conflict about his acting career, what did that mean for them? And after the wonderful day they had had today, she did not want Taylor to leave, ever. She could now finally admit that. Well, take what you can while you can, Tessa.

"About that playing around comment..." she let her words dwindle off.

"Yeah?"

She met his eyes. "I'm ready if you are," she smiled saucily.

Taylor grinned. "Just tell me where the bedroom is, darlin'."

Smiling, Tessa rose, leading him down the hallway to her bedroom.

And it was a Merry Christmas for all.

Chapter
TWENTY NINE

"Hi ya, Frank! How was your New Year?"

Taylor was calling his agent as he relaxed on his sectional, watching snow lazily fall past his windows. January had arrived and it was usually snowy and very, very cold. Cold to the marrow of your bones cold. Taylor admitted he did miss sunny California but he knew if he left he would miss Tessa and Andrew more.

"Hey, Taylor! Wondered when I would hear from you! My New Year was okay, I guess. Had to go to the regular Hollywood bashes for clients and such. Lila always enjoys it. She's been asking about you and why you're not around."

"What did you tell her?"

"I told her you left us for the east coast and I'm not sure if you're coming back. It broke her heart, it did," Frank teased.

Taylor chuckled. "Tell Lila my favorite girl will get lots of hugs and kisses when I return. Which I am planning early spring, I think. I've decided to do the Weinberg project," Taylor informed his agent.

"Good choice! Can I let him know now, or do you want to wait for the formal process of paperwork? I know they want to sign you as soon as possible to re-write scripting."

"I dunno yet. Let me think on that one."

"Taylor—" Frank was exasperated again. "Ya gotta make up your mind and let Stan know what you're doing. How much do you want to film the movie anyway? I also have to negotiate your salary."

"What did I get paid for the last flick?"

"Thirty five mil, but I gotta tell you. I have it on good authority Clooney got more than that for the "Ocean" series and you are bigger box office. You can easily get fifty mil from Weinberg, in my opinion."

"Okay. Let's not get too greedy. Tell him forty five mil for the new pic. If that is not acceptable, I'll pass."

"It will be acceptable. He wants you for his new flick."

"Who is the female co-star?" Taylor was curious.

He could hear Frank flipping pages. "They are looking at Jennifer Garner, Angelina Jolie or possibly an actress of your choosing."

"Scratch Angie. Don't want to work with her."

"Oh? Why is that?" Frank sounded surprised.

"I have my reasons. Again, tell Stan I am considering everything and will make a final decision real soon."

"Okay, Taylor but it would be best to get your butt back here. I have no idea why you would want to be on the east coast in January. She must really be something."

"She is, Frank. She is."

Tessa resumed her duties at the hospital after the holiday break. Andrew was also now back in school and winter had hit Lewiston with a vengeance. It snowed just about every day, lightly but the inches still added up. Thank God Taylor had hired a company to come out to dig them out. They usually showed up in the evening and cleared the driveways and pathways. Every morning when she went to work the snow was magically cleared and she did not even need to shovel. She could get used to that.

She smiled at her thoughts. She was at the nurse's station at her desk working on some charts. Miraculously they were not too busy in the ICU right now and she had more time on her hands than usual. She finished up her paperwork and turned to the nurse next to her, who had just exclaimed in surprise.

Tessa turned in her seat. "What is it, Lois?"

The other nurse was holding a copy of a magazine. "Well, as I live and breathe, Taylor Boudrain is on the cover of *People* magazine with some hot blonde chick. Title on cover: Are they back together again?" Lois flipped to the appropriate page, grinning as Tessa's heart raced.

What?? What was this all about?

"Lois, do you mind if I take a look?"

Grinning, the nurse handed the magazine over as she reached to answer her phone.

Accepting the magazine, Tessa turned back to her station to inspect the cover. Yep, sure enough there was Taylor, glorious blond locks waved by the wind, sunglasses on, holding hands with an actress named Marisa Maloy. Tessa had no idea who that was and quickly went to the story. There wasn't much there. Just a brief story saying the two had been spotted having dinner in LA and speculation if the hot couple were back together. Tessa mentally calculated when the photo was taken from the information in the magazine which claimed it was shot around the last time Taylor had been in California.

Tessa threw the magazine down on the desk, feeling sick to her stomach and very disgusted with herself. While she was having sex with him, he apparently was getting it on the west coast too. Clever Taylor, tell Tessa a few lies about going back west for business and she had swallowed it, naïve as she was. Marisa looked just like his type, a busty beautiful blonde who also was an actress. They did make a glorious looking couple but Tessa could feel her heart breaking into tiny pieces.

Buck up, Tessa. You need to keep your mind on the job. Your patients need you and you don't have time to waste feeling sorry for yourself.

She definitely intended to speak to Taylor about this incident tonight. She felt like an utter fool and did not like the feeling one bit.

After dinner, Tessa took Andrew down to Rose's flat and asked her to keep an eye on Andrew because she needed to go over to Taylor's. Rose smiled at this, very happy that Tessa and Taylor seemed to be getting closer, especially after the holidays.

Tessa left Andrew and Rose in the front living room watching TV as she put on her parka and braved the icy blasts to ring the doorbell to the carriage house. In a few minutes she could hear Taylor descending the stairs and he opened the door to her. He was dressed as usual in faded Levis and a warm black sweater, thick socks on his feet. His blond hair was a bit disheveled and she tried to keep her eyes off of his gorgeous face.

"Tessa!" He ushered her in out of the cold, wondering what brought her over this early in the evening. "Hi, come upstairs. You look like you're freezing!"

She accepted the invitation, stomping snow from her boots and removing them. She moved into his large room and unbuttoned her parka a bit, sitting on his sectional. She could see the remains of his dinner on the bar.

"I'm sorry if I am interrupting your dinner," she remarked.

"No, no. I'm finished! Just gotta clean up a bit." He went behind the bar and put his dirty dishes in the sink and wiped down the bar a bit, glancing up at her. "Can I get you anything, a warm drink? Coffee or something else?"

"No, I'm fine."

He glanced up at her as he finished his chores. She did not look too happy for some reason. Uh oh, what had he done now?

He moved over to the sectional to join her. Obviously she had something on her mind. They had not had sex since Christmas night and he was greatly hoping that was why she was here but her expression did not bode well.

"What's up?" he questioned.

Without saying a word, Tessa removed a magazine she had tucked inside her parka. Silently she handed it to him. "This is what is up."

Taylor took the mag, seeing it was a recent *People* copy and shit, some fool had snapped his and Marisa's photo as they were leaving the Mexican restaurant. They were holding hands (as they usually always did) and the caption blared: Are they back together? Crap, now he could see why Tessa looked upset. She probably thought he was flying back to LA to screw Marisa.

Taylor threw the magazine down on his cocktail table and met Tessa's brown eyes. "So, I guess you are here for an explanation, hmmm?" Taylor ran his fingers through his hair, which he was growing out again.

Tessa's beautiful chin rose. "I don't like to think that I am just some naïve nurse who falls for any little lie you tell me. If you are in another relationship, you should have at least had the consideration to tell me."

"So, I'm found guilty without any chance to plead my case, huh?" Taylor crossed his arms, leaning back.

"Okay, Taylor. I'm willing to listen to your," she rose her fingers in quote marks, "explanation."

Taylor was silent for a moment, studying Tessa. He could see she was really pissed off and one part of him didn't blame her. But Taylor was not used to having to explain any of his actions to any woman. He did what he wanted when he wanted. But Tessa wasn't just "any" woman so he would give her an explanation.

"Tessa, we had dinner at a restaurant. After dinner, we went back to Marisa's place for cocktails. After that, I went back to my place to pack to come back east. Marisa and I are friends, have been for a while."

Tessa gestured to the cover. "It looks like you are more than just friends to me, Taylor."

Taylor sighed. "Tessa, I DO have some female friends. Yes, to be honest, Marisa and I were lovers at one point." He met her eyes directly. "But I haven't been with anyone but you since we became intimate, Tessa. And that's the truth."

Tessa was silent, studying his face. He looked sincere and truthful but it could all be an act. Taylor was an actor and could lie very skillfully and she felt tears prick her eyes and swallowed hard. Oh no, you don't, Tessa. You will NOT cry in front of him.

She stood. "Fine, Taylor. You can keep the magazine as a souvenir," she said sarcastically, moving toward the stairwell.

Taylor gently restrained her. "Hey, Tessa. You are still mad at me. Why? I told you the truth."

She met his eyes. "Did you, Taylor? Did you really? I know actors can lie very skillfully."

At this comment, Taylor's expression closed and he crossed his arms over his chest. "Have I ever lied to you before, Tessa?"

"I don't know, Taylor. I really don't. All I know is when I saw that photo I just felt—very foolish, used and—" she could not say heart broken. She would not give him that satisfaction.

Taylor stepped back a bit, allowing her room to leave if she chose. "I've never lied to you, Tessa. If you want to believe otherwise, that's your choice. Just think on some of the things I have said and done in the past few months. I really thought you knew me better than that. I let you get close—" Taylor stopped. He sighed heavily. "Look, I'm gonna take a trip back west again and despite what you may think, it is for business. I have to meet with my agent about the new movie I'm filming in the spring. I WILL be returning so don't rent the place out. See ya around."

He turned away as Tessa descended the stairs, the tears finally coming.

Tessa composed herself before going into Rose's place. Finally she breezed in and collected Andrew and told Rose he had some homework to do. She did not want to stay and make conversation, she just wasn't up to it after the fight she had just had with Taylor.

She immersed herself in her mommy duties and tried to forget about Taylor. She should have listened to her instincts a long time ago. She had no place in a movie star's life, nor he in hers.

Taylor was very disappointed in Tessa's lack of faith in him. The sudden decision to fly back west was to have some time to step back from the entire situation and re-evaluate what was going on and whether he wanted to be with Tessa or not. He had some serious thinking to do. And then there was

Andrew. Taylor knew if Andrew was not in his life that would cut like a knife. But Tessa's lack of faith had cut like a knife. He felt stabbed in the heart and he had never been hurt by a woman in his life like this. They said everyone eventually suffered from a broken heart but Taylor had never believed that. If you did not fall in love, how was that possible? Taylor did not believe he was in love with Tessa; he was just sexually attracted to her. Then he remembered some very tender moments they had shared over the last several months and knew he was kidding himself. He was falling for Tessa but he wanted a woman who believed in him.

Taylor threw clothes in some luggage and made arrangements to head west. January was too freakin' cold to hang around upstate New York anyway.

Yeah, you keep tellin' yourself that, Taylor.

Chapter
THIRTY

Taylor flew back to LA the next day. It was January tenth so the month was still fairly early and he was glad to be returning to somewhat normal temperatures. LA usually hovered in the low seventies, high sixties in January which was preferable to zero degrees.

As he deplaned at the private airstrip, he could see the limo he had ordered waiting for him. It was raining steadily and the sky was dreary and bleak. Just great. He thought he would be coming back to sunny temps and instead it was rainy and cloudy. Oh well, Taylor. Deal.

He directed the limo driver to his address in Beverly Hills. Then he called Frank on his cell phone as the big limo smoothly carried him onto the main highway.

"Hey, Frank! It's me."

"Taylor, buddy! How are things in Western New York? Are you freezing your ass off yet?" Frank smirked.

Taylor chuckled. "No, hoss. Actually I'm back in LA, only it ain't too sunny. I just deplaned, on the way to my place."

"Oh?" Frank was surprised.

"Yeah, wanted to come back and meet with both you and Stan and plan the upcoming project. I'll probably hang around for several weeks before I go back. Got some stuff I want to take care of here."

Frank laughed. "Plus the weather sucks back east right now."

"Yep. But it ain't too sunny here either, hoss."

"When do you want me to set up the meets with Stan? He told me he will meet anytime you want to."

Taylor ruminated a moment. "Gimme a couple days to get settled in.

Maybe— I don't know, what's today— Monday? Maybe Wednesday. We can meet at your office. Any time that is good for you guys is fine by me."

"Okay, great pal. I'm glad you're back taking care of business. It's been on the back burner too long."

Yeah, lots of things had been on the back burner too long. "See ya soon, Frank." Taylor clicked off and sighed deeply.

After unpacking, he took a long shower to get the kinks of traveling out of his muscles. Then he phoned some friends to see what was happening around town. There were several parties as there usually were and Taylor decided to stop into one a buddy he had filmed with was throwing at his home in Bel Aire.

Taylor dressed in black and headed out to his friend's house. When he arrived, he could see tons of cars parked in front of the place and lights blazed from the huge house. Taylor parked directly behind someone's Audi, blocking them but fuck it, he didn't care. He intended to have a few drinks and party down and try to forget about a certain brunette who haunted him.

As soon as he entered the room, Chris came over to greet him, taking him around the room and introducing him to people he had not met. Many of them were movie stars, actors and singers, people in the entertainment industry that he already knew. He went to the bar and fetched a bourbon and then leaned against it, teal eyes scanning the crowded room. It wasn't long before a woman approached him.

"Hey, handsome. It's been too long."

She was a pretty woman with black hair and blue eyes and he remembered vaguely starring with her in some movie several years ago. What was her name again? Christ, he couldn't recall.

"Hey, you! Cheers!" He raised his glass in a short toast.

"It's Jenn, Taylor. I can tell you've forgotten. That's okay. And I'll have one of those too," she smiled, leaning next to him. She was wearing a white slinky dress that offset her black hair well.

"Ah, yes! Now I recall! Jenny C!" Taylor motioned to the bartender who came right over and pointed to his glass. The guy nodded, going off to fetch the drink. "So, what have you been up to lately, Jenn?"

"Have a new one out with Tom Hanks, *Heroes*. You haven't seen it yet?" She accepted the drink the bartender brought over, stirring the rocks with one elegant finger.

Taylor shrugged. "Nope. I've been kinda incognito. Been out of town for a while. I'm going back again in several weeks 'til spring. Then I'll be filming again. I wanted to take a bit of a break."

"Yeah, you always were a workaholic."

"Not tonight, darlin'," he remarked.

She turned toward him and looked up into his eyes. "Want to take a girl home?" she asked coyly.

Taylor grinned. "No, sweetheart, that's not why I'm here. Wouldn't mind dancing though, if you want to."

She smiled, placing her drink on the bar. "Sure. Let's see some moves."

Taking her hand, Taylor led her over to where couples were slowly swaying together and pulled her against his body. Closing his eyes, he thought of Tessa as the love song played.

Tessa was having a hard time getting through her week. It was mid January and bitterly cold but the weather was not what was bothering her. She could not get the last conversation she had had with Taylor out of her mind. It kept coming back to haunt her and her feelings were so ambivalent.

She knew she was falling in love with Taylor and that was a big mistake on her part. Taylor was a movie star who could have any woman he wanted and after seeing the cover of him with Marisa, she was really depressed. She could not compete with beautiful actresses and models, nor did she want to. She was just herself— Tessa. A mom, a nurse, a widow, a woman who had been on her own for most of her life. When Steve came into her life, all of that changed and she finally felt loved. Losing him was devastating, but at least she had Andrew. When she learned he had a life long disability it only made her love him more fiercely. He needed her so much and *she* needed him. Then Taylor had appeared on the scene and disrupted everything.

Andrew had been asking her all week where Taylor was, his beautiful brown eyes full of hope to see his buddy Taylor again. She knew if Taylor decided to resume his Hollywood life, her son would be deeply hurt. As she would be but she did not have any control over that. Taylor said he would be returning and she hoped fervently that he did, for Andrew's sake. She would just keep her distance and she certainly did not plan to have sex with him again. She was already hooked, body and soul and she knew someday Taylor would leave and she needed to guard her heart. And protect her son.

Taylor met with Frank and Stan Weinberg in Frank's office Wednesday right before noon. The men all sat in the leather wing chairs Frank had situated around a gleaming round table. The script Weinberg had submitted was passed around and they each discussed the merits and the problems with the scripting. Stan wanted to get Taylor's feedback on what he thought about the screenplay and choosing co-stars.

After several hours, they settled most of the details. They decided to go with a very sultry unknown brunette for his co-star, Jeanine Walker. She had one indie movie under her belt and she was so good she was nominated for an Oscar last year but did not win. Taylor liked her work and preferred her over the other actresses discussed. Taylor tried to ignore the fact she slightly resembled Tessa.

When all of the details were settled the men went to a trendy Hollywood restaurant for lunch. It was decided they would meet next week at Weinberg's corporate offices to sign the contracts and all of the legal paperwork. Weinberg had agreed to the salary requirements and informed Taylor filming would begin May tenth in Edmonton, Canada. Taylor hoped it wasn't freezing there mid May. One could only hope.

Taylor spent his remaining time in Hollywood partying and catching up with friends, trying desperately to run away from memories created in Western New York.

Taylor lay awake late the last evening he was in LA. Tomorrow was January twenty seventh and he would be returning to his place in Lewiston and he wondered how Tessa, Andrew and Rose had fared without him. Had they missed him? He had certainly missed them, especially Tessa and Andrew. Rose was like a grandmother he had never had and he knew he was growing very fond of her also. There was no doubt his heart ached being away from Andrew. He missed seeing the little guy so much.

And Tessa. His feelings for her were so mixed up and he tried to sort some things out. Yes, he thought she was beautiful and he loved to have sex with her. But that wasn't the most important thing to him. The memories that haunted him the most were such subtle little things. Her smile, the way her long eyelashes swept her cheeks while she lay sleeping, her tawny brown eyes smiling up into his, her lush lips and what a terrific kisser she was. Her courage in the face of such adversity raising her son with challenges they both faced with bravery day in and day out. He admired her as well as desired her. Did he love her? He turned this question over in his mind. He was not sure yet but he was sure of one thing. He could not wait to get back to Western New York to see her again.

During his Hollywood visit he had not slept with anyone. He just didn't want to and had remained celibate. Of course, she would not believe that. She believed he was capable of lying to her and that hurt Taylor on a level he did not feel any woman could possibly reach.

Sighing, he turned in his bed. He needed some sleep to travel tomorrow.

He landed in Buffalo about noon on January twenty eighth. The wind was blowing and it was cold, but thank God it wasn't snowing. Taylor caught a cab and gave him directions to Lewiston and the guy looked at him in astonishment.

"Lewiston? Do you know how much that's gonna cost ya, buddy?" The driver looked over his shoulder at Taylor in shock.

Taylor looked up from the newspaper he was perusing and met the guy's dark eyes. "Yeah. I do. Gotta problem with that?"

"No, no! Just want you to know it ain't gonna be a cheap trip." He turned back and set the meter as he pulled out.

"Doesn't matter, hoss. Just get me where I want to go."

"Yes sir!" the guy answered, shaking his head as he moved in front of a minivan going too slow.

Taylor hauled his luggage up to his place. Since he had been gone longer than usual, there was more to lug. The driver offered to help but Taylor declined, tipping the guy generously. The man again shook his head in amazement and backed down the drive, moving out of sight.

Taylor unpacked and took a hot shower. He would make himself a small dinner and relax on his sectional and read. He was beat from partying, traveling and being stressed about his personal life.

"Taylor home! Taylor home!"

Andrew was jumping up and down, pointing to the dining room windows.

"What?" Tessa exclaimed.

It was Saturday so she was not working and since it was too bitterly cold to be outside she and Andrew were watching *Spiderman* together.

She moved over to look out the windows and Andrew was right. Taylor was removing luggage from the back of a yellow taxi, speaking briefly with the driver and then he hauled his luggage over to his place, unlocking the door and disappearing inside.

"Go see Taylor?" Andrew asked hopefully.

Tessa's heart was racing and she did not know exactly how to answer Andrew. She wanted to see Taylor again too but he was probably tired from traveling and such.

She tried to explain that to her son. "Honey, I'm sure Taylor is very sleepy from flying on an airplane. We should just let him sleep. Maybe tomorrow we can see him, okay?"

Andrew pouted but he did return to the sofa to watch the rest of the movie and sighing, Tessa joined him, dreading meeting with Taylor again. How would that go? After their last conversation she was very leery. Of course, Andrew and Rose had no idea that the last time she saw Taylor they had argued. But for Andrew's sake she had to make an effort.

CHAPTER
THIRTY ONE

TAYLOR SLEPT IN A bit on Sunday morning. When he finally crawled out of bed he took a long hot shower, dressing in jeans and a warm sweater. Taylor was letting his hair grow longer again for the new flick upcoming in the spring. He swiped his hands through the blond locks then went downstairs to collect the Sunday newspaper. He intended to relax today, just chill on the sectional and read.

When he opened the door, he could see it was snowing lightly and it was still bitterly cold. He collected his newspaper from his mailbox quickly, sparing a quick glance at the larger house. He did not see any signs of any activity.

Taylor went upstairs to his place. Brew coffee first order of the day.

Sighing, he wondered how things would go with Tessa when he finally saw her.

Around noon the buzzer downstairs sounded and Taylor was surprised. He threw down the script he was reading and headed down to answer the door. Tessa and her son stood outside bundled in coats, hats and gloves against the weather.

He grinned broadly, opening the door. "Hi, guys!" he greeted. He motioned them inside and Tessa and Andrew stepped in to the small foyer area.

Tessa looked up at Taylor. "He wanted to come see you badly. This is the longest I could restrain him for. I hope we are not—"

"Nope, nope! I'm not busy!" Taylor stooped down to Andrew and gave him a big hug. "Hey, bud! It's great to see you again! I missed you!"

Andrew grinned, hugging Taylor tightly. "Taylor, miss."

Taylor stood and glanced at Tessa. She was holding what looked like a checkerboard set and several books.

"Would you mind spending some time with him? He likes to play checkers. I also brought some of his books. Would that be a problem?" Tessa looked up into Taylor's face. She could see he had a slight tan from California and he was growing his hair longer again. Had he seen Marisa when he was out west? That was none of her business, of course.

"Checkers? Sure, that's great!" He accepted the items from Tessa, grinning down at Andrew. "I'm a mean checker player, buddy. Better be good to beat me," he warned the little boy.

Andrew giggled and pointed upstairs.

"Let's remove your snowy boots first, Andrew. Then you can go upstairs with Taylor." Tessa proceeded to remove Andrew's boots as Taylor questioned her.

"You're not staying?" He arched a brow.

"No, I wasn't planning to. I thought you and Andrew could spend some time alone, if that's okay with you," she avoided his eyes as she helped her son.

Taylor was very glad to be spending some time with Andrew but he also wanted to see Tessa too. Perhaps some other time. She clearly did not want to stay.

"That's fine. We'll have fun. When do you want me to bring him back over to you?"

She stood. "Whenever. A couple of hours, is that okay?"

"Sure. We'll see ya soon." He turned to the little boy waiting for him on the steps. "Say goodbye to your mommy, Andrew," he prompted.

Andrew came down several steps and gave Tessa a big hug. "Bye, mommee!"

Tessa kissed the top of his head. "See ya soon, tiger." With one last glance at Taylor, she opened the door and exited.

Taylor sighed then turned his attention to Andrew. "Let's go have some fun, buddy!"

"Yeeaaah!" Andrew ran up the stairs and Taylor followed closely.

Around three o'clock in the afternoon Taylor bundled Andrew back up and rang the bell on the back door. He knew it was probably unlocked but he did not want to just barge in.

While they waited for Tessa, Taylor held Andrew's hand, who was smiling up at the man's face. The two of them had played checkers for a while and Taylor let Andrew win every game but one. Heck, he had to challenge him somewhat. He read a few books to Andrew but Andrew preferred to watch television. He was enthralled with Taylor's big screen TV. Taylor finally found a movie they both could enjoy and made some popcorn. When the movie ended, Taylor had not realized so much time had gone by. Three hours. It was time to get Andrew home to Tessa.

She opened the back door and smiled. "Hi! How was your afternoon together?" She took Andrew's hand, leading him inside.

Taylor remained standing on the stairs. "Good. We had fun. Tell your mommy what we did, Andrew."

Andrew frowned for a moment, then he answered. "Checkers! I won! I won!"

Tessa's brows arched. "You did?" She looked up at Taylor.

"Yup, he won all but one game. That is a mean checker player ya got there! High five, bud!"

Andrew fived him back, grinning.

"Well, Andrew it is time to come in and I'll get you a snack, okay?"

"We had popcorn when we watched a movie. Just to let you know," Taylor remarked, shoving his hands in his leather jacket. She had not even invited him in. Hmmm…must still be pissed at me.

"Oh, well I guess you will not need a snack. Just dinner. I'm planning on pizza, something easy. Wanna come by a little later for pizza?" she invited.

Taylor was surprised by the invitation but he knew Tessa did not have a lot of time to spend with Andrew on the weekends and he did not want to monopolize her son's time. She needed to be with Andrew too.

"Thanks, but no thanks. I'm gonna study my script. I've decided on a new project so I need to get crackin' on it a bit. Some other time I'd love to," he ended.

Tessa was surprised he had not accepted her invitation but that was okay. She still did not know what to do about Taylor and maybe she was worrying needlessly anyway. It sounded like he would be leaving soon to film his movie.

"Okay, Taylor. Thank you for taking Andrew this afternoon. He enjoys the time he spends with you." She ushered Andrew up the stairs as she spoke to Taylor.

"I enjoy spending time with him. He is a great kid. Well, I'll see ya." He moved down the steps and across to his place as Tessa closed the door against the cold.

Tessa and her son ate pizza at the kitchen table. Tessa questioned her son about being at Taylor's and she was able to get a few details out of him. Not much, but some.

Andrew looked curiously around their kitchen. "Where Taylor? Pizza?"

"Honey, use sentences. It is 'where is Taylor'. And Taylor had some work to do at his place. So it is just you and me, buddy. What would you like to do after dinner?"

"Go see Taylor."

Tessa was getting a bit frustrated and tried to ignore her frustration. "Honey, we can't see Taylor all the time. Only some times."

"Why?" Andrew's brown eyes searched hers.

This cognitive question flabbergasted Tessa. Usually Andrew did not understand the concepts of what, who, why, where. They were difficult concepts for him to grasp and both Tessa and his school were trying to address this.

Tessa swallowed a piece of pizza and tried to decide how to answer this. She wanted Andrew to keep asking questions and it seemed time spent with Taylor was helping in this regard. "Why? Why do you think?" she asked, holding her breath to see how he answered.

Andrew frowned. "Don't know," he finally answered.

Tessa expelled her breath, hoping for a bit more of an answer or explanation. Slow Tessa. Remember, this is hard for Andrew. "Well honey, the reason is Taylor lives in the back and we live here. So some times we see him and some times we don't." Would this make sense to him?

"Taylor live here then."

Again Tessa was shocked and just about fell on the floor. This remark was totally unexpected and totally out of character for her son. He had solved the problem in his mind and communicated that fact to her. This was *immense* progress! Holy cow! What had Taylor been doing differently that she and his teachers were not? Or was Taylor just one of those people that could reach Andrew?

Finally she looked Andrew directly in the eyes. "Andrew, Taylor is not part of our family. He is just a friend who, for now, lives behind us." She paused. Should she mention Taylor might be leaving someday? No, she just could not do that. Not right now when Andrew was actually talking *to* her and not *at* her.

He frowned again over this answer and she could see he was mulling over her reply. He did not say anything else; he simply continued to eat his dinner.

When Tessa tucked Andrew into bed that evening after reading him a story she decided to ask more questions about Taylor. See what she could get out of Andrew after his surprising remarks at dinner. "Andrew, how do you feel about Taylor?"

Andrew's brown eyes looked up at his mommy and they lit up when she mentioned Taylor's name. Her heart ached. That alone answered her question. Her son loved Taylor. "Taylor friend. I like," he answered.

She hesitated, then asked the big question. "Do you love Taylor?"

"Love mommeee, love Mrs. H. Love Taylor, yes."

Tessa's eyes misted with tears. "Good night, Andrew." She leaned down to kiss his cheek and quietly left for her own room.

Monday arrived and Tessa went to work and Andrew off to school. It was January thirty first, the last day of the month. It was still very cold out but they had not received any additional snow, thank the good Lord.

As Tessa drove into the hospital, she considered the events that had happened over the weekend and felt a talk with Taylor was in order. She would phone him later tonight after Andrew was in bed sleeping. She wanted to know exactly what Taylor was doing and saying that had opened a tiny portion of Andrew's world. Something *she*, his own mother, had desperately been trying to do for years.

"Hello, Taylor."

Taylor had picked up his cell phone from the large cocktail table. He was relaxing on his sectional reading through his script, making notations here and there of changes he wanted made. It was a painstaking process but it gave him something to do. He wasn't a skier and that was about the only thing to do around here in January.

When he heard Tessa's voice, he was surprised. She had been over yesterday so he wasn't expecting to hear from her again until at least the weekend.

"Hi, Tessa. What's up?" he answered.

"Do you have some time to talk? I have some questions concerning Andrew I'd like to speak to you about."

Taylor threw the script on the table and sat up a bit, leaning into cushions. "Sure, I got some time. What did you want to discuss, exactly?"

"Well, after he returned from your place Sunday, he did and said some amazing things at dinner and again at bedtime. He seemed to understand some concepts that he has never grasped before and I was totally shocked. I wanted to ask you what exactly you two discuss or how exactly you approach him— ya know; stuff like that."

Taylor's brows arched at this. "Well, give me a bit more info. What did he do or say that was different?"

"He answered a 'why' question. This is a very difficult concept that even his teachers and I cannot get him to learn. Ya know, 'w' questions like 'what, where, why, how'. These are cognitive questions he just doesn't get. But he answered a 'why' question I asked about you. I almost fell over from shock!"

Again Taylor was totally amazed. "Tessa, I don't do anything differently than you do. Yeah, I interact with him. I ask him questions and stuff. Some questions he answers, some he doesn't. We just— ya know, hang. Like good buddies."

Tessa frowned. "What questions *does* he answer for you?"

Taylor thought for a moment. "He answers basic questions I ask like 'do you like this or that' 'what are your favorite things to do' you know, those kinds of questions to kinda direct me in entertaining him."

"Taylor, he does *not* answer those types of questions for me or Rose. Sometimes, but rarely. That is *huge* progress for him!"

"Tessa, maybe he just needs to be around a guy more often. Boys relate more to same sex people, especially when they are young. Don't get me wrong! He loves you a lot, he talks about you constantly."

"What does he say about me?"

"He tells me 'mommee pretty' 'mommee fun' 'mommee loves me' I love mommee', ya know stuff like that."

Tessa could feel tears prick her eyes. Her son did tell her these things, but hearing it from someone else touched her heart so deeply. Especially because it was coming from Taylor who was special to them both. When was he planning to leave? She needed to know.

"Taylor, I know you have a new movie upcoming. When are you leaving us?"

He sighed deeply. He did not want to leave them, but it was his job to make movies. "May tenth I start filming in Edmonton, Canada."

Tessa took in this information. "Are you planning to stay here until then?" She held her breath.

"Yep. I'm gonna spend my winter and early spring here, studying my script and preparing. I can do that here as easily as I can in LA."

Tessa slowly expelled her breath. Well, that would give her several months to prepare her son for Taylor's imminent departure. She felt her own heart ache. Well, you knew that day would be coming eventually Tessa.

"Okay. Thank you for sharing this information with me. Anything I can learn to help him is important to me."

"Tessa, I'll always keep you in the loop. You know that. And I know you didn't ask, but I'm gonna tell you anyway. Yes, I did see Marisa when I went back west, as well as many other friends. And you're still the only lover I have, baby. You think on that. Bye for now."

He hung up the phone and Tessa placed her receiver down in total shock. Taylor still had the ability to totally amaze and surprise her. She believed him because he had absolutely no reason to lie.

She shook her head. Oh Tessa, what are you going to do?

CHAPTER
THIRTY TWO

FEBRUARY BLEW IN WITH a blast. The first week was snowy and cold and by Thursday they were predicting a full blown blizzard. The forecast was for the storm to start hitting the area Thursday evening and as much as three feet of snow was predicted. There had not been such a bad storm in the area since the earlier storm that had hit in October.

The snow arrived after dinner time on Thursday evening and the wind gusts were up to fifty miles per hour. It snowed heavily all throughout the evening and visibility was very poor.

The snow removal company Taylor hired came and tried to remove some of the snow but it was replaced as quickly as it was removed. Finally they gave up in disgust and informed Taylor they would be by Friday morning to clear the area again. Unfortunately the storm was supposed to remain well into Friday.

Taylor called up Tessa to make sure they were all safe. He knew she would have to go into work on Friday and he insisted on taking her in his Suburban. He didn't want her driving in blizzard conditions and his vehicle could handle the storm. Tessa informed him he would have to get up very early to take her in and Taylor assured her it wasn't a problem. He would be ready to take her into work at five a.m.

At five a.m. Taylor had the SUV running and warm. Since it had been in the garage there was no snow on the vehicle. He had it waiting in front of the carriage house for Tessa. She had informed him she would have to leave around five fifteen or so to make sure she would get to the hospital to start her shift at six a.m.

She came out bundled up around five fifteen and Taylor helped her up into the huge vehicle. When he came around to the driver's side, she addressed him. "You know Taylor, it is really not necessary for you to take me in. My Blazer would get me there, especially since the driveway was cleared."

Taylor backed down the driveway, looking over his shoulder. It was still snowing heavily and the wind howled around the vehicle, shaking it as the snow blasted the windows from all sides.

"Tessa, I don't want you driving in a blizzard. It is much safer if I take you in and pick you up. I don't want to worry about you getting stranded in this mess."

Taylor turned toward the main road as Tessa answered him. "I am accustomed to driving in snowy conditions. You are not," she pointed out.

Taylor used the defroster and wipers, staring hard through the snowy downpour, watching the cars ahead of him. Everyone was driving slowly and he could see the trip would take twice as long as normal. "I think I can handle it, Tessa."

Tessa slowly sighed and settled back in her seat, then she looked over at him. "You will check on Rose and Andrew today?"

"Yep. I'll make sure I carry in plenty of firewood and make a fire at your place. I'll probably hang with them too. I can study my script just as easily at your place. Now, when does your shift end?"

Tessa gave up. Taylor would not be denied and she was secretly relieved that he would be driving her back and forth today. "It ends at five p.m. You can pick me up any time after that."

"Okay, I'll try to be there by then. I'll try to leave early enough to get there at that time. Pick you up at the main entrance?" he asked, looking over at her.

Tessa studied the handsome man wearing a black knit hat over his blond hair. "Yep. The main entrance. I'll wait for you there."

"Sounds like a plan."

Taylor was able to get to the hospital about fifteen minutes before her shift and he dropped her off at the main entrance.

As she descended, she thanked him.

He flashed his famous grin. "No problem, baby. See ya later." He waited until she entered the hospital until he turned the Suburban toward the exit.

The day passed uneventfully at the house. Rose and Andrew spent their time reading or watching movies. Rose did some reading work from Andrew's primer from school and also had him work on some printing. Andrew was so happy with Taylor's presence that he was willing to do anything, as long as he could see his buddy Taylor.

Taylor spent his time on the couch studying his script, tending to the fire and he played several games of checkers with Andrew.

At four fifteen, Taylor left to pick up Tessa. The snow had not stopped and he could see that the snow removal people needed to come by again, the driveway looked like it had about two feet built up from the last time they were by. Taylor made a mental note to call them and kick their asses in gear, which he did by cell phone. They promised to be right over and Taylor hoped it was cleared by the time he returned.

It was very slow going driving to the hospital. Taylor sighed and told himself to be patient. He had allotted enough time to get there right at five.

He pulled up to the main entrance about 5:05 and he could see Tessa waiting inside the glass doors. When she saw him pull up, she came outside and right away the icy blasts blew her hair around.

Taylor came around to open the passenger door for her and grinned. After she was safely in the vehicle, he took his seat and turned to her.

"How was work today?"

"Oh, just another day in paradise. How did things go at home?"

"We were all fine. Hung out, watched movies, played checkers, Rose did some schoolwork with Andrew. Oh, and she made dinner for all of us too, so you don't have to worry about that."

"Bless her." Tessa laid her head back against the leather head cushion as Taylor drove through the blizzard back to her place.

Saturday there was no problem getting the snow cleared away. The company was able to remove all the snow to the sides of the driveway and Taylor took care of all of the shoveling. Tessa was very glad she did not have to deal with this particular storm with Taylor here. He made all arrangements for snow removal and she was hoping this was the last big storm they would get. Since it was still February and they had March to get through yet, the chances of that were slim but having Taylor around to help keep everyone safe was a big relief.

Valentine's Day was coming up very soon and Taylor conspired with Rose so that he could take Tessa for a very special outing. Rose was very excited after Taylor told her his plans and agreed to stay at Tessa's place that evening to be with Andrew.

The day before the holiday Rose, Andrew and Tessa exchanged small gifts, chocolate and such. Andrew always made his mommy a pretty Valentine in school which was always hung proudly on the refrigerator. Tessa was surprised that Rose insisted they do it one day earlier this year. Andrew did not have a problem with it, but Tessa was curious. She questioned Rose but the older woman was unusually vague, saying something about it would be a special change. Her brown eyes twinkled and Tessa knew she was up to something but had no idea what.

That changed Valentine's Day when Rose came upstairs to chat.

She and Tessa sat at Tessa's table sipping coffee about mid-day. Valentine's had fallen on Sunday so Tessa was not working.

As she sipped at her coffee, she wondered what Rose had on her mind. At the moment, Andrew was watching a DVD and was quite content. Tessa had not really seen Taylor for over a week since he chauffeured her back and forth from work during the blizzard.

Luckily lately the weather had not been bad. Cold, but not snowy. They had even managed to have some sunny days. Imagine that in February in Lewiston.

"So, Rose. Why did you want to chat?"

Rose smiled, placing her cup in her saucer. "Well, I wanted to let you know that you are in for a special surprise tonight." She glanced at the clock. It was about three p.m. "Sometime around six p.m. tonight you are being squired out on a very special date by you know who. Tessa, wear your red satin dress and the red heels. And pack a bag. I'll be staying overnight here with Andrew and I've called the hospital and actually was able to finagle a day off for you. I told them Andrew was sick. Okay, I lied!" Her brown eyes twinkled. "But it was for a good cause."

Tessa gasped. "What? What is going on—"

"It may take you a while to get ready. I'd get started if I were you," Rose said calmly.

"Oh, my God!" Tessa ran to her bedroom to burrow through clothes and take a long hot bath.

Tessa had already figured out Taylor was going to take her someplace special so she made sure she paid very careful attention to what she wore. She took Rose's advice and wore her tight red satin sheath, it had straps that would hide bra straps but Tessa chose a backless black and lace bra, a thong and garter to match with black stockings and the red heels. She added a black velvet bolero shrug so she would not freeze. Fussing with her hair, she curled it and then pinned it up haphazardly, creating a mussed sexy tangle of curls. She added the pearl set that Taylor gave her for Christmas and went heavier on the eye makeup than usual.

Then she threw some casual clothes in an overnight case as well as sturdy hiker snow boots. She knew tonight in the heels she would freeze but women had these fashion problems they had to deal with. Walking in snow and ice in high heels was one of them.

She had to admit she was very excited and had no idea what Taylor had planned but whatever it was, she was dressed, ready and primed for it!

He rang her doorbell at six p.m. Tessa shrugged into a long black velvet coat, hugged and kissed Andrew and Rose and grabbed her overnight case and red clutch.

When she opened the door to Taylor, the first thing she saw were a dozen red roses beautifully arranged in a crystal vase. Taylor peeked around the huge arrangement.

"For you," he smiled.

Gasping, she accepted them, looking at the tall man in front of her. Taylor wore a designer black suit (looked like Armani) with a white shirt and red silky tie, a silky red kerchief tucked into the suit coat. He looked absolutely gorgeous and so sexy.

"Oh, Taylor! They are gorgeous! Let me take them upstairs and then I'll join you. Come in," she gestured him out of the cold.

After Rose and Andrew exclaimed over the beautiful roses Tessa placed on the dining room table, they were on their way. Tessa still had no idea what was going on.

Once they were in his vehicle heading north, she questioned him. "Okay. Tell me what the big surprise is already! I'm dying here!" she exclaimed, crossing her sexy legs.

Taylor grinned at her. It was dark already since it was February and she could just glimpse his perfect features in the dashboard lights. "We're going to Toronto, sweetheart! For the night. Made reservations at that big tower they got there. Then we are staying at the Regency in the penthouse suite. I should have left it all be a surprise, but I don't want you to die. Not for a long time!" He tossed her a rueful grin as he drove.

"The CN Tower?! The revolving restaurant above the CN Tower?" she exclaimed.

"Yep. The very same one. Excited?"

"Yes, yes! I've always wanted to go there! I hear the view is spectacular!"

"I know it is February and the weather may be crummy, but I don't plan to spend a lot of time outside."

"Oh?" She arched a brow. "Where were you planning on spending time?" she teased.

"Why, at the restaurant, at their nightclub and at the suite. We'll be inside except for coming and going. I promise it will be a night we will both remember!"

Tessa grinned hugely. It sounded romantic and fun and she was out for Valentine's with a sexy movie star. How lucky could a woman get?

The sparkling lights of downtown Toronto were displayed beneath them. Even the taller skyscrapers were not as tall as the Tower and as the room slowly revolved, one got a view of Lake Ontario also. It was romantic and seductive, which of course was what Taylor had in mind. Tessa knew the evening would end with the two of them in bed and was very glad she had worn her sexy lingerie.

She sipped at her champagne, studying the man across from her. His hair was a bit longer than his collar now, softly brushing the area where his shoulder and neck met. A sensitive area she loved to kiss. She had learned that the last time they made love, which had been Christmas night. She had the hots for him big time and could not wait to have sex with him again. Tessa had been wise after becoming intimate with Taylor. She went on the pill just in case their relationship took this turn after Christmas. She knew Taylor would be moving on and did not want to be left with any surprises. Now was the time for them to enjoy each other.

Taylor grinned over at his gorgeous partner. "What are you thinking about, you?"

Tessa blushed, glancing away. She really did not want to discuss how much she wanted to jump across the table and attack him. "I'm just having a wonderful time, enjoying the view." She gestured to the windows that surrounded them.

Their dinner had been delicious and they were having an after dinner drink in lieu of dessert.

"I'm glad you are having a good time. That is what I wanted. You work too hard, baby. You need to stop and smell the roses once in a while," he remarked.

She grinned. "I know that is your philosophy. Life is fun!"

Taylor smiled. "Of course it is darlin'. But it is what you make it. Some choose to whine and complain. Me, I complain and have fun!"

Tessa laughed. "Actually, I have never heard you complain about anything, Taylor."

"Oh, I complain all of the time in Hollywood. Just ask my agent Frank."

"Do you miss it? Hollywood?" Tessa studied his eyes.

Taylor spun his glass a bit, glancing down then he met her eyes. "There are certain aspects about it I miss. There are more I don't."

Tessa sipped champagne. "That is a very ambiguous answer, Taylor."

He laughed. "Let's just say I like the fun part, the partying and making movies. I miss a few friends, but quite frankly I'm not real close with anyone back there. Maybe Marisa, but we're just good friends. I can talk to her. It is hard to find someone like that in tinsel town."

"You're not still— involved with her— are you?" Tessa always wondered about that.

"Tessa, I already told you. We are just friends now. Nothing more. She knows that and accepts it because she is a friend. I've told her about both you and Andrew."

This surprised Tessa. "You have?"

"Yep. She says I should run far, far away from you."

"And why aren't you?" Tessa's golden eyes teased.

"Because right now in my life, you are the one for me Tessa. You and Andrew too."

"But that could change any time. Isn't that true too, Taylor?" She studied him carefully.

He shrugged. "Don't know. Don't think so. Enough talk. Let's go check out the nightclub!"

Taylor came around to help Tessa out of her chair and they moved into the elevator that would take them up one floor to the new age night club.

After spending a few hours dancing, Tessa declared herself ready to go over to the hotel. Taylor collected their coats and they rode down the tall tower to the bottom. Tessa thought she may have left her stomach somewhere at the top, the ride was so smooth and quick.

The Regency Hotel was located directly across the Tower in a bunch of high rises. Taylor entered and obtained the key to the suite and they entered another elevator that took them to the top floor of the hotel.

When they entered the suite, Tessa could see it was very elegant. Shiny brass lamps, glass table tops, a huge Jacuzzi and a king size iron bed piled with bright red and white pillows. Red velvet drapes now offered a twinkling view of the Toronto skyline. There was a full service bar and a formal dining table and several comfortable sofas and chairs.

Tessa felt pampered just looking around the place.

Taylor immediately went to the bar. "What can I get you?"

"Taylor, between champagne and the glass of wine at the night club, I really do not want anything else. I don't want to wake up hung over tomorrow."

"Ah, come on. One small drink. I'm having a bourbon." Taylor had only sipped at the champagne and had not imbibed as much as Tessa had. He really ordered it for her, he preferred scotch or whiskey.

"Okay. One scotch with a lot of ice!" She shrugged off her velvet bolero as he prepared their drinks. She sat on one of the huge sofas, sinking into the white cushions.

Taylor joined her, handing her a heavy old fashioned glass containing her drink. He clinked his glass against hers. "Happy Valentine's Day, baby!"

"Hmmmm…yes, it has been." Tessa took a small sip, reaching to remove her red heels.

Taylor laid a hand against hers, restraining her. "Leave them on for now, baby. They make those sexy legs even sexier."

"Oh?" She arched a brow.

Taylor swallowed his drink. "Yeah, I got plans for you and your red high heels."

"And what would that be?" Tessa asked innocently.

Taylor relaxed back into the cushions, settling in. "Why, first off, you're gonna strip for me. Want me to put some music on? Or not?"

Tessa gasped. "Strip? I don't know how to strip for a man!"

Taylor grinned. "It's really quite simple. You stand up, remove your clothes, slooowly."

Tessa had had just enough champagne to make her daring enough to give it a try. "Okay. But I'll need music."

She stood as Taylor went to the sound system and found a slow ballad station. "Wicked Game" by Chris Isaak was playing, a perfect song to strip to in his opinion.

Tessa started swaying her hips, closing her eyes, ignoring the man who watched her from the sofa. She listened to the music and lyrics and slowly unzipped the back of her dress, letting it fall down around her feet. She kicked it away, now clad in just her bra, thong, garter belt, stockings and heels. She swayed and danced some more, now opening tawny eyes, watching Taylor, teasing him. She put one stocking clad leg up on the couch, running her hand slowly up and down it. When she reached the top of her stockings, she slowly released the garter and peeled the stockings off. She draped the black silky material over his shoulders and moved away as he tried to grab her.

Taylor could see her fantastic ass as she was wearing a thong. He took in the long limbed beauty before him and knew he could not wait any longer.

He went to her, picking her up and practically threw her on the bed. Ripping off his expensive suit coat and shirt, he climbed on top of her, still wearing his pants. He quickly made short work of her remaining lingerie and sucked vigorously at pink nipples, his hands going to the thong and tearing it off of her. His fingers got busy, parting slick lips and he groaned loudly.

"Oh God! I have to fuck you! Now!" He released his penis through his slacks and the huge organ pointed directly at the entry. He slid it in slowly, slowly and it was long, hard and felt like velvet steel to Tessa. Then he was ramming, ramming, ramming it home. Tessa screamed as he elevated her legs, plunging into her repeatedly, driving them both wild.

They spent the remainder of the evening screwing and using the Jacuzzi. Taylor had never had a better Valentine in his life!

Chapter
THIRTY THREE

THE COUPLE SPENT THE next day exploring Toronto. They bundled up in warm parkas, boots and gloves. There were many stores and various exhibits around the hotel and they strolled along the main streets with other shoppers or workers. They stopped for hot chocolate when they both started to freeze. Mid February in Toronto was very cold, especially with the icy blasts coming off of the lake.

They spent the day in the city and headed back to New York so that they could be home in time for Andrew's bus. Taylor had purchased a very expensive pair of ice skates for Andrew (over Tessa's protests) and could not wait to teach the little guy to skate. Tessa had informed him there was a skating park in the middle of town but she was not a great skater and had never attempted to teach Andrew and she was unsure how he would take to the sport anyway. She felt lessons would be in order for something like that for Andrew and there weren't a lot of social programs available for special needs children. Taylor assured her he had to learn to skate for his movies and he could take them all ice skating and teach them both.

Tessa had her doubts but if it was possible to get Andrew to try something new, she was all for it.

Tessa and Taylor were both down at the bus stop waiting for Andrew at three thirty. Andrew smiled hugely, surprised and pleased to see not only his mommy, but Taylor too! He leapt off the bus into Taylor's arms and Taylor caught him, laughing. Tessa grinned as Taylor kissed Andrew's cheek and set him down. Tessa held out her arms and Andrew ran into them, laughing and hugging her. He had not seen his mommy last night; he had been with Mrs. H and wondered where she was.

He was so excited as they entered Tessa's flat and he told them bits and pieces about his day.

Tessa made dinner for her guys and they spent time in the front living room together.

This was the first time ever that Tessa wished winter would last forever.

True to his word, Taylor took Tessa and her son skating Saturday at the big rink in the center of town. He purchased skates for himself and Tessa and showed both mother and son how to tighten the laces. Tessa stood on the things and promptly fell down!

"Taylor, I don't think I can do this! I can barely stand on these things!"

Taylor came over to her and helped her up. "See how I am standing, Tess? With my legs slightly bowed out and skates turned inward? When you walk in the skates that steadies you a bit. Once we are on the ice, I'll show you how to move your feet. It's really easy once you get the hang of it."

"I don't know, Taylor," Tessa said doubtfully, taking a couple of steps. She followed his advice and at least this time she didn't fall down.

Andrew watched the two adults, smiling. Taylor had already laced up his new black shiny skates and he turned to see other skaters whizz by on the big ice circle. He continued to smile, it looked like fun. Unlike his mom, Andrew had no problem standing in the skates. He waited patiently for Taylor and his mommy.

Taking Tessa's arm, Taylor escorted her to the ice, grabbing Andrew's hand. "Okay, guys! Let's try this!"

As soon as Taylor released Tessa's hand, she went right for the side board to grab it. The skates felt much different on the ice and she felt even wobblier. Her doubt increased but she clung to the side, watching as Taylor held Andrew's gloved hands and patiently showed him how to move his feet on the ice. The other skaters were considerate, giving them a wide berth, smiling at the little boy learning to skate. After a few tentative steps, Taylor released one hand, then another, staying close to catch Andrew if he should fall. Andrew took a few steps and tried to imitate the gliding steps Taylor was doing and fell down. The ice was hard! He giggled and got right back up and tried again. He fell several times but Taylor was always there to help him and after a half hour, Andrew was able to move around the rink tentatively with Taylor.

Tessa watched all of this action from the sidelines. When Taylor tried to coax her out, she slowly tried the gliding motion. She wobbled a bit, but did not fall. Gaining a little confidence, she tried to glide a bit faster and her butt promptly kissed the ice. Man, it hurt! I'll have bruises on my butt tomorrow and I probably already have them from Taylor! She gave it the old college try but she fell more than she skated. Giving up, she decided to watch her guys from the side. She would wave to them each time they passed her and Andrew was doing quite well and his whole face was lit up. He was having fun! She could see Taylor was an excellent skater but she already knew he would be very athletic from his build and the way that he moved.

After a few hours, Taylor and Andrew escorted Tessa off of the ice.

"For being such a good girl, I say I take you both out for pizza. Where's a good pizza place?" Taylor looked down at Tessa, grinning.

She sat in the snow, quickly removing her white skates. "Pizza— and especially a glass of wine— sounds great! There is a good Italian restaurant down the road," she remarked as she removed the skates. She could not get them off quick enough. Quickly she reached for her winter hiker boots, lacing them up.

Taylor grinned, helping Andrew remove his skates and put on his winter boots. Taylor followed suit and answered Tessa. "Sounds good, baby. But don't give up on skating. You didn't do too bad."

"That's not what my butt says!" Tessa shot back.

Taylor laughed as they moved to his SUV to head out for food.

The restaurant was warm and had cozy booths with red checked cloths. It was not too busy at the moment so they received quick service. The pizza was hot and delicious and the wine helped Tessa relax. Taylor had beer with his pizza and Andrew chattered about how much he liked to skate with Taylor. As usual, some of his sentences, words and meanings were choppy but the adults got the gist that Andrew loved skating. Tessa seriously thought about getting him lessons. It might involve some research on her part but she could certainly do it. Taylor would not be around next winter to teach Andrew to skate. She put down her pizza slice and glanced across at Taylor and her son in the opposite side of the booth. This thought depressed her and she did not want her spirits to be down. Andrew had had a wonderful time today thanks to Taylor and she needed to remember the good times when they came to an end. She could not help it. She still felt sad, but tried to conceal her feelings.

After pizza, they returned to Tessa's flat. At the back door Tessa thanked Taylor for teaching Andrew to skate. Since it was early evening, she informed Taylor it was time for a bath for Andrew and he would be going to bed shortly.

Taylor acknowledged this news, waving to them both and descending the stairs to go to his place.

Why had Tessa looked sad when he left?

The week progressed and so did winter. Andrew was off the third week of February from school for winter break. When Taylor heard about this, he planned outings with Andrew and Rose and took Andrew skating several times. The three of them enjoyed themselves, going to movies, out to eat, or just hanging at Rose's place.

Taylor spent his evenings studying his script. Sighing, he realized he would probably only be here two to three more months and would have to leave to film. He was not looking forward to starting his next project as he usually was and he knew quite well the reason why.

After Tessa spent a few weeks avoiding him, Taylor finally phoned her. He asked her to come up to his place to speak to her but she insisted they could speak on the phone. Sighing, Taylor addressed the issue.

"Why are you avoiding me, Tessa? I haven't really seen you since we went skating a couple of weeks ago." He sat on his sectional speaking to her on his cell.

"I've been busy, Taylor," she said evasively. "I work, I have a son to take care of and the weather has been cold so we stay in. I know you, Rose and Andrew had fun over his vacation. I'd like to thank you for all you did for him."

"I didn't call for thanks, Tessa. I called to see why *you* are avoiding me," he repeated. "And you always work, take care of your son and it's been cold for months and I still saw you. So your excuses don't fly, babe."

On the other end of the line, Tessa sighed inwardly. She had been avoiding Taylor because she knew when he left it would break her heart. She felt the less time she spent with him, the fewer memories she would have that would hurt. It was her way of trying to protect herself. She knew ultimately it would not work. She was in love with Taylor and that made her sad, not happy. It would never work between them. However, she should try to hang onto the good memories they could create now. Live, Tessa! That is what life is for.

"Do you want to come over and warm me up? My bed is kinda cold," she offered.

Taylor was flabbergasted. Boy, this woman blew hot and cold.

"Five minutes!" He slammed the phone down, grabbing the key for her place and running over to the bigger house.

Two minutes later Tessa and Taylor were both very happy.

The end of February approached. It was a short month to begin with. Andrew spent his time at school, Taylor spent his time on his script and visiting Rose, seeing Tessa in the evenings.

After Andrew was safely tucked in bed and sleeping, he would go over to Tessa's place and they would have wild sex. He was always careful to leave every night so that he would not be there when Andrew woke in the morning.

Taylor had never been this happy and when he did try to figure out why, he surmised it was the great sex. Taylor loved to have sex and who knew a sexy nurse would be so good at it?

Taylor picked up his script and concentrated on his character and his lines.

CHAPTER
THIRTY FOUR

MARCH ARRIVED BUT THE weather continued to be cold. In the beginning of the month they had several small snow storms. There was not a lot of accumulation and towards the middle of the month there was a slight warming trend and finally some of the white stuff was disappearing.

Taylor spent his time with Tessa and Andrew. He would take Andrew out several times a week after the boy returned from school. It gave Rose a bit of a break and Taylor admitted he loved to spend time with Andrew. He was trying to teach Andrew to talk in sentences and although it was slow going, Andrew tried and made some progress.

As for Tessa, Taylor spent as much time as he could with her after Andrew was in bed sleeping. They would have sex, but they talked too. Taylor inquired about Tessa's family and learned she did not have family. Her parents had been killed in a car accident when she was only about two. She explained she had been with a babysitter at the time. Her parents did not have any living relatives so Tessa was put up for adoption. For whatever reasons, it was not Tessa's destiny to be adopted. The beautiful little girl grew up in foster homes, passed from family to family. When she became an adult, Tessa explained she went to nursing school and never looked back.

Taylor's heart ached for her. Although he had grown up in a dysfunctional family, it wasn't always bad and he had memories of some good times, especially with friends. He also had his mom and knew if he ever needed someone, *really* needed someone, his mom would always be there for him. Tessa did not have family until she married and when Andrew was born. Taylor could now understand a bit better why Tessa was so fiercely protective of Andrew. It was not just his disability but her own background. She wanted to give Andrew the things, memories, love and care that she had never received.

After she told him about her background Taylor was especially tender that evening when he made love to her. He wished he could kiss the hurt away of those painful memories for her.

As the month progressed the weather improved. Most of the snow was melting and one could actually sense spring in the air. The weather was very windy and Taylor took Andrew to a local park to teach him how to fly a kite. Tessa accompanied them and the three had fun watching the rainbow colored kite dance in the sky.

Tessa treasured these moments and memories they were making with Taylor. She did not tell Taylor she was in love with him. She knew he would be leaving them to make a movie soon and she tried to prepare herself mentally for his departure but it was so damned hard. Taylor had become such an integral part of their lives in just months. Tessa was also quite amazed that she had fallen for Taylor too. A handsome famous movie star would be the *last* person she could envision herself with. He was so great with her son and he was a kind, considerate and wonderful lover. Both Tessa and Taylor had danced around the fact that he would be leaving them when spring was in full bloom.

"So, how goes the script?" she asked.

They were relaxing in her living room, sipping wine. Tessa had just put Andrew in bed and they were relaxing together, chatting.

"It goes. I have most of my lines memorized already. But when you get to the set and the live action starts, it is very different than the lines on the page. The story actually jumps to life and you are of course interacting with the other actors. Whole different scenario. Actually, this is the longest I've ever prepared for a project. Usually jump from one project right into the next."

"Why is that? And why did you decide not to do that this time?" Her brown eyes studied his profile as she sipped her wine.

Taylor shrugged. "I always wanted to be busy. If I worked, I didn't have time for introspection. I was running from my past, I didn't want it to catch up with me. Now," he shrugged again, meeting her eyes, "now, this time, after the accident, I had time to do a lot of thinking. And I think I needed that to kind of realign my priorities. Meeting you and Andrew has helped me a lot in that regard."

This intrigued Tessa. "How so?"

Taylor's teal eyes were serious, introspective. "I was the bad ass Hollywood playboy. Everything you read about me was probably true."

At this remark, Tessa's eyes widened.

"But after the accident, I started to think about how easily I could have died, how reckless I had become. Almost self-destructive. When I met you and then Andrew, I realized that life is precious and to be enjoyed. I guess you guys taught me that Taylor isn't the center of the universe." He paused, glancing away. "I know that sounds a bit awkward, but that's the best I can come up with." He sipped his wine, awaiting her response.

Tessa was silent for a moment, tracing the rim of her wineglass. Then she looked up to meet his beautiful eyes. "I never wanted to get involved with you, Taylor. I still have many doubts. Mostly because I know you will be moving on and I don't want my son hurt, or Rose or myself. But you have been so great with my son and when you move on— well, we will miss you." She looked away, sipping at her wine, nervous. This subject was never really discussed between them.

"How do you know I won't be returning?" he asked.

Tessa's head whipped around, her eyes wide and startled. "Say what?" Her brows arched.

"Just because I am going to be away filming a project doesn't mean I am gonna forget you guys."

She searched his eyes for his meaning. "Taylor, when you get back to filming, when you are an actor again, you will be Taylor Boudrain again. Not Taylor Patterson. I get that."

He turned toward her on the sofa. "I was never Taylor Patterson. I have always been Taylor Boudrain." He shrugged. "For whatever my faults, that is who I am and always will be. Taylor Patterson doesn't exist."

"No, I guess he never did, did he?" She stood. "I'm tired tonight, Taylor. I'd like to get some rest. Five thirty comes early."

Taylor stood, placing his wineglass on her table. He softly stroked her cheek. "If you can't take the heat, you should stay out of the fire, baby."

He left through the back door, leaving Tessa to ponder his words.

For the last several weeks of the month, Taylor gave Tessa a wide berth. He did not want to hurt her and felt she needed some time to think through their relationship and decide on the course she wanted to take. He continued to take Andrew on outings here and there and with the weather improving they were able to do more outside activities. Taylor enjoyed the time he spent with Andrew and he missed not having sex with Tessa, but it was probably for the best they both had some time to back off and think about their future—or if they would have a future.

The month of March seemed to move too slowly and then much too fast. With April approaching Taylor needed to do some serious thinking about his future, what he really wanted out of life and who he wanted in that life.

As he looked down at an adorable six year old boy playing basketball with him, he knew the decision was really already made.

CHAPTER
THIRTY FIVE

TESSA AND ROSE SIPPED coffee in Tessa's kitchen, looking out the window at the trees budding. There were several apple and cherry blossom trees in the yard that were beautiful when the weather warmed up enough for them to bloom. The buds were almost ready, in another week they should blossom. It was mid April and Tessa had continued to avoid Taylor although Andrew spent time with him when he was free.

Rose contemplated the woman opposite her who was glancing out the window. At the moment Taylor and Andrew were in the drive playing basketball and they could hear the bounce of the ball even though the windows were still closed. It continued to be a bit chilly.

Rose had sensed the tension between Tessa and Taylor and noticed that they were no longer spending any time together as they had in the past. Although Taylor thought he had been discreet, Rose had still heard him coming and going in the evenings and knew that the two had become lovers and that warmed her heart. Tessa *needed* someone and even if Taylor would not admit it, he did too.

"Tessa, you seem sad lately. What is it?" Rose set her coffee cup down in the saucer, her kind brown eyes studying her friend.

Tessa glanced back at Rose, sighing. "Nothing really. The usual worries. Work, how is Andrew doing in school. I'm tired of winter and want to see flowers and sunshine." She shrugged, sipping her coffee.

"Tessa, we are close," Rose began, "so I am going to give you some unsolicited advice."

Tessa glanced sharply at Rose but she was silent.

"I know why you've been sad. I know that you and Taylor were lovers and something happened and you are no longer. And you miss him. Believe me, he misses you too. Enjoy the time you have to spend with him now. Taylor is a good man," she finished. She picked up her coffee cup, studying the other woman.

Tessa was surprised that Rose had figured out she had been intimate with Taylor. She must have heard him coming and going. Tessa mulled over Rose's words, still silent.

"When does Taylor plan to leave? Does he know Andrew's birthday is just days before he plans to leave to film?"

"No, I haven't told him about that. As you have noticed, we've been avoiding each other. He will probably already be gone by the time Andrew's birthday is here."

"You need to tell Taylor about Andrew's birthday. I know he would want to be here for it. And you should also do it for Andrew's sake. It will be hard enough on your son when Taylor leaves. At least let him know before he leaves," Rose said earnestly, reaching over to touch Tessa's hand gently and patting. "Tessa, trust your instincts. Everything is going to be fine. I know it."

Tessa gave Rose a wan smile. "I don't know about that, but I will inform Taylor about Andrew's special day soon. It is only mid April. We have about a good month yet."

"That is a month that Taylor could be gone in, Tessa."

Sighing, Tessa knew Rose was correct. "Will you keep an eye on him for a bit tonight after dinner? I'll go over and speak to Taylor." She shrugged. "I don't know what I'll say to him, but I'll try."

"Of course. Just let me know when."

Tessa rang Taylor's doorbell about six p.m. Since spring was well upon them it was still light out and actually pretty nice, maybe about sixty. Tessa shoved her hands in her jeans as she waited for Taylor to answer the summons.

Within minutes the door swung open, revealing Taylor. God, the man was gorgeous! Since she had been avoiding him lately, that simple fact had not smacked her in the face for a while. Now her heart started pumping double time and she could feel herself blush knowing he was gorgeous *everywhere*. He was dressed in faded Levis and a white tee, white sneakers on his feet. His hair was almost as long as when she had met him and still glorious looking.

He glanced down at her, startled. "Tessa! Hey!"

"I was wondering if I could come up and talk to you. Rose is with Andrew," she gestured to the other house.

Taylor's brows arched. "Sure. C'mon up." He opened the door wider so she could enter and proceeded up the stairs, Tessa following. She tried to keep her eyes off of his gorgeous butt, but it was hard.

Reaching the top of the stairs, Taylor waved her over to his sectional. "I'm on my cell with my agent right now. Just let me wrap up the call and I'll be right with you. Only be a few minutes."

"Sure. Okay." She seated herself on his sectional, glancing around his place. It really was beautifully decorated. Would he ship all of this stuff back to LA when he finally left? That would be such a shame. He had managed (with her help, she admitted) to turn the carriage house into a home.

At the moment, he was over at his bar, sitting on one of the stools speaking on the phone. She could hear his end of the conversation but it seemed he did not have a problem with that. She waited patiently, heart pounding.

"What did Stan think about that?" Pause. "Why does he want to start sooner? Isn't May still kinda cold in Canada?"

Oh no, Tessa thought. If he started filming sooner, he would miss Andrew's birthday. Tessa thanked Rose and her lucky stars that she was speaking to him before he made that decision, if he did.

His conversation continued. "Nope, at this point I'm pretty set. I've got my lines memorized and how I want to do the characterization. The screenwriters were good, it is well written." He paused again. "Look, Frank. I really don't want to make any decisions about that right now. It is mid April; we still got about a month. And I have a lady waiting to speak to me. I'll call ya later, okay?"

Tessa could hear a deep baritone voice on the other end, which did not sound too happy.

Taylor sighed. "Got it. I'll get back to ya." He clicked off and placed the phone on the bar. He turned to Tessa. "Can I get you anything? A drink, coffee?" Sex? he thought.

"No, Taylor. I'm fine." She waited as he came over to sit on the sectional. "I could not help but overhear. That was your agent you were speaking to?"

"Yeah, Frank. He wants me to go out to the location sooner, like maybe towards the end of this month instead of waiting for May." He ran his fingers through his glorious blond waves as he studied the lovely woman nearby. He had not seen her in a while. Her beautiful brown locks were longer and she had cut her bangs in a sexy style. He could feel himself getting sexually aroused just looking at her. Cut it out, Taylor!

"The reason why I wanted to speak to you is to kinda get an idea of when you are planning to leave to film. I assumed it would be closer to film date, May tenth, right?" She laced her fingers in her lap, nervous, wondering what he would say.

"That was the original plan, yeah. Now they are saying they want me earlier, end of this month." He sighed. "I don't know about that. I have some other business I have to take care of first."

He didn't elaborate on the business and Tessa did not want to push it. That was not her business, but Andrew was. Remember Tessa, you are here for Andrew.

"Well, I really hope you don't leave earlier, Taylor."

This surprised Taylor. "Oh, yeah? The way you have been avoiding me, I haven't felt all that welcome lately," he said bluntly.

Tessa's cheeks pinkened but she met his eyes directly. "That was because I was very conflicted about my emotions toward you and your imminent departure." She shrugged. "I got very close to you and it scared the hell out of me, so I backed off. But I know you have continued to do activities and stuff with my son and believe me, I am grateful for that. Andrew is the reason why I am here right now."

Taylor crossed his arms. "Oh, really?" So she wasn't here to discuss the two of them, but her son. "Okay. I'm listening."

"I know I haven't mentioned this to you, but Andrew's birthday is coming up. Right before you are scheduled to leave to film. His birthday is May seventh and I know he would be really unhappy if you were not here to share the big day when he turns seven..." she paused, studying Taylor, trying to gauge his reaction.

Taylor's brows arched as he took in this information. So, the little guy was going to have a birthday next month. Well, that changed things a bit. He definitely wanted to be here for his little buddy's birthday and he was glad Tessa had told him about it. He was actually thinking of leaving within weeks and did not know quite how to broach that subject with Tessa and Rose.

"I will definitely stay for his birthday. I can't miss my buddy's birthday. I can realign my business calendar, it's not a problem. I don't have to physically be on the set until May tenth. That is what my contract states."

At this answer, Tessa's face lit up and she smiled. "Oh, I am so glad! Thank you, Taylor!"

"I would like to think you want me to stay for your sake too, Tessa."

"I do, Taylor. I truly do. I am conflicted and confused. I just don't know what to do about you, Taylor. I just don't." Worried tawny eyes met his.

He leaned forward, crossing his hands as he studied her. "You're a woman, Tessa. I think you'll figure it out."

Tessa blushed, standing. "Thank you for staying longer. I truly appreciate it." She came over to him and softly touched his cheek. "If you don't want to fall in love with little boys, don't come to Lewiston, New York." And with that comment, she left, descending his stairs.

What about you, Tessa? What happens if I fall in love with you?

CHAPTER
THIRTY SIX

"HEY, FRANK! HOW GOES things in LA?" Taylor was calling his agent the following day after speaking to Tessa. He had to inform his agent— who could thus contact the producer— that he would not be arriving earlier to the set.

"The usual shit, different day. Business has been good lately, so I can't complain. Although it would be better if my top dollar actor was working," he said sarcastically.

"Well, you know I have plans to, hoss. That's why I'm calling. I need to let you know I can't be on the set until about May ninth. Can't make it any earlier than that."

"Taylor, what the fuck?! What's up now? You told me you would probably be ready to leave by the end of—"

"Yeah, well things have changed," Taylor interrupted. "Something important has come up and I don't want to leave until that date. I know the rest of the cast and crew are flying in on May fifth. I'll just take my Lear jet and fly in on the ninth. Should work."

"Taylor, Stan is *not* going to be happy about this. He especially wanted you early to go over scenery, scripting and other details. He wants your input before filming *starts*."

"Well, he'll just have to wait until the ninth, hoss. Can't be there any earlier, that's just the way it is."

"Can I ask what is so damned important?" Frank demanded.

"No. You can't. It's a private matter."

There was silence on the other end of the connection and Taylor knew his agent wasn't happy at all with him. He would get over it. He had in the past.

"I really don't know what you find so damn appealing about that place, Taylor. You need to get your ass back to work," he finally said.

"I will, on the ninth. Got anything else you want to discuss with me right now?"

"Not right now. I'm sure after I speak to Stan we may be speaking again," he warned.

"Look, Stan's a nice guy. But my mind is made up. If you and Stan aren't happy, can't do too much about that. My contract states to be there by May tenth and I will be. Peace, out." Taylor disconnected, knowing Frank was probably having a conniption on the other end. Oh well, he'll get over it.

Taylor made sure he did most of his packing up in April. Any clothes, cosmetics, books or any other items he wanted to take to the shoot he boxed up. He wanted to be organized and ready to go so that he could turn his attention to other matters, specifically Andrew's birthday. He wanted to do something really special for the little guy and Taylor was a bit stumped. With Andrew's disability, it wasn't possible to take him to say Disney Land or an amusement park. All of the sights and sounds would upset him. Hmmm…it was an issue he needed to sort out.

The weather continued to improve as April advanced and the trees and flowers started to bloom. Sunnier days finally arrived and the temperatures climbed into the high sixties, sometimes low seventies.

Taylor was glad to finally see some sunshine. It had been a long winter but it seemed to have flown by. He could not believe it was almost time for him to leave the Pattersons. Sighing, he knew he had to speak to Tessa about that, and Andrew's birthday.

He invited her over to his place to speak to her about Andrew's birthday. It was May first and he really needed to make some plans and he wanted Tessa's advice. He also had several other matters he needed to speak to her about.

She agreed to come over after dinner, leaving her son with Rose. She ascended his stairs and took a seat on the huge sectional. She was wearing a pink summer blouse with her jeans, brown hair tumbling around her shoulders. As usual, Taylor thought she looked lovely and sweet. He ignored his thoughts, wanting to get straight to the point.

"I asked you to come over because I wanted to discuss Andrew's birthday. Are you planning anything special like a party?"

Tessa studied the man across from her. She had not seen him in several weeks and he looked a bit leaner to her than before. Perhaps he was working out for his new movie? He was wearing jeans paired with a navy tee and his blond hair waved to touch the top of broad shoulders. She tried to ignore her physical attraction to this man but it was so damned hard, especially since she had fallen in love with him. And he would be leaving them soon. She brought her attention back to Taylor's question.

"Rose and I usually throw a little party at my place for Andrew with the balloons, cake and stuff. We have him open his presents, take lots of photos. Ya know, a typical little boy's birthday." She paused. "You are, of course, invited over for the party." Tessa's brown eyes studied Taylor closely.

Taylor sighed and ran his fingers through blond waves, then he glanced over at her. "I wanted to do something really special for the little guy. You know, something out of the ordinary that he would really like and remember. But because of his sensory issues, I'm a bit stumped so I wanted to speak to you about it," he began.

Tessa arched her brows. "What did you have in mind exactly?"

"Well, I was kinda thinking of taking him to an amusement park or something like that, but I think that would be too noisy."

"Yes." Tessa answered.

"How about the zoo? Does he like to go to the zoo?"

Tessa was surprised and she had never really thought about that. Andrew loved stories about animals, especially elephants. But to take him where he would actually *see* such a huge creature— that she was unsure about. Plus there were crowds, noise, probably not a great choice. As she hesitated, Taylor continued.

"I contacted the Toronto Zoo and explained the situation. They are willing to close the zoo to the public for one day so that Andrew can visit and see the various exhibits and animals."

Tessa gasped. "How did you get them to do that?!"

Taylor grinned. "Money talks."

"You *bribed* them??"

"Let's just say they were happy to be remunerated. We can still do the party bit. Maybe I can take you, Rose and Andrew a few days before his birthday, if you give me a date so I can let them know. How does this sound to you?"

Tessa thought for a moment. She knew Rose would probably pass on the zoo trip, but Andrew would probably really enjoy seeing all of the animals and if the park was closed for just their use, Andrew should not have a problem with many sensory issues. She was amazed that Taylor had the power to do such a thing. Just how much was he worth anyway? Never mind, Tessa. You don't want to know.

She shook her head in amazement. "You are really something, Taylor. I don't know how you do the things you do. It is impossible in my world."

"But not in mine. Would May fifth work? That is a Sunday and two days before his birthday."

"Yes, okay. We'll try your idea. I like Andrew to have as many different experiences as possible. I am not sure how well it will go over. He may love it, he may be scared to death. But I will speak to him and prepare him for a zoo visit." Pause. "You are planning on coming to the party on the evening of his birthday?" She wanted to be sure he would still be here for that.

"Yes. I've rearranged my business schedule and I'll be here until May ninth. I'm flying out that day to the set. Which brings up another issue." He gestured around at the carriage house. "I don't want you to lease out the place. I'll continue to send you rent and stuff for the time I am gone. I was planning on leaving everything here. Just take the essentials on the shoot."

Tessa was glad to hear this. If he wanted to continue to rent and leave his furniture and stuff, perhaps he would be returning one day. Don't get your hopes up, Tessa. There could be other reasons. Still, she was glad to hear this news.

"I was wondering about your place and if you were shipping your stuff back out west. I will certainly continue to rent it to you if you wish."

"My agent Frank Zimmerman will send you a check every month. I've already instructed him where to send it, so it should not be a problem. Here is his business card." He handed her a gold embossed card with all pertinent details on it. "You still have my cell phone number, correct?"

"Yes I do."

"Once I leave to film you can always reach me at this number. If you need anything, anything at all, I want you to promise me you will call me, Tess." He looked directly into her eyes as she glanced up to meet the beautiful teal eyes.

"Thank you, Taylor. I'm sure we'll be fine." She did not add we were before you were here. We'll make it with you gone. Maybe our hearts will break, but they will mend. She stood.

"Well, if that's everything, I have to get back to Andrew."

Taylor stood too. "No, that's not everything." He leaned down and caught her lips and kissed her thoroughly, licking her lush bottom lip. "Miss me, Tessa," he whispered.

He turned away as Tessa quickly descended the stairs.

May fifth arrived and the weather was pleasant and sunny. Taylor drove them up to Toronto in his SUV. Rose had declined to come on the trip, insisting she would just slow everyone down. So it was the three of them out on an adventure to see lions, tigers and bears.

Taylor was met at the gates by a tour guide and the guide had a cart available which they utilized to get around to the different exhibits. The zoo was very large and there was quite a bit to see.

They checked out the elephant house first. The animals were outside because of the nice weather, munching hay. Andrew was very reticent to approach the big iron bars, but Taylor put the boy up on his shoulders and Andrew was delighted as Taylor took him closer to see the big mammals. Andrew clung tightly to Taylor, giggling as the huge grey animals curiously inspected the little boy in the red shirt. Giraffes came next and Andrew was clearly delighted. The bear house and snake house did not go over well but he enjoyed seeing the rest of the animals and they all had a fun day.

After several hours they were all pretty tired. Taylor took Tessa and her son to a restaurant in Toronto his agent recommended. Fortunately it was quiet and cozy and the three were hungry after their zoo adventures.

Tessa made sure she took many photos of Taylor and Andrew together at the zoo. She knew her son would treasure both the photos and his memories of this day.

After the meal, everyone climbed back into the SUV for the trip back to New York. Andrew nodded right off to sleep, clutching a stuffed elephant Taylor had purchased for him close. He had a tiny smile on his face as he slept. Taylor glanced back at the boy and he felt his heart lift. Sometimes there really were advantages to being a billionaire. Like making little boys who had autism happy.

CHAPTER
THIRTY SEVEN

THE EVENING OF MAY seventh arrived and Tessa had her flat decorated for the big event with balloons, streamers and posters declaring "Happy Birthday Andrew"! Since it was a Tuesday Andrew had school and Tessa had sent him off with cupcakes for his class and party favors. Tessa had requested the day off weeks ago and shopped for all of his presents, wrapped them and baked a special birthday cake. Her day was busy getting everything ready for the party.

The weather was on the cool side today, only about sixty but it was sunny. Tessa was planning to have his party as soon as he returned from school and invited Taylor and Rose up about four o'clock.

Andrew was very excited as he climbed the stairs and entered their home, exclaiming over all of the decorations and the big pile of presents. Rose had already brought up presents and the rest were from Tessa. Taylor had not yet arrived.

Tessa made sure her camera was working properly and took several photos of Rose and Andrew and then Andrew separately. Finally Taylor arrived, his arms full of wrapped gifts. Grinning, he placed them with the rest.

"Taylor!" Andrew screamed, running to his buddy. "Look, look!" He pointed to the balloons and decorations. "Birthday! Me!"

Taylor grinned, scooping him up and hugging him. Then he leaned back to glance down into Andrew's face. "And how old are you today, buddy?"

Andrew frowned a bit. "Six?" he said hesitantly.

Taylor placed him down and held up six fingers. "You are six years old now. When you add one more…" he waited for Andrew to answer correctly.

"Seven!" Andrew answered immediately.

"High five, bud! Right on. You are seven today! Boy, you are growing up on me, kid!" he joked.

Andrew laughed, grabbing his hand to take him over to the huge pile of presents. He pointed to them, obviously delighted.

His mom's voice intervened. "Andrew, we are going to have pizza, cake and ice cream before we open presents. Okay? Everyone is probably hungry."

Taylor turned as Tessa spoke. As usual, she was gorgeous. Today she wore a white sheath dress with short sleeves that had tiny pink roses embroidered on it and high white sandals on her sexy legs. Her long brown hair brushed her shoulders and she turned to go to the kitchen as Rose approached the two guys.

"Here, let's all take seats around the table. The pizza is here and afterwards Andrew you can blow out the candles on your cake!" She knew this was a favorite ritual.

"Yes! Yes! Blow candles!" He moved to the dining table, all smiles.

Taylor followed. "And you will have one more to blow out this year buddy, so you have to blow *really* hard," Taylor informed the little boy, who grinned back at him.

Rose went into the kitchen to help Tessa bring out food as Taylor and Andrew settled at the table. Andrew sat next to Taylor, eagerly awaiting pizza, cake and ice cream.

The ladies joined them and food was passed around. When they finished up, Tessa brought out a huge chocolate cake with seven candles placed on it. She put the cake directly in front of Andrew as they all sang Happy Birthday to him and he blew out his candles, Tessa taking photos of all this action.

"Presents, presents!" Andrew insisted.

Tessa finally relented. "Okay, Andrew. You can now open your presents."

"Yaaaaay!" He ran into the front room where the pile was located and the adults followed him.

Andrew received a special children's computer from Tessa to help him learn academics or to play games. Rose bought him games for his new computer as well as other toys. Tessa had also purchased toys that Andrew had told her he wanted as well as books.

Finally it was time for Andrew to open Taylor's presents and he did so with a big smile on his face. Taylor had been generous. There was a complete library of children's books, a large Barney train set, many board games and other toys that would address his sensory needs. He also bought him a bowling set game that was electronic and could be played alone or with a partner. Andrew exclaimed over all of the gifts and Tessa's eyes widened as he kept opening one gift after another.

Taylor and Andrew played with his new toys on the floor as Rose helped Tessa clean up the pizza and cake items on the dining table.

Rose smiled at Tessa in the kitchen. "Taylor was so generous with Andrew. Andrew will have a lot of fun for months!"

Tessa was busy at the sink, rinsing some dishes. "Yeah. Maybe *too* generous."

Rose frowned. "Whatever do you mean?"

Tessa turned to the older woman. "I don't want Andrew to become accustomed to being— well spoiled. This will all end when Taylor leaves."

Rose continued to frown. "Tessa, Andrew is not in the least bit spoiled. Let him enjoy his special day and the things that Taylor can provide for him. It will give him many good memories when Taylor leaves."

"Will it, Rose? Or will it make him sadder? I haven't even spoken to Andrew about Taylor leaving in two days. I didn't want to spoil his birthday."

Rose was surprised by that. "Why don't you have Taylor talk to him about it, Tessa? That would probably be the best approach. Taylor can explain why he is leaving. Maybe he would take it a bit better coming from Taylor." Rose picked up a platter to dry as Tessa contemplated her remarks.

Yes, that was a very good idea. Her son would only get angry at her if *she* told him Taylor was leaving them. Maybe if it came directly from his new buddy, he would be able to handle it better. Somehow she did not think it would matter who told him. Her son would still be heart broken and that is exactly what she had NOT wanted to happen.

As Rose was helping Andrew organize his gifts and putting them away in his room, Tessa approached Taylor.

"Taylor, can I speak to you a moment in the kitchen, please?" She wanted to be far away from Andrew's bedroom so he would not overhear.

"Sure Tessa." He followed her into the kitchen, seeing everything was spic and span. She and Rose had already cleaned up after the party. It was early evening now, about seven o'clock and he knew Andrew would be going to bed in an hour. He did have school tomorrow.

"Please sit," she waved to a chair. "Would you like a drink, wine or anything?"

"I'll have a glass of wine," he accepted, watching as she went to the cupboard to remove two wineglasses, filling them and sitting opposite him. She offered him his wine and he silently accepted it.

She sipped her wine, silent, studying his face. Taylor already had a tan and it made his gorgeous eyes much brighter. The long honey streaked hair brushed the top of his shoulders and she knew it was longer for filming. He had already informed her the director wanted his hair longer. It was about the same length it was when she first met him. She glanced away from the stunning looking man. She would miss Taylor also. A great deal.

Sighing, she figured she should get to the point.

"You know Taylor, I haven't informed Andrew you are leaving yet. I did not want to spoil his special day," she began.

Taylor's brows lifted at this news. "I thought you were planning on telling him over the last few months. Ya know, here and there to sorta prepare him." He took a sip of his wine, glancing at her over the rim.

She sighed heavily. "There just never seemed to be a right time to tell him. He has been so happy with you here, happier than I have seen him in a long time and I just couldn't——I just couldn't," she ended.

Taylor sighed, sitting back in the chair and crossing his arms over his chest. "Obviously he has to be told."

Tessa took a gulp of wine. "Yes. And I was hoping you could speak to him. It may make it just a bit easier coming from you."

Taylor had expected this remark when she first told him she had not informed her son he was leaving. She was right, though. It was only fair that he spoke to the boy directly. Actually he wanted to. He did not want to leave Andrew without speaking to him directly about his departure.

"Okay. When do you want me to speak to him?"

"Perhaps tomorrow, when he gets off the bus? You will only be here one more day after that. If you want, you can take him on a special outing the last day you are here."

"That's a good idea. I'll think of something special to do." He stood. "In the meantime, I'm gonna go say good night to him and wish him a Happy Birthday."

Tessa stood also. "Thank you for coming today and for all of the gifts. You were way too generous."

Taylor grinned ruefully and left to go to Andrew's room.

Wednesday afternoon Taylor met Andrew's bus. He explained to Rose that he was going to take Andrew out for ice cream and speak to him. So when the little yellow bus pulled up, Taylor was waiting at the end of the driveway.

When Andrew saw who was waiting for him, he smiled in delight. "Taylor!" He ran down the steps to meet his buddy.

Taylor grinned and waved to the driver as the bus moved away. "Hi buddy! I talked to Mrs. H because I wanted to take you for a special treat today. How does ice cream sound?" Taylor grinned down at the little boy who had his backpack on.

Andrew's brown eyes lit up. "Yes, ice cream! Like!"

"I like ice cream, bud. Use sentences," Taylor corrected.

"I like ice cream, bud," Andrew replied.

Taylor laughed as he helped the boy up into his SUV, relieving him of his backpack.

Taylor took Andrew to a local ice cream parlor that had wrought iron chairs for customers to sit and enjoy their ice cream. Taylor bought Andrew a hot fudge sundae and a chocolate cone for himself. They sat at one of the round tables and Taylor smiled as he watched Andrew dive into his sundae. He was soon finished with chocolate sauce decorating his chin. Taylor smiled and reached over with a napkin to wipe away the sauce.

He leaned back in his chair and studied Andrew. This was going to be a very difficult conversation, but it had to be done. He was not going to take the coward's way out and just leave. Andrew meant too much to him to do that.

"Andrew, there is another reason why I asked you out for ice cream today. I have something to tell you. Something important." He watched the boy's face as he spoke.

The beautiful brown eyes swung to Taylor's and Taylor could see he was listening. God, he looked like Tessa! Taylor hesitated, then began. "I have to go away for a while. I have a job. I make movies and that means that I will not see you for a while. I have to leave to do my job." He waited for Andrew's reaction.

Andrew frowned slightly. "Job?"

Taylor could see maybe he was not familiar with this concept. "Yes, big people, adults, have jobs. Like firemen, policemen, teachers or nurses. Your mommy is a nurse; that is her job. My job is I make movies for people to watch on a movie screen. In fact tomorrow after school I will take you to see one of my movies so you can see what I do." Taylor had checked the paper and the last film he made would be appropriate for Andrew to see and it was playing at a theater in town.

Andrew was still frowning. "But why you go away?"

Taylor squirmed uncomfortably. "Because when you make a movie buddy, it takes a long time and you have to go to different places to film them." He caught the boy's eyes. "I want you to know I will be coming back. You just won't see me for a while. Most of the summer and part of the fall I may be gone. But I don't want you to think I have left for good, buddy. I will come back," Taylor assured the little boy.

He glanced at Andrew and could see the brown eyes were bright with tears. "You go away?"

Taylor came around the table and embraced Andrew. "Yes Andrew, but only for a little while. I will come back." He hesitated. "I love you, bud. I *will* come back," he assured Andrew.

The big brown eyes, moist with tears, looked up at him. "Love Taylor, too. Stay, Taylor."

Taylor sighed. "I wish I could buddy, but I can't. But tomorrow we'll go see a special movie. I am in it and you can see what I do. How does that sound?"

Andrew stood, pushing Taylor away. "Go home now."

Taylor rose, his own eyes moist with tears. He could see anything he said now would only make matters worse.

They headed out to Taylor's SUV and in the back mirror Taylor could see tear tracks on Andrew's face the whole way home. He had never felt lower in his life, not even when his dad was beating on him.

Taylor took Andrew upstairs to Tessa's flat and Andrew bypassed his mother and went straight to his room. Tessa could see Andrew was very upset.

She confronted Taylor in her kitchen. "It looks like it didn't go well."

"That's an understatement," he remarked, folding his arms, glancing down at her.

"What did you tell him exactly?"

Taylor sighed. "I told him I had to leave to go away to do my job. I tried to explain that big people had jobs— like firemen, nurses, etc. It didn't matter. I even told him I would take him to one of my movies tomorrow so he could see exactly what my job was. I explained I had to be away for a while but that I would return. It didn't seem to make a difference. He was still upset."

"Well, Taylor. What did you expect? Andrew has grown to love you and you are leaving him. He does not understand the concept that one day you will return, if you even do. This is the LAST thing I wanted to happen!"

Taylor could see Tessa was angry with him too, but hell, she knew this day would come and he really thought she could have prepared her son more for that eventuality instead of leaving it entirely up to him. "Look, Tessa. You knew from the start I would be leaving someday. I'm sorry I hurt anybody here but the fact of the matter is I am an actor and I have to go on location. You guys can certainly visit me on the set this summer when Andrew is out of school."

Tessa crossed her arms over her breasts. "That is not possible, Taylor. Andrew does not fly in airplanes, for the obvious reasons."

"There are trains. You could take one right out of Toronto."

Tessa turned away from him. "Why don't you just go, Taylor? Make it easier on all of us."

He pulled her around gently to face him. "Look, baby. Don't be this way. I told Andrew I would be returning and I plan to. I don't want to leave on bad terms. Not with you, certainly not with your son. I care about all of you, including Rose."

"Let's just say our goodbyes now, Taylor. We'll see what the future holds. Right now, my son needs me." She turned to go to Andrew's room, leaving him standing alone in her kitchen.

Taylor sighed deeply then turned to descend the stairs.

Chapter
THIRTY EIGHT

THE DAY FOR TAYLOR to depart arrived and since it was a Thursday, Tessa and Andrew were both gone. Taylor decided to go over to say goodbye to Rose. He had grown close to her also and did not want to leave without saying goodbye.

He knocked on her back door, his hands shoved in his jeans pockets. He looked around at the flowers just starting to bloom around the stairs and yard and the scent was sweet. It was a sunny gorgeous day, probably mid seventies and he wondered idly what the weather in Edmonton was like.

The door was opened shortly by Rose, who looked up at him in surprise. "Why, Taylor! I thought you might be gone by now."

He grinned. "Not yet. A limo is coming by in about a half hour for me. I just wanted to stop by to say goodbye to you."

She waved him into her kitchen and he followed her in. He could see she was baking bread and the delicious smell filled her old fashioned kitchen. She beckoned him to take a chair and he sat at her table.

"Would you like tea or something cold to drink? I have ice tea, if you prefer."

"Ice tea would be great, Rose. Thank you."

He watched as she went to a cupboard to remove a glass, filling it with ice. She poured ice tea from a heavy glass pitcher with lemons floating it in. Oh boy, the real stuff! Taylor, as most southern people, loved iced tea. He accepted the glass from her, smiling. "Thanks a lot."

"You're welcome." She sat across from him, studying the handsome man opposite her. "It was very considerate of you to come by and see me. I'm glad you did." She watched as he sipped at his tea. "Have you said your goodbyes to Tessa and Andrew yet?"

Taylor sighed, placing his glass down. Then his teal eyes rose to hers. "That did not go over too well, I'm afraid. I took Andrew out for ice cream to tell him personally and he was very upset. Crying. I felt like a total heel." He did not look up to meet her eyes, idly tracing circles around his glass.

Sighing, he continued. "And of course, Tessa was angry at me when I brought him back. So right now you could say neither of them are very happy with me." He finally looked up to meet her kind brown eyes.

She was silent a minute, taking in this information. "Taylor," she began, "you must know how they both feel about you. They have grown very close to you, as I have. For you to leave hurts them and makes them feel deserted." She held up a hand. "I know that is not what you are doing. You are merely doing your job. But Andrew does not understand that concept. He only knows you're leaving and for a little boy like Andrew that is devastating. I think Tessa is upset on many levels. Not just for her son, but for herself. Tessa has not allowed herself to get close to a man for a long time. When she finally did, she fell for you— a movie star she feels that she and her son could not possibly fit into your world." She paused. "They both love you. You know that, don't you?" Rose studied his features.

At this remark, Taylor's brows rose. "I know Andrew loves me, as I do him. Tessa— not so sure about that. We're friends and as you know we were lovers— but as far as being in love with me, I wouldn't go that far. She distrusts me too much."

Rose sighed. Sometimes men were so dense. "She is trying to protect herself and her son. Can you blame her?"

"No. I can't. But when I arrived, she knew I would eventually leave to film and I think she could have prepared Andrew for that eventuality better. Instead, I was the bad guy."

"Tessa is Andrew's mother. She did not want to hurt him for the world. So she put it off. I do not blame her, Taylor. And since you were the one leaving, it is only right that you tell Andrew. I agree with Tessa. But I will miss you. We all will. I understand you have a job to do and so does Tessa." She paused. "She will come around. She just needs some time."

Taylor stood. "Time is something I don't have, Rose. I only have a certain amount of time to give."

Rose stood also and placed a gentle hand on Taylor's arm. "Taylor, you're a good man. You will do the right thing. Whatever that turns out to be."

He leaned down to kiss her cheek. "Thanks for your faith in me, Rose. You have my number. If you need anything, or Tessa does, just call me. Any time."

She watched as he turned to go down the stairs. He turned back to her, gesturing to his black SUV. "You can tell Tessa a company will be coming by to remove the Suburban. No sense in having it just sit here. They should be by in the next day or so."

"I will tell her. God speed, Taylor and stay safe."

"Thanks, Rose."

The limo showed up right on time and Taylor piled his various bags in, making sure the carriage house was locked up tight. He took his set of keys with him as he was still actually renting the place. He put them in a safe place so he would not lose them.

He boarded the private Lear jet that would carry him directly to Edmonton and sighing he leaned back against soft cushions and closed his eyes. He was on his way back to his world. Hollywood. Making movies. Being the big bad actor.

Somehow the appeal was no longer there.

He ignored this feeling and went to sleep, trying to forget three people he would miss immensely.

When Taylor deplaned he was met by Stan. The jet took him right out to the location and Taylor could see it was mountainous and rocky, with lush vegetation. The weather was chillier than back in New York, but not too bad.

Stan escorted him to Taylor's luxurious RV to go over the schedule of the shoot with him. Stan wanted to begin shooting as soon as possible because he wanted the film in theaters by Christmas. Meaning they had about four or five months to wrap the film and that meant shooting twelve, fourteen or sometimes eighteen hour days.

Taylor was used to the hectic pace of shooting films. The high adrenaline rush of filming had always appealed to him. Taylor always lost himself in his characters, one of the qualities of a fine actor. In this particular film he was to play an action adventure hero who had to fight unknown government forces that were trying to destroy the world. There were quite a few action sequences and he would have to do stunt work. The storyline and plot were fast paced and the ending was a real stunner. Taylor had taken on the project because of these details.

He brought his attention back to a question Stan was asking him. "So, are you going to be ready to go in the morning, or are you gonna be jet lagged?"

"Hell, no. I'm ready to go. Slept a lot on the flight and I plan to sleep right now too. So I'll be rested up. How long do you estimate it will take to film and wrap? September, October?"

"Usually these types of films take a bit longer. As you know there can be problems with special effects, techs or whatever. But to answer your question I am shooting for a wrap date of October first, ideally."

October first. About a year after his accident and a year after he had met Tessa. Sighing, he wondered if he would be able to talk her into coming to the set this summer. He could send his Lear jet and possibly she could get a mild sedative for Andrew. He mused on these thoughts, completely missing the fact that he missed them already.

Rose came up to have dinner with Tessa and Andrew Thursday evening. Of course, they all knew Taylor had left earlier that day and Tessa was trying to make conversation with Andrew to lift his spirits. He was very glum and his beautiful lips pouted as he poked at his dinner, barely eating.

Rose decided to save any comments about Taylor until they were alone later on after Andrew was in bed.

The three spent several hours together, talking. Tessa read Andrew several books and he watched his favorite program, Barney. Nothing seemed to cheer him up though.

Finally Tessa said to Rose "I'm going to get him ready for bed now. I think he's toast."

"Do you mind if I stay for a moment? I wanted to speak to you."

"No, of course not, Rose. It will take me a few minutes as you know. But I'll be right out."

Rose nodded, settling in the cushions as Tessa led her son down the hall. She helped him bathe and tucked him into bed, reading him a bedtime story. Then she reached for his Barney to tuck next to him, but Andrew shook his head in a negative gesture.

"You don't want Barney?" she asked in astonishment.

"No. Want elephant. Taylor elephant." The brown eyes looked sleepily up at his mommy.

Tessa looked around his room and spotted the elephant on a rocker in the corner. She picked up the grey stuffed animal. "This elephant?" She was astounded by this.

"Yes. Taylor elephant."

Tessa hesitantly brought the elephant to her son and he took it and placed it by his side where Barney normally resided. He cuddled it close to him as Tessa watched, her heart wrenching.

"You know, you should give your elephant a name. What name will you give your elephant?" she asked.

"Taylor."

"No, honey. Taylor *gave* you the elephant. He needs his own name," Tessa tried to explain.

"Taylor," Andrew insisted.

Tessa felt like weeping. "Okay, Andrew. Taylor the elephant it is. I love you, sweetheart. See you tomorrow. Sweet dreams."

Andrew snuggled with the grey elephant and closed his eyes.

Tessa shut the door and moved down the hall to the living room where Rose was sitting on the sofa. Tessa took a seat in a wing chair and sighed heavily. "Get this. He didn't want his Barney to sleep with tonight. He insisted on having the elephant from the zoo. And he named it Taylor," she ended sarcastically.

Rose was not a bit surprised but it seemed Tessa was and it had not gone over too well. This was the very topic she wanted to discuss with Tessa—Taylor and his absence.

"Taylor came by to see me earlier before he left," she opened casually.

Tessa crossed her legs, settling back in the chair. "Oh he did, did he?"

"Yes, to say goodbye. He also told me that a company will be by in a few days to pick up the Suburban."

Tessa's brows arched. "Yes. I was wondering if he was leaving it here or what."

"We did talk about other things too, Tessa. Mainly you and Andrew."

"Oh?"

Rose sighed, then her brown eyes met Tessa's. "Tessa, don't be angry with Taylor. He has not done anything wrong and he was always honest with you. He was wonderful with your son but he has a job to do. He did not leave you because he wanted to."

"He told you that?"

"Not in so many words, but I can clearly see that he cares about both you and Andrew, more than you know. Taylor just doesn't want to get close to people. It's his nature for some reason. Maybe his upbringing, I don't know. But he got very close with you, Andrew and myself and I think that really scares him. I think he accepted the project to sort everything out. Remember Tessa, he DID say he would be returning."

"And you believe him?"

"Why would I not believe him? He left all of his furniture, did he not? He still is renting from you, true?"

"Yes, and yes."

"Well, that indicates to me that he will return when he is done filming."

"Maybe. Maybe not, Rose. In the meantime I have a heart broken son I must console and somehow try to go on and lead a normal life. Taylor was a fantasy that popped in here briefly and is now gone."

"Do you really believe that, Tessa? In your heart, do you really believe that?"

Tessa was silent. She was so conflicted about Taylor. Taylor had saved Andrew's life. For that alone she would be forever grateful, but she had a life here in Lewiston and a son to raise. She and Taylor came from two very different worlds and Tessa could not see how it could ever work. AND she had made the giant mistake of falling in love with him. She knew it would lead to pain and hurt and that was exactly what was happening. Well, you only have yourself to blame Tessa. But she also knew she would not trade her memories or experiences with Taylor for anything. Sighing, she could see Rose had a point.

She finally looked up at the older woman, answering her question. "I know my heart is very conflicted, Rose. I have strong feelings for Taylor but I have no idea if they are reciprocated. Taylor can have any woman he wants. I am just a mom and a nurse trying to give my son a good life." She stood. "If you don't mind Rose, I am very tired."

Rose stood and came to Tessa and embraced her hard. Leaning back, she looked into the beautiful woman's face. "You don't give yourself enough credit, Tessa. It will be very hard for Taylor to forget you. You think about that."

Rose kissed her cheek and turned to go.

Tessa prepared for bed, ruminating on her conversation with Rose and Andrew's unusual reaction about the elephant tonight. Oh Lord, please let us move on. Please put a smile back on my son's face. I would do anything to see him smile again.

Then take him to see Taylor, Tessa.

WHERE had that thought come from, she wondered as she drifted to sleep.

CHAPTER
THIRTY NINE

FILMING BEGAN THE FOLLOWING day. The weather continued to be cool but sunny, perfect weather conditions when you had to film outside. Stan wanted to get to outside sequences first since the weather was cooperating and many of these scenes involved stunts.

The opening sequences took about twelve hours to film. Taylor had to race over rocky terrain in an open Jeep with the bad guys chasing and shooting at him. Even though the opening sequence would look action packed and fast paced to audiences, it would take several weeks just to film these sequences. Fortunately the weather was predicted to be clear.

Doing such physical filming was always exhausting. When Taylor retired to his RV in the evening, he ate a quick sandwich, took a long hot shower, spent a bit of time going over the scenes for the next day and then hit the sack. He was so tired he didn't even have time to think.

But he did dream, and his dreams were filled with the face of a beautiful brunette.

Taylor and his co-star Jeanine Walker were having breakfast at the food RV. There were many picnic tables scattered around to accommodate cast and crew and at this early hour it was quite crowded. Taylor scooped up some scrambled eggs, bacon, toast and of course, black strong coffee. He needed protein to get through these very physical scenes. As he ate his eggs, he studied his co-star.

Jeanine Walker was about five seven and very slender. She had thick long brown hair and exotic slightly slanted brown eyes with thick lashes, which were her best feature. She was a very intelligent woman and Taylor enjoyed conversing with her but their opportunities to talk had been minimal so far. He had not filmed any scenes with her yet.

Jeanine studied Taylor as he ate his breakfast, occasionally glancing up to grin at her. What a smile! She could see why female fans went ga-ga for him. That smile could melt the devil's heart. She respected Taylor because she knew he was a fine actor but he had a bad boy reputation and Jeanine firmly believed in never sleeping with co-stars. She made movies to act, not to sleep around. Plus she was in a serious relationship right now. Her boyfriend was a race car driver and right now they were separated with her in Canada and Raoul in Argentina.

"So, how is filming going so far, Taylor? Looks like you've had some rough scenes already," Jeanine remarked.

Taylor looked up, chewing eggs and swallowed. He grinned at her. He was getting a deep tan that lightened his hair and brightened his eyes. She could admit he was gorgeous indeed.

"Goin' okay. I'm used to physical chase scenes. Done many of them. I like it better when you get most of them done first off. Then you can concentrate on the dialogue and building the characters and story line. Still the viewers like to see things that go "crash" and Stan knows what viewers want." He sipped at his coffee, studying the woman across from him. "What about you? You nervous about working with Stan?" Stan was a big hot shot producer in Hollywood and many stars would kill to star in one of his flicks. Jeanine had just met Stan for the first time when she arrived on set.

Jeanine's brows rose. Taylor was perceptive. How had he noted her nervousness? "Yeah, a bit. I don't know him well." She paused. "Was it you who wanted me for the film, or Stan?" She knew powerhouse stars like Taylor could request their co-stars.

"Actually a bit of both. Stan suggested you and I like your work. You don't need to worry about Stan. He growls a lot, but he's a big softie. As long as you do your job well, you won't have a problem."

"Action scenes are a bit tough for me. I have a stand-in, but I'll have to do some of the scenes. I know I can act. Can I leap across a cliff? No!" She laughed, sipping her coffee.

"That's why we have all kinds of trainers onset. To help you with stuff like that. The harder stuff will be left to your stunt double. Don't worry. We don't want any actresses with broken necks!"

She chuckled softly. "Neither do I. Neither do I."

Several weeks passed by and they were almost to the end of May. Stan wrapped up most of the outdoor scenes during this time period. Indoor dialogue scenes would be filmed next involving Taylor, male co-stars and Jeanine. The carpenters and stage hands had been busy building the sets that Stan wanted and the producer spent quite a bit of time directing crew and special effects teams.

When Taylor could grab free time, he always studied his script so he could have the mood and dialogue down. He always lost himself when he filmed movies, becoming a different person. During the days and evenings when he was filming, he was a person who had never heard of Tessa Patterson. At night in his lonely bed he berated himself for ever leaving the woman. He tried to get as much sleep as possible because of the grueling shoot. Taylor did not expect to see the Pattersons for a long time. Filming would take up his summer and maybe even part of the fall. Sighing, he concentrated on his script. He needed to make sure every shoot counted, that way he could get back to them sooner. Still there were many things that were out of his control on a shoot and he just had to go with the flow.

Taylor and Stan were going over the daily rushes in Stan's RV. They both watched the monitor intently as Taylor crashed a Jeep and leaped free of the flames. The special effects team had done an excellent job of making the flames appear real and Taylor's natural athleticism made the scene realistic. They both continued to watch as Taylor rolled away from the Jeep, on his belly in the sand, looking up at the burning vehicle in incredulity. Then the thing exploded, debris flying everywhere and Taylor scrunched up his body and put his hands over his head as hot steel rained down around him. He looked up briefly, leapt to his feet and ran fast over a hill. End of scene.

Stan turned to Taylor, smiling as he pushed a button that flicked off the monitor screen. "Good job, as always Taylor. You sure do make those scenes look easy. Makes my job easier."

"Yeah, well I got a sore ass. Do you care about that, Stan?"

Stan laughed. "Nope. But I got painkillers I can give ya."

Taylor shook his head. "No thanks. Don't want to get hooked on those things. I can take my lumps."

Stan relaxed back in his chair, studying the younger man. "That's because you are still young, Taylor. Talk to me in about ten years and we'll see how you feel then. Meantime, drink?" Stan offered.

Taylor stretched out his long jean clad legs. "Sure. What ya got?"

"I know you like bourbon. I have your brand. Your RV is also stocked with it. I saw to that." He poured two drinks, bringing them over to where they were both sitting at the console.

Taylor accepted the drink. "Thanks, hoss." He took a sip. "Yeah, sure tastes good after a day of that," Taylor gestured to the blank screen.

Stan sipped at his drink, studying Taylor. "I'm glad you agreed to do the film. I was worried there for a while you would turn us down."

Taylor sipped contemplatively, tipped back a bit in the chair, his eyes closed. Then the teal eyes met Stan's. "Yep. I took some time off of work. Six months or so. Frank wasn't too happy with me but I needed some time to be off on my own." Taylor felt comfortable talking to Stan about this because they were friends. Stan was one of the few Hollywood producers Taylor really respected. Some of them could be real assholes.

"Yeah, you always were a workaholic, jumping from one project to the next. Never could figure out where you got the energy to do that and still be excellent each time out. Must be innate ability and the fact you're still young." Stan sipped at his scotch, eyeing his star.

Taylor sighed. "That's not really the reason. I didn't need a rest. I just needed— I don't know— a different perspective on things."

Stan's brows rose. This was not the Taylor he was familiar with. Taylor loved to act and was part of the whole Hollywood scene. He was known as a womanizer and a bad boy but Stan knew when Taylor worked he was professional and never partied. So this comment was surprising. "That's surprising. A different perspective. And did you find one?"

Taylor ruminated about his motorcycle accident, thinking about almost dying and then meeting an angel named Tessa who was a mommy to a little boy he fell in love with. Yes, his perspective had changed about many things. He just did not know what to do about it.

Taylor finally answered Stan. "Yeah. My perspective and outlook has changed." He shrugged. "Making movies was the Taylor from a year and a half ago. The Taylor today— not so much."

Again Stan was startled, particularly because Taylor was doing such a fine job on this film. "That is amazing. Your perspective certainly has changed. May I ask why?"

Taylor took another sip of bourbon. "Ya know, I haven't figured that out for myself yet, Stan."

"Well, in the meantime, keep your eye on the prize, Taylor. I want to wrap by October first."

"So do I, Stan. So do I."

CHAPTER
FORTY

THE DAYS WERE SUNNY and mild now that June had arrived. Tessa could usually send Andrew off to school with just a light jacket. The flowers and trees were all fully bloomed and the splotches of color around the yard helped to lift Tessa's spirits a bit.

She had been very down ever since Taylor had left them. He had been gone about a month now and they were making it, but she could tell she wasn't the only one who missed him. Andrew was unusually subdued and his teachers kept asking Tessa if everything was all right at home since they had noticed a complete change in Andrew's demeanor. All Tessa could do was assure them things were normal when she knew they were anything but. She tried to take her son out for fun outings he had enjoyed in the past but nothing lifted his spirits. He went through the motions of going to school and doing what he had to do and Tessa admired his courage so much knowing inside he was hurting. As they all were. Rose tried to boast everyone's spirits but it was really hard for them all.

A company had come by the day after Taylor left and removed his SUV, so there was not even that reminder that Taylor had ever been here. Of course, she had the key to his place and could go in anytime but she did not want to do that. It would just rub salt in the wound seeing his gorgeous place empty without his vivacious spirit to breathe life into the place.

Tessa kept busy with work and since it was mid June, in a few weeks Andrew would be out of school. Rose usually had him all day then but Tessa was now able to arrange to have a tutor/big buddy take Andrew on outings with the extra rent money she received from Taylor.

When her rent check arrived in June from Frank Zimmerman's office she noticed the rent was doubled. Thinking there was some kind of mix up or mistake, she phoned the number Taylor had left her. After going through three secretaries, she finally reached an executive assistant who informed her the amount was correct. Taylor had authorized the amount of two thousand dollars a month in rent. It helped her with expenses for her son so she accepted it silently, thinking if he was going to break her son's heart, at least she could try to help Andrew with the extra money.

Money could not make up for happiness though. She had learned that lesson a long time ago and it really broke her heart to see how unhappy her son was.

Tessa and Rose were swinging on the front porch as they both watched Andrew playing in the yard. He was riding the new bicycle that Taylor had given him for Christmas and Tessa was careful to keep a close eye on him, making sure he didn't get too close to the front road.

As they gently swung back and forth, Rose studied Tessa's face. She looked sad and had a far away look in her eyes and Rose knew she was thinking of Taylor. He was never mentioned much because the two of them did not want to upset Andrew, but school would be out soon and Rose really thought Tessa should think about taking Andrew to see Taylor. How to broach the subject?

She sighed. "Tessa, how have you been doing? With Taylor gone?" There, she had finally said the T word.

Tessa's startled eyes moved to Rose. "What brought that up, Rose?" Taylor was not discussed between them.

"Tessa, you need to stop dancing around the obvious and see how unhappy your son is. School will be ending soon and I think it would be a good idea for you to take Andrew to see Taylor on the movie set. He did say you could do that, didn't he?"

Tessa sighed. "Yes, he said we could all visit the set. But you know Andrew cannot travel on commercial vehicles such as airplanes, trains, boats or whatever. And Edmonton is just too far away to drive there. It is just not possible."

Rose was silent a moment. She glanced over at Andrew, seeing he was sitting still on his bike, just looking down at the ground. Just from his posture you could tell how dejected he felt. "Tessa, look at your son right now."

Tessa obeyed, her eyes rising to see her son just sitting on his bike, not moving, shoulders slumped and she felt like bawling. With tears in her eyes, she turned to Rose. "What do you want me to do, Rose? I would give anything to see Andrew happy again. You know that!"

Rose could see Tessa was upset but she had a point to make and needed to do so. "Tessa, there are ways of getting there if you are really determined."

"Determination isn't the issue, Rose. Andrew's disability is. I would take him in a heart beat if it was possible to get him to go. But you know he cannot handle travel like that. It just is what it is." She paused, looking over at Andrew. She stood. "I have to go to my son, Rose. He needs me."

She moved down the stairs and over to her son and Rose watched as Tessa stooped down next to her son, softly talking to him.

Rose came to a decision. She knew what she had to do. Contact Taylor.

Rose called Taylor's cell phone number direct. She called at eleven p.m. in the evening. She hoped that the time difference would not interfere with getting Taylor. She did get his voice message and sighing, left a message.

Ten minutes later, her phone rang as she was putting on her nightgown. She ran for the phone on her night table, answering breathlessly. "Hello?"

"Rose?" Taylor's voice on the line, with a bit of static and echo because of the long distance.

"Yes Taylor. It's me. How are you? I hope I am not taking you away from anything important." She settled on her bed as she spoke to him.

"Nope. We finished wrapping for the day about a half hour ago. Just thinking about getting something to eat but when I got your message I wanted to get back to you. How are you all doing?"

Rose's heart and spirits lifted just hearing his voice. "Well, to be quite honest Taylor that is the reason I called you. Tessa and Andrew are not doing well at all."

Taylor's voice was alarmed. "What do you mean? Is everyone okay?"

"Oh, everyone is fine physically," she hastily reassured him. "It's just Tessa and Andrew are not doing well at all. They are both very depressed with your absence Taylor. You mentioned they could visit the set and Andrew will be out of school after next week. I wanted to discuss how we could get them there to see you. They both need to see you." She didn't mention she felt the same way. "Do you have any ideas of how we could accomplish that?"

There was a slight pause and then Taylor answered. "Yep. Been thinking about that myself. I could have my private Lear Jet pick them up and bring them directly here. I have investigated and purchased special head phones that should obliterate most of the noise of the jet for Andrew. Plus, if Tessa could get a mild sedative from her doctor just to calm him a bit, I think it could work. When does he get out of school?"

"June seventeenth is his last day. That is about a week away."

"Okay. Run this by Tessa and see what she thinks. I'll make sure you guys get the royal treatment. And I want you to come too, Rose."

Rose smiled. She wanted to go also but wanted to be invited and was pleased he was including her. "Okay, Taylor. I will speak to her and see what kind of arrangements we can come up with. They are both so sad it is breaking my heart." She wanted him to know just how badly he was missed.

Taylor sighed heavily on the other line. "I miss you all too. I try to run away from that fact filming every day, but every night all I do is long to see the three of you again. If you could come out, that would be great. I'd love to see all of you."

"I will speak to Tessa and get back to you Taylor."

"Okay, Rose. And thanks for making this overture. I know Tessa would not do so."

"I don't know Taylor. I would not be too sure about that. She will do anything to make her son happy."

"Okay. I'll talk to ya soon."

"Yes. Good bye, Taylor."

Rose replaced the receiver, a satisfied look on her face. As she brushed her long thick silver hair out, she tried to decide how to approach Tessa about this.

Rose went upstairs the next evening to speak to Tessa when she knew Andrew would be in bed. It was about nine p.m. and the little guy should be asleep by now.

She ascended the back steps and knocked lightly on Tessa's kitchen door. "Tessa? It's me, Rose." She entered the kitchen that was dimly lit with just the stove night light on.

"Rose?" Tessa entered from the other room. "What brings you up here at this hour?" It was unusual for Rose to come up after they said their good nights after dinner. "Something wrong?"

"No, no. I just wanted to speak to you when I knew Andrew would be asleep."

"Oh, okay. Well, would you like some decaf coffee, tea or anything?" Tessa offered.

Rose took a seat at Tessa's table. "No thank you. I just wanted to chat a bit."

Tessa turned a light on low and sat opposite Rose. The older woman was wearing a light pink satin robe over her nightgown. Tessa was still wearing her jean shorts and light blouse, sandals on her feet. Since she had been out gardening lately she had a light lovely tan that enhanced her long legs and pretty face. She studied Rose's face and could see her friend was worried about something.

"You know you can come and talk to me anytime, Rose. What is up? You look upset."

"Do I? Well, maybe that is because I am so concerned for you. For both you and Andrew. I can't help but notice how unhappy you both have been since Taylor left. I love you both and can't bear to see either of you unhappy."

At these remarks, Tessa's expression changed. Her concern changed to nonchalance as she tried to pretend everything was fine. "We're okay, Rose. We're making it."

"No, you're not. And no you are not making it. And neither is your son Tessa. And you *know* that! I spoke to Taylor," she continued.

At these words, Tessa's head snapped up. "Oh?"

"Yes. Since Andrew will be through with school soon, I called him to suggest that perhaps we could visit him at his set—"

"Rose," Tessa interrupted, "you know that is—"

Rose held up a hand. "Please let me finish, Tessa." Tessa was silent, and Rose continued. "Andrew is not doing well lately. You know it and I know it. He needs Taylor. He just doesn't love him, he *needs* him. To go to see him would help Andrew a great deal. I know you are worried about the logistics of getting Andrew there but this is what Taylor has proposed." Rose explained to Tessa the plans Taylor had come up with. "What do you think about this?"

Tessa was silent as she thought about Rose's comments. She knew her son missed Taylor greatly as she did, but they had to learn to live without him. Taylor would not always be in their lives and they had to get used to that. But her son was so miserable and she knew Rose was right. A visit to see Taylor would greatly lift his spirits. Tessa had vacation time too. Since they basically never vacationed she had at least four weeks she could take at any time. She usually used part of that when Andrew was off in the summer to do fun activities and spend time with her son and she had many good memories of summer moments. It would make her son very happy to see Taylor again. She could get a low dose sedative that would help calm her son enough to fly on a private plane. A commercial plane would not work but a private plane would be much quieter and they would be able to cater to Andrew's needs.

Sighing, she looked up at Rose. "Okay. I agree this is a good idea. I'll have to put in for some time off. Perhaps we can leave around the twenty seventh if that works for Taylor."

Left unsaid was Tessa would not be contacting Taylor. Rose would be.

Rose smiled and patted Tessa's hand. "You are making the right decision,

Tessa. And don't worry. I think Andrew may handle this trip much better than you think."

"I hope so, Rose. I hate seeing my son so unhappy. If this will help him, I'm all for it."

Rose stood. "I'll speak to Taylor and make the arrangements." She hugged Tessa. "Good night, Tessa." She turned to exit the kitchen as Tessa sighed, ruminating over the conversation.

CHAPTER
FORTY ONE

TAYLOR LOOKED UP INTO the clear azure sky. The sound of a jet approaching roared overhead and in the clearness and open space, Taylor recognized his private jet. It was sleek and white with his initials "TAB" scrolled down both sides in azure blue and turquoise. It was a fine looking machine and just as fine on the inside. Cushy pale blue carpets, white supple leather seats and teak mahogany accents throughout made for a pampered luxurious ride. Taylor had purchased the jet two years ago and hired an ex-Air Force captain as his pilot. The sleek baby made it easy for him to come and go as he pleased (except for winter storms, humph!) and Taylor liked the freedom the jet afforded him.

Now he shaded his eyes from the bright summer sun as the jet landed smoothly on the helo pad. The movie set was located twenty miles outside the city of Edmonton and the set was a mini city onto itself. He waited in anticipation as Ron landed the jet smoothly and hoped the trip had gone smooth also, especially for the little guy. He could not wait to see Andrew and Rose. His feelings were ambivalent about Tessa since they had not left on the best of terms but at least she had agreed to bring Andrew to the set for two weeks. Taylor had to be satisfied with that.

Stan had just started shooting interior scenes which would be good. There was less noise in interior shots although lighting was very bright. However there was always noise on a shoot no matter where you happened to be but he had explained Andrew's disability to Stan and Stan agreed to make every effort to accommodate Taylor's guest's disability. This relieved Taylor. That fact alone would go a long way to making things easier all around.

Taylor approached the jet as he could hear Ron shutting down the engine. His baby purred like a kitten and then silence reigned and the elevated stairs were activated. As Taylor drew nearer, he saw Ron first who waved to Taylor, wearing aviator sunglasses. Taylor waved back as he moved closer to the stairs.

When they were fully deployed, he waited impatiently at the bottom for his guests to deplane.

Rose appeared first, wearing a gauzy scarf over her silver hair and a yellow summer dress, clutching her purse. She noticed Taylor and waved then looked behind her. Taylor waved back and Rose slowly descended the stairs. He met her at the bottom, giving her a big hug. He knew she was the main reason he was receiving this special visit.

"Hello, Rose! How are you? It is so *good* to see you!" Taylor declared. He leaned back as he embraced her, smiling down into her face.

Rose looked up at the tall man embracing her. Taylor was wearing his mirrored sunglasses out here in the bright sunlight. His tan had deepened and he looked very fit and healthy. He wore cut off jeans and a white muscle tank, black thongs on his feet. Rose hugged him back tightly; she had missed him so much. "I'm fine, Taylor. Just fine. And the flight was amazing! I've never been so comfortable flying!"

Taylor grinned down at her. "She's a little beauty, isn't she?"

"Oh yes!"

Rose and Taylor turned to see Tessa at the top of the stairs speaking to her son who was holding her hand tightly. Taylor could see she was wearing tight white slender jeans with a cropped red swiss dotted top and white sandals. Her hair was pulled off of her face in a ponytail and she wore sunglasses, a white purse slung on her arm. She was bending down speaking softly to Andrew who appeared next to her wearing jean shorts, a light green shirt and sneakers. The little boy seemed to be afraid of the long metal steps in front of him.

"Excuse me, Rose." Taylor said, mounting the stairs to help.

Reaching the top of the stairs, Taylor greeted Andrew. "Hey, buddy! It's been too long! I miss you! Come here and give me a hug!"

At the sound of Taylor's voice, Andrew looked up in amazement, his beautiful eyes wide. Although his mommy had told him he would see Taylor at the end of the trip, he did not know that was possible. He didn't know why, it just was. But here was Taylor! His beautiful smile instantly appeared and he launched himself into Taylor's arms. "Taylor!" he screamed in delight.

Taylor caught the child in his strong arms, hugging him tightly, closing his eyes. They were a little misty and he did not want Tessa to notice that. Finally he turned to greet Tessa.

She looked beautiful as always. She smiled tentatively at him. "Hello, Taylor. Thank you for inviting us."

Taylor still held her child. "How was the flight? Did everything go okay?"

"Considering the circumstances, yes. He was very frightened at first, but once we were airborne, he was fine. He is having a problem with these metal stairs though," she gestured to the airplane steps. "He is afraid to step onto them."

"We can take care of that very easily." Taylor looked down at Andrew. "I'll carry my buddy down and he won't have to touch those nasty 'ol steps. Sound good, bud?"

Andrew's arms went tightly around Taylor's neck and he buried his face in Taylor's shoulder. "Yes," he mumbled, trembling.

Taylor quickly trotted down the stairs, holding the boy tightly, knowing he was frightened. He could hear Tessa descending after them. They reached the bottom safely and Taylor placed Andrew on his feet.

"There ya go, buddy! Safe and sound!" He glanced at the two women and smiled. "Welcome to my world!" He waved his hand and the women could see a bustling mini city about fifty feet away from the cement pad they were standing on. It was hot out here in the sun too. "Ron will close the jet down. In the meantime, let me take you to your RV. We have a special one set up for you guys right next to mine." He looked down at Andrew who was glancing warily at all of the activity.

"Here buddy, take my hand," Taylor instructed and Andrew instantly obeyed. As long as he was with Taylor and his mommy, he felt safe.

"We go there?" He pointed to the set where cameras, techs, lights and people scurried around buildings erected in the middle of nowhere.

"Yep, bud. It is where I work. It is called a movie set." As they walked toward the set, he turned to the women. "A gofer will get your luggage and bring it to your RV for you. Right now, I'll take you right over to your RV so you can relax. You're probably tired after the flight."

The women smiled, following Taylor as Andrew looked around curiously. He was wearing ear plugs his mommy gave him so the noise was muted for him but he was still frightened seeing all of the motion and people. He gripped Taylor's hand tightly, not wanting to let go.

It took only above five minutes or so to arrive at the RV. Tessa and Rose were both surprised by its size. It was huge, sleek and modern. It looked like it could easily sleep five people.

As Taylor opened the door for them to enter, they gasped. The RV was as luxurious as a penthouse suite in any elegant hotel. Pale blue and white cushiony sofas and seats were piled with dark blue cushions, glass cocktail tables, shiny brass lamps and gold chandeliers were in the main room. They could see halls leading off to various areas and Taylor gave them a tour. The hallways led to a huge master bath with a separate shower and Jacuzzi, a main bedroom luxuriously decorated, several other guest rooms, smaller but equally nice and another private bathroom. There was also a media room, complete with large screen television, DVD and surround sound. Their kitchen had a large table with cushioned benches and Taylor showed them their refrigerator was fully stocked. Tessa was amazed. They would certainly be comfortable here. Air conditioning was on low at the moment and the temperature was a comfortable seventy one degrees.

Tessa and Rose placed their purses down on the kitchen table as Taylor took Andrew into the media room on the other side of the RV to show him how everything worked.

Rose glanced at Tessa, eyes wide. "This is amazing! It is huge and gorgeous! A mini apartment!"

"Not so mini," Tessa was thinking the place was as large as her flat, or maybe just a bit smaller. She was not expecting anything like this.

She went to the refrigerator and checked out the contents. Lunch meats, fruits of various kinds, freshly chopped veggies, milk, juice, coffee and fruit juices and diet soda were included. Also several bottles of Kendall Jackson Chardonnay, lemonade, iced tea. Checking the freezer, she could see it was well stocked with ice, ice cream and meats and fish of all types.

Taylor entered the kitchen alone. "You can also order meals from the food RV. All you have to do is pick up this phone," he showed them a grey phone hung on the wall, "and dial F for food and they will bring you anything you want."

Tessa closed the door and turned to Taylor. "Wow, Taylor! We were certainly not expecting— well— all of this!" She gestured around them.

Taylor replaced the phone and Tessa could now see his beautiful teal eyes since he had removed his sunglasses. God, she had missed him! But she would never tell him that.

"Where is Andrew?"

Taylor gestured behind him with his thumb. "In the media room. I showed him how to use all of the remotes and he is watching a DVD. I noticed the ear plugs and removed them. Good idea, by the way."

"Yes, they helped him on the trip," she remarked.

Taylor gestured to the kitchen table. "Sit, sit. You must be tired." He went to the refrigerator and poured three glasses of lemonade. Bringing the glasses to the table, he handed them around, seating himself as the ladies also sat.

Tessa removed her dark glasses, sipping at the frosty drink. It tasted heavenly and the plush cushions were comfortable and soft, a chocolate color.

Rose sipped at her lemonade after removing her scarf. "Well, Taylor. We are impressed. We never expected anything like this!"

Taylor chuckled. "Wait 'til you see mine. It is even bigger, with far more amenities. But then, I'm their BIG star!" He laughed, white teeth flashing.

"So, Taylor. Are you working today?" Tessa wondered what was on the schedule.

"Nope. Not today. We're going to film some night scenes so I have some time to show you guys around the set, introduce you to some people. And just to let you know, everyone here is aware of Andrew's disability and will try and accommodate him as much as possible. I would recommend using the ear plugs onset, though. It will be noisy— sometimes more so, other times not so bad." Taylor sipped at his lemonade as he studied Tessa. God, she was beautiful and her slight tan really brought out her tawny eyes.

Those eyes now swung up to his. "Thank you, Taylor! I am so grateful you did that. I was very nervous and unsure how this whole experience would go for Andrew. But it was wonderful to see his smile when he saw you." She didn't mention it was the first smile she had seen in ages.

Finishing up his lemonade, Taylor stood. "I can take you all for a short tour right now. I'll introduce you to Stan; he's the producer/director. The big wig, if you will. Maybe some co-stars too, if they're around."

"Let me get Andrew and we'll be right with you," Tessa said as she rose, placing her dark glasses back on.

"I think I will relax with my lemonade for now, Taylor. You two go ahead, though. I will be able to see everything soon, I'm sure." Rose stretched out her feet, snuggling into chocolate cushions.

"Sure thing, Rose."

When Tessa appeared with Andrew, who had his earplugs in again, Taylor ushered them outside.

"Let's go, guys. Lot's to see and do."

Taylor only gave a very short tour of the set, about twenty minutes. He knew if it was too long it would be too much for Andrew to handle. He took them over to Stan's RV and introduced them. Stan smiled, shaking hands. He was going over the schedule of the shoot and Taylor didn't stay long.

He showed Tessa and her son the set and how the carpenters built certain buildings to look real from the front, whereas a back view just showed recently sawed wood. Tessa was amazed at all of the activity. There were people everywhere and huge cameras and lights and catwalks.

The food RV was probably a ten minute walk from their RV. There were a few cast members there eating lunch and Taylor's co-star Jeanine Walker was among them.

Taylor introduced the two women and Tessa carefully took note of

Jeanine, curious about Taylor's female co-star. Did he have love scenes with this woman? Oh boy, that would be tough.

Jeanine was about an inch shorter than herself, slender and had exotic beautiful brown eyes. She looked a bit Eurasian. She had long brown hair and her nose was a bit long and sharp. Although she wasn't a classic beauty, she exuded sex appeal. Any man around her would immediately lust after her. Tessa was not familiar with Jeanine's work at all but she was pleasant and friendly. Tessa also knew Jeanine was checking her out just as intently. Tessa smiled and shook hands, and also met a few male co-stars. Everyone was friendly and kind toward Andrew, greeting him with smiles and high fives. Andrew smiled, fiving people back, chattering about his buddy Taylor. Everyone grinned down at the beautiful little boy. Tessa was very glad to see the people she had met so far were kind to her son. That had been a huge worry for her too. Hollywood people had reputations as big snobs. That wasn't true in Taylor's case, so perhaps she did not need to worry.

Taylor wound around back to their RV, not wanting the little guy to get too tired or cranky.

They entered the RV and Rose was at the kitchen table, reading a magazine, sipping lemonade. "Well, hello! How did it go?"

Andrew ran to her, smiling. "Got to see set. Wood. Buildings." He grinned hugely and Rose returned his smile.

"I think you will have fun here watching Taylor work, Andrew. Don't you think so?"

"Yes!"

Tessa was in the process of pouring Andrew an icy drink of water after being outside for twenty minutes and she could see he had a bit of a sunburn. Next time she would have to use the sunblock she had brought along liberally.

After Andrew had his drink, he looked up at Taylor. "Taylor, 'edia room?" He pointed toward the media room.

"Sure, buddy. Let's play some video games. I'm gonna win too!"

Andrew giggled as he ran to the other side of the large RV, Taylor following close behind.

Tessa joined Rose at the kitchen table with her own lemonade. She was hot too after their jaunt outside.

Rose arched a brow.

Seeing this, Tessa laughed a bit. "I know, I know. You don't have to say it. 'I told you so'".

"Then I won't say it!" Rose quipped.

CHAPTER
FORTY TWO

TESSA SPENT THE EVENING in their RV, snuggled into one of the comfy sofas, reading a novel. Rose had just retired and Andrew went to bed early, around eight because he was so exhausted from the busy day. Tessa laid her novel down and ruminated about their first day on the set.

Taylor had left them about five p.m. saying he needed to get back to prep for night scenes. She knew he was now working at ten o'clock at night and could not believe he had the energy after escorting them all over the set today and spending time with Andrew. Before he left he gave Tessa three gold badges for them. He explained the badges indicated they were VIP guests, meaning they would be treated well on the set. There were hundreds of people on a set he explained and not everyone would be aware of Andrew's disability, but as soon as they saw the gold badge it would automatically guarantee they would be treated well. Especially for the times Taylor could not be with them.

Tessa picked up the badge on the table next to her. It was a gold foil adhesive circular label to be worn on one's shirt. In bold black calligraphy it read: Guests of Taylor Boudrain. Hmmm...Taylor really was a king in his own world.

The movie set was fascinating and in the latter part of the afternoon she and Andrew were able to observe a short scene being filmed outside. She had already warned Andrew he must always be quiet like a mouse when scenes were filmed and she did the "ssshing" motion. Andrew copied that, smiling. He was very good when they were watching the scene. Whenever they were onset she had his earplugs in and Andrew was quite content to watch the scene with Taylor standing with him. Tessa worried about the times Taylor would not be with them, such as when he was filming.

He had also told her the next day they were filming indoor dialogue scenes from late morning to mid afternoon and he would come by and get the three of them so they could watch the filming. Tessa wondered how that would go with Andrew observing.

Sighing, she picked up her book to read a bit more before lights out. She would find out tomorrow.

Taylor came by about eleven in the morning. Tessa made sure Andrew was liberally covered with sunblock. They were all dressed in cool clothing. Tessa had Andrew dressed in a jungle print Hawaiian shirt and khaki cargo shorts, brown suede sandals on his feet and a tan ball cap to shade his face. She and Rose were dressed in white— Rose in a white sundress with a wide white hat to protect her from the sun's rays and Tessa chose white shorts and a white sleeveless top with white sandals. She opted for a wide white straw hat and tucked her abundant hair under it so it would not make her hot.

When Taylor arrived, he was already in costume. He was wearing a pinstriped 1930's style grey suit with a black bowtie and was carrying a dark grey fedora. Tessa had a basic idea what the film was about from reading and helping Taylor with the script but had no idea what to expect on set.

"Hi guys!" He greeted them all. "Ready for a day on the set?" He flashed his famous grin.

They left their RV, smiling at Taylor. They all had their gold badges on display and Andrew had his earplugs in.

"Taylor!" Andrew ran to his buddy to hug him.

Taylor leaned down to hug the boy back and standing, took his hand. "Let's go over to the set. It's not too far, shouldn't have to be out in this sun too much today. Which is a good thing!"

"Yes, it is hot already!" Rose declared.

Taylor turned to her. "The set is air conditioned so you guys should be comfortable while you watch."

"Thank God for little favors!" Tessa declared.

They reached the building the scenes were to be shot at. It was an entirely enclosed building, unlike some sets they had already toured.

As they entered, Tessa could see they had the huge spotlights already set up and the cameras pointing at the focal point of the action, which seemed to be an office. A desk, files, shelves, chairs, books— a typical office. Taylor had explained he would be filming a scene with a male co-star and most of the scene was dialogue. He did explain towards the end of the shoot there would be a fight scene and if she did not want Andrew to view that, she could then remove Andrew. She was to signal Stan when this action started.

As the three entered the set with Taylor, Stan came right over. Smiling, he greeted Taylor's guests and pointed out three directors chairs close to the action.

As Rose, Tessa and Andrew took their seats, Stan addressed Taylor in a low voice. "Now, the boy knows he has to be totally silent, correct?" Stan wanted to make sure Andrew would not be interrupting scenes as they filmed.

"Yes, both his mother and I have discussed that with him," Taylor answered.

"Okay. We're set and ready to go. Let's punch it!"

Taylor moved behind the desk and seated himself.

"And action!" Stan's voice.

Taylor's protagonist entered the office door and the two actors spoke their lines, interacting in the scene. As they did so, Andrew squirmed in his chair, clearly wanting to run up to the set.

Tessa leaned down to whisper "Andrew, you must be still and quiet. Please read your book." She had brought it along to distract him for just this reason.

"No, see Taylor," Andrew insisted.

"Cut!" Stan's voice.

Obviously Andrew's reply had been too loud for the scene.

Taylor made a ssshing motion to Andrew. Andrew mimed Taylor, sssshing.

Tessa was very embarrassed. It had only taken the first cut for Andrew to disrupt matters.

"Take two. Action!" Stan's voice again.

The actor re-entered the office and the scene progressed. This time Andrew was very quiet, watching intently as the action unfolded.

It took two hours to film the entire dialogue scene and Tessa was amazed it took this long to film a segment that would probably be five minutes in the movie. They had needed ten takes because the second actor kept fumbling lines and cues.

Finally Taylor approached Tessa when they had a break.

"We're going to be filming the fight scene next. I have to beat the guy up, basically. You probably don't want him to see that," Taylor informed Tessa.

"No, I don't. I think we'll go back to our RV. We're all hungry and this has been tough on Andrew having to be still for so long. We need a break too!" She laughed a bit.

"Okay. I'll come by when I'm finished for the day. It will probably be around dinner time, six or so."

"Okay. Do you want to have dinner with us in our RV? I can make us some dinner." Tessa's brown eyes searched his.

"Sounds good, Tessa. See ya later."

He turned to go speak to Stan as Tessa collected her son and Rose and they left the set.

As they ate lunch at the kitchen table, Rose remarked about how amazing an experience it was watching a movie being filmed.

"I had no idea so much work goes into the making of a film. When you watch one, everything seems so effortless. And Taylor is amazing to watch in action too!"

Tessa took a bite of her ham sandwich. Andrew had finished up his lunch and was in the media room relaxing.

"I have never seen any of Taylor's previous movies. I agree. He is totally a gifted actor."

Rose's brows lifted. "You have NEVER seen one of his movies?!" This shocked Rose. She had assumed everyone had seen at least one Taylor Boudrain film.

"No, Rose. All of my movie time is spent with Andrew. You know that."

"Well, I thought maybe like on a date, you may have gone to a movie or something…"

"Yeah, here and there. But I never saw a Boudrain film. Not for any special reason. Just never saw one. But now I am seeing one being filmed! It is exciting!" Tessa admitted. "Oh, and Taylor is coming by for dinner after filming. Six or so. Should I make steaks?"

"That would be good. I'll make some of my famous potato salad!"

"Sounds terrific! I know he'll love it!"

The two ladies spent the hot afternoon in their RV, preparing dinner for Taylor. Andrew napped in the afternoon so he would be refreshed when Taylor came.

Taylor knocked on their door about six fifteen. Tessa opened the door to him, smiling, motioning him in. She could see he was now in regular clothes, jean shorts and a pale blue tee, black suede thongs on his feet. His glorious hair brushed the top of the tee.

"Hi, Tessa! All done for the day!" He entered the RV and looked toward the kitchen where he could see Rose placing food on the table. "Hmmm… something smells awesome!"

Tessa motioned him into their kitchen. "We grilled some steaks and there is Rose's potato salad, corn on the cob and strawberry shortcake for dessert."

"Oh man! I don't eat this good when you guys aren't here. I gotta be careful in these two weeks! Can't put on any weight!" He chuckled.

Andrew ran into the kitchen from the media room when he heard Taylor's voice. He hugged Taylor's bare legs tightly. "Taylor! Missed!"

Taylor hugged the boy back. "I missed you too, buddy. How did you like seeing me work?"

"Sssssh!" Andrew made the shushing motion.

"Yep, I know that was hard for you buddy, but you were so good about it and I am proud of you. High five!"

Andrew giggled, fiving Taylor.

Rose motioned everyone to the table. "Come sit down, everything is hot and ready."

They all took seats around the table and dug in. Rose asked Taylor different questions about the filming and he casually chatted with both her and Tessa about acting and what directors wanted in scenes. He also informed them scenes for the next day would be shot outside and it would be hot.

"I don't know how long we'll be able to stay for an outdoor shoot Taylor, but we'll definitely want to see that."

"There is more action involved. You'll get to see me do stunts, instead of just dialogue scenes."

"I thought the dialogue scenes were fascinating," Tessa remarked. "Since I've never seen any of your movies, it was quite an experience to see you act."

Taylor's brows arched. "You never saw a Boudrain movie?! What's wrong with you?" he quipped.

Tessa and Rose both chuckled and Rose answered him. "She never even saw one out on a date. Imagine that!"

"Boy, Tessa. I'm lucky the general public doesn't think like you! I'd be out of a job!"

Tessa looked up into his twinkling teal eyes. "Somehow I doubt that, Taylor."

Taylor laughed and they enjoyed their dinner. Afterwards Taylor played some video games with Andrew until he was too tired to keep his eyes open.

Taylor left them. "See ya on the set tomorrow!"

Tessa smiled as he left the RV. "We'll be there!"

CHAPTER
FORTY THREE

THE OUTDOOR SET WAS busy with people scurrying around on their various tasks. Today they were shooting a scene where Taylor would have to help rescue his co-star Jeanine after she fell over the lip of a cliff. There were quite a few special effects team personnel needed. They all waded around the two stars making sure their vests and lines under their shirts were secured. Taylor had filmed such scenes in the past but Jeanine had not and he could see she was frightened. Her stunt double would be doing most of the work with Taylor but Jeanine would be required for scenes at the very tip of the cliff—and it was a *loooong* way down!

Taylor conversed with the effects team, Stan and Jeanine as he waited for the Pattersons and Rose to come to the set. He told them they were filming early, nine a.m. and he did not know how that would work out for the little guy. So far, they had not shown. They needed to be in place before action started too.

Glancing up briefly from his conversation, Taylor could see the three approaching the set. It was hot out here in the sun and they all had dressed for the weather with light cool clothes, hats, shades and sandals. He waved to the three and Tessa returned the wave as they approached closer.

"'Scuse me Stan, Jeanine," Taylor remarked, moving over to the three.

"Sure." Jeanine watched curiously as Taylor greeted his guests. She had been informed by another co-star that Taylor *never* had guests on a set and assumed these people, especially the woman, were special to Taylor. She admitted he had good taste. The woman was beautiful and friendly.

"Hi guys!" Taylor greeted the three.

"Hi, Taylor! We're excited to see an outdoor shoot but it sure is hot out here!" Tessa remarked, glancing up at him through her shades.

Taylor grinned down at her. "I know. It's only gonna get hotter as the day goes on and we'll probably be at it for hours. Just signal Kev here," he threw his thumb over his shoulder at a young guy with a goatee standing next to him, who waved as his name was mentioned, "when you guys need to leave. He'll signal Stan so we can stop action. Kev is also gonna look out for you guys. Anything you need or want, Kev gets for you. Drinks, whatever. We have your chairs situated back further from the action. You won't be as close so little slight noises are not a problem, but as usual, no talking. Good to go, little guy?" Taylor looked down at Andrew and the little boy smiled back and grinned.

"Yes. Good, go!"

"All righty, then. Kev— they're all yours. Gotta go work guys. I'll see ya later on, it will probably be after dinner but I'll stop by for a bit."

"Okay. Thank you, Taylor," Tessa responded.

Taylor grinned and waved and loped over to the edge of what looked like a steep cliff to Tessa. Looking across the ravine, sure enough she could see the other side of the huge crevasse. And Taylor was going to do *stunts* there?! Oh my Lord!

Kevin smiled and introduced himself and escorted the three guests to their chairs, noting they all wore gold badges. Kevin knew right away that meant they were to be treated like royalty.

He seated the three in their chairs and looked down at them through his shades. "Can I get you anything right now? Cold drinks, snacks, anything?" he asked. "I'll be sitting right here with you guys." He gestured to another director chair.

Tessa smiled up at him. "Thanks, but we are set for now. I brought a cooler with water bottles and some cokes. Would you like a cool drink?" He sure looked hot already.

Kevin's brows arched. "Do you have regular Pepsi?"

Tessa opened the cooler. "Yep." She tossed him an icy bottle and he accepted it with thanks as Tessa took out three waters. They settled in to watch the action. They all were slathered with sunblock and although it was early it was probably already close to eighty.

Taylor and Jeanine were in the midst of filming a scene where Taylor leans over the edge of the cliff and tries to catch her hand and drag her back to safety. He had an invisible safety harness on, as did Jeanine, but the woman had the more dangerous stunt in this particular scene because she was over the cliff and hanging.

After Stan was satisfied with the shots of Jeanine, her stunt double was called in for the more difficult rock climbing needed for the shoot. The stunt double wore a long brunette wig which was tied into a ponytail for the shoot. Taylor's long blond locks blew in the breeze and they filmed one scene after the next. These shoots actually went pretty quickly considering all of the action. Only ten shots were needed but the three people involved were very professional and were able to pull the shoot off quickly, within two hours.

At eleven a.m. Taylor approached his guests, who were still seated and watching. Kevin was with them and he could tell they were all hot, probably more so than he was because he had been moving around in the action shot.

Taylor stopped in front of the three, hands on his hips. "Okay, Kev. You're good to go." He dismissed their new friend and Kevin grinned and said goodbye, heading toward another part of the set.

Taylor turned back to his guests. "Come on, you guys. I've got a twenty minute break and ya'll look like you're frying."

He gestured with his head back toward their RV.

The three stood, Tessa taking Andrew's hand. They had gone through five waters each and she knew they all needed bathroom breaks and they *were* frying! "Yes Taylor! We're hot and need a break. You must too! I can't believe the action I saw! You were literally hanging off of that cliff!"

Taylor grinned down at Tessa. "Actually you saw one of the easier stunts. We are doing some night stunts tonight involving a train. I don't want you guys there because it will be too noisy for Andrew. But this particular set is located far enough away that you shouldn't even hear anything."

"Watching you make a movie is really fascinating, Taylor! It is an experience I will never forget!" Rose remarked.

As they approached the RV, Taylor flashed his famous grin. "Yeah, I like making movies and the stunts are a fabulous high. It satisfies my need for thrills!"

Tessa snorted. "You must have an active thrill meter."

Taylor opened the RV and the cool air wafting out was heaven to the four of them. They all entered the RV and Tessa immediately sent Andrew to the bathroom. Rose excused herself also as Tessa got out the lemonade pitcher and poured four drinks.

Taylor and Tessa took seats at the table and gulped at their drinks. Taylor finally answered her comment. "You of all people should know I have a high thrill meter, baby," he said softly.

Tessa blushed. This was the first time since she had seen him again that their past intimacy was mentioned.

He noticed her blush and grinned. "Didn't mean to embarrass you or anything." He smiled.

Tessa sipped at her drink, then answered him. "You can do that quite easily and you know that, Taylor!"

He laughed as Rose and Andrew returned and Tessa took her turn in the bathroom.

Taylor did not see the Pattersons for the rest of the day. Mid-afternoon he napped a bit and went over his scenes for the shoot for the evening. They were shooting as soon as the sun went down, around ten p.m. The shoot would probably take at least five hours or so to film, maybe until three in the morning. Fortunately he did not have any scenes at all the next day (which was unusual). Stan was filming shots with co-stars so he would have the day free to spend with his guests and he planned to take them into Edmonton to explore the city. He had never been there. He knew they were famous for their hockey team but that's about all he knew about the city.

The shoot that evening involved a moving train and Taylor leaping from car to car— sometimes below, sometimes above the engine— chasing the bad guys. He again wore slacks, a long sleeved shirt rolled up and a fedora (which miraculously stayed on for the shots). The clothes were hot but it was cooler in the evenings, low seventies, so it wasn't too uncomfortable.

It took fifteen shots before Stan was satisfied and they finished up about three thirty in the morning. Since Taylor had been in makeup at eight a.m. this morning it was a long day for him and he was exhausted.

He headed to his RV to sleep. Before he conked out, he left Tessa a voice mail to let her know the plans for the next day.

Taylor flopped into his comfortable bed and it was lights out.

CHAPTER
FORTY FOUR

TAYLOR MADE ARRANGEMENTS WITH a local limousine company to take his guests into Edmonton the next day. He hired a company that was very familiar with the city and explained Andrew's special needs. There was a gigondo mall in the city— the biggest in North America— but Taylor explained something loud, noisy and big would not work. He was informed there were many other sights to see, including a large horticultural complex. Since it was now early July the flowers would be amazing. He thought both the ladies would appreciate that and the little guy too.

Taylor knocked on Tessa's RV door about eleven a.m. Tessa opened the door, smiling down at Taylor, motioning him into their cool RV.

"Hi!" she greeted. "We're almost all ready. I just have to put a few more things in my purse for Andrew. Come in and say hi to him. He's in the media room."

Taylor moved up the step into the RV, glancing around. Rose was sitting at the kitchen table and she greeted Taylor. She was wearing a cool pink gingham summer dress and white comfortable shoes. Tessa also looked cool and sophisticated (as she usually did, no matter what she wore) in a sleeveless royal blue sheath dress, with delicate ruffles decorating the bodice. She had low sling back sandals on and her hair up in a high ponytail. The style was very cute and made her look much younger, like a teenager. Taylor had gone for cool clothes too. He wore khaki cargo shorts with a white tee and brown Teva sandals.

He grinned down at her. "I'll do that. I'll bring him out. The limo is here and waiting. Charlie is ready to show us all of the sights."

Tessa arched a brow. "Charlie?"

"Charlie is our limo driver. Knows the city like the back of his hand. I've explained to him Andrew's special needs so he knows which sights Andrew can handle and those he can't. We'll have a good time," he assured her.

"I'm sure we will." She grabbed her sunglasses and purse as Rose did the same.

Taylor went into the front of the RV to get Andrew. He found the little boy watching (what else?!) Barney. As soon as he entered the room, Andrew jumped up, forgetting all about his show.

"Taylor!" he squealed, running to his buddy with open arms.

Laughing, Taylor hugged the boy close, then looked down at him. "Guess what, buddy? I don't have to work today, so I am taking you, your mommy and Mrs. H into the city to see some things. I don't want you to be afraid. Mommy and I will be with you all of the time. It is a big city and some of the buildings are tall, but we won't be going to any of them. Only fun places you will like."

"McDonald's?" Andrew questioned.

Taylor grinned and chuckled. "If you want to go to Micky D's we can make it a stop on our trip. Whatever you want to do, bud."

"Be you, Taylor," Andrew's big brown eyes studied the man holding him.

"Be with you, Taylor," Taylor corrected.

"Yes."

Grinning Taylor took Andrew's hand and they headed out for their Edmonton adventure.

The limo was long, white and luxurious. Charlie was a middle aged man with dark hair and was quite a talker. He filled his guests in on all pertinent details of the city they were about to visit. The population, the University of Alberta, the trendy Whyte Avenue district. Today he explained they would be touring Fort Edmonton Park, the Muttart Conservatory and the state Legislature Building. He explained these sights were beautiful and the noise level should be acceptable for Andrew. Tessa had made sure he had his earplugs in. She also had dressed him in cool clothes so he would be comfortable. He wore chocolate cargo shorts paired with a tan tee and his comfortable suede sandals and a ball cap.

As they drove into the city, he chattered with Taylor, asking him questions about his movie.

The drive was short as the movie set was fairly close to the city. They stopped at the conservatory first so that everyone could get out and view the splendid array of flowers. Tessa took many photos of Taylor, Rose and Andrew.

Taylor had also brought along an expensive camera and took photos of the group and many of Andrew.

Next it was on to the state legislature building. Since it was well after lunch and July, there was not much activity in the building itself. It was a grand old building with interesting architecture with turrets and a basilica. They also toured a large library that was just gorgeous with gilt moldings and a star spattered ceiling. There were endless shelves of books.

They did lunch at Micky D's and continued their day shopping. Taylor insisted on buying Andrew some Edmonton shirts and caps, despite Tessa's protests. He purchased a beautiful silk scarf for Rose and a gold twisted chain necklace for Tessa. He knew it would look lovely next to her tanned skin.

After shopping it was off to dinner at a restaurant that Charlie suggested. It was quiet and off the main drag and they all relaxed and enjoyed a leisurely meal.

Tessa took many photos of Taylor and Andrew together. She knew once they left (which would be in about seven days) these photos would help to ease Andrew's unhappiness when they had to leave.

The Fourth of July was tomorrow and Tessa had already explained to Taylor that Andrew did not do fireworks. Taylor explained he would be working all day tomorrow and the crew were planning on shooting off fireworks, but not near the RV's. Tessa was planning on a quiet Fourth of July spent in their RV.

They had a fun day but by early evening the four were ready to head back to the set.

Taylor tipped Charlie generously, telling him he had been a wonderful host.

"Ya know Mr. Boudrain, you being a big movie star and everything. I didn't know how well this would go over, especially with a boy with special needs. But I must say you are one of the kindest clients I have ever had. And I'm not just sayin' this cause you just tipped generously." The guy shrugged a bit. "Just wanted you to know. You're nothing like your reputation implies."

Taylor tipped his finger to his forehead. "Thanks, hoss. You have a good one." Taylor turned to follow the ladies and the boy that had already headed over toward the RV's.

Charlie smiled as he turned the limo and drove away.

Tessa invited Taylor in for a bit to relax for a while. She knew they would not be seeing him tomorrow on the fourth so she wanted to spend as much time as possible with him while he was off. He agreed to come in for a glass of wine and to visit with Andrew a bit longer.

Andrew was very tired and only managed to stay up about a half hour with Taylor. Tessa put him into bed in his guest room as Rose chatted with Taylor.

When Tessa reappeared, Rose stood, sighing. She moved over to Taylor and kissed his cheek. "Thank you for the wonderful day, Taylor. I will never forget it." She turned to Tessa. "I am tired too, dear. I'm going to go to my room now." Smiling, she moved down a hallway leaving the two of them alone.

Tessa felt a bit uncomfortable. This was the first time she had been alone with Taylor since they had arrived four days ago.

She reached over to top off his wine but Taylor put his hand over his glass. "No thanks, baby. I have to work early tomorrow. Limit myself to only one on those nights."

"Oh, I see," she replied as she sipped her own wine.

"You plan to stay in the RV for the fourth?"

"Yes. It will be cooler for us in here and we are all pretty beat from today. It will give us a nice breather and then the following day we can watch you work. What is your schedule like for the day after the holiday?"

Taylor thought for a moment and then remembered. "We're doing some night scenes, I believe. Which means I can spend some time with you guys during the day. Sound good?"

"Yep. And thank you for all you did for us today. We all enjoyed ourselves immensely and Andrew will have many fond memories to take home with him."

"What about you, Tessa? Will you have fond memories to take home too?" He arched a golden brow, studying her.

Tessa blushed, sipping slowly then she placed her glass down. "I already have many fond memories. This just adds to them."

This comment surprised Taylor. Usually she did not tell him what she was thinking. She was a very private person and it was hard to get close to her, even though they had been *very* close physically. He knew that probably stemmed from her background. It was hard for Tessa to trust people, especially men and she was really letting her guard down around him. How did she feel about him? He knew she liked to have sex with him and was grateful that he was close with her son, but how did she feel about *him*, Taylor— the person— not the movie star.

"You're awful quiet tonight," she remarked.

Taylor decided to be honest. The only way they would get closer would be through talking to each other. "I was thinking about you Tessa and wondering how you feel about me." His teal eyes met hers steadily.

Tessa was startled by this remark, not expecting it at all. Taylor usually was lighthearted and carefree and did not talk about anything serious. She also did not know quite how to respond. She was in love with the man across from her, but he was a famous movie star and in her mind she and her son would never fit in his world. Nor did she want to.

She finally answered him. "I have feelings for you, Taylor. I like you a great deal. I appreciate everything you do for Andrew."

There was a bit of silence as Taylor contemplated her words.

Tessa decided to ask him the same question. "How do you feel about me?"

Taylor met her lovely brown eyes. "I think I'm falling in love with you," he answered, studying her lovely face.

Tessa nearly fell out of her chair. This was the *last* comment she expected. She took several gulps of wine, not sure how to answer or react to this news. She placed her glass down and met his eyes. "Are you sure about that, Taylor? Or is it you just like the sex?"

He sighed heavily. "Tessa, is that all you really think I want from you? Hell, I can get sex anytime I want from anyone. No, it isn't just sex. And you already know I love your little boy, and Rose too."

"Taylor, what are you trying to tell me here? That you want us in your life? How would that work Taylor, with you being a movie star, coming and going and leaving Andrew for extended periods? I just don't see how our relationship could work."

Taylor's teal eyes studied her intently. "You need to look on the positive side, not the negative. You can make anything work if you want it enough." He leaned forward a bit. "The question is Tessa: do you want it enough?" He whispered the last five words.

Tessa blushed, pulling back.

Taylor rose, gazing down at the lovely brunette. "I gotta get up early so I'm gonna leave now. I think you should give my words some thought. I'll see you the day after tomorrow."

He went to the door of the RV and his tall form disappeared as he quietly closed it.

Tessa sighed, finishing up her wine. What was she to do about Taylor? She had no idea.

CHAPTER
FORTY FIVE

THE FOURTH OF JULY was spent in the Patterson's RV. Andrew played a computer game Taylor had taught him and Tessa and Rose prepared a meal. They all spent their time leisurely, Rose doing some knitting and Tessa read a novel. Or she tried to read a novel.

Her thoughts kept going back to the previous evening when Taylor had confessed to her that he thought he was in love with her. She really did not know if she could believe him or not. She was very sure he had never said the words to another woman and for Taylor to even *say* those words to her she realized had to be very difficult for him. She knew Taylor well enough to know that. But it opened up a whole can of issues/complications that Tessa was not sure she could deal with. She had quite a bit on her plate just raising her special needs son. That was a huge challenge in and of itself. Tessa did not need the complication of a man in her life who had such a famous career. She knew if things ever did get really serious between herself and Taylor she and her son would be shoved into the limelight. That was the last thing Tessa wanted for Andrew. It would be an issue that would be very hard for them all to handle.

Tessa sighed, trying to concentrate on her novel. There was still some time to see how everything shook down. For now she planned to enjoy their vacation and take each day as it came.

Later that evening they could hear the distant boom of fireworks going off. Tessa had already explained to Andrew that he might hear some noises, but assured him it was okay. It was part of the special effects needed for the movie. Andrew accepted this explanation and after watching a few television shows went to bed happily, knowing he would be seeing Taylor tomorrow. He had missed his big buddy.

The Pattersons and Rose went to the set the next morning early. Taylor had informed Tessa they were starting to film at about eight a.m. so she had to get everyone moving early. It wasn't a problem with her son, he was eager to see Taylor again. However Tessa was not quite as eager as her son, wary about seeing Taylor again.

Rose chatted casually as they walked to set seventeen where the shoot was to take place. The shot was indoors so there would be air conditioning so it would be more comfortable for them. They were all dressed in casual cool attire as usual.

Approaching the set, Tessa could see a ton of people scurrying about. Taylor had already explained the various roles of the people working on the movie, but there were so many people Tessa could not keep them straight in her mind. Many young women and men hurried about on their various chores and she could see the lighting and camera crew getting their equipment set up. She looked around for Taylor but did not spot him. However she did see Stan standing with a cameraman, speaking to him. When Stan spotted the Pattersons, he excused himself and strode over to them.

"Hello!" he greeted. "Welcome to set seventeen. We have your chairs all set up for the action." He indicated four chairs set up near the sound stage that faced the action directly. "We'll be doing some interior dialogue scenes between Jeanine and Taylor. I think Taylor is still in makeup. Please, make yourselves comfortable. And Kevin," he waved the young man over, "is here to see to whatever you may need."

The young guy approached, waving at the ladies and fiving Andrew. The three smiled and sat in their seats as Kevin settled next to them.

Tessa leaned down to Andrew. "Now remember Andrew," she murmured, "be quiet as a mouse. Sssh!" She did the shushing motion.

He smiled, repeating the motion silently.

"Good boy!" she praised him.

It took another twenty minutes before the stars were in place and action began. Tessa could see the set was an interior room of a hotel. A luxurious brass bed with a lacy white satin duvet dominated the room, with the requisite vanity, dressers and mirrors. Gold velvet drapes hung at windows and it looked like a typical elegant 1930's style boudoir.

At the moment the action involved Taylor and Jeanine having an argument. Taylor was dressed in what looked like a satin emerald green robe and Jeanine wore a white peignoir set, lacy and fortunately not see through. Tessa was a bit uncomfortable with this scene with Andrew watching.

When Stan called for a brief break, Taylor headed over to the four of them. He smiled down at Andrew and greeted him. Then he turned his attention to the two ladies.

"I just wanted to suggest to you Tessa that you might want to have Kev here show Andrew some various sets he hasn't seen yet." Taylor's attention went to Andrew. "Kevin wants to hang a bit with you buddy and I'm gonna be tied up. Would that be okay?"

Tessa figured out Taylor was sending her son out with Kevin because most likely there was a love scene coming up. Oh God, how would she handle that, especially after their last conversation?

Andrew looked at his mommy for permission and Tessa leaned over to speak to him. "That sounds fun, Andrew!" She looked up at Kevin. "How long will you be gone? And will you be in the sun a lot?"

Kevin showed her a bottle of sunblock he was carrying. "We will be for a bit. Then I plan to take him over to the food RV for ice cream, if that's okay with you. And I think we'll be gone about an hour."

"Okay. That sounds fine. You will bring him back here?"

"Yep. I'll bring him right back to this set." He turned to the little boy. "Are you ready, bud?"

"Yes, yes!" At the mention of ice cream, Andrew was willing to give up watching for a bit. He happily took Kevin's hand and the two exited the set.

Taylor looked down at the two women. "As you've probably already surmised, we are going to film a love scene. It is not too hot and racy— we're going for a PG rating— but I figured you would not want him seeing me kissing another woman." Taylor's expression was inscrutable as he looked down at Tessa.

She looked away briefly. "Yep. Good idea."

Taylor smiled. "Well, off to work. I'll see you soon after the shoot. I've got a bit of a break." He turned to return to the sound set.

As he moved away, Tessa nervously clasped her hands in her lap. It would be very difficult for her to watch a love scene involving Taylor and she had almost volunteered to go along with Andrew but that would be cowardly and also leave Rose alone.

Rose sensed her tension. She patted Tessa's hand gently. "Don't worry, Tessa. It will be over and done with. And you know Jeanine and Taylor are just friends."

"Yes. I know."

The two stars took their places on the bed for the scene and Stan called out "Action!"

Taylor threw Jeanine onto the bed, quickly undoing the buttons on her sheer robe. Jeanine's cleavage showed and Taylor planted tiny kisses on the top of her breasts as the actress continued to berate him. Taylor moved up her body and started kissing the lush lips passionately. They were really getting into it, Taylor's hands diving into her hair as they rolled across the bed, continuing to kiss.

"Cut!" Stan's voice. "Okay, we need to change the lighting a bit for take two." When the lighting was re-adjusted, he spoke. "Take two!"

The passionate kissing started all over again. Oh God, Tessa thought. How much more of this will I have to watch? Taylor kissed Jeanine just as passionately as he had kissed her and she was really uncomfortable watching a man she had been intimate with kiss another woman like this. She tried to keep telling herself it was acting, but it certainly didn't *look* like acting! She also felt Taylor could have warned her about the love scene too and given her the choice whether or not to view it. But she knew that was a cop out. Taylor was just doing his job and she had to get used to the fact that part of his job was making love to other beautiful women. But it was not easy.

After three takes, Stan was finally satisfied and Tessa was glad the next several scenes were again dialogue. Kevin returned soon with Andrew and they all watched the remaining action. Finally Stan dismissed everyone and people disassembled as they went off to their various activities.

Taylor approached his guests and grinned. "I have to go change into some street clothes. I have about a two hour break, so we can catch some food if you'd like."

"We will go back to our RV and prepare something. You can come by and eat with us," Tessa offered.

Taylor grinned down at her. "Sounds good. See ya soon buddy, Rose."

Tessa prepared sandwiches for the four of them and tossed a salad. Iced tea and lemonade with tons of ice were also offered. Taylor showed up at their RV twenty minutes later and Rose ushered him in and over to the table. Taylor was now wearing faded jeans and a white tee.

Andrew was very happy to be having lunch with Taylor and chattered away. Taylor grinned and inserted comments here and there. He also chatted with Rose but Tessa and Taylor really were not speaking much to each other.

Tessa knew they only had several more days left here, maybe four or five. Five. They had to be back July tenth and today was the fifth. Five days to try to settle things between herself and Taylor. She ate her lunch, silent as she listened to her son happily chatter to Taylor.

When they finished up lunch, Taylor stood to leave. As Andrew hugged him goodbye, he motioned Tessa to the side. Andrew and Rose moved into the media room so Taylor could speak to Tessa.

"Just wanted to invite you to my place for dinner tonight. I don't have to work and if Rose can keep on eye on Andrew for a few hours that would work. I think we should talk about some stuff." He shoved his blond hair back as he spoke, studying her.

Tessa blushed a bit. "Okay. What time is convenient?"

"Around six p.m. work for you? That way you will be back by Andrew's bedtime." Taylor was well aware of the bedtime ritual with mom and how important it was to Andrew.

"Sure. That works."

"Okay. See ya then." He opened the door and exited the RV.

Tessa sighed as she watched him go.

Tessa was not quite sure if the dinner was to be considered casual or not, so she went for in between. She chose a strapless fitted red sundress with red low heeled sandals. She put her hair up in a loose French twist and added the gold twisted chain Taylor had purchased for her in Edmonton. She went a little redder on the lipstick than usual and inspecting herself, she thought she would do.

Rose and Andrew were already in the media room. They had finished dinner up an hour ago as Tessa prepared for her dinner date.

Promptly at six p.m. there was a knock on the door and Tessa opened it to reveal Taylor. He wore a pair of dark tan cargo slacks paired with a cream colored polo, brown suede sandals on his feet, his glorious hair brushing his shoulders. She sighed in relief. She had chosen attire correctly.

"Hi," she greeted him.

"Hello," Taylor replied, studying the drop dead gorgeous woman. He loved it when she wore red. She looked terrific in it.

"Are you ready for dinner? Hungry?" He helped her down the few stairs of the RV and they walked over to his.

She looked up at the tall man in the sun. The rays stroked his blond waves and lit up his gold hair. She looked away quickly as he ushered her into his RV.

Entering, she gasped, looking around. She thought their RV was elegant and spacious but Taylor's was twice the size. Again there were plush sofas and chairs, tables, lamps and chandeliers. The color scheme here was white and dark hunter green. He actually had a large dining table that she could see was set with elegant china and two white candles that were lit. It was romantic and elegant.

As she moved to the table, he followed her. "I made dinner. I didn't even call the chef," he grinned down at her. "I grilled some steaks, mashed potatoes, tossed a salad and there is lime sherbet for dessert. Oh, and also champagne," he waved at a silver chased ice bucket draped with white linen holding a bottle of expensive champagne.

"Well, I'm certainly glad I didn't wear my jeans," Tessa quipped lightly.

Taylor pulled out a chair for her, seating her. "You're fine no matter what you wear, Tessa. You always look classy."

Tessa remained silent, watching as he went to the ice bucket to remove the champagne, filling both of their crystal flutes. If Tessa did not know any better, she could swear she was dining at a fine restaurant. There was a platter of steaks steaming on the table and her china bowl contained a colorful salad and mashed potatoes waited in a bowl. Taylor served her food and then moved across from her, serving himself.

Then he raised his glass in toast. "To us, Tessa."

Tessa clinked her glass and smiled slightly. "Thank you. You really did not need to go to all of this trouble. A hamburger would have sufficed."

Taylor arched a brow as he cut into his steak. "Now, Tessa. Is that really what you thought when I invited you to dinner? You can get a hamburger at the RV for God's sake!"

Tessa cut into her beef, and it was cooked just the way she liked it, well done without being burnt. He had remembered. Taylor was very good at remembering all the little details. And who knew he was a romantic? Well, Valentine's Day was certainly romantic she recalled but she had the feeling that was out of the norm for Taylor. He was more a thrill a minute type of guy.

She contemplated him as she chewed her food.

"What exactly did you want to discuss?" she asked.

Taylor picked up his champagne flute, sipping as his teal eyes studied her intently. Placing it back down, he answered her. "About the scene today— I guess I should have warned you I would be doing a love scene with Jeanine…"

"Yes. That would have been nice to have first hand knowledge," she replied.

"Well, I didn't see you guys on the fourth. And I know you only have a few more days here on the set and it is hard for us to talk when we are constantly surrounded by people. That is why I suggested this dinner," he explained.

Tessa continued to eat her dinner then she looked up to meet his eyes. "Well, I have to be honest Taylor. Seeing you do a love scene with another woman was very uncomfortable for me."

Taylor met her eyes. "Yes, I thought so and that is another thing I wanted to discuss. You know that was just *acting*, correct? Jeanine and I do not have a thing together. We're just good friends."

"It looked very real to me, Taylor. That is the way you kiss me." She blushed and looked away.

"No, Tessa. There *is* a difference." Pause. "Tessa, look at me."

Tawny eyes turned back to his face.

"Look into my eyes. What do you see?"

"I see beautiful teal eyes. Eyes that could seduce any woman."

Taylor sighed. She was not getting it. Perhaps because she did not want to? "Tessa, I admit in the past I have slept with some leading ladies. It was all part of the big Hollywood star gambit. But I don't do that anymore. Not since I met you, babe."

Tessa studied his teal eyes and believed him. It still did not change the fact that he was a movie star and she led a very ordinary life and the twain did not meet. Which bard had said that one? She couldn't remember and quickly picked up her champagne flute to drain it. Placing it down, she finally answered him. "I believe you about that, Taylor." At these words, she saw a look of relief on his face. "But, and this is a big but, you are a movie star. I am a nurse from Lewiston, New York. I don't travel in the circles you do, nor do I have any desire to. This is why I don't think we can make it. There are just too many differences. You know it and I know it. And I have to protect my son. He needs privacy."

"Tessa, I have enough money to buy anything, even privacy. If you are afraid of being thrust into the spotlight with me, perish the thought. I keep my private life *very* private."

Tessa actually laughed at this comment. "Oh yes! The way the cover of you and Marisa was private. The way your bad boy Hollywood antics were private. The way your many affairs were private! That is privacy I cannot afford."

Taylor shoved his plate away, frustrated. "Tessa, you're not getting me here. You are speaking of a different man, not the man I am today. That Taylor does not exist anymore. I thought you got that."

Tessa looked down, playing with her silver a bit. She finally looked up. "Taylor, with you I don't know what is real and what is acting."

"Then you don't know me at all, Tessa," he said quietly.

"No. Perhaps I don't. I know you have been kind to my son. Believe me Taylor that means the world to me. But it also upsets me. In a few days we will be returning to our life and Andrew misses you like crazy. I have to deal with that and believe me it is so..." she could not go on, tears appearing in her eyes.

"Tessa, the last thing I want to do is hurt you or your son," he began in a subdued voice. "When I finish this shoot, I plan to come right back to you guys. We are going to be wrapping here the end of July and then filming for two more months in Chicago. Stan plans to wrap the film by October first and I will be right back to Lewiston October second." His teal eyes studied her intently as he spoke.

Tessa was surprised to hear they would be going to a second location. Chicago actually wasn't all that far from Buffalo and it might be possible to drive to the second set. Did she want to do that? Or should she just make a clean break?

"Why do you want to return, Taylor? Isn't your life in Hollywood making movies?"

"I want to return because you, Andrew and Rose are the most important people in my life besides my mom. I know your son will miss me. I will miss him too, but you can assure him he will be seeing me again. Can you do that for me?"

Sighing, Tessa finished up her meal, throwing the linen napkin on the table. "I always try to reassure my son, Taylor. Sometimes it works, most times it does not. He does not understand that you are here today and gone tomorrow. And that's just the way it is. I need to get back." She stood and Taylor also rose.

He came around the table to stand in front of her. Tall, lean and gorgeous. She looked up into his tanned face and her heart turned over. She loved him intensely but was not prepared to tell him so.

He leaned down and kissed her lips very gently. Leaning back up, he spoke. "We probably won't get another chance to talk privately before you leave. Just know that I'm thinking of you, Tessa. All of the time, despite your doubts and hang ups."

Tessa smiled ruefully. "I am reminded of you every day because of my son Taylor. You are never out of my thoughts either." She touched his cheek gently. "Take very good care of yourself, Taylor."

She turned and left the RV.

Taylor watched her go, his heart breaking. What did he need to do to get through to this woman?

CHAPTER
FORTY SIX

THE DAYS PASSED AND Taylor worked on filming. The Pattersons and Rose were usually present for early morning or mid-day shoots. Sometimes he had evenings off and he would spend some time chatting after dinner with them. Most of Taylor's time was spent working and he did not see too much of Tessa. He regretted that he would not have more private time with her before she and her son left the set.

The cast and crew had grown fond of Taylor's guests, especially Andrew, and they informed Taylor they were planning to throw a little "going away" party for the three. It was to be held in the big tented awning that Stan used for parties for the crew here and there.

Stan made sure some of his staff decorated the tent with colorful streamers and balloons with special posters and back scenery devoted to the party. He ordered the chefs to put out a bountiful spread of food and everyone got into the spirit of surprising their guests on their last evening on set.

After Taylor finished filming on July ninth, he went over to the Patterson's RV. It was about six p.m. and he knew the Pattersons were getting ready to leave in the morning and Tessa had mentioned they were packing. Taylor had come to collect the three to take them over to the special party where hundreds of people were waiting to say goodbye to them. He knew Andrew might be a bit intimidated with all of the people but he was hoping since it was a party for them the little guy might be able to handle it.

Taylor approached the RV and knocked lightly on the door. Soon it was opened by Tessa. She was wearing jeans and a white eyelet summer top, her hair tumbling around her shoulders. He tried to ignore his sexual attraction to this woman but it was damn hard.

"Taylor!" Tessa did not expect to see Taylor until tomorrow morning when he escorted them to the jet.

"Hi." Taylor shoved his hands in his jeans. He was wearing his ubiquitous white tee shirt and sneakers. "I just wanted to show the three of you something. Can you come out with me," he gestured outside with his head.

Tessa looked behind her. "Well, we are packing up. Rose and I have most of it done but—"

"It's kinda important, Tessa. Can you go get Rose and Andrew?" Taylor's teal eyes looked up at her as he stood at the bottom of the steps.

"Okay, sure Taylor. Be right back."

She disappeared back into the RV, leaving the door open and he could hear her as she went in and called to Rose and Andrew. Soon the three appeared and Andrew instantly smiled as soon as he saw his big buddy.

"Taylor!"

"Hi, bud. I'm here to show you, mommy and Mrs. H something special. Can ya'll come with me?"

"Yes, yes!" Andrew moved to take Taylor's hand, not even waiting for his mommy's permission.

Taylor smiled down at the little boy. Tessa had him dressed in cute carpenter jean shorts and a red and white striped tee, sneakers on his feet. Rose joined them also, wearing a mint green printed dress.

Tessa and Rose shrugged as they followed Taylor, having no idea what was going on.

Finally they could see a huge tent up ahead with balloons, big bows and streamers with candle lights flickering and big spotlights shining on the interior to light it up. The tables were beautifully decorated with linen and bunting and as they moved closer, Tessa could see huge posters and signs wishing them a safe journey home and thanking them all for visiting. They were throwing them a send off party! Tessa was so touched.

Taylor grinned back at her. "Not my idea, babe. The cast and crew wanted to do this for you guys. 'Course, I agreed."

As the three guests moved under the tent, people came up one by one to say goodbye. It took a bit of time but the cast knew Andrew could not handle a bunch of noise and people around him. Andrew was all smiles, especially when he saw the big cake the chef had made.

Tessa gasped when she saw the elaborate spread of food and the decorations. The staff had gone to quite a bit of trouble to throw them a very nice send off.

After everyone greeted the Pattersons, Taylor spoke. "On behalf of my guests, I want to thank y'all for going above and beyond. You've all been so kind to my guests and I want to personally thank every person here. It is rare to see such camaraderie on a set. Thanks." He turned to Tessa. "Tess, you want to say anything?"

Tessa had tears in her eyes. "Thank you from the bottom of my heart."

At this there were cheers and clapping.

"Now, let's eat and have fun!" Taylor declared.

Everyone smiled and grabbed plates, letting the guests of honor serve themselves first. Tessa, Andrew, Rose and Taylor filled their plates, followed by Stan and the rest of the cast and crew. There were steaming lobsters, sliced beef, chicken cordon bleu, an array of all types of salads and fruits, shrimp, clams, corn on the cob and cold beverages, both soft drinks and beer and wine. Stan had spared no expense for Taylor's guests.

The Pattersons filled their plates and sat with Taylor, Stan, Jeanine and a couple of other co-stars at a head table. The rest of the crew continued to file past as they filled their plates.

The food was delicious and Tessa could not believe this was actually happening. Hollywood was throwing a party for *them*! This was the last thing she had expected when Taylor knocked on the door and she smiled over at him as she conversed casually with one of the male co-stars seated next to her. Andrew was on her other side and she helped him with his food, cutting up his portions. Fortunately there was food he liked (probably thanks to Taylor) so Andrew was able to enjoy the big feast too. He was all smiles as he chattered to Taylor who sat on his other side, Rose next to Taylor.

Everyone had a great time. After food, there was a big bon fire. Since Taylor had taken Andrew camping in the past he was not afraid of the fire. The cast and crew sat around and some chatted, others had another libation but one of the co-stars was telling funny stories about a comedy he had recently starred in. The Pattersons joined in the laughter and fun as they watched the flames and conversed with various people.

Soon it was time to disperse. The cast had to work in the morning and the Pattersons would be boarding Taylor's jet to head back to New York.

Rose went ahead of Taylor and Tessa, taking Andrew's hand. She informed Tessa she would get Andrew ready for bed and finish up the remaining packing. She wanted the couple to have some time alone on this last night.

Tessa and Taylor walked slowly on the set, glancing up at the huge silver stars in the black velvet night. The summer evening was balmy and warm with a slight breeze and it was a gorgeous night to be outdoors. Taylor glanced down at Tessa, smiling.

"Did you enjoy the party?"

Tessa smiled. "Yes, I did. And Andrew and Rose loved it too. That was a very nice gesture, Taylor. Andrew will have many more good memories to take home."

"Told ya, Tessa. It was the cast's idea."

"Yeah, well I know you had something to do with it. And I was completely surprised! I never expected that at all. It was so— so— elaborate!"

Taylor chuckled. "That's Hollywood. We don't do things in a small way. But it is unusual to have that type of a party onset. Stan was fine with it so we did it." He looked down in the dim light to see her features. "I wanted to send you guys off in style."

"Thank you. And we *will* miss you, Taylor."

They continued to stroll slowly as Taylor answered. "I'll miss you guys, too. Everything I said several days ago is true Tessa. I'll be coming back when this film wraps. I have assured Andrew of this fact too."

"I think he will be better about you being away now Taylor since he has actually seen what you do and *why* you are away. He understands that you are doing your job and that you will return. Before— he just could not grasp that concept. I think he will be happier. The summer will be a long one for him but if he knows he will see you again that will go a long way to alleviate his hurt feelings. It has been so good to see my son smile and I have you to thank for it."

Taylor grinned ruefully. "I'm as fond of the boy as he is of me."

"I will miss you too, Taylor."

Taylor stopped and leaned down to kiss her. It started out gently and soft, but soon they were kissing passionately. Finally they broke apart, both breathing harshly.

Taylor tenderly touched her cheek. "Good night, Tessa. I will see you early in the morning at the helo pad."

"Yes. Good night, Taylor." Tessa entered her RV, her cheeks pink and lips slightly swollen from being so thoroughly kissed.

The jet was waiting on the helo pad. Ron had the jet checked over and the stairs deployed. The engines purred smoothly and he went over his instrument checklist as Taylor said goodbye to his guests.

Taylor embraced Rose first, finally leaning back to kiss her cheek. "Thank you, Rose. For everything. Have a safe flight back. I will miss ya." He grinned down at her, white teeth flashing. It was very bright out here in the sun but Taylor was not wearing his sunglasses and Rose looked up into beautiful teal eyes.

She kissed him back on his cheek, leaning up. "God bless you, Taylor." She smiled, turning to board the stairs.

Taylor turned to Tessa and Andrew. "Ya gonna have a problem with the stairs, buddy?" Taylor threw his thumb toward the metal stairs.

Andrew smiled. "No. No 'fraid stairs!" he declared.

Taylor grinned, high fiving Andrew. "Good deal, bud! Now c'mere and give me a hug and kiss!" Andrew was lifted into strong arms as the blond head moved close to the darker one, hugging the boy tightly. Andrew closed his eyes as he returned the hug, then he leaned back. "See ya soon?"

Taylor smiled, placing Andrew back down on his feet. "Yep, bud. As soon as possible. Real soon," he clarified.

Andrew smiled as he turned and accepted Rose's hand to help him up the stairs.

Taylor turned to Tessa. She was wearing a white summer sundress that clung in all the right places, her dark hair pinned up. She removed her dark glasses so that her tawny eyes met teal. "I know we basically said our goodbyes last night, Taylor. I just want to add that you are a very special person. I don't know how or why you are in my life, but I consider it a blessing." She leaned up to kiss his cheek briefly. "Stay safe," she whispered.

Taylor pulled her close before she could board the stairs. He leaned down to whisper in her ear. "You stay safe too, darlin'." He gently kissed her lips and released her, watching as she boarded the steps.

The three waved to him from the top of the steps, then Ron activated the stairs upwards. He waved goodbye also as the door to the jet hissed closed.

Taylor waited on the helo pad until the jet was no more than a tiny speck in the clear endless sky.

CHAPTER
FORTY SEVEN

THE PATTERSONS ARRIVED BACK in Lewiston on July eleventh, a Saturday. This gave Tessa the weekend to unwind from the trip and attend to household chores. There was laundry to do, a house to clean and a little boy to entertain. Since she had to go back to work on Monday, Rose would be caring for Andrew again and the buddy program would take him on outings here and there.

They had all enjoyed the trip and seeing Taylor again but they were happy to be home. The trip had been exhausting for all of them and Tessa was thankful she at least had the weekend to catch up on some sleep before going back to work.

Life settled into its usual pattern for them. Andrew would question Tessa about when he could see Taylor again but Tessa was vague in her answers to her son. She was not quite sure when they would see Taylor and did not want to get Andrew's hopes up. However her son was doing much better since the trip. The remaining weeks in July he was his usual happy self so the trip to Canada had really helped lift his spirits. Tessa was so grateful. It had broken her heart to see how unhappy her son was after Taylor left them.

As the summer waned, Tessa tried to sort out her feelings for Taylor. Even though he claimed he supposedly was falling in love with her Tessa did not know quite what to believe. Anything could happen between now and October and Tessa was well aware Taylor was a babe magnet. He could have any woman he wanted. He could possibly take up with Marisa again. Or another woman of his choosing. Tessa realized she did not quite trust Taylor even after everything he had done for them. She was still wary about a serious relationship with the man. He was a movie star and she was a nurse. A nurse in love with a famous movie star.

August first arrived and it was a Saturday. Tessa took Andrew to a local park that had a wading pool with a huge fountain in the middle of it. There were also playgrounds around with swings and such, but Andrew always wanted to go in the water. It seemed to somehow help calm him with his sensory issues and Tessa had seriously thought about getting a pool at one time but it would be too much work for her alone. She would love to do it for her son if it was feasible but for now they relied on local beaches or pools.

It was a hot day, in the mid eighties, and Andrew and Tessa were dipping their toes in the water, sitting on the concrete edge of the pool. Andrew was wearing navy blue and white board shorts and had already been in the pool for a while. He was taking a break with his mommy and they both sipped from cold water bottles.

"Having fun, kiddo?" Tessa looked down at her son through her dark glasses. She was wearing white cargo shorts with a white camisole top, her hair up in a ponytail. She was grateful for the occasional breeze. It was hot out here in the sun. Other children laughed and splashed nearby. Most of the moms chose to watch the action further away on the lawns. Tessa loved the water herself and relished the cool water on her toes.

Andrew smiled up at his mommy. He was getting a nice brown tan from being outside this summer and his slender body was evenly toasted which enhanced his long lashed brown eyes. "Yes! Water!"

Tessa smiled as she dipped her toes, then Andrew spoke again.

"When Taylor done job?"

Tessa was a bit startled. This was the first time Andrew had mentioned Taylor's profession. Usually he just asked where Taylor was. "Well, remember the movie set?" she questioned him.

Andrew's eyes widened and he nodded.

"Taylor is still there, working on his movie." She knew he was probably in Chicago by now. He did mention to her that August and September the filming would be moving to that location. Still she had no plans to go to the set in August. She planned to spend time with her son on outings together as they usually did in the summer; like today.

Andrew frowned a bit at her response. He was silent, so Tessa prompted him.

"Andrew? Is there something wrong?"

After a moment, he looked back up at his mommy. "Miss Taylor."

"I miss Taylor too, honey. But he has a job to do. When he finishes his job, maybe we will see him again."

Still frowning, he continued to question her. "Long time?"

"Andrew, please use sentences. I don't know if it will be a long time. I know it won't be until summer ends." She paused. "You will be going back to school in September. You like school and then maybe a little after that, we'll see Taylor." Tessa hoped this was the case for Andrew's sake.

"I see Taylor summer over?" he eagerly questioned.

Tessa sighed. "Yes, Andrew. When September comes, or October when the leaves start to fall, Taylor will return."

"Summer end now then!" he declared.

Tessa chuckled. She splashed him a bit with her foot. "Are you ready to leave, bud? We're frying out here!"

Andrew stood. "Yes, yes! Leave! Summer be over!" He grabbed his sandals.

Tessa grabbed hers also, knowing she would have to explain they had at least two months before summer would be over and Taylor would return. If he did.

The two walked to Tessa's SUV, holding hands, Andrew skipping along by his mother's side.

Andrew spent his time in August in the usual manner. Tessa took him to a local hotel that had an indoor water park. It was a bit noisy but he could tolerate it with his ear plugs. She also took him to the science fiction movie Taylor had made and Andrew was so excited seeing his buddy up on the screen. He kept pointing and saying "Taylor!" loudly. Fortunately they were at a matinee that was sparsely attended and he was not annoying anyone. Tessa was quite fascinated as she watched a man she had been lovers with act in a movie. There were many stunt scenes and action scenes in this movie also and Taylor performed his stunts as flawlessly as he acted. She knew this was the last movie he had made right before his motorcycle accident and the fact that he was in such great physical shape probably contributed to saving his life. She knew from the details of the accident she had been given that most people would not have survived such an accident. Taylor very well could have been killed that day. Instead he had lived to enter hers and Andrew's lives and they had not been the same since.

Sighing, she settled in her seat with her popcorn to watch the action.

Soon August waned and Tessa took Andrew back to school shopping. She made sure he had enough new outfits, socks, underwear, shoes, sneakers, a new windbreaker jacket and bought him a bigger backpack. She let him choose it himself and he was excited talking about getting to see his friends and Mrs. C again. Tessa was just so grateful school would be starting soon. It would give Andrew less time to brood about Taylor whom they had not heard from since July in Edmonton. Remember Tessa, Taylor is a movie star, he is very busy. You will just have to be as patient as you have told your son to be.

She wondered how things would go when they finally did see him again. She had no idea.

CHAPTER
FORTY EIGHT

THE FINAL WEEKS OF July were a whir of activity for Taylor. He ate, slept, worked and did it all over again. The pace of filming had intensified so that the cast and crew could pack it in to go to the second location. Taylor was too exhausted to think and when he did he was haunted by thoughts of Tessa. How the hell had he fallen for *her*, out of all of the women in his life? He finally falls for a nurse who wants nothing to do with Hollywood and Hollywood was Taylor's bread and butter. He was now independently wealthy apart from being an actor because he had been wise and invested in hospitals, real estate and other ventures. Next year he would probably add another billion to his current value. But none of that really mattered anymore to Taylor.

Stan kept him busy. They were always going over shots, rushes or scripting when Taylor was off-screen, which was not too often. Stan was very professional and kept everyone on pace and the few minor glitches that arose were handled quickly. Thus they were moving right along. They were on target to leave for Chicago right on time, August first.

The flight into Chicago was long. Finally the exhausted cast and crew arrived at O'Hare and deplaned and boarded several limos waiting for the stars and the producer/director. The rest of the cast and crew took shuttle buses to their various hotels. Since Taylor was a big star, Stan had put him up at the Drake Hotel, the most luxurious hotel in the city.

Taylor flopped his luggage on the huge bed and placing his hands on his hips, looked around curiously at the huge suite. Your typical luxurious hotel suite. Everything pristine, elegant and orderly with a wet bar, large private bath and breathtaking views of the city's skyline dominated by the Sears Tower.

Taylor quickly unpacked and prepared to catch some z's. He had to be on the set early for make-up. Stan wanted to get right to work as did Taylor. Two more months in Chicago and then he could hop his private jet back to Western New York.

Taylor slept soundly that night and his dreams were sweet.

The movie set was erected right smack dab in the middle of downtown. Stan had already received the permits and authorization for police protection for the set from the city of Chicago. A city always wanted to host a movie shoot because it brought in big bucks from tourism. As soon as Taylor approached the shoot in the area he could see roped barricades all around that kept the crowd back from the action. There was already quite a crowd at this early hour. Thousands of people ringed the area watching as the techs set up equipment. Soon some of the stars started arriving and cameras whirred and flashed. When Taylor appeared there was a roar from the crowd and frenzied screaming and flash strobes. Since Taylor had only been up for a half hour the flashes were half blinding him, but he affably waved back to his fans anyway, stopping along the barricades to sign some autographs. His fans went wild at this action and Taylor's bodyguards tried to move him along at a quicker pace but Taylor took his time, chatting with people, especially the kids. He gave one little boy the studio ball cap he was wearing and everyone smiled at Taylor. He waved goodbye and proceeded to the set where Stan was waiting for him.

Soon Taylor was in makeup and costume and they began a day of shooting the film on the streets of Chicago.

Filming wrapped about seven p.m. and Stan and Taylor met to eat at the restaurant in the Drake hotel. The men sat at a private booth so they would not be bothered by news media or fans and Stan had a gofer as a lookout.

The restaurant was elegant; lots of shiny brass and glass chandeliers, frosted blue etched glass panels and frothy plants provided some privacy. As they settled at their booth, the waiter brought over drinks. The men relaxed, sipping at their drinks and talked business for a bit. They ordered their dinner and then Stan turned the chat personal.

"So, Taylor. Do you miss your friends back in Western New York?" They had not really discussed Taylor's guests in Edmonton. They had both been too wicked busy.

Taylor sipped at his bourbon leisurely, setting the heavy glass down. His teal eyes met Stan's dark eyes. "Yeah, I miss them like crazy. But I want to get the shoot down and concentrate on that."

"Well, you've succeeded. You're doin' a heckuva job, but I didn't expect otherwise. The woman, Tessa. Are you involved with her? I know it's not my business but— just curious." Stan sipped at his scotch.

"Involved? Yes, we're very close. As you know I adore her son. Tessa is one classy lady and I admire her." Taylor shrugged. He did not want to get into the intimate details of his relationship with the woman. Taylor was a gentleman and did not kiss and tell.

Stan studied Taylor's face. "After this project, what will you be heading into next?" Stan knew Taylor usually only took a few weeks off between projects, if that, working non-stop.

"I haven't decided on a next project." Taylor did not meet Stan's eyes.

The waiter showed up with their entrees and Stan waited for him to move on before replying. "Why is that? Usually you can't wait to get back to work."

"Well, let's just say I'm in the mode of looking a bit more before leaping." Taylor shrugged. "Got other business ventures as you know and they need attention too."

"Yeah, you're one of the lucky few actors that would never need to make a film again in your life and you'll still die with more money than you can spend." Stan chuckled a bit.

"The thing is: I love acting. When I left Texas, I didn't know what the hell I would do with my life. I just knew I needed to leave, move on, see other places. I never dreamed I would become an actor. The fact that it has made me so wealthy is a dream come true. So now I like to give back a bit, I guess."

"All of that 'giving back' as you put it is what has made you wealthier," Stan pointed out.

Taylor shrugged. "That's one of the benes, but I do it to help people. And don't you *dare* tell anyone I told you that! I'm the badass actor, remember?"

Stan laughed. "Oh yeah. Real bad. I saw you signing all of those autographs today and even giving a kid a ball cap. I don't think you're fooling anyone but yourself there, Taylor." Stan paused. "You've changed. Meeting this family in New York has changed you."

"Yeah, my whole world was turned upside down when I met them. I'll never be the same."

The shoot continued through August. It was usually always hot, sticky, muggy. Stan tried to do as many night scenes early on in the month as possible because it was cooler, saving outdoor scenes for the latter part of the month when perhaps the weather would improve. The cast and crew put up with the elements and did their jobs. They were accustomed to filming in heat, freezing cold, rainstorms and equator weather. The night scenes involved many stunt scenes between Taylor and his male co-stars and Stan concentrated on these scenes in the upcoming weeks.

Taylor did his job and tried to keep personal thoughts at bay. He usually worked in the evenings, spent mornings going over his script and sleeping in the afternoons. Waking early in the evening, he would grab a quick bite and head to the set. Thus life in Hollywood/Chicago.

August was moving along and fortunately, so was filming.

Taylor was dining at the Drake this evening with Jeanine. He knew she missed her boyfriend Raoul as much as he missed Tessa. They had become good friends while working together and they casually chatted in the elegant restaurant.

Jeanine was wearing a strapless red dress that looked terrific with her dark hair and flawless tan, golden earrings dangling from her earlobes. She looked scrumptious and he knew every man in the restaurant was checking her out. He had opted for black dress slacks with a white shirt with a matching black vest. His long glorious blond waves brushed the top of his shoulders and the candlelight picked out golden streaks among the honey strands.

They were casually discussing the film, politics and other subjects as they leisurely enjoyed their dinner. August was almost over and with any luck they would finish the shoot in one more month. That was the deadline Stan was shooting for.

"Taylor, do you miss Tessa?" Jeanine casually toyed with her champagne flute, studying the gorgeous man opposite her. If she wasn't in love with Raoul she would be wanting to jump Taylor tonight, Tessa or no Tessa. She smiled at her thoughts.

Taylor sighed, his teal eyes rising to hers. "Yep. Do miss her a bunch. And Andrew and Rose too. They are sorta the family I never really had and I've become close to them all."

"Especially Tessa, correct?"

Taylor grinned ruefully. "Was it that obvious?"

Jeanine chuckled. "Oh yes. Whenever she was around, you could not keep your eyes off of her. I really did feel superfluous, you know!" she teased him.

"C'mon. I know you have eyes only for Raoul," his eyes twinkled at her.

She laughed gaily. "Yep. But it does not mean I am blind, Taylor. You're a gorgeous man and the nice thing is you haven't let that go to your head. So many actors are just so arrogant and stuck up." She sipped champagne, eyeing him over her flute.

Taylor chuckled. "Ya know, when I first hit this town that was a perfect description of me. I hope I have been man enough to grow up a bit."

Jeanine leaned forward. "You are one hell of a man, Taylor. That Tessa is very lucky indeed. I hope she knows just *how* lucky."

Taylor was introspective as he met her eyes. He shrugged. "Tessa's got a lot on her plate with her son and all. And she does not want to be part of the whole Hollywood scene for that reason."

"I'm sure you have explained they do not have to be. Many stars keep their families out of the limelight. It is a wise thing to do when you are such a famous person."

"Yeah, I've kinda gone there with her, but she doesn't really get it. She is very protective of Andrew and I can certainly understand why. But she feels that is why we cannot have a closer relationship. Because of the boy and the effect my career would have on their lives."

"Taylor, do you want my advice?"

"Sure Jeanine. Shoot."

"Take each day as it comes. I could tell by the way she looks at you she has very deep feelings for you. I am a woman, I know. She just needs to work some things out. When she does, she will be there for you Taylor. The question is: can you be there for her?"

"Yeah, that's the question, isn't it?"

CHAPTER
FORTY NINE

FILMING CONTINUED IN CHICAGO. Since they were now in the beginning of September the weather was not as muggy and outside shoots were more comfortable. Stan finished up many outside sequences before they would move on to their final destination which was a suburb outside of the city. They had to blow many things up for the grand finale of the movie and Stan had already gained all of the permission papers he needed from the city for these particular shots. They were highly dangerous too, but Stan had the best explosive/special effects team in Hollywood.

Taylor was just so glad the shoot was moving along so well. He recalled just around this time of the year— mid September— he had met Tessa and his whole world had changed. He missed her so badly sometimes he could not believe it. He never would have thought he could develop such deep feelings for a woman. Not Taylor the Hollywood stud. Taylor had been celibate for months and he was not used to that feeling. Not having sex was driving him crazy too. He was a young guy with raging hormones and he knew he could satisfy that urge at any time but he just did not want to do that. Even though he and Tessa weren't formally in a relationship (at this point) it would still feel like cheating to him. So he kept his dick in his jeans and did his job.

Today they were filming inside. It was a nightclub scene in a very noir style for the 1930's. Lots of flashing lights glared, the big band blasted away with their horns and art deco furniture was placed about. The shoot involved Jeanine and Taylor dancing, having dialogue at a table and finally a shoot out where Jeanine is wounded and Taylor carries her over his shoulder to safety.

The shoot was quite complex and took them the whole day to film it, well into the evening. Twelve hours total.

Taylor was exhausted but when Jeanine invited him to meet her for a drink at the bar, Taylor accepted. He needed to unwind and talk to a friend.

He found her waiting for him at the elegant bar at the Drake. There were several other people at the bar, most of them men and all were eyeing Jeanine. She ignored the stares as she waited for Taylor, absently sipping a martini. She was dressed in a white slinky sleeveless jumpsuit that draped around her figure nicely. Her long hair was pulled back off of her face in a loose ponytail.

As Taylor approached her, she looked up and smiled. Grinning, he seated himself next to her. He had opted for a white shirt and black slacks. The bartender hurried over and Taylor pointed to Jeanine's drink.

"I'll have what she's havin'," he remarked.

"Yes sir." The bartender went off to prepare the drink as Taylor smiled at Jeanine.

"Tough day today, wasn't it?" he said.

"You bet 'cha! That's why I'm sitting here, trying to unwind from all of that. The few films I have done did not have this much physical activity. I've done mostly dialogue flicks."

"And quite well too, Ms. Oscar Nominee."

She laughed. "Yeah, coming from a guy who already has one. And before you even turned twenty four!"

"That was a while ago. I'm getting older. Aren't we all?"

"It wasn't that long ago. Only two years as I recall. You're what— twenty six now?"

"Not yet, darlin'. Still twenty five. Birthday is in October, so almost."

"October." She sighed. "I hope we are done then. I want to head down to Argentina and see Raoul and take a looong break!"

Taylor laughed as he accepted his drink from the bartender.

"I know where you will be headed," she continued. "To Western New York."

"Yep. Got unfinished business there."

Jeanine eyed him curiously. "Business? Since when is love 'business'?"

Taylor glanced at her, then sipped at his drink. "I have a lot of decisions to make about what I'm going to do about the whole situation and haven't quite worked everything out yet. I do the love the boy. The woman— she is still an enigma."

"Why is that, Taylor?"

He shrugged. "Tessa is a private person, hard to get to know. Sometimes I think she has feelings for me, other times I think she just wants me gone, out of her life for good." He sipped at his drink, idly eating the green olive off the stick.

Jeanine was silent a moment, stirring her drink, then she looked up to meet his eyes. "Taylor, the woman has a lot to sort out. She has a son that needs special care, every day, twenty four/seven, 365. Even though she has a caretaker it is a huge responsibility. She also has a stressful job. I have a sister who is a nurse, so I know. Now you come along, a gorgeous handsome movie star and she falls for you. But she is worried for her son. She probably feels stuck between a rock and a hard place. She is conflicted and trying to sort things out as far as you are concerned and in the meantime be a good mom. I don't know Tessa real well but the vibe I got from her is she is very dedicated to that little boy."

"Yeah. I know all of that. Life is complicated. Nobody ever said it would be easy. And I never thought I would fall for a nurse, of all people!" Taylor grinned ruefully.

"We don't pick love, Taylor. It picks us. And if we are lucky enough, we realize it and hold onto it." She signaled the bartender for another drink. "And on that note, let's have one for the road. Then nap time for me. Six a.m. comes early."

Taylor chuckled as he accepted the second drink. "Thanks, Jeanine. You have been a good sounding board during this film. And a good friend. I hope Raoul knows how lucky *he* is!"

"He does. And when he forgets I remind him real quick!"

"That's my girl!" They clinked glasses.

The month moved along and so did filming. They were preparing to film the final sequences outside of the city. Stan had received permission to demolish an old warehouse outside the city (after handsomely paying the city of Chicago for a building they would probably demolish anyway). The cast and crew all moved out to the second location. They would have to commute back to the city when they were done filming since they were all still up at hotels there.

Everyone did their jobs professionally and efficiently. The special effects team had some problems with fire control and Stan had to work with the team to iron out these issues. Finally the right mixture was found that would be needed for the scenes and Taylor and Jeanine and Erik (the bad guy in the film) filmed scenes in the burning warehouse. It was hot, exhausting and filthy. Every evening when Taylor returned to his hotel room he showered thoroughly, especially the long blond locks. He *still* could not get the scent of smoke out of his hair or skin. How did people who smoked cigarettes stand that?

There were many scenes to wrap up in this final stage of the movie and Stan kept everyone hustling. They worked fourteen hour days but nobody complained because the end was in sight. Everyone was eager to move on to their next project or just take a vacation.

Stan filmed final sequences on September twenty ninth and thirtieth. October first Stan was throwing an elaborate wrap party at the Drake Hotel to thank his cast and crew.

Everyone circulated in the elegant ballroom of the Drake Hotel. Hundreds of people mingled, enjoying cocktails and the elaborate spread of food. Since the party was being held at such an extravagant location, dress was not casual as it usually was for some wrap parties. Black tie was the order of the day and everyone dressed up, getting into the festivities, glad the movie was wrapped. Now Stan would work with the foley people, music and sound editors to edit, polish, clip the movie into the final product. They had finished up right on time, the very last day of September.

Taylor wore a collarless black tux. He chatted with some keygrips and cameramen that he had become friendly with. He circulated, speaking to several co-stars and minor stars.

Taylor went to the bar to fetch a bourbon and Stan was there so he spent quite a bit of time speaking to Stan.

Afterwards he danced with Jeanine for about an hour, slow dancing to the big band that Stan had hired, keeping in the spirit of the 1930's movie. Both stars thought about their lovers as they swayed together.

Taylor had already made arrangements for his private jet to take him back to Buffalo, New York in the morning. He could not wait to get back to the Pattersons and Rose. As he swayed slowly with Jeanine, he closed his eyes, Tessa's beautiful face in his mind.

Soon I'll be coming home to you, baby.

CHAPTER
FIFTY

SEPTEMBER WAS FINALLY OVER in Lewiston and October had arrived. Life went on in its normal pattern— Tessa worked, Andrew returned to school and Rose resumed her caretaking duties for Andrew. As usual the weather was gorgeous in the autumn and the trees blazed with glorious colors. The weather had been pleasant and sunny, usually in the low seventies and Tessa was still able to put light clothes on Andrew for school. It was just about this time of year a year ago when Taylor had entered their lives.

All three of them missed him intensely and were looking forward to his supposed return on October first. However October first and second came and went and there was no sign of Taylor.

Andrew had been questioning his mommy all day about when Taylor would be arriving but Tessa did not have any answers to give her son. All she could do was try to reassure him he would see Taylor soon and hoped the movie star would not make a liar out of her.

Tessa was upset that Taylor had not arrived back in Lewiston when he said he would be returning. As they entered October and he did not return she was starting to worry. She did have his cell phone number and could call him at any time but she did not want to do that. A stubborn pride kept her from calling him even though she knew her son was impatiently waiting to see his big buddy. Tessa figured it was up to Taylor to contact them, not vice versa.

She tried to put Taylor out of her mind as she worked. They had been very busy in the ICU lately. There was a full moon in October and for some reason it made people crazy. They were dealing with many car accident victims and other various types of accidents. Her days were busy and full and so were her evenings caring for her son. Eventually she would put Taylor from her mind. It was just a matter of time, but her heart ached for her son whom she knew missed Taylor a great deal. It made Tessa angry at Taylor for making a promise to her son and then reneging.

The nurse's summons buzzed and Tessa hurried to room number three where an elderly man who had been in a car accident was. Tessa did her job, compassionately caring for her patients.

There was no room in her life for a movie star anyway.

Taylor arrived back in Lewiston late the evening of October third. Wearily he unlocked the door to his carriage house, hauling his bags up the steep stairs. The place was dark and he quickly flicked on lights, throwing his bags down at the top of the stairs.

The place had that unused lived in feel, an empty sensation that rooms seemed to take on when not inhabited by human beings. He shrugged off this weird thought and prepared to leave a message for Tessa.

His damn private plane had been down for repairs for two days. Ron said the engine needed some parts and even though he had had them expedited, it still took two days to get the jet up and running. Taylor was seriously thinking of taking a commercial flight when Ron assured him he could take him back the third. Taylor acquiesced. He would rather fly back on his private plane than deal with the hassle of airports. He had not called Tessa about the delay because he had wanted to surprise them with his return. After he found out he would be late, he did not want to call with disappointing news. He figured when he got back he could then see them and explain what happened.

He stumbled to bed and threw off his clothes, completely forgetting his earlier thought to give Tessa a call. As soon as his head hit the pillow, it was lights out for Taylor.

October fourth dawned and Tessa was up bright and early as usual to go to work. She grabbed her coffee and headed out to her Blazer. She glanced over at the carriage house and it was still shut up tight, just as it had been since May. She shook her head in disgust as she started her vehicle, backing down the driveway. So much for promises from famous movie stars. She *knew* she should never have allowed herself or her little family to get close to Taylor. Well, live and learn Tessa.

She swung her vehicle toward the hospital where she knew another busy day would await her. There was a tiny baby in the ICU that Tessa had been assigned to and she spent her time with him all day, consoling the family as they came in. Their newborn was in an incubator awaiting surgery and Tessa's heart broke for them. She knew exactly how they felt and she needed to have her head in the right place. Work— not whether or not Taylor would return.

Taylor slept well into the afternoon. He was exhausted after the grueling shoot, then waiting around for days to get back and finally arriving late.

When he finally shook the sleep from his eyes and checked his watch it was three p.m. Shit! He had to get up, shower and go over to the main house to let them know he had returned. He also had to have Tessa drive him to a car dealership so he could purchase some wheels since the Suburban was no longer here.

Flinging the covers back, he headed to his shower.

He groomed his long hair back, shaved carefully and chose a dark hunter green Henley to wear with his faded Levis, choosing work boots to wear. Glancing at his watch he could see it was just about three thirty.

He quickly trotted down the stairs. He intended to be at the bus today to see his little buddy. He couldn't wait!

He went outside and Rose was just coming out her back door. When she spotted Taylor, her eyes widened in surprise.

"Taylor!" she screamed, running to him to hug him.

Taylor grinned hugely, returning the hug tightly. "Hi Rose. It is great to see you again!"

They were interrupted by a toot toot of a bus. Together they turned to go down the drive to meet Andrew's bus which was waiting at the end of the driveway.

When Andrew came down the stairs and saw the tall man standing next to Mrs. H. his smile came out like a rainbow. His big brown eyes filled with love and adoration and he threw himself into Taylor's arms.

Taylor caught him, hugging him tightly. The two embraced at the end of the driveway, the man gently rocking the boy and Rose watched this reunion with tears in her eyes.

Tessa had had a very stressful day. The baby had died in surgery and she and the doctor had to tell the heart broken parents. Tessa had cried right along with them. She usually kept her composure at work because her patients needed her to be strong for them but when the infant died, she could not help herself. Her brown eyes were moist with tears and the mother had fallen into her arms crying. Tessa consoled her and the father and she knew there was nothing worse than losing a child. She had come very close herself the day Andrew had ran away to the railroad tracks. He could have died that day if not for Taylor. She owed Taylor a great debt. He had saved her son's life only to break his heart and Tessa could not forgive Taylor for that. Count your blessings Tessa, she told herself as she drove back to her home. You have Andrew and Rose and that is all that matters.

Her eyes were still a bit moist and red from crying. Sometimes Tessa really hated her job. Today was one of those days.

Taylor, Rose and Andrew were in the kitchen in Rose's flat. They were all sitting around the table chatting, catching up with each other. Andrew was telling Taylor all about his new school year. Taylor did not quite understand everything that Andrew chattered about but he got the gist that Andrew liked his new teacher Miss Reuben and there were even a few more girls in his class. Rose explained he was still in the same school but had moved up a level therefore his teacher and some of his classmates had changed. He still received all of his other therapies and Taylor could see that Andrew's use of sentences had improved a bit.

Rose served them all apple cider as they sat and chatted. It was a pleasant sunny afternoon and the three were in high spirits, very happy to see each other again. Taylor explained to Rose that he did not get back earlier because of problems with the jet and he had not been able to purchase a vehicle yet.

As the three chatted, they heard Tessa's SUV pull up about five fifteen. They each waited expectantly for Tessa to enter soon afterwards but they did not hear the car door. A good five minutes went by and still no Tessa.

Rose was concerned. She stood and looked down at Taylor. "Taylor, can you keep an eye on Andrew for a moment, please?"

"Of course, Rose," he answered as he watched her leave through the back door, his brow furrowed also. What was going on?

Rose approached Tessa's red Blazer. It was parked right in her usual space and Rose could see Tessa's profile in the driver's seat but the door had not been opened.

Getting closer, she could see Tessa's head was down and her shoulders shaking. Oh my God! Tessa was crying!

Rose immediately went to the door, opening it and leaning in toward Tessa. "Tessa! My goodness! What is wrong?"

Tessa's hands immediately flew to her face, trying to wipe away the tears and repair any damage to her makeup. "Nothing Rose, really. I'm okay. I'm just a little upset…"

"Yes, I can see dear. What is wrong? Are you sure you're all right?" Rose's brows were knit in concern.

Tessa exited her vehicle, reaching for her purse and hitching it onto her shoulder. "I'm okay, really. Just a bit upset. It was a very stressful day at work today. The baby died," her voice choked as she said the last words.

Rose knew about the tiny infant in the incubator because Tessa always shared work concerns with her. Rose gasped and placed her arms around Tessa. "Oh, dear! I am so sorry!" She stood holding Tessa for a moment and Tessa clung to her, taking comfort in Rose's embrace.

Rose finally leaned back. "There is someone here who might cheer you up a bit," she said tentatively.

Tessa walked with Rose toward the back door, composing herself. She did not want Andrew to see her tears. "Oh? Who would that be?"

"Well, I'll kinda let it be a surprise," Rose answered as they entered the house and moved into the kitchen.

Tessa looked up and could see Taylor sitting at Rose's kitchen table with her son. Andrew was all smiles as he chatted with Taylor. Taylor's teal eyes swung to Tessa. He was wearing a deep green shirt and the color intensified the teal eyes and his hair was still a glorious mass of wavy blond. He had a tan and he looked magnificent but Tessa was not in the best of moods and she was still pissed off that Taylor had not arrived when he said he would.

She put her purse down and glanced at the man at the table. "Well, well. Look who we have here. Taylor Boudrain." Her tone was sarcastic and both Rose and Taylor reacted in surprise. Rose frowned and Taylor gave Tessa a tentative smile.

He stood and moved around the table to where she was standing. "Hello, Tessa." He did not embrace her because her vibes were screaming "leave me alone". Was she mad at him for coming home late? It could not be helped but Tessa did not know that.

Tessa turned to her son. "Hello, Andrew!" She leaned down to hug him. "How was your day?" She ignored the man standing awkwardly in Rose's kitchen, her focus on her son.

Taylor was really confused now. Rose motioned him outside and he followed her, wondering what he had done wrong now.

He followed Rose down the few steps and turned to her, waiting for some type of explanation.

The older woman gazed up at Taylor, shading her eyes from the bright sunlight. "Taylor, when I came out to get Tessa I found her in tears in her SUV," Rose began.

At these words, Taylor pushed his blond locks back off of his face. "Oh, Christ! I *knew* I should have called about being late, but I wanted it to be a surprise—"

"Taylor that is not the only reason Tessa is upset right now," Rose interrupted.

The teal eyes moved back to Rose. "Yeah? What's going on?"

Rose hesitated. She really thought Tessa should be speaking to Taylor about this issue but the timing was all wrong. So it was left up to her.

"Tessa has had a patient in her care very recently. A tiny infant that needed surgery. Today the baby boy died. He didn't make it," Rose met his eyes.

Taylor gasped, his eyes tearing up a bit. Now he could totally understand Tessa's mindset and why she was not jumping up and down with joy to see him. Plus he had arrived late and she most likely assumed he was not returning at all. He knew she had always doubted him about that. And now this. Christ!

Taylor finally met Rose's eyes. "Perhaps now might not be the best time to see her. I'll wait a little while and come over a bit later. I'll give her a call to see when would be the best time."

Rose smiled. "That might be the best way to go for now. I want you to know she isn't angry at you. She's just had a tough couple of weeks and when you did not return—" her words dwindled off.

"Yeah, I get it Rose. I fucked up— 'scuse me! I messed up again!"

Rose placed a hand on his arm and squeezed. "No, Taylor. Do not berate yourself. We are *all* very happy you are back safe and sound. Even Tessa. Call her later."

"I will," Taylor answered as Rose turned to go back into her home.

Taylor sighed as he turned and did the same.

Taylor phoned Tessa at nine p.m. Andrew should be in bed and it was still early enough that he could go over and talk to her.

"Yes," she answered her cell phone and her soft voice melted his heart.

"Hi Tess."

"My name is Tessa, Taylor," she retorted.

Oh boy, how would this talk go? "Okay. Tess*a*," he emphasized the a. "May I come over and speak to you?"

"No Taylor. I'm exhausted. I've really had a stressful day and I just want to be alone." He could hear the tiredness in her voice.

"Please Tessa," he asked softly. "I need to see you."

Tessa could hear the entreaty in Taylor's voice and sighed. She might as well get this first meeting over with now when they could speak alone without Andrew present. "All right. But I don't want you to stay long. I really am tired."

"Okay. I'll be right there."

Shortly Tessa's downstairs bell rang and sighing she moved down the steps to open the door to Taylor. She had changed into jeans and a summer gauzy yellow blouse and put her hair up. She wore minimal makeup and she knew she had circles under her eyes. Taylor on the other hand had looked magnificent earlier as he always did.

When she opened the door to the tall man, she waved him silently up the stairs. He followed her into her main living room and she waved him to the sofa, taking a seat in an opposite wing chair. She curled up with a fluffy white quilt and just stared at him.

Sighing, Taylor rose and picked her up, quilt and all and brought her over to the sofa. He cuddled her close and whispered to her "I know about the baby, sweetheart. Rose told me. We don't have to talk at all." He hugged her close.

At these words and feeling his strong body encircling and comforting her Tessa burst into tears. She cried and cried and Taylor's eyes filled as he hugged the woman he loved close.

Not exactly the homecoming he was expecting but it felt so good to be holding her close once again.

CHAPTER
FIFTY ONE

TAYLOR HAD LEFT TESSA sleeping peacefully in her bed. After the crying storm she fell asleep in his arms and he carried her tenderly into her room, leaving her clothes on, tucking the pale pink satin duvet and sheets around her. She murmured softly, cuddling into her pillows. Taylor spent several moments glancing down at the beauty sleeping in the bed. Even with puffy eyes, her hair slightly mussed and no makeup on, she was still beautiful. His heart ached for her. She had had such a stressful day and he had added to it without meaning to.

He went back to his place and proceeded to further unpack, placing his clothes in his armoire and throwing dirty laundry in the hamper. He went around and dusted and vacuumed the place, opening the windows to get the stale air out of the place— to make it feel more like home.

Home. He was home. Wherever Tessa, Andrew and Rose were was home to him.

He finally took a long shower and went to bed himself.

The next morning, he was up bright and early. It was a beautiful October day so he threw on some sweats and went for a run. He paced himself hard, letting the sweat pour. He needed this physical exertion to help clear his head. Tessa. They needed to work out some things and he needed to make some decisions about his future. Taylor had quite a bit to think about as he jogged. He went further than his usual five miles; he pushed for seven and made it easily. All of the physical stunt work had left him in excellent condition. Absently he pondered the fact he had a birthday coming up in two weeks.

Twenty six. Hmmm…still fairly young. He still hadn't hit thirty candles yet. Startled, he wondered about Tessa's age and her birthday. He had never really asked her about that. Considering Andrew was seven he mentally calculated she was probably a few years older than him.

Taylor dismissed his thoughts, pouring himself into the run.

When he returned to his place, he took a hot shower, shaved and groomed his long hair back off of his face. He donned jeans, a royal blue ribbed sweater and boots. Since it was Friday he knew Tessa and Andrew would be gone, but he wanted to see Rose again and chat.

He headed out into the bright sunshine and rang her bell. Since it was mid morning, she should be around.

His summons was answered shortly by the attractive older woman. Her brown eyes twinkled up at him as she smiled. "Hello, Taylor!" She ushered him into her kitchen and he grinned back.

"Hi Rose. Just thought I would come by to visit for a while if you're not busy." He took the proffered seat at her table.

"You know me, Taylor. I always love to have company, especially when it is you. What can I get you? I have some apple pie and coffee. Can I tempt you?" She smiled at him as she went to her cupboards.

"Tempt me?! That sounds like heaven!" Taylor tossed her a grin, settling at the table. He looked around. The old fashioned kitchen was immaculate as usual. Rose was wearing black slacks with a long white blouse over them. He could not recall ever seeing her in slacks, but October was here and the weather was getting cooler. Her thick silver hair was pulled up in a black sparkly clip. He smiled as he watched her move about her kitchen, getting him food.

She brought over a huge slice of pie and a big mug of black coffee. She sat opposite him with her own coffee and smiled as he dug in.

"Ummmmmm…" he closed his eyes in sheer bliss. "This is heaven, all right."

Rose chuckled as Taylor enjoyed his snack. When he was through she offered him another slice but he declined, patting his belly. "Gotta stay lean and mean, Rose. No thanks." He sipped at his coffee.

She chuckled, removing the plate and taking it to the counter. When she returned she remarked "Lean, yes. Mean, never."

Taylor put down his coffee mug, glancing at her. "Oh, I've been mean many times. Sometimes I had to be, just to survive."

"Yes. Your childhood, is that what you are referring to?"

"Yeah, that— but other things too. To make it in Hollywood you cannot be a pussycat. You have to be hard as nails and have nerves of steel. And an ego! Don't forget the ego! It's almost expected of you."

Rose frowned a bit. "But Taylor— that is not the type of person you are now."

Taylor sighed, idly pushing his mug. "No, I guess not. At least, I hope not."

There was a bit of silence and then she questioned him. "Do you have any plans to go back to work? To do another project in the near future?"

His teal eyes lifted to meet hers. "No. I don't have anything up and coming yet. My agent will be bugging me soon. The movie you were able to observe me filming will be out at Christmas. He'll be on my case to do something else soon, but I'm not exactly ready to hop into another project."

Rose sipped at her coffee. She arched a brow. "Why is that? I know you love to act."

Taylor sighed. "Yeah. That has been my life for about seven years now. I have a birthday coming up in a couple of weeks and it gets ya thinking about what you want for your future..." His words dwindled off.

Rose gasped at this news. "A birthday? When?" she asked eagerly.

Taylor met her eyes. "Rose, I don't want to make a big deal out of it. Really. I've had birthdays for years and never celebrated them. It's just another day for me. I was usually always working." He paused. "Except for last year."

"You had a birthday while you were here last year and did not tell us! Taylor, why not?" she scolded.

He shrugged. "Wasn't important. Healing up was."

"Well, now you are healed and we are definitely going to have a little party. You know Andrew would love that Taylor. Please tell me when it is."

Taylor sighed. "Okay. It's the twentieth, in about two weeks. Don't go crazy! Some of this pie and good company will do me just fine."

Rose snorted. "We'll see..."

"And I don't expect presents either, okay? I got more stuff than I know what to do with."

Rose's eyes twinkled. "Of course not, Taylor."

Taylor grinned ruefully. "Let's change the subject. I notice Tessa hasn't been doing well. The job has been stressful lately?"

Rose sighed. "Yes. Even before this baby boy she was assigned to died, she had many patients coming in from many accidents. I think it reminded her too painfully of your accident." She paused. "There was a motorcycle accident and the young man, unlike you, did not make it."

"Wow," Taylor said in a subdued voice. He knew Tessa had quite a bit to deal with in her private life. To have so much stress in her business life too had to be awful. Tessa was a strong woman and could usually handle that aspect of her job, but he had been gone and that put extra stress on her because of Andrew.

He looked up at Rose. "It seems Tessa and I have quite a bit we need to talk about. I went up to see her last night. She was not doing well."

Rose smiled slightly. "Yes, I thought I heard you on the backstairs."

"I just want to help her, Rose. I don't want her to be unhappy."

"Then just be there for her, Taylor. That is what she needs."

Taylor pondered those words long after he went back to his place.

Tessa was at her work station, trying desperately to get caught up on paperwork. She was so behind because the ICU was so busy and taking care of the patient's needs came first. Tessa worked like an automaton, exhausted, stressed out but doing what she needed to do. Some information on her charts blurred a bit and she blinked her eyes, reaching for her coffee cup.

"Tessa?" She heard the head nurse's voice behind her and turned in her chair.

"Yes, Grace?"

Grace came over to Tessa's station and leaned against Tessa's counter, crossing her arms and looking down at the other nurse. Grace was stockily built, in her mid fifties and was a kind soul. She ran the ICU with a firm but fair hand and was respected by all of the personnel and doctors. She and Tessa had been friends for five years now, ever since Tessa had been assigned to ICU.

"Tessa, I need to talk to you about something."

Tessa straightened, meeting Grace's eyes. "Yes, what is it, Grace?"

"Tessa, you are not doing too well lately. I can tell when a nurse is burning out and you are very close to doing so." Tessa attempted to interrupt but Grace raised a hand. "Tessa, you are a fine nurse. Perhaps too fine. You care deeply about your patients and there comes a time when that can take a very deep toll on you. You are very close to that point. I don't want to lose an excellent nurse such as yourself. I've put you on a two week hiatus, starting Monday. You need to re-energize, refocus, relax, spend some time with that adorable little boy. You will be compensated for the time and I am not putting it in as vacation time, I'm putting it in as personal time for you. I can do that occasionally," Grace smiled down at her. She patted Tessa's shoulder. "So after today, go home and get some rest."

"But— I'm needed here! We are so busy! I would feel really-"

"Tessa, no arguments! Take the time. You need it." Grace straightened up, smiling down at her friend. "See ya in two weeks. I've got your shift covered. No need to worry."

She walked away as Tessa turned back to her charts. She was secretly relieved that she would have some time off. Grace was right. She could not help her patients if she herself was dead on her feet.

And she could spend so much more time with Andrew! Then she remembered that Taylor was back. She was not sure what would happen there. He had been so wonderful last night, just letting her cry and finally carrying her to bed. She woke up in her clothes and wondered what had happened. Then she recalled how he had comforted her and simply been there for her.

As usual the simple thought moved through her head. What was she to do about Taylor?

Taylor spent some time in the afternoon with Andrew shooting hoops. Rose called him in about four thirty to get ready to go upstairs since Tessa would be home soon. The two spent an hour together, laughing and having fun. Taylor had the basketball net at the lowest setting but Andrew still had a very difficult time making shots. Taylor patiently explained how to aim and shoot to target the net. Andrew tried and when he finally made two in a row, Taylor praised him, giving him lots of high fives. Andrew was all smiles to be spending time with his buddy Taylor again.

He went into the house with Rose and as they climbed the stairs to the upper level, he directed a question to Rose. "Mommee, sad again?"

Rose was startled by this question. So, even Andrew had noticed how stressed and upset Tessa had been. If Tessa knew that, it would only add to her stress. Rose decided to deal with this issue herself.

They entered the kitchen and Rose had Andrew sit at the table with her.

"You know your mommy has a job, right Andrew? She is a nurse and works at a hospital," Rose began.

Andrew frowned slightly. "But why mommy sad?"

Rose looked directly into his beautiful brown eyes. "Your mommy's job is sometimes hard, Andrew. Like how you find printing to be hard sometimes?"

Andrew understood this concept. "Yes. Hard. Printing."

"And you know how that can make you feel unhappy because it is hard for you?"

Andrew shook his head in a positive gesture.

"Well, that is what mommy is going through right now. Her job is hard and it makes her a little sad. It will pass and she will cheer up. Especially with Taylor here."

"Yes, yes! Taylor make us happy!"

Rose smiled at the little boy. "Yes, Andrew. He does."

CHAPTER
FIFTY TWO

TESSA DROVE HOME FRIDAY after her shift, exhausted. Grace was right. She was burning out and if she could not handle her job, soon it could spill over into her home life and affect her relationship with Andrew and Rose. The *last* thing she wanted was for her job to have a negative effect on her home life. Home was her sanctuary and her security. Without Andrew and Rose in her life, she would not have any reason to go on. She realized she had been depressed for several weeks and hoped her son had not picked up on that because she did not want him to worry about her. She was supposed to be there for him. She also realized she needed someone there for her. Yes, Andrew and Rose were very important to her but Tessa needed someone who could comfort her, hold her and just listen and be there for her. That is exactly what Taylor had done the other evening, just simply been there for her. Sighing, she knew that would not always be the case but she should be glad. She was blessed with two weeks off and she intended to use them wisely.

Relaxing and being with her son and not worrying about a thing.

When Tessa pulled into the drive, she noticed a brand new vehicle in the spot Taylor usually parked in. Emerging from her vehicle, she looked more closely. It was one of the those fancy Escalade SUVs, the upgraded one with all the fancy stuff on it. It was a beautiful deep burgundy color. So, Taylor had purchased a new set of wheels for himself. Sighing she slung her purse over her shoulder. It must be nice to buy whatever you wanted whenever you needed it. Her Blazer was several years old and she was seriously thinking of replacing it soon. With the extra rent money she received from Taylor it should be feasible.

She entered Rose's kitchen and looked around. No one was in the room. "Hello?" she called tentatively.

Rose and Andrew came out to greet her from the front room. When her son threw his arms around her and hugged her hard Tessa thought, this is what it is all about. Love. This is why I strive so hard everyday. This is why I work, live and breathe. Because of Andrew.

Tessa visited with Rose for a bit then she and Andrew went upstairs together.

"Guess what, buddy?" Tessa looked down at her son as they entered the kitchen. "Mommy has some time off of work and we can spend LOTS of time together! I'll be home every day and you won't have to go to Mrs. H's after school. You and mommy can hang out and do fun things together."

Andrew smiled. "You be home?"

She stooped down to his level. "Yes! The hospital has let me take some time off and we can do whatever you want after school!"

"Taylor too?" The brown eyes questioned her with hope in them.

Tessa sighed, straightening. "Yes Taylor too, if he wants to come along." Tessa had hoped Andrew would want to be alone, just the two of them but she could understand that he would want to see Taylor also. They had grown so close.

Tessa started to prepare dinner and she expected Andrew to go into the living room to watch television but he lingered in the kitchen. She glanced up at her son who was standing near the table, just watching her curiously. This was very unusual so Tessa turned to her son.

"Mommmee not be sad with Taylor here?" His brown eyes moved to her face, hope and concern in his eyes.

Tessa's heart ached. So her son had noticed how stressed she had been and was hoping Taylor could cheer her up.

Tessa took her child in her arms and whispered down to him "All I need is you, Andrew. You are the one that makes me happy."

His brown eyes searched hers, clearly wanting a further explanation. Tessa smoothed his hair back. "I am happy Taylor is back, honey. I did miss him but you are the one that mommy needs most. I don't know if you understand me or not Andrew, but you are my heart." She placed her hand over her left breast.

Andrew's smile broke out and it was like seeing the sun after a thunderstorm. He hugged her tightly. Tessa rocked her son gently in their kitchen, tears pricking her eyes.

Rose came up to visit after dinner for a while. She wanted to discuss some things with Tessa. The two settled at Tessa's kitchen table as Andrew played with some toys in his room. Tessa was curious when Rose mentioned earlier she wanted to speak to her.

As they sipped coffee, Rose smiled up at Tessa. "I am glad you have two weeks free, Tessa. That will help you relax and you can spend more time with Andrew."

"Yes, I am looking forward to that. The job was getting really stressful." She hesitated. "Even Andrew noticed. He mentioned something to me this evening about it and I was totally astounded. I did not realize just how bad it was, I guess." She looked down at her cup, not meeting Rose's eyes.

Rose was surprised that Andrew had mentioned such a thing to his mommy. Sadness and emotions were sometimes difficult concepts for Andrew but he was so in tune with his mommy that he had noticed.

"Well, he will do much better now knowing you will be home with him. And that Taylor has returned too."

At the mention of Taylor's name, Tessa met her eyes. "I see he purchased himself a fancy new vehicle."

"Yes. Just today. He said he needs it to get around. He was going to ask you to take him to a dealership but then decided against it seeing you had so much on your plate." Rose hesitated and then continued. "Did he tell you he was late returning because his jet needed repairs?" Rose's eyes searched Tessa's.

Tessa was startled. "No. Taylor and I haven't really had a chance to talk yet."

"Oh, I see."

Tessa blushed a bit. "He came up to see me the first night he was back but we did not talk much. I was too upset." She shrugged. "I kinda lost it, crying. He held me and the next thing I knew I woke up in my bed the next morning." She looked down, tracing the rim of her cup.

"Oh. So you haven't really talked about anything yet then?" Rose persisted.

Tessa shrugged. "No."

"So he doesn't know you have two weeks off?"

Tawny eyes met Rose's. "No. Not yet."

Rose hesitated, then decided to go ahead. "You know, Taylor has a birthday coming up. In two weeks."

Tessa's brows arched. "Oh, really? In October?" She frowned. "I can't remember him celebrating one last year."

"That is because he did not. He said he doesn't usually celebrate his birthday, he just works. I thought it would be nice to do something for him. Any ideas?"

"When is his birthday?"

"The twentieth."

"Hmmmm…a little less than two weeks away…" Tessa was silent, mulling over this information.

"I know Andrew would probably like to have a party for him. If you want, we can do it at my place. I can make a cake and stuff," Rose offered.

"No, no. I'll do something at my place. I just need to figure out what. Andrew will be thrilled to celebrate a birthday with his big buddy."

Rose silently sipped her coffee, wondering about Tessa and Taylor. Their relationship seemed to be in a stall. Even with Taylor home they were not really communicating. Although Taylor had only been home several days, Rose thought Tessa would be interested in seeing Taylor again. Sighing, she figured that was up to Tessa and Taylor to sort out. She smiled, drinking her coffee and turned the conversation to other subjects.

After Rose left, Tessa helped Andrew bathe and put him into bed, tucking the elephant next to him after bed time stories. She gave him extra kisses that evening and he giggled and laughed, returning them. She tickled him and laughed with him, lying next to him for several minutes, just enjoying being together. Finally she kissed him tenderly and left.

Tessa usually read for a while before going to bed. It usually relaxed her and then she would head off to bed. Tonight her novel did not hold her interest. She thought about Taylor and all of the things that were left unsaid between them. She also wondered if he was planning a new project in the near future.

Shrugging, she picked up her book. She figured she would see him around at some point and they would talk. She tried to ignore the fact that she missed teal eyes smiling down at her.

Taylor finally broke down and bought himself some transportation. He needed to get out to shop for food and other essential items.

When he returned home, it was shortly before five and he knew Tessa would not be back from work yet. He carried his purchases upstairs and prepared to fix himself a small dinner. They had not really seen each other for a couple of days since he had returned. He had spent time with Rose and Andrew but Tessa continued to be elusive.

Taylor knew he would probably have to make the first move because Tessa would not.

He moved to his cocktail table and picked up his phone.

Tessa could hear her cell phone chirping. She put down her novel and answered. "Hello?"

"Hey, Tessa. It's Taylor."

The familiar masculine voice sent tingles up and down her body. She tried to ignore that as she answered him. "Taylor. Hi."

"Mind if I come over for a bit? Haven't seen ya around and I wanted to talk if you're not busy."

Tessa sighed inwardly. Yes, it would probably be a good idea to talk. "Sure. Come on over. The back door is unlocked."

"Okay. Be there in a few."

Tessa met Taylor in her kitchen. She was still wearing her jeans and sweater, socks on her feet. The tall man before her was gorgeous as usual. She noticed his hair was still long from filming. He wore jeans and a denim shirt.

"Would you like a glass of wine or anything?" she offered.

"No, no. Just wanted to chat a bit."

"Okay. Well, come into the front room. Andrew is in bed. He went a little while ago."

Taylor settled on her sofa and she settled a little further down from him, facing him.

Tessa was silent, just studying Taylor and he sighed.

"Tell me what the other night was all about. I know work has been hard for you lately, but for you to totally lose it is unusual. Anything else bothering you?" he questioned.

Tessa looked away briefly then met his eyes. She shrugged a bit. "Work has been tough, yes. And then you didn't return and Andrew was anxious about that, constantly asking me questions about you that I, of course, could not answer…"

"Tessa, all you had to do was call me on my cell phone. I'm always just a call away."

"I really felt it was up to you to call us. You were the one that was gone. I figured you would call when you were returning. Then when you didn't return, I did not know what to tell him."

Taylor sighed heavily, crossing his arms over his chest. "Tessa, when are you going to learn to trust me?"

Tessa glanced away, considering his words. It was hard for her to trust a man. She had been let down by the men in her life constantly. Therefore she did not want to get close to a man, especially *this* man who was a famous movie star. She was in love with him and someday he would resume his Hollywood life. Yes, he wanted to be with them for now but that could change.

She finally answered him. "Taylor, it is not a matter of trust. It is a matter of protection. I am trying to protect my son and myself. Someday you will leave us for good. Yes, now you want to be with Andrew and myself, but that might not always be the case. Don't you see how difficult that is for me, Taylor?" Her brown eyes were sad and concerned.

"Tess, I've been doing a lot of thinking lately. About my career, about us, about Andrew, about everything. I haven't laid everything all out yet but the one thing I can assure you of is I have no plans to leave any of you in the future."

"Are you telling me you are going to rent my carriage house indefinitely?" She arched a brow.

He leaned a bit closer. "No, Tessa. What I am telling you is to trust me."

"Trust. Such a simple word, with such a huge meaning. I find it hard to trust men, Taylor. I've been hurt too many times," she said.

Taylor stood. "See, that is where you are making a big mistake. Comparing me to other people in your past. I'm not them, Tessa. I'm Taylor, and I have always been around for you. I think you and I both need to work out some separate issues before we can be together. And I *want* us to be together." He leaned down to softly kiss her lips. "Good night, sweetheart."

She watched as his tall form moved to her kitchen and she could hear his footsteps descending the stairs. Tessa sat and ruminated about what Taylor had said.

Then she got up to go down to lock the back door.

CHAPTER
FIFTY THREE

TAYLOR WAS UP BRIGHT and early on Saturday morning. He showered quickly and went down to collect his newspaper. He had called and re-subscribed so he could keep up with local events. As he collected his paper, he glanced over at the other house. It was a sunny gorgeous October morning, the sky was an endless blue and it was crisp and clear. It would be a perfect day for a fall outing; pumpkin picking or apple picking. He recalled the Pattersons doing that last year just around this time. He wondered if Tessa would want to take Andrew to a local farm. After their conversation last night he was a bit unsure and wary. Taylor felt Tessa needed some time to think about some important issues, as he did.

Sighing, he took his paper upstairs to peruse it to see what was happening this weekend.

A couple hours later he heard car doors slamming and glancing out his front windows he could see Tessa's Blazer moving down the driveway, turning onto the main road. Sighing, he turned away from the windows. So they were off on their own adventure for Saturday. He needed to decide what he wanted to do for the day.

He also needed to decide what to do about Tessa. If he was planning to stay here in Western New York he needed to make some decisions about his life in Hollywood-whether he would be returning to acting or not. This thought startled him. He had never considered doing anything but acting ever since he passed his first screen test and received a bit part in a movie. That part had blossomed into his current career. Taylor had not had a hard time making it in Hollywood as some younger actors did. By the time he was twenty, he was a major star. Now he was turning twenty six shortly and it made a man re-evaluate what was important in the grand scheme of things. He knew someday he wanted a family. A wife, children, the whole picket fence routine. He also knew that he pretty much knew who he wanted in those roles but there was still a long way to go before he felt Tessa and he would or could be together for the long haul.

He also needed to find some activity to occupy himself if he planned to stay in Western New York. Taylor was an active person and did not want to idly twiddle his thumbs while Tessa worked and Andrew was in school. So he had some decisions to make...

Tessa took Andrew out to a local farm to pick pumpkins on Saturday morning. It was gorgeous and sunny, a perfect day to be outdoors. She thought briefly about inviting Taylor and then discarded the idea. She did not get to spend too much time with her son and she wanted to be alone with him. With her two weeks off she would have plenty of time for that and the thought made her happy. She grinned back at Andrew in the back seat as she drove.

"We have to get some *really* big pumpkins, little guy! We need some cool jack o lanterns and Mrs. H will want some smaller ones to make her famous pumpkin pie!" Tessa was wearing dark glasses as she glanced at her son.

Andrew looked up, smiling. "Yes! Pumpkins! Orange! Smiles!"

Tessa grinned back. "Yep. We will carve them closer to Halloween, but for now we'll enjoy the farm. They have a petting zoo too. You can see ponies and sheep. It will be fun!"

Tessa pulled into the lot where other families were emerging from vehicles too, children chattering and adults smiling. The farm had a store that sold autumn decorations. Everything from haystacks, corn cobs, gourds, stuffed scarecrows and of course, all kinds of produce and pies. Tessa and Andrew always enjoyed just looking around the store.

After Andrew picked out several pumpkins, Tessa took him into the store to shop. She held his hand firmly so he would not be jostled by the people crowding in. An old fashioned popcorn maker was popping popcorn and Tessa purchased some for Andrew. She also bought a pretty fall figurine she thought Rose would like. As for Taylor, she shrugged mentally.

"Mommee!"

Tessa's attention went to her son and she could see he was pointing to a straw shaped Stetson hat that had a red and white paisley print bandana on it. Taking it down from the stand it was perched on, she handed the hat to

Andrew. He inspected it and looked up with beseeching brown eyes. "Get Taylor?"

Tessa figured Taylor probably had more Stetsons than he knew what to do with but she knew it would make her son happy to purchase the hat for Taylor. "Sure honey. We can get the hat for Taylor if you like."

"Yes, yes!"

Tessa moved to the long line to wait as Andrew munched popcorn.

Tessa and her son spent several hours out. After visiting the farm, Tessa took her son to lunch. When they returned to her place, right away she noticed Taylor's new SUV was gone. So he was out somewhere. She did not blame him. Who would want to stay home on such a beautiful day? Rose had taken her little car to go grocery shopping. Usually Tessa shopped for them both but Rose occasionally did. Today was one of those days.

She and Andrew exited her vehicle and she could see Rose had returned. Her small car was parked in the back of the huge garage where it usually stayed. Once in a while she would use it to take Andrew on outings but usually it was garaged.

Tessa went to the back of her SUV to unload their purchases. At some point today they would have to go visit Taylor to give him his Stetson.

Carrying items upstairs with help from her little guy, she tried to put Taylor from her mind.

Taylor had decided to drive into Buffalo for the day. The local paper had announced there was a big art show going on all weekend and he decided to check it out.

He walked among the crowds wearing his mirrored sunglasses. He did not bother to tie his hair back and the blond locks blew in the slight breeze. He wore faded Levis paired with a dark green tee and his cowboy boots. As he went from booth to booth inspecting wares, people recognized him and eagerly asked for autographs. Taylor complied and soon there was a huge crowd around him. Taylor dutifully signed autographs until the last fan left. It took several hours and his hand was a bit cramped but hell, it was the least he could do. He asked the locals about sights to see in the area and they all recommended he check out the waterfront.

Taylor drove down to the Marina and checked out Lake Erie and the mouth of the Niagara River. This would be a great place to own a boat, maybe a spacious sailboat. With winter coming up he decided not to get one now but in the future… he really did not know what the future would hold.

Taylor toured Buffalo alone. Although hundreds of people had greeted him and were very friendly, he still felt alone.

After catching a quick bite to eat, Taylor returned to his carriage house. He still had the rest of the evening ahead of him and was not quite sure how he would spend it. He had bought a painting from a local artist he really liked that would look great in his place. He went around to the back of his SUV to haul it out and opened his door, carrying his new artwork upstairs. He knew just where he wanted to hang it too.

Taylor was in the process of hanging his new acquisition when he heard his cell phone chirping. Probably Frank wanting to know why he was still in Western New York after a week. Sighing he moved to answer it.

"Yeah?" he answered.

"Taylor?" Tessa's voice on the line.

"Hi, Tessa."

"Are you busy right now? Andrew and I would like to come see you, if that is okay."

This news surprised Taylor. "Sure. Come on over," he invited.

"Okay. We'll be there soon."

Taylor hung up and tilted the artwork a bit more to the right. He was curious about the visit and soon his buzzer sounded.

He trotted down the stairs and opened the door to Tessa and Andrew. Tessa was dressed in jeans and a light blue sweater and looked fabulous as always. The little guy was also wearing jeans and a red tee shirt. He was holding a white plastic bag and grinned up at Taylor, his long lashed brown eyes lighting up when Taylor appeared.

"Hi guys! C'mon up," Taylor motioned them upstairs.

They ascended the steps and he followed them. He still had his hammer and some nails on the big cocktail table from hanging the new picture.

As the three entered the big room Tessa immediately noticed the new artwork. It was a beautiful piece that meshed all of the colors of his décor in a stylish design. It was breathtaking and he had placed it in the center of his front windows.

Tessa turned to him, eyes wide. "That is a beautiful piece of artwork. Where did you get it?"

Taylor moved to the sectional as he answered. "I went into Buffalo today. They had an art show going. I saw this piece, liked it and picked it up." He motioned them to the sectional. "Come sit down," he said as he removed the hammer and nails, placing the items in a closet.

As Taylor settled on the comfy sectional, Andrew ran over to him, brandishing the bag he was carrying. "Taylor, for you!" he said happily.

Taylor slowly accepted the bag, looking over at Tessa. She smiled, waiting expectantly for him to open the bag. Taylor did so and lifted out a Stetson made from straw with a bright bandana on it. He molded the crown and visor into the shape he preferred and placed it on his head.

He turned to Andrew. "How does it look, pardner?"

Andrew clapped, smiling. "Yes, yes! Fits! I like!"

Taylor hugged the boy. "Thank you for thinking of me today, Andrew! You rock!"

Andrew giggled as he snuggled next to Taylor. Tessa was on the opposite side of the huge sectional as she watched her son with Taylor.

"We visited a farm today to pick pumpkins and such and they have a gift store. Andrew picked out the Stetson for you."

Taylor squeezed Andrew again. "You are the best, Andrew!"

Andrew pointed at his mommy. "Mommy helped!" The brown eyes looked up into teal.

Taylor swung his gaze over to Tessa. "Thanks, mom!"

Andrew giggled as Tessa rose.

"Well, we really should let Taylor get back to whatever he was doing, little guy. We should go."

Andrew frowned. "No. Stay Taylor!"

Taylor intervened. "It's still kinda early. If you want to leave him here for a while, he can stay and visit. I'm not doing anything important."

Tessa studied the two guys on the sectional and sighed inwardly. "Okay. Please bring him back a bit before bedtime."

"Sure thing."

"Yaaaaah!"

Andrew was all smiles as his mommy descended the stairs.

Taylor spent a couple of hours with Andrew. They watched a movie and played a couple games of checkers. Taylor had invested in a nice set when he learned Andrew liked to play the game. About quarter to eight he took the boy back over to the larger house, ringing the bell.

They waited as Tessa descended the stairs, opening the door to the two of them.

"Hi!" Taylor greeted, holding Andrew's hand.

"Hello. Did you two have fun?"

"TV! Checkers! Lots fun!" Andrew informed her, still clutching Taylor's hand.

"Well, that is great honey but now it is time for you to come in and get ready for bed." She held out her hand and reluctantly Andrew dropped Taylor's to accept his mother's.

"See Taylor tomorrow?" Andrew asked hopefully.

Tessa's gaze swung to the man standing at the bottom of the steps. "Well, that is kind of up to Taylor, Andrew. I don't know what he has planned."

Taylor shrugged. "No plans."

Tessa met his eyes. "Well, there is a local art show here in town too. I was planning to take both Rose and Andrew. If you would like to join us, we can all go."

"Sure. I guess so."

Tessa ushered Andrew up the stairs. "I'll be there in a minute, honey." As Andrew ascended the stairs, she turned back to Taylor. "Thank you for letting him spend some time with you." She paused. "I didn't know you wanted to go into Buffalo. I could have taken you in and shown you some of the sights."

Taylor shrugged. "You guys were gone and I wanted to do something so I headed in. I had a good time. I don't expect you to babysit me, Tessa. Don't worry about it. See ya later." Taylor turned to go to his own place.

As Tessa shut the door and locked it she could sense Taylor's aloofness. How would tomorrow go?

Sunday was another gorgeous day. The four of them went into downtown Lewiston and spent hours looking at all of the displays and vendors. Taylor bought some balloons and special toys for Andrew but nothing really caught his eye so he did not purchase anything else. Tessa and Rose enjoyed looking at all of the paintings and Taylor spent time with Andrew. They went off on their own exploring. They found a pretty fountain in the middle of the green and spent time there throwing a Frisbee around and enjoying the gorgeous day.

After lunch and some more browsing Tessa and Rose were finally ready to head back. Everyone piled into Taylor's new SUV and he drove them back to Tessa's place.

Rose noticed that Tessa and Taylor had barely said two words to each other.

CHAPTER
FIFTY FOUR

TESSA WAS HOME ON Monday and was able to see her son off to school. She went through the normal routine for the morning and blew kisses to him as he headed off on the little yellow bus. She said a silent prayer for his safety then moved up the driveway noticing Taylor's SUV parked in the regular spot. Since she had two weeks off she would probably be seeing more of Taylor than usual and Tessa was unsure how that would go. It could be a good thing or an annoying thing. Shrugging, she went upstairs to her flat. She planned to use the time she had free today doing housework and running some errands. That way on the weekend she would have more free time to spend with Andrew. She would also get to see him in the afternoons too. Her two week vacation gave Rose a much deserved break also.

Sighing, Tessa moved upstairs and prepared to begin her day.

Tessa returned from shopping about two thirty and pulling her Blazer into the driveway right away she noticed Taylor's vehicle was gone. So, he was out for the day again. Well it wasn't really any of her business what Taylor was doing. She needed to put away groceries and prepare a snack for her little guy. He would be home in about an hour.

After putting away grocery items, Tessa went down into the yard to rake some leaves while she waited for Andrew to return. As she came out, she noticed the SUV still had not returned. She frowned a bit as she went to the storage area in the garage to collect her rake. It was a bit chillier today and Tessa wore her quilted aqua vest over a teal sweater with jeans and oxford work boots. She had tied her magnificent mane back into a ponytail and wore dark glasses as she raked the mass of leaves into separate piles.

Within an hour the bus arrived and Tessa hurriedly made her way down the drive to greet her son.

Laughing, she gave him lots of hugs and kisses and the two went up into their home. As they did so Tessa again noticed the SUV was still gone.

Tessa invited Rose up for dinner and they all casually chatted in the kitchen. Andrew went off to watch television as Rose helped Tessa clean in the kitchen.

"I noticed Taylor's vehicle has been gone all day," Rose remarked casually. "I wonder where he is off to." Her brown eyes lifted to Tessa and the other woman shrugged.

"I don't know, Rose. I am not exactly privy to his schedule." She placed platters in the cupboard as she answered, averting her eyes.

Rose sighed. "I noticed yesterday you and Taylor were not speaking much. Is there a problem?"

Tessa met Rose's eyes. "No. No problem."

"I see."

"Taylor does his thing and we do ours."

"Tessa— that is not exactly how things have been in the past and you know it," Rose persisted.

She moved to Tessa's table to sit as they finished up. Tessa followed her, taking a seat.

"I don't know if you've noticed, but his SUV is still gone and it is six p.m. He has been gone all day. I can't possibly think of anywhere around here that Taylor would be gone all day," Rose said.

"It's still gone?" Tessa's brows arched. "I hadn't noticed. I've been busy with Andrew." She got up to look out the kitchen window and sure enough, no sign of the SUV. Hmmmm…

She returned to the table, shrugging. "Don't know what his plans were for today Rose. He didn't tell me."

"What are you planning to do tomorrow? Would you like to go to the mall and shop a bit?"

"Sure, Rose. Sounds great."

"Okay. I'll be up around ten and we can get a start."

"Yep. We can do lunch and stuff. It will be fun, just us girls!"

Rose smiled and shortly left for her own apartment.

As Tessa was preparing to get Andrew ready for bed, she finally saw the SUV pulling up the driveway and parking. In the dim light she could see Taylor emerge from the vehicle and move over to his place, unlocking the door and disappearing inside. So he had been gone well into early evening somewhere. Truly a mystery but none of her business, she surmised.

She was looking forward to her shopping date with Rose. The two of them had never really had any alone time. Usually Andrew was with one or the other of them. Tessa did not really have any close girlfriends. She had acquaintances at work but no one she was really close with. Most people did not understand about Andrew's disability and did not try to and thus Tessa tended to be a loner. Rose was not only Andrew's caretaker; she was Tessa's best friend.

Tuesday morning the women were up and out early. As Tessa drove the Blazer down the driveway they both noticed that Taylor's SUV was right where it was usually parked. They both looked at each other and shrugged and went off on their shopping adventure.

Taylor noticed Tessa's SUV leaving about ten in the morning and was puzzled. It was a week day morning and usually Tessa was working. She and Rose had entered the vehicle and were off somewhere. He had already gone for his run and showered up and was on his second cup of Joe. He had heard the doors slam and looked out his front windows to see the two leave.

Yesterday he had driven into Rochester on business. He had been gone all day and into the evening because of the commute and the reason for his business. He had finally made a decision about what he would do with his time here in Western New York and quite a bit of time would be spent commuting back and forth to Rochester.

He went over to his cocktail table and looked over the new designs for the hospital.

Tessa and Rose returned about two p.m., carrying shopping bags and chattering. They had enjoyed their day out together but Tessa had to make sure she was home for Andrew's bus.

She came out at three twenty to rake a bit more and immediately noticed Taylor washing his Escalade. He wore mirrored sunglasses, jeans and had his glorious hair tied back.

Tessa moved over to the SUV. "Hello, Taylor."

"Hey, Tessa." He was standing on the footboard washing the roof and he continued with his chore as he answered her. She was very curious about where he had been yesterday but did not want to question him since it was really none of her business.

"Gorgeous day, isn't it?" she remarked, putting her hands in her jeans pockets.

"Yep. Good day to be outside," he answered, still not looking up.

Tessa felt a bit at a loss. Usually Taylor was interested in chatting with her and as she hesitated, he rinsed out the sponge and finally looked up.

"What are you doing home on a week day?" He glanced down at her.

"Oh, I have two weeks off from my job. The head nurse gave me some time off. Rose and I went shopping today," she casually mentioned.

"Yeah, I saw you leave." He picked up the sponge again and started scrubbing the windshield.

"I noticed you weren't around yesterday..." she tried to get a bit of information.

He straightened and looked down at her. "Yeah. Had some business to take care of. I may be gone here and there occasionally."

The yellow bus pulled up at the end of the driveway so Tessa was unable to question Taylor further. "Well, see ya around," she said as she moved to the end of the driveway.

"Yeah, sure." He went back to his chore and Tessa moved away, her brow quirked in puzzlement.

Business? What type of business?

She collected her son and when he saw Taylor he ran right over to chat with him. Tessa reminded him he had to come in for his snack. Andrew begged to come out to shoot hoops with Taylor afterwards. Taylor acquiesced and Tessa sighed. Her son was more interested in spending time with Taylor than herself right now. She smiled. That was okay. She was glad her two guys got along so well.

Her two guys! Where had *that* thought come from?

The week continued and Tessa was able to go on little outings either alone or with Rose. She did not see too much of Taylor. Several times a week his SUV was gone and she surmised he was taking care of his mysterious business, whatever that was.

Afternoons were spent taking Andrew to a movie, or to Micky D's or out for pizza or visiting the park. The weather continued to be nice, sunny but cool. Andrew had the following Monday off too because it was Columbus Day so they had the whole day to spend together. She recalled how last year Taylor had taken Andrew camping that weekend. A whole year had passed by. It seemed unbelievable to Tessa. A year had come and gone and Taylor was still here. Still here and conducting mysterious business.

As Taylor's birthday became closer, Rose and Tessa tried to decide what to do to celebrate the day. They planned out what they would have for dinner and Tessa planned to make a cake. Tessa also had been busy making sure they had a special present ready for Taylor. She hoped he liked it. Since she basically had not spoken to him for the whole two weeks she had been off, she needed to call him and invite him over for his birthday. She would be returning to work the following Monday. Taylor's birthday fell on a Thursday.

She called him several evenings before his birthday on one of the days the SUV was present.

"This is Taylor," he answered.

"Hey, Taylor! This is Tessa!" she returned.

Taylor was startled. He had not really seen Tessa for a while. "Hey! What's up?"

"You know what's up, you scoundrel, you! Your birthday is Thursday and we all want you to come to my place for a special party."

"Told ya, Tessa. I don't celebrate my birthday."

"Well, we do. How is five? Can you be here at five that night?" She still had several days off and would be able to have everything ready with Rose's help.

Taylor checked his business calendar. He had meetings all day in Rochester that day and really could not make it Thursday. Friday was free though. "Sorry. Can't do it Thursday. I'm free Friday though."

Tessa was a bit let down by this news. What was so damn important? Well, at least he had agreed to come Friday. They would just push it ahead a day. "Okay. Friday it is. We'll see ya then, Taylor."

"Okay. And thanks for thinking of me. It really wasn't necessary."

"You know Andrew will love to have a party for you, so for his sake, I thought you might want to do something special. If you really don't want to do this, tell me!" Tessa was getting a bit exasperated. She had gone to a lot of trouble to make it a nice day for him.

"No, no! I want to come! I'll be there Friday. Can't wait to see y'all again."

"Okay, Taylor. Friday it is. See ya then." Tessa hung up the phone, sighing. What was it with Taylor lately?

CHAPTER
FIFTY FIVE

TAYLOR WAS IN ROCHESTER for business meetings and was taking a short break for a stroll in the hallway of the office high rise. His phone chirped in his pocket and he removed it, clicking to answer.

"Hello?"

"Taylor! Cripes! Where ya been?" Frank on the other end being his usual cheerful self.

"I've been around, hoss. What's up?"

Taylor leaned against a wall, looking out at the city through large glass windows as he spoke to his agent. Frank continued to berate him.

"What's up is I haven't heard from you in three weeks! Heck, even when you had your accident I heard from you within two! Is everything okay back there, kiddo?" Frank's voice now sounded concerned and Taylor sighed inwardly. Sooner or later he and Frank needed to have a long talk. Now was not the time.

"I'm fine, Frank. Really. I've just been busy with some different enterprises I got runnin'."

Frank was puzzled. The children's cancer research hospital that Taylor was a major donor in was now up and running and there was really not too much that needed attention there at the moment. "Enterprises? Such as what?"

Taylor did not want to get into the whole scenario with Frank yet. "Oh, I just got a few irons in the fire," Taylor returned casually.

Frank sighed. "When are you coming back? Are you EVER coming back?"

"Sure, I'll be back, hoss. Got business there too, as you know."

"Speaking of which, we need to discuss a new project for you."

"Not yet, hoss. Soon though." Taylor wanted to reassure his agent to mollify him.

It worked. "Good. Give me a call soon so we can work on that Taylor."

"Will do, Frank. I'll call real soon."

"Okay, Taylor."

Frank clicked off and Taylor sighed. He had quite a bit to settle— with everyone.

Taylor's meetings lasted until seven and it was after eight before he finally made it back to Lewiston. Checking his watch, he could see it was about eight fifteen and it was already dark out. Looking up at the bigger house, he could see lights lit in both the upper and lower levels. The Pattersons and Rose had settled into their evening routines. Startled, he realized today was his birthday and tomorrow they were expecting him for a little party. What had Tessa said, five p.m.?

Taylor hauled his briefcase up to his place. He needed to get some extra sleep. He was exhausted from commuting so much and spending time in board meetings.

He threw off his clothes and fell face down on his bed, asleep immediately.

Tessa and Andrew decorated their apartment with streamers, balloons and big posters saying "Happy Birthday Taylor". Andrew was very excited and got into the spirit of helping to decorate. He also had a special present to give to Taylor and his mommy had helped wrap it and put a big gold bow on it. Andrew could not wait for Taylor to arrive and open his presents.

Tessa made lasagna for dinner and tossed a huge salad. She made a large chocolate cake. She figured most men liked chocolate cake. Since she really did not know what age Taylor was turning, she just put on enough candles to look decorative.

Rose helped her get the dining table set up and bring the food out when it was ready. It was five to five and they were all excited, waiting for Taylor to make an appearance. They had even dressed for the occasion. Tessa put a pair of black slacks on Andrew paired with a bright red polo shirt. She wore a long sleeved silky red knit dress with black pumps and Rose opted for a navy floral patterned dress.

Tessa made sure the wine glasses were ready and poured Andrew some soda. Glancing at her watch, she could see it was exactly five p.m. As she fussed with napkins, she heard the buzzer about five minutes later.

She descended the stairs to open the door to Taylor and gasped in surprise. He had cut his hair again, quite short, just brushing the collar of a grey shirt he wore open at the collar which he had paired with jeans and cowboy boots. The cut looked terrific on him and he looked a bit leaner too, like he lost some weight. She smiled up at him.

"Hello! Happy birthday!" She motioned him inside and complying he moved into the house, smiling down at her.

"Wow! You didn't have to dress up, Tessa! But I've always loved you in red!" He grinned as they moved up the stairs.

"It's a special occasion. So we dressed for it!"

They moved into her kitchen where delicious smells emanated. "Hmmmm…something smells good."

Tawny eyes rose to his. "I made lasagna. I hope you like it," she said uncertainly.

He grinned broadly. "Love it!"

She smiled at his response as Andrew came running into the kitchen when he heard Taylor's voice, Rose not far behind him. He launched himself into Taylor's arms and grinning Taylor caught him and hugged him.

"Taylor! Birthday, you! Happy!"

"Andrew, it is happy birthday, Taylor," Tessa corrected.

"Yes!" he said, smiling from ear to ear, holding Taylor's hand. "Come see!" He led Taylor into the dining room as Tessa and Rose brought food in.

Taylor looked around at all of the decorations and posters and smiled. They had really gone all out for his birthday. Nobody had ever really celebrated his birthday for him except one time he recalled his mom had. When he was seven or something. So long ago, just a distant memory. And now at twenty six he had a little family that cared enough about him to throw him a party. Taylor was truly touched.

"Wow, guys! This is terrific! I'm really surprised!" Taylor turned to grin at the two women.

"Presents too," Andrew informed him.

Taylor smiled as Tessa directed everyone to seats. She served the food and everyone dug in, chatting and laughing.

Finally Rose brought up the big question. "So, Taylor. How old are you today exactly? We did not know how many candles to put on your cake."

Tessa looked up at this question, very interested in the answer. She had no idea how old Taylor was.

"I turned twenty six yesterday, Rose."

Rose gasped a bit. "Twenty six! My, so young!"

Tessa was surprised also. Taylor must have been quite young when he first became famous.

She rose. "Speaking of candles, I have a big chocolate cake with candles on it just for you, Taylor!" She went into the kitchen to get the cake. She placed it in front of Taylor and lit the candles and they all sang happy birthday to him.

Grinning Taylor blew the candles out with help from Andrew, Tessa taking photos of this action. Afterwards they all enjoyed the cake and Taylor told her everything was delicious. She had really gone to a lot of trouble to make his birthday dinner nice.

Finally Andrew tugged Taylor's arm, directing him into the front room. "Come, Taylor! Presents!"

"Well, we have to wait for mom and Mrs. H. Andrew." They were both still cleaning up a bit.

The two women joined them shortly and Tessa told Andrew he could give his present to Taylor.

Smiling, Andrew presented Taylor with a square wrapped gift, waiting breathlessly for him to open it. When Taylor did he could see it was a beautiful color eight by ten framed photograph of Andrew. He was wearing the teal hunter green and plaid shirt and his beautiful brown eyes shined in the picture and he had a tentative smile on his face. It was a gorgeous photo of the little boy he cared so much for. Taylor's eyes got a little misty.

He leaned forward, scooping Andrew into his lap and buried his face in Andrew's neck, choked up a bit. Then he looked directly into the beautiful brown eyes. "Thank you, Andrew. I love it."

Smiling, Andrew leaned forward to return the embrace, hugging tightly.

"It is his current school photo. I thought you might like to have a copy of it," Tessa remarked.

Taylor swiped a bit at his eyes and glanced up. "Yep. I know just where I'm going to put it too."

Andrew jumped up. "Where, where?" He was excited.

"Right on my night stand table where I can see you every night and every morning."

Andrew smiled and hugged Taylor again.

Tessa finally presented him a present from herself and Rose. It too was square but much larger than the first present. It took Taylor a few minutes to get all of the wrapping off but when he did he gasped in surprise. Tessa had taken one of the photos of the four of them together at the Muttart Conservatory in Edmonton and enlarged it, framing it in an elaborate gold frame. It showed the four of them surrounded by flowers, Taylor stooped down next to Andrew in the front, with the two ladies flanking them on either side. It was a beautiful photograph of all of them and the splendid array of colors from the flowers made it particularly striking. He could not have asked for a better birthday present.

He looked up at Tessa, teal eyes moist. "I love it, baby!"

He came over to kiss her cheek, turning to kiss Rose also. "This is the best birthday I've ever had. I'll cherish both of these photographs."

Tessa blushed. "I was hoping you would like it. You have so many things it is hard to know what you might like…"

"You and Andrew and Rose picked the perfect gifts! I love them both!"

They all grinned hugely. Then Tessa offered Taylor wine and she and Rose settled in the front room with wine also, talking casually and Andrew sat snuggled next to his big buddy.

Around nine Rose took Andrew into his room to get him ready for bed and Tessa went in to give him kisses. Rose left shortly after that, after wishing Taylor a happy birthday again.

Tessa topped off their wine and smiled softly at the man sitting beside her. "So, twenty six years old. You're still a young kid!" she teased.

Taylor grinned in the low lamplight. "What about you, Tessa? You never did tell me when your birthday is or your age." He studied her lovely features as he drank his wine.

"We missed my birthday both years. It is September tenth. I had it right before your accident the first year, and last month when you were filming! As to my age— let's just say I'm older than you!" Her brown eyes teased him.

"Come on, Tessa! Give! If I couldn't be here for the special day, at least tell me how old you are! I'm curious."

"Okay. I just turned thirty one." She sipped at her wine as she waited for his reaction.

Only five years older than him. Hmmmm… he always had preferred older women. They had more going on upstairs usually and were better sexual partners than younger women. That was definitely the case where Tessa was concerned.

At his silence, she teased him. "Too old for you Taylor?"

"Actually, I was just thinking that is the perfect age. I prefer older women," he grinned.

"Oh really?"

"Yep. Usually smarter and more sophisticated than their younger counterparts."

Tessa was silent, studying the handsome man. The new hair cut was full and soft. She knew he had silky thick hair and she loved to run her fingers through his beautiful blond mane. She blushed, glancing away from him.

Finally she asked a question. "What is this mysterious business you have been going away for?"

At her question, his expression closed up a bit. "It is a bit of a surprise. I don't want to mention what it is until I have the final details worked out. Then I'll tell you all about it."

"I'm assuming it is an acting job?" She arched her brows.

"Nope." He sipped slowly at his wine.

"You're involved in something that is not dealing with your career?" Tessa found this hard to believe.

He met her eyes. "That's right."

Tessa's brows knit in puzzlement. It wasn't like Taylor to be so mysterious and now she was really curious. She changed the subject. "I go back to work Monday. My two week hiatus ends then," she remarked.

"I wish I could have been around to spend more time with you, Tessa. But I'm glad you got a break. You needed one badly."

"Yeah. I'm doing a lot better, a lot more relaxed. I got to spend quite a bit of time with Andrew and that was wonderful! And Rose and I went on our girl outings so I had fun!"

Taylor grinned and finished up his wine. It was going on ten o'clock. He stood and Tessa rose also. He approached her and stroked her cheek softly. "Thank you for the wonderful birthday, baby. I'll remember it for the rest of my life." He leaned down and softly kissed her lips. Tessa moaned a bit then he broke off the kiss.

He collected his presents and then turned to her. "If you're not busy tomorrow night, do you want to do dinner? I can take you out somewhere if you like," he offered.

Tessa's heart pounded hard. She would love that. "Yes. I can have Rose come up to be with Andrew. What time?"

"Does six work?"

"Sure," she replied as she walked into the kitchen with him.

He turned a final time to softly touch her hair, stroking his hand down the soft tresses. "Good night, baby. Thank you again." He descended the stairs and Tessa could hear him lock the door from the outside.

Sighing, she turned to go bathe and get ready for bed.

Chapter
FIFTY SIX

Tessa dressed carefully for her dinner date with Taylor on Saturday evening. She chose a backless black velvet dress with a matching black velvet cropped jacket with long sleeves. She wore black high heels and chose the stunning pearl set Taylor had given her for Christmas last year. As she brushed her thick hair out, preferring to leave it down, she ruminated about the past year.

She could not believe a whole year had come and gone already. It was just about this time last year Taylor had taken her to Shamuses. She was unsure where they were going tonight but she was certain it would be special and she wanted to look especially nice. In the half year that Taylor had actually been in residence he had touched all of their lives in different ways. Hers, Rose's and Andrew's and they were all better off for it. Sighing, she picked up her black velvet clutch and headed to the front room where Rose and Andrew were watching television.

As she entered the room, Andrew gasped, jumping up to come over to hug his mommy. "Mommy pretty!" he exclaimed.

Smiling, Tessa bent down to kiss his soft cheek. "Thank you, honey. Mommy is going out to dinner with Taylor this evening so I may not see you for a while."

He looked up into her face, his brown eyes shining. "You go Taylor?" He seemed very happy with this news which was such a contrast to his reaction last year. So many things had changed…

"Yes, honey. We're having dinner together and you will have Mrs. H for company. I'll be home later on. It will probably be after your bed time. Be a good boy for Mrs. H," she leaned down to kiss him again.

"I will, mommy!" he promised as Rose chuckled.

The bell downstairs rang right at six p.m. Tessa descended the stairs to open the door to Taylor. It was a gorgeous October evening, crisp and clear and the lamp light lit up the area around the door.

Taylor was wearing a dark grey suit with thin light grey stripes, a pale blue shirt paired with a silky silvery tie with a subtle print. With his new shorter hair cut, he looked like a prosperous business executive. He was still drop dead handsome and she knew she was a very lucky woman indeed to have such a man.

She smiled at him. "Hello! I'm ready!" she greeted.

Smiling, he offered his arm, helping her down the steps and politely seated her in the Escalade. Taylor always displayed those polite southern manners and that was just one of the many things Tessa liked about Taylor. She had been out with some real clods who did not know the meaning of manners. As she settled in her seat, she glanced over at him as he sat in the driver's seat. The blond hair was carefully styled and fell slightly past his collar. He had a perfect profile and the dying sun kissed his features and hair.

As he started up the vehicle, she asked a question. "So, where are we going for dinner tonight?"

He smiled. "I thought I would surprise you."

She laughed a bit. "That's Taylor! Just full of surprises!"

"Hey, gotta keep you on your toes! Otherwise, you'll start taking me for granted!" he teased.

Even though Tessa knew he was teasing, his words still struck a chord with her. Yes, there were many things about him that she took for granted and she really shouldn't. Tessa tried to dismiss introspective thoughts. She only had one more free night and day before going back to work and she planned to enjoy herself.

As he continued to drive, Tessa could see he was taking the route to Shamuses. "Are we going to Shamuses?" she asked.

He turned to grin at her. "Yep! I thought we could sorta make it a tradition. We went there last year just around this time. I know you like it," he replied.

Tessa smiled, very happy to hear this news.

When they entered the restaurant, the hostess greeted them politely. "Reservation?" she asked, smiling.

"Yes. Taylor Boudrain for two," he answered.

Tessa's eyes widened when he used his name and the hostess became all flustered. "Oh yes, Mr. Boudrain! We have one of our finest tables waiting for you! And the owner himself will be waiting on you! Please follow me."

Tessa rolled her eyes slightly. It seemed like she could not gush enough.

The table they were seated at was also by the windows as last year but it was slightly elevated which gave one a better view of the valley and scenery. Taylor pulled out the posh chair, seating Tessa politely and the hostess waited, all smiles, for Taylor to take his seat. When he was seated, she gave them both elaborate menus.

"Harvey will be right out to attend to you. Please have a wonderful dining experience tonight!"

"Wow! Quite the greeting," Tessa remarked as the hostess moved away and picked up her menu. She arched a brow. "What made you decide to use your name? Thought you were trying to fly under the radar, as it were."

Taylor's teal eyes met hers in the candlelight. "Not anymore, darlin'. If I'm going to be living around here, coming and going, livin' my life I'm gonna to do so as myself. I *will* make sure that where I am living is totally private for the obvious reasons. But when I'm out in the community, I'll be Taylor Boudrain."

"Well, get ready to be mobbed by the masses," Tessa warned.

Taylor shrugged. "A few people have already recognized me at stores and such. Everyone's been great, they don't bother me. Usually they want autographs." He shrugged his shoulders. "No big deal."

Before Tessa could comment, a middle aged man with thinning brown hair approached their table with a huge smile. "Mr. Boudrain, this is a pleasure!" He shook Taylor's hand. He smiled over at Tessa. "M'am, good to see you. I am Harvey Shamus and I own this establishment. I will be your server this evening. I hope you both enjoy your dining experience."

Taylor glanced up. "Well, thank you Harvey. Glad to hear that and all. I think we need a few minutes to kinda look over the menu."

"Take your time, sir. In the meantime, can I get you anything to drink?"

"Yeah, we would like a pitcher of ice water and a bottle of Perrier Jouie," Taylor said the French name casually as though he was ordering a coke.

"Yes, yes! Of course! One of the finest brands of champagne made! Very good taste! I shall be right back, sir." He left to go attend to his duties.

"Well, well. Quite different than the service we received last time. Not that it wasn't wonderful, but it wasn't *fawning* either," Tessa remarked as her eyes went to the bulky menu.

Taylor glanced up from his menu. He shrugged briefly. "I'm used to it, Tessa. Just take it in stride."

"That's easy for you to say!"

He chuckled.

When they placed their menus down, Harvey was right there to take their orders. They ordered quickly, handing the bulky menus back. Smiling, Harvey accepted them and left so they could chat over their champagne which he had already served.

"So, ready to go back to work Monday?" Taylor asked casually, swirling his champagne flute. The candlelight painted romantic colors around their table and it softly touched Tessa's lovely features. As usual, he wanted to throw her on the floor and have wild sex with her. He took a sip of champagne, trying to distract himself from erotic thoughts but it was damn hard.

She sighed a bit. "Yes. I'm ready to go back. The two week rest helped me a lot. I'll miss the time I had to spend with Andrew but life and work must go on." She sipped at her champagne, studying the handsome man across from her. "Speaking of work, you still won't tell me what you've been up to? I can keep a secret, you know."

He flashed his famous grin. "It is not a matter of secrecy. It is a matter of completion. I want all details complete and nailed down solid before I reveal what I am working on. But just to let you know, it involves staying here in Western New York. I don't have plans to go back to LA."

Tessa was very surprised by this news. "What about when you make another movie? You WILL be making another movie I assume?" Her tawny eyes searched his but he just shrugged.

"Drink your champagne, darlin'. And tell me how that adorable little boy is doing in school."

Tessa sighed. She could see she would not get any more details about the mysterious project.

The couple talked casually as they enjoyed the extravagant meal.

When it was time to head back to Tessa's place, she could feel the slight effects of the champagne and knew she had a little buzz going. She laid her head back in the luxurious cushions and closed her eyes as Taylor drove back.

Arriving back at the carriage house Taylor parked and glanced over at Tessa. He wanted to have sex badly. He had been celibate for months and months and he decided he wanted to do something about that tonight. Was she in the mood? It had been a long time since they had been intimate.

He came around to help her down from the vehicle and as she started to walk to the back door, he restrained her and she glanced up in surprise. "Can you give Rose a call on your cell and tell her you might be late? Would she have a problem with that?"

"I'm not late. We're home," Tessa stated the obvious.

Taylor sighed and met her eyes in the moonlight. "Yeah. I know we're back but I want to take you up to my place."

Tessa's brows arched. She had a guest bedroom that Rose had utilized in the past and she knew Rose would not have a problem staying overnight. However Tessa had not requested that in a long time but Rose would probably be very okay with it.

Sighing, she glanced up into his beautiful teal eyes. She knew what going up to his place meant. Having sex and Tessa admitted she wanted it probably just as badly, if not more so, than Taylor.

She removed her cell phone from her purse and hit one for home. Rose immediately answered.

"Hi Rose. It's me. I was just wondering if it would be a problem if you stayed over tonight." Pause. "Not a problem? Okay, I'll be over at Taylor's if you need me." Another pause. "Yes, all right. See you in the morning." She clicked off and turned to the man who was standing next to her just moments ago.

He had unlocked his door and it was standing wide open. He came over to her and picked her up in his strong arms, carrying her over to the entrance of the carriage house.

He kicked the door shut.

Tessa sighed, stroking the muscles on Taylor's chest. They were both sweaty and totally exhausted after having wild sex three times. She loved to snuggle after sex and Taylor did too. He smiled down at her as her fingertips softly stroked his skin. It felt heavenly. But everything about Tessa was heavenly. She was his angel and he knew he was in love with her and never wanted to leave her, ever again.

He flipped onto his side, propped up by his elbow. He gently traced a bit of cleavage showing above the sheet she clutched to her breasts. "You are so beautiful, baby," he said softly.

Tessa smiled. "You are too, you big hunk of man!" She leaned up to kiss him leisurely then snuggled against him. His fingers continued to stroke down her back. Her skin felt as soft as the velvet dress he had removed earlier.

"Tessa, when I am with you, the whole world fades away. The only thing I can think of is you. How you taste, smell, the way you kiss, the way you moan when I enter you…I'm in heaven and you're the reason why. I know it is a song cliché, but what can I say?" He shrugged. "It's the truth."

Whiskey brown eyes looked up into teal. She searched his eyes and they were tender and soft. She loved Taylor with her whole being but there were still too many unanswered questions. And now there was this mysterious business he was involved in. "You are such a mystery, Taylor," she whispered.

"No, I'm not darlin'. What you see is what you get."

Tessa stroked back blond locks. "Enough talk. Let's make love again."

Tessa opened her legs wide and Taylor filled her and gently started to move inside her.

Tessa saw stars again and gave herself up totally to sexual bliss.

No matter what happened in the future, she would always have these memories.

CHAPTER
FIFTY SEVEN

TAYLOR HEADED INTO ROCHESTER on Monday again for business. He had meetings with top executives at a local children's research hospital. Taylor was in negotiations at the moment to work out the logistics of building an off shoot hospital in the Western New York area. Taylor would retain controlling shareholder interest and thus would basically own the facility but he needed the expertise of the personnel at this particular hospital. They were renowned in the area for helping children with special needs. Taylor wanted to build such a facility in his area and they were currently speaking about looking at a large sprawling lot of land for sale in Lockport New York, which was about a fifteen minute ride from Lewiston.

Taylor wanted to nail down final details very soon so construction could begin. The next phase after purchasing the property would be to hire architects and a construction firm for the project. All told, everything would take at least a year to come to fruition.

It was finally decided they would all go out to look at the property in Lockport together on Wednesday. The realtor and developer would be there to show them around and give details and area survey maps. The property was one hundred acres and Taylor was purchasing it on his own.

After taking care of these details, he headed back to Lewiston and pulled up early evening, about dinner time. As he pulled into his park space, he glanced over at Tessa's red Blazer parked in its normal spot.

Taylor sat in his vehicle a few minutes and recalled Saturday evening and the wild and tender sex that followed it. He shook his head. What was he to do about Tessa?

Taylor spent Tuesday meeting with a local university in Buffalo. He visited the medical office and spoke to the dean. The dean was all smiles having a famous movie star visiting the campus. He took Taylor around to classes and Taylor greeted students and signed autographs. He was mobbed and the dean offered to call school security but Taylor waved this away, chatting with fans and signing one textbook or notebook after another. Grinning, he answered questions about co-stars and other questions about making movies. Word got out he was at the University and the local television stations showed up to tape the event.

Taylor basically ignored the media as he spoke with fans. Then he waved goodbye and continued his tour with the dean. Taylor was quite fascinated with the medical school and wanted to learn as much as possible.

He left late in the afternoon to return to his place. After dinner he planned to go over to Tessa's to see if Andrew wanted to shoot some hoops. He had not seen his little buddy in a few days and he missed him.

Rose breathlessly climbed the stairs as fast as her old legs would carry her up to Tessa's flat.

Entering the kitchen, she called out. "Tessa! Tessa! Where are you?"

Tessa entered the kitchen from the other room. It was early evening and they had just finished up dinner. Taylor had come by earlier and shot some hoops with Andrew and then went back to his place. Tessa could see Rose was excited about something.

"What is it, Rose?"

Rose moved quickly into Tessa's living room, where Andrew was watching a game show. "Quick, quick! We must turn on the local news! Taylor is on the news!" Rose declared.

"What?!"

Tessa immediately picked up the remote and switched it to Channel seven's evening news. Sure enough, there was Taylor clad in a brown leather bomber jacket and jeans surrounded by fans at the University of Buffalo. The reporter was speaking and Tessa turned up the volume a bit:

The University of Buffalo received a surprise visit from the famous movie star Taylor Boudrain. Boudrain explained he was in the area to tour various medical school facilities and was impressed by UB's program. As he toured, he took the time to sign autographs and answer questions for fans, as shown here. We were unable to speak directly with Boudrain but his many fans gave us commentary:

A young blonde shown: "He was the best! So polite and absolutely gorgeous!"

A young guy with brown hair: "I wanted to speak to him because I am majoring in dramatic arts. He encouraged me to follow my dreams. It was such a thrill!"

An older faculty member: "I was just as excited as the students. Such a handsome man! What a surprise for all of us!"

And there you have it folks. Thanks Taylor for making Buffalo's day!

In other news…"

Tessa clicked back to Andrew's game show as Andrew pointed at the television. "Taylor! Taylor on TV!" he exclaimed loudly.

Rose grinned as Tessa speculated. Hmmm…did this have anything to do with his mysterious business?

Tessa phoned Taylor on his cell.

"Hello. This is Taylor," he answered.

"Taylor! Did you catch the evening news?" Tessa asked.

"No, Tessa. I just finished up with dinner. Why?"

"Why?! You were big news at the University today. It is all over the local news! Andrew, Rose and I just watched. Andrew was so excited to see you on the news. You could have told me about it earlier when you were here," she lightly chided.

"Tessa, it wasn't a big deal. I'm on the news frequently. I forgot you guys might be watching. Guess I should have mentioned it, but I was having fun with Andrew."

"Is there a certain reason you are touring medical facilities, Taylor?"

His voice became nonchalant. "No. No special reason. Just wanted to check it out."

Tessa sighed. She could see he was still keeping his secrets. "Okay, Taylor. By the way, you looked great and everyone else thought so too."

"Why, thank you m'am."

"Are you going on another mysterious outing tomorrow?"

Wednesday Taylor had to meet with the developer and hospital personnel at the Lockport sight. "Yep. I'll be gone for a little while. Not quite as long as today and Monday. I'm gonna be in the area again tomorrow."

She sighed. "Okay, Taylor. Keep your secrets for now." She sounded a bit petulant.

"Tessa, you will know what I am doing and very soon. Just want to wait for the right time to tell you, baby."

"Okay. See ya around, Taylor."

"You bet 'cha!"

Taylor met with the developer and realtor and toured the Lockport property. It was a sprawling wooded lot actually located in the Town of Lockport, not the city. A major highway was very close by and Taylor considered that an asset. The property was large enough to accommodate the facility Taylor wanted to build.

After touring the property, the developer and realtor left and Taylor discussed the merits of the property with the hospital personnel from Rochester. They were in agreement with Taylor that it would be an ideal location.

Now Taylor had to get his lawyers together to negotiate a fair price for the land.

Taylor got on his phone and got busy.

After attending to all of these details, Taylor headed back to his place. It was close to three thirty and he could be around to help Rose get Andrew off of the bus and spend some time with him.

Taylor was still hanging out with Andrew at about five fifteen when Tessa finally returned from work. Taylor offered to take them all out to a local pizzeria restaurant for dinner. Everyone piled into Taylor's SUV and he drove to the restaurant he and Tessa had visited last winter after skating. It did not seem all that long ago.

Halloween was coming up very soon and Andrew chattered away. He wanted to be the sci fi hero Taylor had played in the movie Andrew had seen. Taylor was flattered (and a little disturbed by the fact he could now be considered a Halloween character to kids-yikes!) that Andrew wanted to be one of his characters. It was a bit surreal.

The four of them enjoyed their dinner and then Taylor took them all back to Tessa's place.

"Do you want to come up for some wine after I get Andrew in bed, Taylor?" Tessa invited as she climbed the stairs to her flat. Rose had already entered her flat downstairs.

"Sure. I have some paperwork I gotta go over, then I'll come by. I'll just go in and say good night for now."

After hugging and kissing Andrew, Taylor returned to his place.

He hoped wine with Tessa meant sex with Tessa.

When he returned a little later he found out it sure enough did. And Taylor was in heaven.

CHAPTER
FIFTY EIGHT

HALLOWEEN ARRIVED AND TESSA prepared to take her son trick or treating for yet another year. Taylor told her unfortunately he would be in Rochester for business meetings until well into the evening and would therefore regrettably miss going out with them. Since Andrew was one of the characters he had portrayed, he had been looking forward to seeing that. Tessa assured him she would try to take a few photos so Taylor could see Andrew trick or treating.

As they traipsed from house to house, Tessa was able to catch a couple shots, not too many. There were other kids and she always needed to keep Andrew moving along. As usual, he tired quickly but he did a few more houses than last year. He also kept asking her where Taylor was and Tessa had to reassure him he would see Taylor the next day. Taylor was unable to make Halloween with them because of work. Andrew accepted this explanation and happily offered up his candy pumpkin holder.

Soon it was time to head back and as they walked up the drive, Tessa could see the Escalade was still gone. She sighed, wondering what was so important in Rochester. She was disappointed that this year, as last, he had not been around for Halloween.

She shook off her mood, escorting her son upstairs as he chatted to her in broken sentences about trick or treating. Tessa smiled down at her little guy. Andrew had enjoyed himself and that was all that mattered.

Taylor had finalized all legal paperwork to purchase the property in Lockport. He was now the sole owner of the sprawling property and he had spent the day in Rochester with the hospital executives going over a business plan to go forward to build the hospital. They met with several large architectural firms that had built state of the art buildings around the country and Taylor informed them he wanted drawings, art schematics and a quote on pricing. After all of that was complete, he would then need to select a construction firm with the help of the architects he eventually would hire. They were finally getting closer to the bottom line of actually beginning construction in about a month or two. Taylor preferred a month. That would be November and not quite as cold as December. He planned to surprise Tessa with this project. He was doing it so that children in Western New York who had autism and other developmental disabilities would have access to the best quality care in their own area. The project was time consuming and he was in Rochester more than Lewiston and he knew this frustrated Tessa, especially since she did not know what he was doing. He hoped it was all worth it in the end. In fact, he knew it would be.

Wearily he went up to his place about ten p.m. on Halloween evening. He regretted missing seeing the little guy as his last character, but there was no help for it. Fortunately tomorrow he did not have any meetings scheduled. He could hang out with Andrew and Rose until Tessa returned.

Taylor threw off his clothes and crawled into bed. He was asleep immediately.

Tessa was up very early as usual and it was still dark out. She prepared for work, brewing coffee and Rose came up at her regular time, five thirty. Tessa usually left around five forty to make her shift at six. She chatted briefly with Rose, went in to kiss her son and taking her travel mug of coffee, she descended the stairs to go to her SUV. In the dim morning she looked up at Taylor's place. All of the blinds were down and his SUV was present. He had informed her he would be home today and she was glad to hear that. Lately she had not seen much of him and she admitted she missed him.

Sighing, she started up her SUV and turned the defogger on to clear her windows. She shifted into reverse and headed off to work.

Taylor and Rose were both down at the end of the driveway to meet the bus at three thirty. Andrew was very excited to see Taylor and gave him all details of his Halloween adventure. Rose chuckled and interjected comments here and there. The three moved into Rose's kitchen and she went about preparing Andrew a snack.

After snack, Taylor took Andrew out to shoot hoops. Andrew was doing much better at the sport and Taylor was actually able to move the basket net a notch higher. Sighing, he realized that Andrew was growing and time was flying by. He thought about Tessa and all of the important things he had to tell her. Since tomorrow was Saturday, he planned to ask her to go with him on a special outing. He had already spoken to Rose who said she would be happy to keep Andrew for a few hours.

The architects had submitted a preliminary sketch done in full color of how the building would look sitting on the property.

"Taylor! Taylor! Watch!" Andrew's voice interrupted his thoughts.

Taylor grinned, bringing his attention back to the little boy. "That was a heck of a shot, buddy!"

Taylor took the ball and dribbled it around and shot one straight in. Nothing but net! Andrew giggled.

Taylor spoke to Tessa and asked her to come on a special outing with him on Saturday. Rose had already agreed to watch Andrew he explained and he had something special he wanted to show her.

Tessa was mystified but agreed to the outing. It was November second but the weather continued to be balmy for Lewiston. It was in the fifties and she wore a denim jacket over her sweater and jeans with low boots on.

Taylor picked her up shortly past noon and they were on their way.

She glanced over at him as he drove. His hair had grown out a bit. It was longer, falling past his collar but nowhere near as long as it was when she first met him over a year ago. She could not believe so much time had flown by. He was as gorgeous as ever. Today he was wearing a teal Henley with his jeans that complimented his eyes, with a grey fleece vest thrown over it. He wore oxford work boots.

As he drove she tried to get some information about where they were going but he remained mysteriously silent or changed the subject.

Finally Tessa sat back in frustration and waited until they reached their destination. Taylor obviously was not going to spill the beans.

Tessa could see they were entering Lockport. The city was not far from Lewiston and the total drive time to the sight they were at was about twenty minutes, give or take. All Tessa could see was sprawling trees on the outside of the city, which she knew was actually the Town of Lockport. Taylor descended from the SUV so Tessa did the same, frowning slightly. Okay, what was so special about an empty lot in Lockport?

Taylor gestured over to the wooded lot and Tessa could see there was a "For Sale" sign and underneath it was added a "Sold" sign. She looked up at Taylor curiously as he went down a short incline that took one closer to the woods. Tessa estimated it was a very large piece of property and she knew this area was zoned for commercial use. She followed Taylor, still having no idea what was up.

He finally halted and looked up at the blue sky and the many trees that were all starting to lose their leaves. Leaves crackled underfoot as they walked in the woods and Tessa was glad she chose to wear boots.

"See this, Tessa?" He encompassed the wooded lot with arms outstretched.

"Yep. It is a wooded lot, lots of trees losing their leaves. Is this what you wanted to show me?" She stared up into his face, removing her dark glasses.

Taylor did the same so that she could now see his teal eyes. "Yep, but it is a very *special* wooded lot."

"Oh yeah? How's that, Taylor?"

He grinned down at her. "Because I own it, honey."

Tessa was really puzzled now. "You bought a wooded lot in Lockport? Why?" Tessa was genuinely confused.

Taylor motioned her back over to the Escalade and Tessa followed him. He went to the hood of the large vehicle and spread out a large piece of paper that Tessa assumed would be the survey for the lot.

When Taylor had the paper totally spread out and Tessa looked down at a drawing of a beautiful state of the art hospital, she gasped. Tawny eyes moved to his in complete confusion. "This looks like a hospital," she remarked.

"Yep. My business in Rochester has been meeting with Lloyd Children's Hospital in Rochester. As you know—"

"They are renowned for helping children with special needs," Tessa answered. She glanced up at Taylor then back down at the schematic drawing. "I'm still a bit confused here, Taylor—"

"The big surprise is: I am building a similar hospital right here on this spot we are standing on. A state of the art hospital devoted to helping children with special needs, especially those with autism and other developmental issues. This hospital will be named after your son. I'm using his initials to keep his identity secret. It will be named the ASP Research Children's Hospital." Taylor knew Andrew's middle name was Stephen.

Tessa gasped, tears coming to her eyes. She looked more closely at the drawing and could see it would be a huge facility and that many children would benefit from having such a hospital in the Western New York area.

She looked up at Taylor with tears in her eyes, then she jumped into his arms, squeezing tightly. "Oh, Taylor! It is wonderful! *You* are wonderful!" she choked through her tears.

As Taylor held the woman he loved, he knew all of the hard work that lay ahead of him would definitely be worth it.

The couple embraced in the sunlight next to the huge sprawling lot. It was the beginning of a dream which would one day be a wonderful reality.

CHAPTER
FIFTY NINE

TAYLOR SPENT MUCH OF his time commuting back and forth from Rochester. He was usually gone most of the week and Tessa, Rose and Andrew only saw him on weekends. There was much to do now that the final plans had been drawn up and accepted for the new hospital. Taylor and his co-sponsors had hired a very well known architectural firm famous for their futuristic designs. Taylor wanted the building to be attractive but user friendly. Many details went into the planning of such a huge complex and Taylor could see that his initial groundbreaking ceremony would not occur in November as he was hoping. If they stayed on track and their plans did not go awry, they should be able to break ground right before Christmas. Taylor hoped very much this was the case. He was planning a big ceremony for that special event.

He was interviewed quite frequently in the local press and it soon became national news that Taylor Boudrain was building a new hospital for children in the Western New York area. The area was all abuzz about what it would mean in terms of jobs and benefits for the Buffalo area, a city that had just about died out because of steel mills and manufacturing jobs leaving the area. Such a huge facility as Taylor was building would revitalize Buffalo and put the area on the map as THE place for families who had children with special needs to turn to. There was such a lack of facilities for these children, especially those suffering with autism.

Taylor was interviewed by all of the big magazines: **Time, Newsweek, The New York Times** and he also appeared on *Sixty Minutes*. He was asked many questions about his acting career but Taylor always steered the conversation back to the new hospital and what he hoped to accomplish. Right now, that was his main focus and his main task.

"Taylor, what the fuck!? I gotta watch my *own* star on Sixty Minutes to see what you are up to?" Frank's voice on the other end of the line was irritated and upset.

Taylor sighed. He had been meaning to meet with Frank but with the million and one things he was involved in, it just had slipped his mind. Any free time he had he spent with Tessa and Andrew.

"Sorry, hoss. I really am. I *have* been meaning to call you. I've just got so much on my plate right now—"

"Yeah, one of which is not your acting career!" Frank interrupted. "So, Taylor. Are you gonna be a medical entrepreneur or are you gonna do what you do best? Act?"

Taylor sighed. He really did not want to give Frank this news over the telephone. He preferred to do it face to face but Frank was forcing his hand. "At this point Frank, I don't have plans to make another movie."

Frank gasped. "Are you telling me you are no longer acting?"

Taylor sighed. "Yeah, I guess that is the gist of it."

There was a long silence. "Taylor, you do know you have an acting contract with me that you have not fulfilled. We still got two years on it, my friend."

"Yeah, I know. And as you know, I can buy my way out of it. But I don't want to do that to you, Frank. You've been a loyal and a good agent." Taylor paused. "How about this? I need a public relations firm for my new enterprise. I will bring you in at twice the amount of our contract. As the business grows as I fully expect it to, you will make even more money on your investment. What do you think of this?"

Frank ruminated on the other end. It was a very tempting offer. Taylor could make much more money in the future if he acted, but if he chose not to Frank would not see any money coming from this particular client. If he accepted this deal, he would make bundles. It was a very attractive offer and Frank had many contacts in public relations that could really help Taylor's new project get publicized properly.

"I like the idea," Frank finally said and Taylor sighed in relief on the other end. "Let me get with my lawyers and we'll fly out to meet with you."

"Great! I'm glad to hear that, Frank. I don't think you will regret this."

"Taylor, I've never regretted our business relationship. Yeah, you can be a pain in the ass, but you DO know how to make money!"

"I'm not in this for the money, hoss."

"Well, I am. I'll contact you soon about when we'll be in and we'll settle all details."

"Sounds good, Frank."

"Ciao, buddy."

Taylor sighed, relieved and pleased that he had Frank onboard. He was an expert at wheeling and dealing and Taylor preferred to leave all public relations to another person. He did not want his fame interfering with the project and having Frank's firm handle those aspects would help greatly in that regard.

The Pattersons and Rose were celebrating Thanksgiving. This year Rose was well enough to have the dinner at her place, as was their tradition.

Taylor joined them and they all spoke casually around the large dining table. Tessa and Rose asked many questions about the new hospital project and Taylor filled them in on what was currently going on.

He helped the ladies clean up afterwards and then went into the front room to spend some time with Andrew. He played several games of checkers with him and then read some Thanksgiving stories to him about Pilgrims and such. Then he had Andrew read to him. As the boy sat on his lap, slowly reading the words to him Taylor thought: this is what it is all about. This is why I want to help people so much, because this little guy has taught me to love. He kissed the top of Andrew's head and glancing up he caught Tessa smiling at both of them.

After Andrew was tucked in bed and sleeping, Tessa and Taylor slowly made love. He grabbed her hands, pressing them down as he looked deep into tawny eyes as he slowly shoved his penis into her. All the way out, all the way in. Her eyes were filled with bliss and she moaned. Taylor leaned down to cover her lips, silencing the moan and kissing her deeply. His woman. His love. His angel.

Thanksgiving came and went and Taylor finalized details for the ASP Hospital. Frank came into town and Taylor signed a public relations deal with Frank's firm to run ten years. Frank was scheduling a press conference the day of ground breaking which was tentatively set for December fifteenth. If the weather and the work moved along apace, they would be able to meet the deadline.

Taylor was also throwing a big bash at the Hyatt Regency in Buffalo and all of the big wigs he knew were invited— politicians, both local and national, actors, actresses, famous people from all walks of life. Taylor also visited Andrew's school and met with various parents and invited these parents and their children to the special event that was celebrating their efforts to help their children. Taylor wanted not just the glitterati there but the regular folks who were the true impetus behind the project.

Everything was coming together and Taylor also had another big surprise for Tessa. But he wanted to wait until all details were finalized.

When Taylor had free time, he always spent it with his new family— Tessa, Andrew and Rose.

As December approached the weather turned colder, plunging down into the thirties and sometimes twenties. Taylor and the Pattersons decorated for the holiday season and the big Victorian duplex was decked out with many twinkling lights and candles in the windows, making it festive and beautiful against the backdrop of evergreens it was snuggled into.

Taylor kept commuting and commuting. Now his days were mostly spent in Lockport as the sight had been cleared, all the trees removed and the construction firm readied the area for the first shovelful of dirt.

Mid December approached and Taylor frantically tried to Christmas shop as he worked. His life was busy and full and he had never been happier.

CHAPTER
SIXTY

TESSA WAS DRESSING ANDREW for the big day. December fifteenth had finally arrived and the official groundbreaking for the hospital was scheduled for eleven a.m. Rose, Tessa and Andrew would be attending the event along with Taylor. She had to dress her son in warm clothes because it was frigid out, in the low twenties. She chose a pair of black corduroy slacks paired with a red shaker sweater and warm black boots. She had purchased new winter coats for the two of them for the event. Andrew had a new wool grey topcoat and Tessa purchased a winter white long coat with an empire waist and warm fur cuffs and a winter hat with matching fur. She wore a warm emerald green turtleneck sweater dress and tall lined black boots. She wanted to look especially nice because the press would be there in droves. Tessa wanted to protect Andrew as much as possible for anonymity reasons and Taylor assured her he would only be photographed for the ground breaking ceremony where he would join Taylor in the formal shoveling part of the event. Tessa was not allowing Andrew to attend the formal ball that evening. There was already a big video display that would be shown in the backdrop with autistic children and Tessa had given permission for Andrew's current photos to be used as well as photos of him younger; as a baby, toddler and younger boy. She had made arrangements with his teacher Susan Reuben to come stay with Andrew because Rose would be attending the formal ball.

Tessa buttoned up Andrew's coat and pulled his red knit hat over his ears. It was very cold and they would be out in the weather for several hours. "All snug and warm, buddy?"

His big brown eyes lit up. "Warm. Taylor come?" he asked hopefully.

"Yes, honey. Taylor should be here any minute along with Mrs. H. We are all going to the new site for the hospital. Now you know what you have to do, right?" She had been over this story and used picture cards so he would not be afraid.

"Yes! Help Taylor shovel! Even if people around! No afraid!"

Tessa leaned down to hug her son tightly. "That's my boy!"

Rose also wore a pale pink wool coat over her dress with warm boots and a white fur hat with a fur muff to tuck her hands into. Taylor picked them all up and they piled into his SUV. Taylor wore a dark grey suit with a red tie and a grey wool top coat. His hair had grown out a bit and brushed the collar of his coat. He wore shiny black oxford boots, well aware of how muddy the sight was but now it was starting to freeze. One of the reasons he did not want to delay any longer for the first shovelful ceremony. He wanted the construction workers to get right to work on the project and since it was winter, ground digging would be more difficult.

Smiling he drove to the site where they could all see the media gathered around with their lights, cameras and reporters were all over the place. Frank would also be at the ceremony and he had hired a security firm to keep people and press well away from Taylor and his family.

Taylor greeted Frank, shaking hands. Frank was dressed similarly to Taylor with a black suit and topcoat on. Taylor, Tessa (holding Andrew's gloved hand tightly) and Rose waded through the people, the security people leading the way. Finally they reached the sight for the ceremony which was surrounded by yellow tape and bunting with big yellow ribbons. The puzzle logo sign for autism was interspersed on the bunting and all cameras were aimed at the action.

Several politicians spoke first and then Taylor took the podium, speaking about his vision of bringing a better tomorrow for those children who suffered with various disabilities. His speech was well received and Taylor waved as people cheered and flash strobes went off.

Finally it was time for Tessa to bring her son over to Taylor and she stood to the side as Taylor led Andrew over beside him and then Taylor presented a shovel that had a large yellow bow on it. Having Andrew stand next to him, he showed the little boy how to put his booted foot on the shovel next to his. Andrew did this and Taylor pushed and the shovel moved into the dirt with the man and boy's feet on it and Taylor heaved a mound up and out. Clapping and cheers erupted as again flash strobes winked and Andrew smiled up at Taylor. This photograph made the local news and was on the front page of all of the local papers, as they would find out later.

Tessa moved to take Andrew's hand as the three of them waved to the press. Bending down, Tessa spoke softly to Andrew and he hesitantly moved to the microphone.

"Thank you," he said in a very subdued voice, turning to take his mommy's hand again.

There were more cheers as Taylor waved and the security people again moved Rose, Taylor, Tessa and her son through the sea of people.

Now it was back home to rest up a bit before the big party being held at the Hyatt Regency.

Tessa and Rose had shopped for gowns together. There was a special boutique in a nearby town that sold very unique and beautiful gowns. Tessa chose a deep red strapless satin gown that clung to her figure and had a very slight train in the back with a side slit to about knee length. Rose chose a deep coral gown overlaid with tiny pearl beads that sparkled and flashed. They both chose footwear and accessories. Rose planned to borrow Tessa's pearl set because it would compliment the gown perfectly. Taylor had already presented Tessa with a gorgeous diamond necklace and dangling diamond earrings to match. When she protested (as he knew she would) he just kissed her into submission. It worked! Tessa accepted the gems.

As Andrew rested at home with his teacher, Tessa and Rose went to Tessa's salon and received the royal treatment; pedicures, manicures and their hair done. Tessa went for an elaborate updo to show off her shoulders and the gorgeous jewelry. Rose did an elaborate French twist with a golden sparkly comb inserted into the thick silver waves.

The two ladies prepared for the elaborate ballroom party, not really knowing what to expect. Both were very excited and as the time neared for Taylor to pick them up, Tessa and Rose spent time with Andrew who exclaimed over how beautiful they looked. Tessa explained that Andrew could watch the event on television with Miss Reuben. Some of Andrew's classmates would be at the event with their parents but Tessa had drawn the line there, only allowing Andrew's presence at the ground breaking. She knew a ballroom full of people would be just too much for him to handle and she would be busy socializing with Taylor.

Andrew was very excited as his mommy explained there would be pictures of him shown on television. Andrew was not quite sure what all of the fuss was about but he was sure it stemmed from his big buddy, Taylor.

Taylor showed up at five thirty to pick up the ladies. He wore a formal black tuxedo with a red cummerbund and a silky red kerchief tucked into the lapel. He wore a black topcoat and he helped both Tessa and Rose into their furs (which Tessa insisted be faux). Tessa's was a silver grey fox and Rose's a gold mink. They had matching muffs to keep their hands warm. It was now a very frigid fifteen degrees out.

The extravaganza was to start at six p.m. and it was about a half hour drive into Buffalo. Taylor made sure his SUV was warmed up for the ladies, who both wore heels. They chatted excitedly about the event as he drove into the city. Buffalo's skyline sparkled with Christmas lights and spotlights for the grand party. Buffalo was lit up and ready to party.

When they arrived at the Hyatt, there was a red carpet leading into the hotel. Velvet roped barricades kept back crowds of hundreds of people but the press were allowed free reign, snapping photos of various dignitaries and stars as they arrived. When Taylor appeared with both ladies by his side, the crowd erupted. Taylor smiled and took the time to quickly sign some autographs, then they were rushed inside out of the cold by the security detail. Tessa and Rose also smiled and waved at the crowd and Tessa thought what a very odd feeling. I now know how Taylor feels on occasion. It was a heady rush to have so many people interested in you and taking photos, they were practically blinded by flash strobes.

They entered the elegant hotel where a concierge came right over to relieve them of their outer wear. Frank was there with his entourage to escort them to the head table. His wife Lila was by his side in a silver lame gown, jewels twinkling at her neck and ears. Taylor introduced everyone and they proceeded to the head table.

There were many speeches and then the collage of autistic children was shown on a very large screen as they dimmed the lights. "My Wish" by Rascal Flatts played as the various children were shown which opened up with a beautiful shot of Andrew looking directly into the camera with his big long lashed beautiful brown eyes large as life. Various photos of him were interspersed with classmates and other children whose parents had submitted photos.

Afterwards Taylor spoke emotionally about how meeting Andrew had changed his life and how helping children with autism had sent him down a different road in his life than he had ever expected to travel. He spoke briefly and then invited everyone to enjoy the dinner and the entertainment afterwards. He seated himself next to Tessa among clapping and she leaned close to kiss his cheek.

"You were marvelous," she whispered.

He grinned back. "Thanks, baby. But everything I said is true. Y'all have changed my life and I will never be the same."

The dinner was elaborate and delicious and the guests could choose dessert from a huge display arranged at the back of the ballroom. Fancy sugar and ice sculptures captured the holiday theme as well as the theme for the party. Frank had hired a band that was currently playing "Moonstruck" and Tessa and Taylor danced together as Rose danced with a gentleman that had asked her.

Taylor smiled down at Tessa. "Do you think the little guy saw the festivities on TV?"

"I'm sure he did. He was all excited when I told him he would be on. He did not quite understand why, but I know he watched."

Taylor looked down at the beautiful woman in his arms. She had chosen to wear his favorite color on her— red— and with the diamonds flashing at her décolletage and ears. Her beautiful hair was swept up revealing well toned arms, gorgeous cleavage and her beautiful features perfectly made up. He wondered what he had ever done in his life to deserve such a perfect woman.

He bent down to kiss her lush lips tenderly as they danced to the romantic song.

Tessa was in pure heaven.

The event was a huge success. They raised five million dollars which would go to help run the new hospital. Taylor and his ladies went out with Frank and Lila after the event wound down around midnight. They went to the Hyatt bar to enjoy cocktails as they talked about the event and what Taylor's plans were going forward. Everyone was very excited and in high spirits.

Frank and Lila went out of their way to make Tessa and Rose feel comfortable. Tessa admitted she liked Frank very much and could not understand why Taylor had complained about him in the past, but as the evening wore on she could see that it was just how they rolled and it worked. Taylor's banter was *meant* to annoy Frank and Frank understood that and didn't take it personally.

After a few hours, everyone was tired from the very long day. Frank and Lila retired to their hotel room and after the ladies bundled back up in their furs, Taylor drove back up to Lewiston.

Taylor joined Tessa checking on Andrew after Susan left. It was very late, about three in the morning, and they both gazed down at the beautiful child asleep in his bed with his elephant cuddled next to his face. Tessa kissed his cheek and Taylor followed suit.

Joining hands, they went to Tessa's room, this time to sleep after the long eventful day, falling asleep in each others arms.

CHAPTER
SIXTY ONE

TAYLOR DECIDED TO TAKE a few weeks off from his development project. The holidays were coming up and he had some very special surprises planned for Tessa and needed the free time to get organized and ready for Christmas. He also wanted to spend time with Tessa, Rose and Andrew because he had been so busy the past few months he had barely seen them.

He went into Buffalo to do some Christmas shopping and wore his dark glasses and a knit cap pulled down to try to hide his identity. It didn't work. His face was even more famous in the area now because of his recent project and he was swamped. He signed as many autographs as he could and the security people at the mall finally moved the people along. Taylor was secretly relieved. He did not want his Christmas shopping to make the six o'clock news for the obvious reasons.

Taylor spent several hours shopping for his little family. He dropped easily fifty grand but that was a drop in the bucket for Taylor. Besides, he knew if he overdid it, Tessa would not be happy. For some reason she hated it when he spoiled her. Well, she would just have to get used to it, he chuckled to himself.

As the holiday approached Tessa also did her shopping, both separately and then with Andrew and Rose. She went to the mall in Niagara Falls and was really stumped about what to give Taylor this year. She wanted to get him something really special. She went shopping on her own for his gift. When Andrew and Rose shopped for him they would all go together but Tessa wanted to be alone when getting Taylor's gift.

She went to a jewelry store and looked among the selection for men. They had the usual watches, bracelets, rings, gold chains, etc. None of these were special enough. Then she spotted a gorgeous gold medallion that was circular and had what looked like an intricate small figure engraved with calligraphy writing surrounding the circular pendant. She asked the salesman to show the item to her and he explained it was the medallion of St. Christopher and anyone wearing it would be protected by the saint. He brought the velvet box out so Tessa could take a closer look. It was twenty four karat gold and the figure was beautifully detailed and the calligraphy was in Latin. She wanted it very badly; it was the perfect gift for Taylor. It would look terrific against his golden skin and she wanted him to be safe. With Taylor's sometimes reckless behavior and after losing Steve, she always worried about Taylor's safety. She asked the salesperson how much it was. When he told her two thousand dollars, she almost fainted from shock! She did have some money saved up however from the extra rent money Taylor had been giving her. She could afford to buy it although it would put a dent in her savings.

She handed back the pendant and asked the clerk to wrap it for her. Smiling, he complied, wrapping it in gold foil paper with a fancy gold bow attached. Tessa wrote a check for the amount and left the store. She still needed to get him other presents, she would feel bad just handing him one. She continued shopping and picked up some men's cologne (she knew he liked Stetson and it drove *her* wild!) so she picked up a gift box of that. She bought him some beautiful soft warm sweaters, slippers and other things she thought he might like.

Finally she headed home. She had blown quite a wad of money and she still had Andrew and Rose to shop for! Oh well, she grinned. Christmas was for giving to loved ones. She did not care if she went into the poor house to do it.

Christmas Eve finally arrived and Rose spent some time with Andrew, Tessa and Taylor. About nine p.m. she left to go to her place and Tessa tucked Andrew into bed after reading him a Christmas story and admonishing him to sleep tight. Andrew solemnly nodded. He was able to spend Christmas Eve with Taylor this year and that was a big thrill for the little boy. Smiling, Tessa kissed him and returned to the front room where she could see Taylor tending to the fire.

Tessa went to her liquor cabinet and poured them both brandies in brandy balloon glasses. She knew Taylor preferred the drink when it was colder and after trying it, Tessa found she liked it also. Smiling, she offered him his glass as he settled next to her.

He grinned at her, accepting the drink and nuzzling her neck. "Wanna neck on the couch, baby?"

Tessa almost choked on her sip of brandy. Grinning, she snuggled next to him. "We can't yet. Andrew probably isn't asleep and I know you! You'll moan!"

"Baby, its Christmas eve. I might howl!"

Tessa giggled, taking a sip of the brandy. "You know, you can't stay over tonight. He gets up very early on Christmas so you'll have to leave before your regular time."

Taylor sighed. "Then we can't waste any time, baby. Let's get to it!"

"Taylor, we still have to put all of the gifts under the tree! You have to eat cookies and milk!" she reminded him.

"Oh yeah," he responded. "Well, that won't take long and *then* we'll get right to it. Right?"

"You are a horny devil!"

"Yup! And I admit it, too!" He sipped at his brandy, his teal eyes bright against his slightly tanned face. He had been spending a lot of time out at the site and as a result he had tanned up a bit. His golden mane was getting a little longer too.

Tessa sighed just looking at him. He was a beautiful hunk of a man.

"What was the sigh for, baby?"

"I'm going to go peek in on Andrew. See if he's asleep." She put her glass down on the table and headed down the hallway. She returned within minutes. "He's sound asleep and I closed his door. Let's get this Christmas business over with so I can jump your bones!"

"But baby, what was that you were just sayin' about—"

She jumped on top of him. "Okay. I'll jump your bones now!" She bit his neck lightly and they proceeded to have sex on the couch.

Around midnight Santa Claus came.

As usual, early Christmas morning Andrew was up around six a.m. and it was still dark out. Rose came up and shortly so did Taylor to watch Andrew open his gifts from Santa Claus.

Taylor had not even showered or shaved yet. He just threw on some jeans and a warm navy sweater. The ladies were still in their warm robes and he could see Andrew was wearing Christmas pj's.

Andrew was so excited and opened all of his gifts from Santa, his mommy and Mrs. H. Taylor promised him he would bring his gifts over a little later after everyone had the chance to shower up and dress.

Andrew was quite content to show off his various toys, books and DVD's to Taylor and Taylor played on the floor with him for a little while. Then he went back to his place to get ready for the holiday. He had some very special gifts, especially for Tessa.

Rose went downstairs to dress and Tessa bathed Andrew and dressed him in an emerald green sweater and black corduroy slacks for the holiday. The bright green color always brought out his beautiful brown eyes. After he was ready for the day, Tessa put on a Christmas DVD so she could also shower and get dressed.

After showering, she chose a soft velour red jumper and a white turtleneck to wear underneath. She twisted her hair up so she could wear the pearl and gold earrings Taylor gave her last year. Adding black pumps and applying her makeup, she was ready for the day.

Shortly Rose came up wearing a black skirt and a gold lame blouse, her hair clipped up with a gold comb. Tessa was in the process of making sure her camera was working and then took several photos of Andrew, then Rose and Andrew together.

Taylor arrived carrying a sack of gifts. He had so many there was no way he could get them over to the house without it. Grinning, he set it down near the Christmas tree and turned to hug and kiss everyone. Taylor chose black dress slacks and a teal silk shirt Tessa bought him last year and as usual Tessa thought he looked marvelous.

Tessa and Rose went into the kitchen to prepare the meal and Taylor spent time with Andrew. After dinner, Taylor would exchange gifts with the Pattersons and Rose.

They all enjoyed their Christmas dinner, chatting casually about various subjects. Tessa had a beautiful Christmas centerpiece on the dining table with several tall red candles lit. The chandelier was on low and the Christmas tree lights sparkled and glowed. Andrew and Taylor had chopped down a special tree as they did last year. Everyone was merry and enjoying themselves.

Soon it was time to open gifts. After Taylor helped the ladies clean up after the meal they all headed into the front room to have a second Christmas opening party that day.

Andrew opened his gifts first. As usual Taylor had been very generous. He purchased a special laptop computer for Andrew that was designed to be used by special needs children. He also bought him software, both educational and entertainment, so that Andrew could learn as well as play. There were also many other toys that he knew Andrew would like and a special Christmas copy of "Beauty & The Beast Enchanted Christmas"— a very hard DVD to find nowadays. Tessa gasped. She had been trying to find that for Andrew forever because she knew he would really love it. *She* loved to watch it, but it went into the Disney vault and had not been seen in ages.

"However did you find that?" Tessa questioned.

Taylor wiggled his brows. "I got connections." He turned to Rose as Andrew played on the floor with his various toys. "Your turn, Rose."

Smiling, Rose opened her gifts from Taylor. He purchased a silky robe with cabbage roses swirled over it, pink and mint green. It was lovely and Rose gasped, feeling the material. The second gift was a warm black fur muff. Andrew came over and buried his face in it and everyone laughed. She opened her final gift and gasped when she saw what the square black velvet box held. He had purchased a triple pearl strand necklace for her with a diamond clasp, with matching diamond and pearl earrings.

She gasped, her eyes wide, looking up at Taylor. "Oh, Taylor! This is too much! You should never have—"

Taylor came over to her and kissed her cheek. "I wanted to, Rose. You are priceless. Enjoy them and wear in good health!"

Tears were in Rose's eyes. She stood and hugged Taylor tightly.

Normally Tessa would open her gifts next but Taylor asked if it would be okay if he opened his gifts first. He wanted to save Tessa's for last.

"Sure. Not a problem, Taylor." She went over to the pile of gifts from the three of them and presented them to Taylor.

Taylor opened Andrew's gift first. It was a fairly large box and heavy. Taylor arched a brow. "Got me stumped again this year, buddy!"

The little boy stood next to Taylor and just grinned as he waited for the man to open his gift. Taylor did so, stunned when he saw a beautiful pair of cowboy boots. He lifted one out and could see they were a very unusual deep wine/burgundy color. They were intricately stitched and gorgeous. Taylor loved them! His famous grin appeared and he hugged Andrew close. "You picked the perfect gift, buddy! Again! I just love them! I don't have any at all nearly this nice! Thanks, dude!" He high fived Andrew and the little guy was all smiles.

Taylor turned to Rose's gifts. She had purchased him a warm caramel colored cashmere scarf and a brown leather bomber jacket. It was longer than the one he currently owned and he knew she had spent quite a bit of money. His teal eyes rose to the older woman. "I love it, Rose! But God— this is much too expensive—"

She interrupted. "I don't want to hear it, Taylor!" She grinned.

He came over and kissed her cheek and whispered. "Thank you. I love it. And I love you too."

She blushed as he moved away.

Finally it was time to open Tessa's gifts and she had about five or six for him. Glancing up at her, he spoke. "Hope you didn't go overboard, baby."

Tessa just grinned mischievously.

Taylor opened several gifts. She had bought him some very nice warm sweaters in a variety of colors, warm thermal gloves, a Stetson cologne set and warm slippers. "Oh man! Everything is so nice, babe! Thank you!" He rose to come over to her but she put up a finger. "I have one more." She presented him a smaller gift wrapped in gold with a gold bow.

Taylor arched a brow, slowly un-wrapping the gift. When he saw the gold pendant winking and flashing in the lights, he gasped, tracing the carving of a figure on the circular gold pendant.

"It is a medallion of St. Christopher. Anyone who wears this pendant will be protected by that saint for the rest of their life," she explained.

Tears filled teal eyes and he looked up at her, choked up. Tessa came to him and hugged him tightly. Then she took the pendant out of the box and put the medallion on him. She fussed with the placing on his upper chest where his silk shirt lay open a bit. Stepping back, she admired him. It looked beautiful on him as it flashed and glowed as she knew it would.

He stood, taking her in his arms and kissed her long and deeply, uncaring they had an audience. Andrew clapped and Rose smiled.

Finally Taylor stepped back. "I love it. Thank you."

She smiled as she sat in a wing chair and everyone brought her their gifts. She opened gifts from Andrew first. This year, Rose had taken him shopping for her, so she totally did not know what she would be receiving. She gasped as she opened Andrew's gift. It was an expensive bottle of perfume she had admired and liked but had never indulged herself in. Gasping, she hugged her son. "Oh, Andrew! It is perfect! Thank you!" He smiled happily as she opened the remaining gifts from her son. Chocolate, a sterling silver framed photo of Andrew from last Christmas and a beautiful red sweater completed his gifts. Tessa loved everything and kept kissing him profusely. Andrew giggled. Rose had purchased Tessa a very nice leather hobo handbag, an aqua cashmere sweater and a pearl bracelet. Tessa thanked her, kissing her. Rose had opened her presents from Andrew and Tessa earlier and as always she received gifts she loved and cherished.

Finally it was time for Tessa to open Taylor's gifts and she could see a dozen waiting for her. "Taylor, you really—"

"Babe, just open them!"

Blushing, Tessa did so. He had also purchased her a variety of cashmere sweaters in a rainbow of colors. Also a very nice pair of tall brown leather boots, buckles on the side. Tessa gasped, stroking them. Then she opened several boxes that contained satiny nightgowns, lingerie and a red satin robe.

Tessa glanced up, surprised by this.

"As you can see, I raided Victoria's Secret."

Tessa laughed and turned to the few remaining gifts. There was another bottle of sexy perfume and warm red leather gloves. At the bottom of this pile was a large white envelope that said OPEN ME. Glancing up in puzzlement at Taylor, he just grinned back.

Tessa opened the large envelope and pulled out what looked like an official certificate. Reading it, she could see that one Taylor Boudrain had been accepted into the doctorate program at Yale University. "What— I don't understand—"

Grinning, Taylor put his hands in his slacks. He explained. "I applied to Yale to become a pediatric doctor with a specialization in autism. They are renowned for their program there. I can take all classes online, so no, I won't be moving to New Haven, Connecticut. I decided if I am going to build a state of the art hospital for children I'm going to walk the walk, not just talk the walk." He paused. "I am giving up my acting career to become a doctor. I'm gonna fast track it too. Should have my degree in about seven years."

Tessa burst into tears of happiness and jumped into his arms. "Oh, Taylor! I couldn't be more proud of you! This is SUCH a surprise! This means you will be staying here! This means— oh God— I am just so HAPPY!"

Rose and Andrew inspected the formal announcement as the couple embraced in the middle of the room.

Taylor stepped back from Tessa and held up a finger as she had earlier. "That ain't all, babe. I have one more present for you. Can you please sit in the wing chair?" He indicated the burgundy wing chair by the fireplace.

"Taylor, absolutely nothing could top that last gift! You are amazing! C'mere!" she beckoned.

"No, I am serious Tessa. Sit here, please." He had a very solemn look on his face, much different than the effusive joy he had just shown.

Puzzled, Tessa obeyed. Then Taylor turned to Rose and Andrew and gestured them close. "Please come closer, you two. You're part of this too."

Rose stood and took Andrew's hand, leading him next to the chair. Rose stood on the other side.

"Perfect." Taylor took a silver and gold wrapped small present from his pocket and handed it to Tessa. He stood in front of her and waited as she slowly removed silver paper and gold spindly ribbon. A black velvet box was revealed and when she lifted the lid, she saw a single diamond ring. It had to be five carats easily and was an exquisite marquise shape. It flashed and sparkled in the glow of the Christmas lights.

Taylor took the ring out as Tessa gasped. Her gasp was echoed by both Rose and Andrew. Taylor knelt in front of Tessa and slowly slid the ring on her left hand. "Tessa, will you do me the honor of being my wife?" he said solemnly.

Tears were running down Tessa's face as she swiped at them, gasping, admiring the gorgeous ring. "Yes! Oh yes! I love you so, Taylor!"

She stood and they again embraced and then kissed in the middle of the room. She kept crying and he tenderly wiped her tears away. "Baby, you're supposed to be happy, not sad. If you don't like the shape or the design, we can take it back and get whatever you want."

"No, no!" she gasped between breaths. "I love it! I am just so— Taylor, you are just so full of surprises! I NEVER expected anything like my two last wonderful gifts!"

"Just as long as you're mine, darlin'. That's what is important to me." He turned to Rose and Andrew. "Come over and say hello to the future Mrs. Boudrain."

Laughing and crying, Rose, Andrew and Tessa embraced. Then Taylor gathered everyone into his arms for a big group hug.

SEVEN YEARS LATER

TAYLOR, TESSA AND ROSE watched Andrew being chased by his two year old sister, Angela. The children laughed and played in the huge landscaped yard in the back of the home Taylor had built in Lewiston. It was located on a very private wooded lot and possessed ten acres and had a beautiful in-ground swimming pool with lavish landscaping all around that Tessa had designed.

Andrew, now fourteen and tall for his age, glanced back teasingly at his little sister as his much longer legs ran further into the yard, Angela's little legs trying to pump fast enough as she giggled and tried to catch her older brother. Angela had blond honey streaked hair and Tessa's big tawny brown eyes. She was a beautiful child and thought the sun rose and set on Andrew.

Rose chuckled as she watched from her rocking chair, gently moving it back and forth as she kept an eye on the children. When Taylor built their huge sprawling house he had included a miniature suite for Rose to have her own living space. She still helped Tessa out with the children but since Tessa was now a full time mommy and Rose was aging, Rose was really more of a companion to the children.

As Taylor had predicted his hospital was up and running within a year. It fast became known as THE place to go to get a diagnosis and treatment for children with autism and other developmental disabilities. Taylor's degree from Yale in Pediatric Medicine had just arrived. Taylor had already had Tessa's old Victorian duplex converted into an office to see patients in and he would be hanging his shingle out very soon. He had a *long* list of patients waiting to see him so his practice would be off and running in no time.

Taylor glanced at Tessa seated next to him watching their children play. At five months pregnant, she was starting to show again with their second child. They knew they were having a boy this time and he would be named Trevor Allen (using Taylor's middle name). Taylor had long ago told Tessa that after he came out of his comma in the hospital his first thought when he saw her was she was an angel and he had died and was in heaven. Thus, they had named their daughter Angela Rose. Taylor chuckled at the memory.

Tessa glanced over at her handsome husband. "What was that chuckle for, you devil?"

Taylor thought she was just as beautiful at thirty eight as she was when he first met her. She glowed when she was pregnant.

She had left her nursing career soon after they married and moved into their present house so that she could help Andrew more. As she landscaped around their new house, she discovered she had a real talent for it and other neighbors had asked her to do theirs. Soon she had a little thriving side business going. It kept her busy but not too busy so she could be available for her children. Andrew was going through adolescence and it was a difficult time for him. Fortunately his little sister helped cheer him up. Andrew absolutely adored Angela.

Taylor answered his wife. "Oh, I was just thinking about when Angela was born and why we chose her name." He nuzzled her ear. "You know, you just glow when you're pregnant, baby. Have to keep you that way, Im'a thinkin'."

Tessa blushed. "Taylor! I'm thirty eight now! Can't be breedin' no babies when I is close to forty! This is it for us!"

Taylor sighed heavily. "Yeah, but not for the sex," he whispered in her ear. "I plan to stay active in that regard for a *looong* time!"

"Just like a man to think about sex when his wife is sitting here five months pregnant." Fortunately they were sitting a little further away from Rose and she did not hear their conversation. Her attention was on the children, making sure they were both safe and in sight.

"When you open your office on Monday, you are going to have lines out the door. Just remember when the young mommies come in and flirt with you that you're married, gorgeous!" she teased.

He nuzzled her ear again. "Tess, baby. You're the only one for me and you know it!" His hand gently rubbed at her belly and Tessa shivered at his touch, as she always did.

"So you don't regret it, do you? Leaving Hollywood for Lewiston? Giving up being a famous movie star?" Her brown eyes searched his.

"Tessa, I needed a purpose in life and back then that was my purpose. Now my life is dedicated to you, our family and helping children as much as I can. I don't want to be a star. I want to be your man." The gorgeous teal eyes smiled down at her.

"But Taylor, you ARE a star. You were a famous movie actor back then, but you weren't a star in the true sense of the word. Now— you are a star. You are beautiful, both inside and out. That is what makes someone a star." She stroked his cheek.

He leaned close to kiss her.

"To be a star— yeah it can mean many things. As long as I have you, Andrew, Angela, our new son and Rose, I'm complete. I've come full circle. I ran away from my family only to find my family."

They kissed tenderly as the children giggled and laughed in the background.

The End